THE TROUBLES KEEPER

SUSAN MAY

The Troubles Keeper

INTERNATIONAL BEST SELLING AUTHOR

SUSAN MAY

PRAISE

Wow! Susan May is a gifted story teller and I can't wait to read what she publishes next! **Julie Wall (<u>Musingsfromaworkaholic.com</u>)**

I, for one, have already put her on my 'if she writes it, I will read it' list. **Madelon Wilson** (*Good Reads Reviewer* USA*)*

Not since Odd Thomas have I enjoyed a character as much as I do Rory Fine! **Carolyn Werner** (*Good Reads Reviewer USA)*

A unique take on a serial killer and the author is brilliant at creating a storyline that leaves the reader breathless. **Maureen Ellis** (*Good Reads reviewer UK)*

Watch out Stephen King Susan May is coming up on the outside with her outstanding story telling. **Lynn McCarthy** (*Good Reads Reviewer Australia)*

Susan May is Australia's best kept secret. Her name belongs to the A-List suspense writers Parthenon, next to Stephen King, Gillian Flynn,

Dean Koontz or Glenn Cooper. **Jorge Lopez** *(Good Reads Reviewer USA)*

I absolutely loved this book just as much as I did Susan May's others and more. **Jane Culwell** *(Good Reads reviewer USA)*

Susan May proves once again why she is the foremost genre writer of the suspense/thriller/supernatural novel. **Judy Clay** *(Amazon reviewer USA)*

'The Troubles Keeper' kept me spellbound. **Sandy Jones** *(Good Reads Reviewer New Zealand)*

Like reading some of the big authors' best works. **Angel Koychev** *(Good Reads Reviewer Italy)*

Great characters and a bit of supernatural powers makes this a really enjoyable novel. Susan May at her best. **Louise Wilson** *(Good Reads reviewer UK)*

Well-written and the characters are so real. **R.J. Abell** *(Author of The Wildest Kind of Pretty USA)*

A dark thriller combined with fascinating science, eerie supernatural occurrences, gruesome (unique, never read this before) murders, breath stopping suspense, beautiful love, and inspiring acts of kindness between human beings. (**Loretta Paszkat** *Fiction Addiction Book Club Canada*)

The story carried on with a furious pace that grabbed my butt and made me sit down and read. **Bill Craig** *(Good Reads Reviewer USA)*

Wow! A very interesting concept. Brilliantly paced and an awesome adventure of suspense. **Ramyakrishna** *(Good Reads Reviewer India)*

I didn't want to put it down so much so I stayed up until 4:00 in the morning the first night and it was well worth it. **Sandy Good** (*Good Reads Reviewer USA*)

Very intriguing and awesome story **Kaila** (SJ's Book Blog *USA*)

If you like the Odd Thomas books from Dean Koontz, you will love this book with another lovable character. **Jason Perry** (*Good Reads Reviewer USA*)

An interesting Paranormal thriller, with a nice romance and a side touch of science fiction! I loved it. **Faouzia** (*Good Reads Reviewer Germany*)

The writing is exceptional. The story is full of twists and turns. I couldn't put it down. An amazing plot. I didn't know who the killer was until the very end. What a sicko!! **Irene** (*Good Reads Reviewer USA*)

You need to do: Buy this book. Book a day or so off work. Kick any humans that you live with out. Find comfy reading spot. Get under a nice warm duvet. Grab snacks and supplies (will need a lot for the last few chapters). "Are you ready?" READ! **Mike Rice** (*Good Reads Reviewer UK*)

An amazing story with an excellent plot that was very well written and hard to put down. **Jim Phillips** (*Good Reads Reviewer USA*)

Wow, what an amazing story absolutely loved reading this, nice short chapters that are packed full of action. **James Hayward** (*Good Reads Reviewer UK*)

After the first several chapters I was so hooked that I stayed up all night to keep reading. **Christy Mun** (*Good Reads Reviewer USA*)

I have never seen my fingers move across the pages on my Kindle as fast as they were during the last third of this novel. **Peg McDaniel** (*Good Reads Reviewer USA*)

I fought my urge to sleep many nights, and was very frustrated at life getting in the way of reading! **Annelien Mes** (*Good Reads Reviewer USA*)

If you loved David Mitchell's Slade House then you will thoroughly enjoy this suspenseful, creepy, supernatural bus ride with Rory Fine. **Jo-Ann Duffy** (*Book reviewer @Duffythewriter*)

Once in a while you come across a novel that is genuinely unique; that touches upon ideas that you've never seen written about before. **Eldon Farrell** (*Author of the Descent series*)

This book has the things I'm looking for in a novel - interesting characters that grow, change and adapt to their challenges as an imaginative story moves along. **Scott** (*Good Reads Reviewer USA*)

Beautifully written, great concept. **Nadja Ezzat** (*https://fit-and-beautiful-heart-reads.blogspot.de/ Germany*)

Rory, Mariana, Beth Ann all become like family and you want them to make it in the end. **Melissa White** (*Good Reads Reviewer USA*)

Lots of twists and turns - a good read and a wild ride! **Diane Lybbert** (Passionate Bibliophile and *Good Reads Reviewer USA*)

Once again I have the chance to live this author's work. I say live because that's what you do after she draws you in and ties you down. **Teri Hicks** (*Good Reads Reviewer USA*)

It was a fun. I will look for more Susan may novels. **Ron Keeler** (www.ron877.com *Indonesia*)

What do we need to make a good book? Interesting characters - They are for sure! Blooming relationship - yeah! Bad one behind the scene - present! Good plot - it's brilliant! **Ola Iliasviel** (iliasviel.word-press.com *Poland)*

The Troubles Keeper has a touch of everything to keep the reader entertained throughout. **Tracey Allen** (carpelibrum.net *Australia)*

Definitely one I'd recommend checking out. **Carrie Glover** (carries-bookreviews.wordpress.com/ *USA)*

Will be one enjoyed by lovers of the dark entity which invades these pages. **Brenda Telford** (*Good Reads Reviewer Australia)*

Wonderful book from beginning to end. **Michele Castillo** (*Good Reads Reviewer USA)*

The book is electrifying to the very last page. **Shannon Gardner** (*Good Reads Reviewer USA)*

I think I fell a little in love with Rory. A thrilling book from beginning to end. **Debra** (*Good Reads Reviewer* Canada*)*

The Troubles Keeper won't remind you of another book because it is a totally original idea with interesting and well-developed characters. **Mike** (*Good Reads Reviewer* Canada*)*

Susan once again proves that there isn't any place she won't go for a good story. **Jan Paramski,** (*Good Reads Reviewer* USA*)*

This is the first book that I've read from this author and I already can't wait to read more! **Tami Walker** (*http://www.theinspirationlady.com/* USA*)*

The Trouble's Keeper had me pumping "Hard" on the elliptical! I read while exercising. This book was so exciting that suddenly my hour is up. **John N. Kristiansen** (*Good Reads Reviewer* USA*)*

I love this book! You've done it again Susan! Rory is the most amazing of all of your characters. **Alecia** (*Good Reads Reviewer* USA*)*

Another amazing book that will keep you hooked to the last page. **Anisia Kokkinopoulou** (*Good Reads Reviewer* USA*)*

I don't normally read this genre of book ... started it and it was so hard to put down. **Paula Adams** (*Good Reads/Net Galley Reviewer* USA*)*

The plot is unique. The main characters come alive and the writing is captivating. **Karen Brozina** (*Good Reads Reviewer* USA*)*

This was a very original, well written thriller with just a hint of romance. **Irene Cole** (*www.wellwortharead.blogspot.com* USA*)*

A book to make you think, smile and sense a tingling chill or two. **Richard Latham** (*Good Reads Reviewer* United Kingdom*)*

With the genres of paranormal, crime, and suspense all twisted together, fans of any or all of these will find something they like. **Sharon Berge** (*Good Reads Reviewer* USA*)*

This is one of those stories that you will not want to put down. **Stefanie Rizzi** (*Good Reads Reviewer* USA*)*

I usually don't dive into this genre but Susan May's stories are excellent. **Trisha Georgiou** (*Author/Poet* USA*)*

Action, science, mystery with a touch of romance. **Angie Dokos author of Mackenzie's Distraction** *http://www.angiedokos.com/* USA

This book is not easily defined into a simple genre. **Cathy Geha** (*Good Reads Reviewer* LEBANON)

Odd Thomas and Chris Snow fans would love this book. **Diane Lynch** (*Good Reads Reviewer* USA)

New and interesting, the ending was superb and was delivered expertly. **Jenelle Roberts** (*Good Reads Reviewer* Trinidad & Tobago)

Susan May has taken us somewhere unbelievable and made it believable. **John Martin,** Australia (*Author of Major B.S*)

This book grabbed my attention right away ... really couldn't put it down! **Danielle Covelli** (*Good Reads Canada*)

It's easy to follow but hard to figure out ... what a ride. **Ushma Patel** (*Good Reads USA*)

It barely took 5 pages for the love at first write! **Hallie Fletcher** (Good Reads USA)

THE TROUBLES KEEPER

SOMETIMES TROUBLES AREN'T JUST IN YOUR MIND

Bus driver Rory Fine possesses a unique and wonderful gift, the power to relieve others of their troubles for real! With just the barest of touches, the worries and woes of those he helps simply fade away. All remain unaware why in being near him they feel happier and more able to face life's challenges. He's just one of those nice guys who make you feel good.

Despite his special gift and friendly nature Rory can't seem to gather the courage to mumble more than a hello to the one passenger who means everything to him, a girl he might just love. That is, until an evening commute during a hell of a storm when he stops the bus and invites the sullen passengers to play a little game. Tap his palm as they leave and he'll take their troubles and transform their mood. This might also be the perfect chance to speak to the girl who's stolen his heart.

. . .

On board, though, lurks a killer, and he leaves behind something far darker than everyday troubles. Now this sweetheart of a bus driver must discover the killer's identity and somehow stop a relentless evil. To do so, he'll need to face a heart-breaking event from his past and overcome his greatest fear. And he'll need to find a way soon because there's more at stake than just his true love's life... only the very fabric of the world.

From international best selling dark thriller author, Susan May, comes another page-turner keeping readers up way past their bedtime. Board The Troubles Keeper for a non-stop killer suspense ride you won't want to disembark.

WHAT READERS SAY...

⭐⭐⭐⭐⭐ "Susan May seems to be following in the footsteps of **Stephen King.** I, for one, have already put her on my 'if she writes it, I will read it' list." Madelon Wilson (Good Reads Reviewer USA)

⭐⭐⭐⭐⭐ "A unique take on a serial killer and the author is brilliant at creating a storyline that leaves the reader breathless." Maureen Ellis (Good Reads reviewer UK)

⭐⭐⭐⭐⭐ "Love love love! Great Book. Great story. Quick pace. Twists and turns and makes you HAVE to know!"

⭐⭐⭐⭐⭐ "Not since Dean Koontz's Odd Thomas have I enjoyed a character as much as I do Rory Fine!" Carolyn Werner

To the late Frank Capra, director of It's A Wonderful Life. Your film made me look at life differently.

To my husband Franco and my children Bailey and Harry, without you I have no good words.

DEDICATION

The Moving Finger writes; and, having writ,
Moves on: nor all thy Piety nor Wit
Shall lure it back to cancel half a Line,
Nor all thy Tears wash out a Word of it.

The Rubaiyat of Omar Khayyám

1

He examines his work. Certainly not the best he's done but not the worst either. He's improving and becoming more artful. More certain and confident. There's magic in this moment; the *just after* moment when he can breathe again. *In. And out.* A drowning man reaching the surface to suck in pure air so he can survive.

Disappointment rushes in as he feels her last breath. He feels the failure like an ache inside ripping at his core. He felt so certain his search was over, but he was wrong.

He'd found her on the bus. Something had attracted him to *that* bus. Surely the girl, he'd thought. He'd sat behind her as they had traveled downtown. Pretending he'd dropped something, he'd leaned forward. In the closeness he smelled her hair like a bee smells nectar. Sweet. Enticing.

After the bus ride she'd met a friend. A girl just like her, unsuspecting and unaware. As she'd touched her friend, greeting her with a kiss, *there* was the glow, the shine of what lay beneath, inside, where only he could reach down.

At the cinema she was merely four rows away when he saw the shine. Surrounding her, glowing in the dark, a gentle halo of gold as she leaned to her friend to whisper something. They'd laughed, before returning their attention to shared popcorn and the film.

From the multiplex he'd followed, watching from a distance from doorways and shop fronts, pretending to peer into windows. She'd shouted a goodbye to the other—her final goodbye. She hadn't known, so certain there will always be just one more. Does anyone ever recognize their last of anything?

All hope is gone as she slumps. One leg stretched before her, the other bent back beneath the chair like a mannequin awaiting display. Moments before her hands gripped the chair's arms like claws. Now they lay unfurled and limp.

Blood flows in rivulets from the thin, white line carved in her forehead. Red against shiny white bone and pale, translucent skin. Shimmer-black hair falls about her face; strands caught in the blood. He considers brushing them aside to examine the incision, but he's lost his taste for her. He doesn't like the way the face muscles have slackened and her skin droops; how the eyes lay open, staring at him. Above those windows to the soul, white muscle and bone shine through.

As he studies his work he sees his mistake. The hole above her brows, slightly off center, not neat enough. Wrong. Or perhaps not wide enough. The pink-beige flecks of brain matter mingle with the blood. Wrong. The incision is also too deep.

Her fault.

She'd moved, even after he'd explained—in detail, always in detail—why she should be still. Usually they listened. Sometimes not. His concentration had wavered and allowed her to move. He grew stronger with each one though, and soon his control would be absolute and he wouldn't need to bind them.

A long sigh escapes his lips. The need remains, tearing again at him like a climax almost there, but fades away. He wanted, *so wanted* for this to be The One.

He sighs again. No matter, he tells himself—even though this does matter—The One is in this city somewhere out there. He senses her like a hum in the air.

He leans over her, the girl he thought, hoped, would open the door to home. From her brow, he wipes a drip of blood, which hangs like dew. Squeezing and smoothing the blood between his fingertips he thinks back to the bus ride. Something is there behind the curtain of his mind. A strange, little catching lingers, scratching at his awareness, crawling into his subconscious, seeking a memory, a very distant memory.

Now hovering there before him.

The redheaded bus driver.

Could this really be him?

What an ironic twist.

Maybe, *maybe,* this one now just blood and bone and empty flesh, is a sign, a glowing flashing marker. Not The One, but fate's message sent for him. He rolls the idea around inside his mind like the last peppermint in a packet, to be savored, considered.

In that slippery, sliding moment, his disappointment begins to heal. If the bus driver has appeared at this moment, this very day, then there *is* a reason. All he needs to discover is why. He'll take his time. He'll watch. Surely the reason will be revealed.

Reasons usually do.

2

Y ou could blame what happened on the weather.

If not for the sizzling and humid summer evening, the moisture hanging heavy in the air, clinging to everyone's skin, heralding a storm flying toward us, I might never have done what I did.

Rain or shine, storm or blue skies, everything was all fine by me. The weather might get other people down but never me. I knew better.

"Fine" was a great word.

My wonderful mama used to say: "*Fine* by name—Rory Fine, that is—and *fine* by nature."

She peppered my life with that word from the day I entered this world. Until she drew her last breath, haggard and weary, she still insisted *everything* was fine. Always had been and always would be, no matter how much Adversity knocked at her door she wouldn't allow those bad thoughts in.

According to her, my manners were fine enough for the President, should he ever come to visit. My friends, my quite average school results, my smile, my sandy, red hair—the butt of schoolyard jokes—

my stories, everything, was just fine. Nothing earned her reproach. Nada.

"You're the finest thing in my life," she'd say.

"And you're the finest in mine," I'd reply.

The day she left this earth was certainly Heaven's finest and the saddest day I'll ever live. Her last words, spoken in broken syllables and wisps of sound to me, her sobbing seventeen-year-old who'd kept vigil by her bed hoping for a miracle.

"Don't ... cry, my darling boy. God smiled the day you were born. Have a *fine* life my son. That is your destiny."

She may have revised her prediction if she'd known about this hell-hot day that awaited, nine years down the road. There was too much of what St. Alban folk call the Madness Air. The kind of hot that never helps anyone's mood. Or troubles.

A slight breeze blew in off the Dawson River, trying for all it was worth to cool things down just a little. Without that freshening whisper people'd be crawling up the walls by nightfall. Three days straight the heat had invaded our city and sure made my job all that much harder. At the end of a day, all the passengers wanted was to get to their air-conditioned or fan-cooled homes. You know how people look when they've had enough, their muscles stretched beyond capacity and energy on low flow? Well, this described my passengers today. Every single one of them.

I've been driving buses for five years now. A peculiar job for a young man, I know. I know. At twenty-six I should be exploring the world, making my mark, building some kind of résumé to show I've done something with my life and secured my future.

For me though, this job is perfect fitting like a glove with my other more important work. *Life Job*, as I think of my sideline business.

Probably what I do is a smaller scale version of solving global warming by switching off a single light bulb one lamp at a time. So a big job. *Big*. Yet, one by one, I switched off those bulbs, because who knew the effect that might have? Think of my intervention as saving one butterfly that might flap its wings in Bangkok and, in flapping those little wings averts a bushfire in Australia and saves a town. You know the Butterfly Effect, right? That's me, the Butterfly Effect guy. Except, I call this thing I do troubles keeping, which makes me a Troubles Keeper.

I love this job, both jobs, most days. Looking for greener pastures doesn't enter my mind. Even if those thoughts did, I couldn't leave, because in the last six months all had changed. I simply can't leave until everything plays out.

3

Mariana entered my life via the bus's front boarding steps. She delicately boarded the bus, gliding like a dream. Her smile, followed by a casual "hello," hit me like an electric spark that traveled up my spine and charged my soul. Think those zap things that restart hearts. Her smile did that to me. *Smile. Spark. Zap.* Now I'm magnetized to her. *Nope, I can't leave now.*

I'm in glorious, wonderful, very fine love.

The day she hit me with that warm smile was cold, wet, and nasty; not a day you'd expect love to come a knocking. She climbed aboard my bus, soaked and bedraggled, golden-blonde coils, dark with moisture, poking out from beneath her raincoat hood.

Mariana pushed back the hood of her green-with-pink roses patterned coat, looked down her front, then back at me.

"Sorry. I'm dripping. Raining crazy out there. Am I okay?"

Droplets ran down her jacket to puddle on the charcoal-colored steps as she stared at me through running-mascara-blackened eyes. A gentle, magical light switched on instantly brightening that cloud-darkened day.

I heard my Mama's voice whisper in my ear. *Rory, she's the finest,*

most beautiful natural woman in the world. I like her. I know Mama,
me too.

I remember that day like yesterday, remember I'd wanted to say
something smart, something flirty and light. Normally I'm good with
a quip. Witty Fine, some call me. Something happened to my brain or
my heart or whatever had joyfully twisted inside my chest. My voice
had been suddenly held hostage so the best I had managed was a nod
toward the back of the bus and a limp smile.

"Thank you," she'd said, pulling and pushing at her coat as
though removing a layer of skin. More drops flew about her. Then
she had moved down the aisle, her coat now over her arm. The last
glance I had snatched in my mirror was of her seating herself next to
Mr. Ogilvy (gray-haired, weary eyes and always missing his son).

Six months ago that had happened and still I hadn't worked up
anything close to enough courage to squeak more than a "hello" or
"have a nice day." I guess that's why today I became bold and took a
risk. On reflection, what possessed me?

Love. Unexpressed love.

On this stifling day, air sticky with invisible moisture, the high-
light was my anticipation of Mariana's stop. Nearly two years now, the
nine-zero-five was my regular route, traveling through City Central
with its towering buildings, bustle of shops and department stores,
clutter of lunch bars and cafes, and thousands of workers navigating
the streets, seemingly always in a rush. From the city we enjoyed a
picturesque two-mile drive along the wide and glistening-blue
Dawson River, the focal point of the city. Then, on to East Village
(doesn't every city have an East Village?). Here we passed the
ramshackle, no-longer-in-use, ancient cemetery. Then along
Ellsworth Road, the epicenter of the village, dotted with small
boutiques, sweet, fine eateries nestled beneath low-rise residential
apartment blocks, (sprung up like well-watered saplings since the
reinvigoration of the area).

The route terminated at East Village train station by Benedict
House, so named to conceal the building was really a halfway house
for addicts on the mend. Then the route reversed back the same way.

Three hours after I'd swung the bus out the gates, I drove back into the depot for a break, before repeating the journey all over again.

What most people would consider a mundane job—same streets, same view, same stops and starts—I enlivened by getting to know my regulars. In fact, I did more than get to know them, more than transport them from A to B. I helped them. I changed lives.

They never understood, of course, why on the odd occasion their commute left them happier, more content than when they'd boarded. Maybe they thought the change in mood was due to my friendly smile, or the chance to relax while someone else drove, or that anywhere was better than where they'd just left.

But the difference was me. My touch. My gift to them, delivered without a trace, without a sound, without anybody knowing why suddenly the world seemed a brighter place; the troubles they carried when they left their homes that morning now not so heavy.

I didn't need a thank you or to leave a florist's calling card: *Here's a gift because I can, because I want to make the world a better place.* I didn't need acknowledgment; all I needed were their smiles, their improved moods, and to see extra bounce in their steps as though they no longer toted that emotional backpack.

Troubles. They stick to skin like glue, like gum to the sole of a shoe. They slide into the crevices of your heart, slither into your veins, and tug at you from the inside until they become something dark and heavy and not so easy to shake.

The length of time you allow them to take up residence, that's what makes all the difference between the good, the bad, and the ugly days. Sure, you can brush them aside—and most good folk usually do—but what gets you is the sometimes; the sometimes when shrugging off troubles may not be so simple.

I took away the sometimes.

Dawson River was my favorite stretch. Some days the word *fine* just wasn't enough. The sun rising, yellow and pink, a present to those awake, and the sun setting over glistening water, warm gold, a splendid vista that made you believe in all things good. Some days the river didn't need the sun to shine. Rain splashing its surface, urged small white-tipped waves to rise up like dancing handker-chiefs. I knew this river like a friend. We shared a secret; in fact, we were allies.

This five-fourteen afternoon run was my favorite. Not just because of Mariana, either. My best work was done in these hours. If people ever needed relief from their troubles, the time was after a hard day's work. But, for whatever reason on that day, most passengers seemed to feel the weight of life more than usual. I guess that's why I did what I did, before I'd thought the whole thing through.

4

He peers through the bus window at the ominous clouds. The light drops of rain, quickly turn the gray of the sidewalk to a mottled black. He likes this dark brand of sky. People are less aware, far more concerned with getting to shelter, staying dry, worrying about plans made more difficult by the heavens spilling down.

Though he walks freely among them, beside these scurrying creatures of habit, there's always a risk he'll be recognized for his true self. Rain feels like an invisible cloak; the humidity like soft, protective fiber against his skin.

Until he found *him* on this bus in the late afternoon, he had spent the day traveling the bus routes, attempting to ascertain if what he felt yesterday was because of this bus, or this man, or a random connection to something else. *Now he knows.* He'd moved seats numerous times, reached out and brushed a few of those around him. *Nothing.* Just a nagging frustration growing within that he may have been mistaken.

Now as he watches him—yes, and the man *is* him—he understands like a faded memory reinvigorated by an old song or the whiff of an intangible scent. He *knows* his search is over.

With each stop he studies the driver, cobbles his memories

together, and wonders why he hadn't sought him out before. Of course, he may help him to open the door. *Friend or enemy, though?*

The way he looks at the girl, all golden hair and a smile, as she climbs aboard and skims past the driver, reveals so much. This makes perfect sense; the two of them special lights in a world filled with half-opened doorways and empty rooms. They are both of the same design.

As she maneuvers down the aisle, the girl places a hand on the seat back in front of him. He reaches out nonchalantly to touch her. Electric fire, blue and sharp, rushes through his skin.

She could be The One.

He soaks in this knowledge, and the peace this thought brings. This long search could be over. Her brow lifts playfully as she looks down at his hand; surprise crosses her face. He smiles and withdraws the hand, feigning embarrassment. She smiles. Unsuspecting. No reason to fear. A random accident of physicality, a moving bus, an unbalanced body.

Now she is his and he can source her at will. A thrill plays through him and goosebumps rise on his skin. For the next fifteen minutes he slides between exhilaration and frustration that he must wait until tonight. He'll follow, but he's learned through experience that timing is everything.

Then the bus stops and the driver stands facing down the aisle. He introduces himself. *Rory Fine.* Has the man recognized him? Surely the bus driver cannot know or he would have noticed a reaction.

As the bus driver talks he begins to understand. This isn't a random chance meeting that he is here on this bus with her. Something grander is at play. He just needs to figure out exactly what that means.

5

I looked down the aisle, acutely aware of everyone's stare. Why had I stopped the bus? That's what they were thinking. I'd never done this before, so my regulars will be just as bemused as the random first-timers. I didn't prepare for this. What I was about to do today just seemed right. My Mama always said: *When someone has a gift, keeping that gift to themselves is wrong.*

Well, I may use my gift wherever and whenever I can, but I keep this secret for good reason. First, I'd sound crazy. Pure and simple, as sure as the sun rises and the Dawson flows, I'd end up locked away. That's if I could even explain troubles keeping. Second, I learned as a kid, this knowledge is dangerous in the wrong hands.

You know the idea that everything is energy? Even a stone laying there solid is *still* moving. You can't see the movement, of course, but if you got down to an atomic level, you'd see there's plenty going on. Same goes for emotional energy. There's a lot going on. Even if you can't see it, you sure can feel something.

Putting the evil eye on someone (malocchio), cursing a person, feeling blue, and wishing someone every happiness, or good health, even prayer. These are physical descriptions for something you cannot see.

Why did I stand in front of all these good folks taking a big chance? With Mariana looking at me, maybe thinking, *what's with this guy*? Why would I bother with troubles keeping? Snatching up worries from strangers? Yep, no money in that. Recognition: nil. Kind of tiring, if I'm honest.

Maybe I like the way people smile when troubles flow away. Maybe helping others gives my life purpose and keeps the balance of good and bad in check. The idea of yin and yang is kinda cool.

I thought this would turn out to be just another normal *pick up troubles and float them away and aren't I a swell guy* day. But I was wrong. Something dark had boarded my bus. As I opened my mouth I couldn't know that this simple action would levy a cost I'd struggle to pay.

I smiled and in my most confident go-along-with-me voice said, "If I could have your attention, please. I noticed everybody looking glum." Insert reassuring smile here. "Hope you don't mind, but I'd like to help."

A busload of puzzled eyes stared at me.

The game was on and I hoped we'd all be winners.

6

Thirty-four Minutes Prior

Five-fourteen p.m. and I'd run ten minutes late for the last thirty minutes of this run. Not late-late, but late enough that a few boarding passengers wore *disgruntled* like a red flashing vest.

Despite threatening *nasty* ahead and spitting down on us, the weather hadn't seen fit to send enough decent rain to cool the city down. Yet. A downpour was coming though; the clouds hung low and the humidity thickened by the minute.

Every time the doors opened at a stop, the heat rushed in as though attempting to steal a ride. Tracks of sweat rolled down my face, despite the air-conditioning.

The minute rain threatens, the traffic multiplies as though to manufacture cars you just needed to add water. *Getting nowhere fast,* rang through my head and a silent prayer that the cooling afternoon breeze would skim up the river and drop the degrees by ten.

On an average day this run was usually full. Two extra buses scheduled within minutes of mine caught the overflow of stragglers. Today though, I was the bus behind. Some regulars had actually waited for my bus and that brightened my day.

There were no passengers until the third stop on the route: Green Wall Road. Mrs. Daley was always there with a smile and an over-sized brown bag clutched tightly to her body. If we're talking fruit for a body-shape, she was a pear. Fifteen years she'd been a cleaner at Metro Inn, but maybe not for much longer. Earlier this week she'd told me, with a hopeful smile, she'd applied to the accounts department of the hotel. "My back," she said, "is near quitting with all the bending over bathtubs and beds. I gotta get out of this work."

"Nothing great," she said, when I asked about her day as she climbed on board. "Same old, same old, Rory." She winked at me, the skin wrinkling around her eyes. "But any day above ground's better than the alternative. Probably be cooler down there though. Which *would* be nice."

I threw her a smile and pressed the hydraulic release. The doors closed with a groaning swoosh. Her back must be complaining today, even if she hadn't. She clutched at the railing on each alternate seat as she slowly made her way to her usual seat, mid section on the right. From the rear view I watched and waited until she'd nestled herself down. My final glimpse: she retrieving a blue wool ball and knitting needles from her bag. She'd promised me a scarf for this winter. She knew my mom was gone.

Not all passengers were quite as habitual as Mrs. Daley, but regulars like her gave me a sense of being part of a family, part of a team.

Next stop, Limestone Avenue. Six more travelers. Only one a regular: the woman with brown, wavy hair. She had white alien-looking eyebrows and moved like a person who felt watched and judged. Never a smile. Her sadness went deep. The other three: a group of mid-twenties women dressed for a cocktail party, loudly climbed aboard. Fashion detailed and mini-skirted, with vibrant red lips, heavily mascaraed lashes, and hair straightened to shining silk; they laughed at a private joke, too busy talking to each other to notice my smile. I still smiled. Smiles are free. You can never give away too many.

Seven minutes later, we were into the south end of the central business district. Tailor-suited lawyers, financiers, and corporate office workers inhabited this area. A better dressed group of passengers filed silently into my care. The two earlier buses would soon reach capacity, they'd quit stopping and I'd become the main bus.

At Capital Tower, the two I called the lovebirds always waited. Mark—tall, dark, with a sharp edge to his face. Tracy, much shorter, with cheeks like those models you see, all bones and tight skin. Both somewhere in their twenties. They'd just become engaged, and were usually happy and handholding and sweet as a passion fruit popsicle.

Uh-oh, not today. No entwined hands. No smiles. They looked more like a quarreling brother and sister as they angled past with a brief, sad smile from Mark and nothing from Tracy, except a glare at Mark.

I followed them in the mirror, curious. I liked watching love, wishing happiness for everyone. The two still sat beside each other— that was good—two rows from the back. Maybe I was mistaken, maybe they were okay. Then Tracy slumped into the window seat and turned her back on Mark, pursed her lips, and stared out the window.

That did not look good.

I itched to see them back as they had been yesterday: love birds happy in their love cage. As I drove, I thought about what I could do to help. Maybe this couple and that moment was what prompted me later to take the risk.

Over the next four stops an ebb and flow of passengers continued, some on, some off, as we passed through the entertainment area of the city. Southbridge was a four-block assortment of restaurants and theaters, with a small two-lane section of Chinese supermarkets and eateries like every Chinatown in every large city. The young miniskirt women alighted at Terrace Street, still giggling and talking. They made their way along the sidewalk like a gang of models (or was that a glitter of models?), beautiful and young, oblivious to the stares of passersby.

Mr. Bradley, bushy eyebrows, crumpled suit, and knobby ears (who had a habit of pulling on those knobby earlobes as he spoke) made his way onto the bus as though he'd scaled a five-hundred-step Asian temple.

He didn't look happy, either.

"Good evening Mr. Bradley." I tried to sound chipper and upbeat. Sometimes an ordinary, send-a-good-vibe worked almost as well as troubles keeping.

"Evening Mister Rory. How are you, son?"

I saw now as his eyes met mine that he didn't look good, like the light in them had been turned down. He had grown worse. His troubles weighed down his every step. He had so many worries even I couldn't help him to any great degree. I tried, of course. You always try.

"As fine as I can be in this heat." I caught myself—no negativity. You let a glimpse in and that pessimism grows. "Still, this air-conditioning's darn wonderful, so I won't complain."

"Sure is hot. Days like this, my body reminds me I'm a long way from young."

"Better close the door quickly then. Keep the cool air in," I said, pressing on the lever. "Might have to sleep in here tonight."

He continued on, and as he did, mumbled, "Might have to join you. Yes, I might."

Three rows behind me, he claimed a seat, shuffling in as though climbing into a deep chasm. I watched in the mirror as he opened his newspaper and began to read. Most catch the news on their smart phones or tablets these day, but Mr. Ogilvy was stubbornly old school.

We had that in common. I barely remembered to carry my phone. Who'd call me and who would *I* call? Since middle school I'd steered clear of relationships. When you have my gift, you need caution more than you need friends. Better to be a friend to everyone, but close with no one. Safer. People don't die that way.

As I navigated the bus into traffic, I noted half way through my route the bus was unusually full. No doubt, weather played a factor. Nobody wants to walk even a few blocks in the heat or with rain threatening. The engine groaned with the extra weight.

Traveling by Joe's Pizzeria I felt a tug. No, not from the food, although they did make the best pepperoni and mushroom you'll taste this side of the Dawson. No, the tingling and my heart beating faster were for a whole other reason. From this point on, I could barely focus. No trick of thought control could take my mind away from the next stop and the passenger waiting there.

Nile Street bordered the end of the central city area. Here, shops were older, cobbled together in a ramshackle fashion, as they'd remained as they were built nearly a hundred years before. This area of the city awaited reinvigoration, if renewal ever came. Shop signs touted Lucky's Laundry, Elizabethan Used Book Store, Nile Street Real Estate, and the bright note of this passage being Wanderings Deli, two doors down from the stop. Rows of bucketed flowers and fruit sitting on either side of the door sung out a colorful hello to me every day. I often wished I could stop and buy flowers for her, but then would I ever have the courage to present them?

Nile Street was Mariana's stop. *This* was where the sun rose and set in my day. Every time I saw her waiting there, I had to fight to keep a love-struck grin from swallowing my face. Of course, I didn't do the normal thing, the smart thing, like smile, say hello and connect. Nope. I kept my head down, nodded, or looked the other way. Occasionally when she said "thank you" or "goodbye," I managed a "No problem."

My mama would have said, "Rory, spit those words out and take your chances." But she wasn't here to encourage me, and I had no reason to feel encouraged, so I watched Mariana from the mirror with downturned eyes. Pretty darn feeble, *I know.*

Mariana worked part-time at Sterling's Records, a block from Nile Street. Of course, I didn't garner this tidbit from her. Several months prior, I learned this by accident. The only time I had dared speak to her, and my face still reddened at the thought.

7

That day, Mariana stood at the Nile Street stop staring down at her phone, wearing a loose, black Macklemore and Ryan Lewis t-shirt emblazoned with *I'm Gonna Pop Some Tags.* She'd look amazing in anything, even old sweats.

Be still, stupid heart, I remember thinking. Every time I saw her I felt a lightness like flying in a dream and my breath always stuck in my throat. Mariana barely looked up from her phone as she'd climbed the steps and continued down the aisle. That's why she didn't notice something had fallen from her bag.

I called out to her without even thinking—"Ma'am!"—before realizing who I was addressing. Instantly my cheeks matched the color of my hair.

She didn't turn or stop, but continued to stare at her phone and kept moving down the aisle.

"Ma'am, excuse me." My voice, though louder, sounded reed-thin and awkward. The *me* came out cracked and whiny like I was a hormonal teenager.

Mariana paused in the aisle and looked up. Mrs. Daley pointed toward me, and I shrank in my seat as Mariana turned and gave me a quizzical gaze. A million fireworks instantly exploded in my head.

Like a puppeteer controlled my hand, I clumsily pointed to the piece of paper lying innocently on the floor. I wanted so badly to get out of my seat and reach for the slip. That would be chivalrous. That would be good mannered. But I felt glued down to the spot. My body, like my voice, belonged to someone else.

"You've drop-pped ... something. Something there." My finger moved, but in a limp embarrassing way. "From, from your bag." I got the sentence out, but my voice faltered on "bag."

She looked in the direction of my pointing digit, which then slowly curled back into my palm.

"Oh. Thank you," she said, floating back down the aisle and bending gracefully to pick up the errant paper. I expected her to turn and walk away, the moment over. My face still glowed red, the awkwardness thick in my pores, hot and uncomfortable. I couldn't have felt more exposed had I danced naked down the aisle.

Clutching the slip in her hand, she smiled, then turned to continue away before stopping, as though a thought had occurred to her. She looked down at the paper, paused, then retraced her steps to the front of the bus and held the slip toward me.

"This is a flyer from my work, actually. I'm meant to give them to friends. And family. Anyone who's interested, in fact."

She looked at me and actually smiled. I shrank inside; I didn't feel worthy of her smile.

"Do you like music?" *Her voice sounded like music.*

The flyer hung between us. If I took that simple piece of paper, what did that mean? If I answered her question in the affirmative, then would she ask what music I liked? Then, would I answer the wrong music, music she hated and ruin any chance I might have? Would she laugh but not in a good way?

"I, um, I, I don't know," I said.

Mariana cocked her head to the side, an eyebrow raised.

Oh, that was dumb. Of course I liked music. Who doesn't like music?

Every time I opened my mouth, my voice sounded like a squeaking, badly-played violin. I was too scared to say anymore, so I said nothing. Like a mute. Like an idiot. Like a lovesick idiot.

She wrinkled her brow, then said, quite brightly, as though my lack of response was perfectly fine and she hadn't noticed I was a mute idiot, "Okay, well, if you do ... like music, I mean, we're having a sale at Sterling's Music. I work there. Overstocked, my boss says. He blames iTunes."

"I love music," I said, even though I couldn't name any of the latest hits. Enough went on in my head without adding music and lyrics to the mix. But I did *like* music when melodies entered my consciousness. Tunes just didn't usually factor highly in my world.

"I might lose my job if sales don't pick up. If you know anyone who likes music, can you tell them too, please?"

Mariana reached inside her bag and drew out a handful of the flyers and passed them to me. "You could give them to passengers. Yes —that's an idea! Could you?" She smiled sweetly, expectantly, unaware of the impact of her smile on me.

My tongue felt knotted, my mouth dry. The best I managed was to take the flyers and nod. Then I couldn't stop the nodding like I was a crazy bobble head.

Finally, my tongue unglued. "Hmm. Sure." I snatched the flyers and stuffed them in a shelf in the bus dashboard. I'd just been kind of rude, I thought, but that response was the best I could do when she stood so close. She must have thought I didn't care and wouldn't hand them out. That I didn't care she might lose her job. But I did. I cared for everything about her. Why couldn't I act self-assured like the hero in a movie who always gets the girl?

Perhaps because I was just Rory Fine, bus driver with a peculiar little gift.

I knew my face had turned tomato-red, so I tried not to look at her. Sweat had formed on the back of my neck and beads of moisture popped on my face. I wanted to say what I thought: "Sure thing, I'd do anything for you." Then she might reply, "Wow, so kind. Let's have coffee and get to know each other."

Yeah, in my dreams.

Instead I said, still squeaky-voiced, "No problem." Then I turned back to the wheel so I didn't have to see the look on her face that would say, *What a weirdo. And rude. Really rude.* But I heard her voice behind me: "Thank you. You're a sweetie."

I looked at her in the mirror, moving only my eyes, not daring to move a muscle in case I lost control. She moved back up the aisle and found a seat. Unaware, I'm sure, she'd unraveled my day.

I flipped the indicator, making an overly exaggerated movement of checking the side mirror—to say *I'm good, really, I'm in control*—before easing the bus out into the traffic.

That was terrifying. And hopeless. And embarrassing. That day was certainly 'no fine day.'

One of those flyers sat on my night table for several days, as though having that piece of paper there kept Mariana close. I'd even visited Sterling's once during the sale to find her not there. I don't know if I felt relief or disappointment. Next time she boarded, I mumbled, "I came to the store. For the sale?" Which would have been fine, but my brain disengaged. I then repeated "I do like music. Yeah, I really like music" twice.

Mariana raised an eyebrow and said, "Thank you, good of you." Then she laughed. "I'm glad you like music. Hope there's more of *you* out there somewhere." Then she was gone.

I turned back to the wheel and that small moment haunted me for weeks, the seconds repeating in my head relentlessly with what I could have, should have said.

After that, Mariana never said anything more to me than *hello, thank you*, and *goodbye*. I spoke plenty to her in my head, but I found nothing I could say aloud that didn't sound weird or make me sound like a stalker.

Nearly three months to the day, here we were again, and music or flyers or anything so simple wasn't what began our conversation again. An impromptu idea, which filled my head when I noted the universal gloom on the passengers' faces was what gave me the shove. I might not have the courage to speak to Mariana, but de-glumming a busload of people? That I could do.

8

U p ahead, Mariana stood like a beautiful statue. Even among a crowd of waiting people, she was noticeable. Her outfit today was one of my favorites: a rose-bronze metallic miniskirt and a gray off-the-shoulder slouch shirt with hearts embroidered on the sleeves. Tan-bronze lace-up ankle boots accentuated her perfect legs. So cute and unaffected.

The breeze created by the bus's arrival blew her blond curls across her face, and she reached up to push errant strands behind her ears.

Maybe the weather, maybe the idea forming in my head made me brash for a moment, but as she climbed the steps, I began to speak. "How, how are you? Hot, really hot, right?" Stupid, obvious thing to say, but at least my voice didn't sound like an eighth grader.

She smiled, actually looked delighted. Or was that wishful thinking? "I'm great. Despite the heat. How are you, nice bus driver?"

Nice bus driver.

"Fine," I said, my face beginning to heat. *Nice bus driver?*

My next words had a life of their own. They ran together like a sped up recording. "*Iseeyousoften. Seemsrude* not to, to … *introducemyself*. Rory, Rory Fine. Fine by name, fine by nature."

Oh, heck. *Fine by name, fine by nature?* The words had sounded good in my head. Ridiculous though, hanging out there.

Mariana lifted an eyebrow again, and because I'd totally lost my mind, I continued on. "Um, just don't call me Lion."

She looked puzzled.

"You know, *roar*, as in Ror-eee. A lion, you know? Roars?"

Mariana coughed a polite laugh as though she thought my quip half funny.

"Your name?" I asked, even though I knew her name, even though I bordered on sounding creepy now, but I'd committed. "Nothing weird that I'm asking. Just, you know, I see you quite often—not that I was paying attention, no, I mean I *do* pay attention, but not because you're a girl. Because you're a *regular*. I pay attention to my regulars."

Was my voice getting high again?

"Oh, yes, right," she said, tilting her head to the side and puckering her lips like she couldn't figure out what she really thought. *What had I done?*

"I'm Mariana. Just don't call me Marry. I'm too young."

My turn now to look confused.

"Marry. A nickname?" The words came out better, less frantic; at least my voice had lowered an octave.

"No, it's a joke, silly. A joke because you made a joke. Mariana. Marry? M-A-R-R-Y. Forget it. Such a stupid thing to say."

"Oh."

The sound came out like a sigh, not a word. *Again.* Again, words deserted me. Until I spoke a line no guy says to a girl who'd stolen his heart, ever. "Well Mariana, nice to have you on-board."

Nice to have you on-board? *Nice to have you on-board,* like I'm some kind of over salted sea captain? I pushed my face into what I hoped was a charming grin.

"Thank you."

Mariana smiled at me, white teeth and sparkling green eyes. "And thanks for always being such a friendly bus driver. Rory ... Lion Rory."

She laughed and our eyes met. I felt something. Maybe I saw a glow come to her face, a flicker, a magical thread darned between us, stitched together by the silly conversation.

But I panicked. The smile slid from my face and I abruptly turned away. Now my voice was quiet; no charm and no emotion. "Okay, then—well, I'd better hurry or I'll be a *late* bus driver."

I left her standing in the aisle, dismissed like I didn't care.

"Of course," I heard her say over my shoulder. I imagined I felt the slight displacement of air as she turned. As I always did, I watched her in the mirror for a moment longer, before she wandered down the aisle to sit across from Mrs. Daley.

My breath caught in my throat as I forced my foot on the accelerator and guided the bus onward. I glanced upward in the mirror one more time. She'd begun to read. She always read.

For the next ten minutes I drove on auto-pilot. I didn't dare check on her again. My focus now was on controlling my thumping heart. *What was that feeling that passed between us? Was there even a feeling?*

Passengers climbed aboard and exited for the next half dozen stops. Only a few regulars now. The mother and her boy who rode once a week. Dawn, I think was her name, and her young son Tommy, who sometimes carried a guitar case that looked far too big for him. Visiting her sister, I think she told me once. She always hugged him so close once seated, her arm around the back of his shoulders, as though afraid he might run away. Once, I heard him ask why they didn't drive. She'd said something about the safety of riding a bus.

Overhearing conversations went with the job. A driver's a ghost. Nobody thinks twice about spilling his or her secrets in earshot. I'm a spectator and eavesdropper of a live reality show.

Near the Butler Street stop I started to note something strange in the air. A dark mood had snuck onto the bus, easing its way inside each time I opened the door, as if the approaching storm had joined us for the journey.

The fifteen to twenty people still on the bus had stopped talking, the silence heavy and claustrophobic. Anger, frustration, irritation and melancholy. A collective gloom.

While stopped at traffic lights I surveyed the passengers in the mirror. Most stared absently out the window—even if they were in an aisle seat. The darkening skies seemed a magnet. Many probably wondered if they'd arrive home before the storm. A few, most notably Tracy and Mark, were clearly unhappy with more than the weather.

Mariana still read her book, but even *she* frowned. Normally, even while concentrating, she wore a subtle smile like everything she read amused her.

When troubles have clearly invaded someone's life, I'd deliver my special brand of help. Clearly more than one person on this bus had palpable troubles like the pall of a heavy morning fog. I drew my gaze from their misery to look ahead through the oversized windshield. Speckles of rain dotted the glass, and the automatic wipers threw themselves into removing the offending liquid.

We were well away from the city center, and these remaining passengers were mostly homeward bound. The bus route would terminate in twenty-five minutes. I needed to say something to Mariana when she alighted, try to recover from my blunder. What to do or say though, that wouldn't sink me deeper into creepy-guy-ville?

At each stop as I waited for passengers to disembark, I ran scenarios and quips through my mind. They all sounded great—in my head—but who knows when they left my mouth? In between these thoughts, I kept playing mental eeny-meeny-miny-mo with the passengers, thinking who might I help tonight.

The sweetheart septuagenarian Ellen, who visited her daughter's home twice weekly to babysit her grandchildren gave me the idea. She slowly made her way toward the front as I neared her stop, her cane tapping as she went. Normally, she'd touch my arm and thank me profusely as if I'd personally escorted her home. "Happy evening Rory. You're a lovely boy," she'd say.

Tonight though, even Ellen threw me a curt "thanks" before disappearing into the night, tapping along the pavement, mouth taut as though her lips were sewn together. I thought to myself: now why didn't I pat her arm as she passed, pull those troubles from her, so she didn't carry that extra weight home with her?

Something *was* different today and, like the humidity, a heaviness hung in the air. Worry, troubles, negativity had taken residence in the passengers to form a collective melancholy like a contagious yawn. Tracy and Mark with their quarrel. Mr. Ogilvy's sadness even deeper. Ellen, even Mariana. Everybody just looked miserable. What was the cause? The hour? The weather? The approaching storm?

As if hearing my thoughts, in the near distance flashes of jagged white breached the dark sky. Thunder rumbled. The storm was nearly upon us, feeling omnipotent and hungry, seeking my bus, my passengers. How could I allow poor Ellen to go out there carrying the heaviness I saw in her, when I could have done something?

If they all carried home the melancholy, the gloom would spread to everyone with whom they would interact in the next few hours or even days. A multiplier effect of misery.

These people needed me. I couldn't allow them to get off coated in angst and worry. The streets of every city were filled with the destitute, the results of accumulated moments of troubles left to fester.

A crazy idea popped into my head and took hold. I pushed the thought away, telling myself this held danger. But the darn notion wouldn't let go. I'd never used my gift for more than a few persons at any time. Just because I'd never tried though, didn't mean this was impossible. Maybe I could even learn something.

There was another benefit too. *Mariana.* Maybe this would give me a chance to talk to her. Maybe she'd even be impressed. Then, who knew after that?

"Yes," I mouthed silently, as another flash of lightning lit the sky, a perfect backdrop to a critical decision. Okay, so I would lift every passenger's troubles as they disembarked. Lighten each person's load. There was absolutely no reason I couldn't make this work. If I felt myself become overloaded, I would simply stop.

Yes, I could do this.

One catch. I needed to physically make contact with each person. Probably not a great idea to grab passengers, even if we were on first name basis. *So how to do this?*

As we approached Riverside Drive, the half-mile width of open river came into view. The sky was so dark now where the water ended and the sky began was blurred. The little tips of white I'd seen on a previous run had grown to form undulating waves lashing the shore. Small boats and a ferry bobbed and rocked as the blustery wind heralded the imminent storm. Big, juicy drops of rain now hit the road and pavement. The complaining squawk of the accelerated windshield wipers scraping across the glass reached inside the cabin.

As I stopped at a red light, I glanced back into the bus interior. Nearly every passenger stared tight-lipped, toward the river on our left, probably dreading the prospect of walking into the melee.

Fifty yards ahead a tall man in a thick, dark trench coat waited at the next stop. He reached out an arm from beneath a black umbrella to signal me to stop. I didn't recognize him.

I eased the bus to the curb and released the doors. Trench Coat climbed aboard and navigated to stand a few rows from the front. He didn't smile or acknowledge me but merely added to the sullen atmosphere like he was another pebble in a bucket of misery. You couldn't blame him. Despondency filled the air.

My mama used to say: *If you stand by while others are in need, then that's bad karma, right there, and bad karma is a heck of a thing to wear.*

That was that.

In the next thirty seconds I would do something wonderful or make a complete fool of myself. Since the bus was already stopped, now was as good a time as any. I pushed on the hand brake in the console and pulled myself out of my seat to stand in the aisle. Several people near the front noticed and stared like they couldn't believe I had legs. Everyone else continued to glare out the windows.

Calm was a necessity with my talent, so I inhaled a deep breath and took a moment. *Calm. Be at peace.*

I didn't look at Mariana. I might have lost my nerve, if I had. Instead I looked to the left of her across the aisle at Mrs. Daley. She now smiled at me, a puzzled look on her face. That smile gave me courage.

I cleared my throat, the sound feeble yet ridiculously loud in my head. One of my hands, with a mind of its own, rubbed up and down

my other arm, now held rigid at my side. Before doubts could intercept my actions, I opened my mouth and spoke the fateful words.

"If I could have your attention, please."

A smattering of people turned toward me, puzzlement painted
across their faces.

"I noticed everybody looking decidedly glum." I inserted a reassuring smile. "I think I can help. I'll still get you to where you're going
on time—you too, sir." I nodded at Trench Coat, still in the aisle and
fussing with his umbrella. He tilted his head back to look at me.

Everyone had stopped now, their attention on me. I thought I
noticed Mariana look up, but I didn't dare look at her.

My heart wanted to escape my chest and run screaming from the
bus. As I felt the full focus and emotions of the passengers, I wanted
to run too. But if I stopped now I'd look pretty ridiculous. The only
way out was forward.

This was more stressful than normal. When my mind was
peaceful I had more control, and lifting the troubles of all these folk
would require the utmost control. I needed to relax.

Breathe. Breathe. Breathe. Hold. Exhale. Calm Rory, calm.

Thankfully, my heartbeat seemed to be slowing. I needed to get
this done.

"Some of you know me. We've spent many trips together, haven't
we? Some don't, I know, and you're thinking, 'Is this guy nuts or
what?' So ... my name is Rory Fine. Watching you all tonight made
me think of something my mama always said: *'Life's too short not to
smile.'*"

A couple in the second row to my right nodded agreement.
Several others looked at each other. I dared a glance at Mariana.
Nothing. I looked past her, so I wouldn't lose my nerve. Then I think I
stopped breathing.

Breathe. Breathe. And go. Keep going.

I sucked air in until my chest hurt, and continued.

"Today, with this weather, the storm coming—" I made a motion
over my shoulder, through the windshield toward the heavy, dark
clouds over the Dawson. "—seems to me anyway, the weight of every-

one's troubles might be a tad heavier than usual. I see the slump in your shoulders, the look in your eyes like you've had enough. You might have noticed the mood is about as stifling as the air."

Tracy, who seemed glued to the window, as far from her fiancé as she could get, vigorously bounced her head. Young, apprentice chef Glen, with his tied-back, don't-give-a-damn ponytail, who always seemed distant and ready to explode, nodded too.

"Just a guess," I continued, "but everyone seems overly caught up in their troubles tonight." I paused to take another breath. "And taking these worries home to your loved ones, that ain't fair. If nobody's waiting on you, still unfair. *To you.*Brooding alone won't solve a thing. So here's an idea. I'm gonna get back in my seat and keep driving and stopping, as usual, but when I get to *your* stop, you'll see my hand held out. As you pass by, I want you to touch my palm and leave all your troubles with me. Just swipe those bad boys away."

Blank stares met my words. Were they thinking *He's crazy*? Any bravado I possessed had begun to leak from my pores, and despite the air-conditioning, I felt sweat beading at the back of my neck.

Moments moved by slowly. I think I even heard ticking in my head. Then a blond woman, sporting pigtails, smiled and began to clap. My gaze traveled around the bus, as more and more smiles illuminated faces and others joined in clapping. Even Tracy's straight-lined lips softened.

I could possibly do this, I thought, and make a real difference to a lot of people. If I could keep their troubles, free them, maybe they wouldn't have that fight with their spouse, which steered to separation and divorce. Or yell at their children and hurl words that might remain with that child for the rest of their lives. Or they'd sleep better without worry as a bedfellow and the next day they might not make a mistake that would cost them their job. They might not argue with a parent on the phone who asked too many times, *What's wrong?* Estrangements begin with the tiniest of things.

At the greatest, and the least, they would feel happier, more content, and kinder, always kinder. Maybe, just maybe, they'd pass the sentiment on, which might create a ripple effect, to spread kindness and care instead of heartache. Multiple waves of goodness beginning here on this bus, on this night. From me.

The clapping had become applause, and I risked a glance at Mariana. She smiled and clapped along. *Happy days.*

I held up my hands to the side and patted the air, to signal for the applause to stop, and said, "Then, I'm taking those troubles and throwing them into the Dawson where they can't bother anyone again."

Someone chuckled. Murmurs and whispers bounced around the interior. But people were smiling. Just the thought of handing off their troubles had done something magical.

"What do you say? Hand over your troubles, or ..." My voice was now assertive, assured. "... I won't move this bus another inch."

Someone clapped again from the back. I couldn't see who. Another joined the single clap. Then another. A whistle shrilled from the back from the twenty-something suit. Joey, George? His tie always looked too loose. Mark reached across and grabbed Tracy's hand. She didn't pull away. Mariana clapped joyful, bouncing claps. Ellen, the single mother of two who never saw her children—holding down three jobs will do that— suddenly didn't look so tired, so beaten down.

Now all I needed was to manage their troubles for the rest of the trip. Apprehension flooded in. Would I have the strength? That was a lot of troubles to keep. Even for a few hours. Unknown troubles keeping waters, and I hoped I wouldn't drown in the emotions. But, I'd already dived in, so somehow I had to find a way to manage.

"Let's go," I said, as I turned around and slipped into my seat, gripping the wheel a little firmer. It seemed to have gone pretty well. After this, everyone would believe slapping my hand was nothing more than a symbolic gesture. Their change in mood? That would be the power of suggestion. Me, take their troubles and throw them in the Dawson, well, that couldn't be real? So my set-up was good.

Tonight I would help all these people. Really make a difference, like in Mama's and my favorite film *It's A Wonderful Life*, where Jimmy

Stewart's character George Bailey changes the destiny of the whole town just by standing up to evil ol' man Potter.

Just as it did for George, my story would have worked out, if not for one thing. Something else had come aboard, something I'd never encountered. Something evil. Troubles I could handle. This dark, twisted thing was a whole other world, and I was ill-prepared.

9

He's found himself again on this bus. There's something here, and now he's beginning to understand why he's felt so drawn. The girl. She's a beacon flashing bright. A pretty blonde too, but he sees below the superficial exterior.

This event proves most intriguing. The bus driver, this Rory Fine, he fascinates him.

Pass your troubles into my palm.

Quite the ploy. He wonders if they understand, if all these people will play along. But their applause answers the question.

If they only knew, troubles are unavoidable. They'll just travel back to find you. That's their nature, their physics. These people would do better to accept their fragility, the inevitability of the darker side of life. The certainty they crave is not fate's modus operandi.

He watches with amusement as the bus driver's act plays out. His attention is on the girl, The One, who might be the answer to his quest. Will she play along? This seems so beneath her ability. Then, perhaps she doesn't know what lies beneath her skin.

Her fingertips on his before means they are now forever connected; she belongs to him. He feels her breath inside his mind. He pushes at the excitement that wells within. And waits.

A thought occurs. Will this Fine recognize him for who he is? Is this merely a tactic to reveal him? Perhaps the man is smarter than he seems. He feels naked and revealed. But for them, time is almost up; the game has already begun.

10

So now probably the dumbest, most ill-conceived plan or, if it worked out, the smartest thing I would ever do, was about to begin.

As I slowed the bus for the next stop, I glanced in the mirror every few seconds as an Asian man, his hair in the short sides, long top style every man or boy under thirty now wears, moved toward the exit. The earphones plugged into his head and a faraway look on his face told he lived in a music-powered world.

Hard to know what he'd do as he wasn't a regular, and if he didn't play along, he might set the tone for everyone else. If he ignored me, I might end up left high and dry, my palm waving in the wind like a lost kite.

He'd passed the side door, so good. He still came toward the front and my hopes rose. I extended my palm, face up. Waiting. When he drew almost beside me, I looked up expectantly, wiggling my fingers. The bus grew eerily quiet and I felt a dozen eyes staring.

He didn't even glance at me, so intent was he on whatever fed into his ears via those little, plastic buds. A thick feeling traveled from my chest to my stomach as he stood at the door, one foot suspended above the first step. I still kept my hand outstretched.

I pressed the release for the doors and he began to step down. I'd begun to convince myself his ignoring me didn't mean anything, although I thought it did. Probably really did. Suddenly he stopped and turned, pulling one of the buds from an ear as he did.

"Oh," he said, as a hand snaked out.

My own reached up to meet his. Our hands collided, the smacking sound loud, as a smile erupted on his face. Without even a nod, like this action was no big deal—probably wasn't for him—he pushed the ear bud back in, turned, and jumped down the steps to the pavement. The rain had stopped and he paused, looking up at the dark, threatening sky. Then, as though he'd seen sunshine instead, the smile on his face widened into a grin.

The door swooshed closed and laughter came from the back of the bus, followed by a few hand claps. Success. But I didn't have time to revel in triumph. The minute our hands met, a tingle had erupted across my palm and fingers as though the surrounding air was electrified, each molecule a spark of chaotic, brilliant life. The gentle buzz worked its way up my arm, tiny swirling particles trembling with emotion, traveling to my vault space.

A familiar feeling swept through me. The vitality of life, emotions, experiences all condensed into a single stream of energy. The thousands of times I'd done this, I knew this energy as unique to each individual. Now a warmth journeyed from my arm through my chest. I thought of this feeling as a wisp drifting through my heart and soul. The energy didn't stay there long—to allow that would be dangerous. Never could I risk others' emotions seeping into my own. Mentally, I took a deep breath and shunted the emotion on to *The Attic.*

Yep, the attic. Not sexy, but the imagery works for me, and when I was younger that was the best I could conjure. After all these years the concept had stuck. The attic was the place where I held all the troubles, a kind of emotional vault.

They say *go to your happy place* or *build a shield around your heart.* This was mine. Your mind can create most anything, just like hypnosis can make you do nearly anything. The attic was a necessity to protect from the troubles keeping fallout. I'd learned early on, after the tragedy at school—even before I slipped into my teens—that I needed some basic rules to live with my gift.

One: Never give in to fear or doubt.

Two: The attic must remain completely in my control, impenetrable by anyone or anything except me.

Three: Never keep troubles inside the space longer than forty-eight hours.

Troubles, you see, have a way of coloring your view of the world. Imagine the increased darkened shades when those troubles belong to others, when there's a constant daily influx. Inside the attic I'd placed boxes everywhere. Some small, some large, some thin-walled, others thick and reinforced—strengthened with cast-iron will. These containers safely captured and stored the arriving troubles.

There's the nature of troubles too, for which I had to allow. Troubles are ratty, uncomfortable things; they desire their freedom. Oh, and I do give them their freedom eventually, but not necessarily *where* they want. That's the magic key.

Which brings me to my final rule, numero quattro: When handling said troubles, even during disbursement, never allow curiosity to cause you to look at them or become involved. *a)* they're not my business, and *b)* I can't afford the thought process or the angst they'd cause me.

I'd prepared the attic for the large quantities of troubles I would send from the passengers, placing a box ready, fortified for trapping them. They needed respectful and careful handling. Imagine tiny, dark fish caught in a net, desperately struggling to escape. Once inside, I'd wrangle them into a suitable box, slam shut the lid and, if they were particularly nasty, add a chain and lock.

How do you control troubles with imaginary rooms and locks?

Well, using the nature of imagination and energy, I believe. That's all we're dealing with here. Imagination turns experiences into anxious feelings, troubles and sadness or, on the flip-side, excitement, happiness and contentment.

The system worked. I held the troubles safely until I found the time—usually that day or night—to throw those pesky pieces of negative energy into the river, the best place I'd found for release.

Major troubles didn't plague Earphones Boy. Serious troubles felt heavy, carried a dull thickness, and, as they traveled to the attic, they fought, annoyed to have relinquished their hold over their owner.

As I funneled the troubles into their waiting box and took off, rain came down again, heavy, and wind-driven. As we traveled past Earphone Boy, he seemed unperturbed, his step lighter. A long, slow smile lit his face. He'd likely put his change of mood to my gesture, or the music, or a dozen other reasons, which made more sense than a bus driver whisking away his troubles for *real*. Two hundred yards before the next stop, passengers had already made their way down the aisle. Mrs. Daley, Mr. Ogilvy and two others—a grizzled and graying man and a well-styled, auburn-haired twenty-something girl waited in the aisle near me. I pulled into the stop and swung about to face them. Mrs. Daley stared at me, then the glint of a smile appeared as she held out her hand as though she was about to pay me. Our palms tapped and she mouthed 'thank you,' before heading down the steps. The others followed, walking by with a raised hand slapping or brushing my outstretched palm. Each face erupted in a grin on contact. The girl giggled as though she'd heard the world's funniest joke.

The feeling of lightness for them would be subtle—at first. They wouldn't notice the full effect until later. For me, not so wonderful in keeping so many people's troubles at once. Enormous waves of energy rolled over me. Even though I kept a smile fixed on my face, my arm had begun to numb. My heartbeat rose, pumping like an engine. Handling this many troubles was more difficult than I'd imagined. Mr. Ogilvy, always sad, was the tipping point. I'd shaken his hand occasionally, when I knew the weight of his lost son was beating him down. With focus I had managed to handle those deep, flickering, fighting emotions of his. Tougher now with the multiplier of so many others.

But I managed, and every one of those troubles was encased in a box, unable now to hurt anyone. I heard the click of the locks and the slam of the attic door as I returned to the world to note the four passengers follow each other down the steps. Just as Earphone Boy had done, upon reaching the pavement they walked taller, their steps lighter. Mrs. Daley looked several years younger, even nimbler. The doors swung shut behind them.

Mrs. Daley paused on the pavement and stared through the door's long window, her brow furrowed. She felt the difference. Then a smile crossed her face, and she turned to Mr. Ogilvy and kissed his cheek before turning back to send me a little wave. I waved back, feeling proud, as I began to hum "What a Wonderful World."

Even the weather played along; the sudden shower had stopped and the moon peeked out through a break in the thick clouds. The night felt less dark.

The route now took us off Riverside, leaving the river behind as we entered Ingleton. From here, two more stops and Mariana would get off. My bravado faded at the thought. What would happen when we touched?

Our hands would meet and her troubles and her emotions would temporarily become part of me. Absolute focus was needed to not look into her worries. I didn't want to know anything she wouldn't want shared. Our relationship consisted of a dozen sentences and a look I probably imagined. Here I was worrying about protocols when I needed to keep my mind on the job.

Tracy and Mark were up next, standing two streets before their stop and still not looking at each other. Tracy's lips looked glued together. Mark stood meekly behind nearby.

Would they be my first rejection? The two people who looked as though they most needed my help. Even a few hours without troubles might give them a chance to talk, to work out whatever had wedged between them.

I curved the wheel right and braked to pull into the curb. The moment I brought the bus to a stop I checked in my mirror. Tracy flicked her loosely braided hair behind her shoulder. She looked like she would run the minute the doors opened. She moved down the aisle toward me, but Mark didn't immediately follow.

This time, I didn't turn but simply held out my hand as though my arm was a human turnstile barrier. I wiggled my hand in the air.

Come on you. You know you want to try the Troubles Keeper's service

She began to move toward the front. Mark now followed behind at an arm's-length.

My hand wiggled again. I hoped the movement said: *Come on. Come on now.*I continued to stare ahead, out the front window. Less confronting, I thought. I watched their feet move beside me and held my breath.

Would they?

But Tracy had continued on down the steps, ignoring my hand, and there was only one pair of feet left standing beside me. A hand covered my palm, strong, warm. *Mark.* A tingle began. Sparks moved through the connection in our cells, twisting their way, burrowing into me.

Sadness, tremendous crushing despair, slipped into my grip. Deep, sharp, painful, and overwhelming sadness. *Recent.* As the energy pressed through me, I felt every flicker. Love is a powerful emotion, matched only by anger. When they're fresh and intertwined like this, they're incredibly intense. They needed to be moved into their waiting boxes immediately, but their potency made this difficult. They lingered, clutching at me, clinging like gum on a shoe. I wrestled with them, little fishes of pain. Then, in the following moments, I had them scooped up and in my control and in the attic, safely stowed, so they could harm him no more.

When I turned to look at Mark, a tear glistened in the corner of his eye. He reached up and touched a finger to the moistness. Holding out his hand, he stared at his finger, a puzzled look on his face.

Some noticed and some didn't. He, like Mrs. Daley, felt the lifting, the absence. Without troubles, joy fills the space left behind. What Mark did with that space in the next few hours would determine whether the troubles would return. Respite allowed for perspective, change, a resolution, a different choice.

He looked up from his finger and stared at me as though we'd never met. Then back down again at his finger. Slowly he reached out a hand toward me. My hand met his and we shook.

Barely above a whisper, he said, "I ... I actually feel better. Like a weight lifted. This has been a terrible day. I was sitting there, just now, thinking my life's gone to hell. I've done something stupid. I couldn't ... I just didn't know how to fix."

I understood. As I locked the troubles in the attic, I saw everything that had happened. I felt his hopelessness and his desire to mend that which had been broken. He loved Tracy very much.

An encouraging smile settled on my lips as I offered, "Where there's a will, there's a way, right?"

"Yeah. Yep, you're right." He spun around to face his fiancé, who was glaring up at him.

"Tracy?"

Tracy still stood on the sidewalk, her arms tightly folded across her chest. She did not look happy. She looked just as angry as she had when she'd first climbed aboard.

"Tracy, please. He's right. You do feel better. Please. Just try. I'm begging you."

A few spots of rain plopped on the pavement, big and heavy. Here came another patch of the weather again. A flash of lightning lit her face; a second later a crack of thunder smacked the sky. Tracy jumped. So did I. And Mark.

Then Tracy moved as though the sound was a prearranged signal. She climbed the steps, ignoring Mark's outstretched hand, and slid past him to me, her arms held stiffly by her side. She didn't glance at Mark, instead her gaze fixed upon me, and in her eyes I saw something. *Hope.* Whatever had driven them apart, I knew then I could help.

Her delicate hand, with nails manicured in a perfect pale pink, reached out to me. In return, my hand, fingers taut and extended, found hers.

I smiled a reassuring smile. "This won't hurt a bit. I promise."

Every eye on the bus felt fixed on us as we touched. Tracy's eyes closed.

There they were. The tangled troubles flowed into me, a snaking ball of angst and hurt, so fresh and newly evolved the emotions felt wild. And sticky. And ugly. This time I was ready, and I threw every ounce of energy at the troubles, to deliver them to the attic.

Normally, I'd pay no heed to the exact nature of the trouble. *Mind your own,* my mama always schooled me. As I hurried the energy through, everything became clear. No lover's tiff here. He may have betrayed her, but this was more complex. Something she'd done too. This is why you don't look. There're always two sides. Now both sides were locked inside the attic. Maybe now these two had a chance.

Tracy's face softened as she opened her eyes, the anger and sadness dissolved away. She stared at me with the same puzzled look Mark had given me moments before. Her eyebrows drew together and, instead of letting go, she gripped my hand tighter.

"What just happened? What did you do?"

She turned to Mark, standing only feet away. "I don't understand."

Usually at this point I would offer something like: *See the power of positive thinking* or *just call me Doctor Feel Better.* Before I could say anything Mark spoke.

"I don't know how this thing works, but, Tracy, this just feels like … like we made a mistake."

His arms went around her waist and he pulled her toward him. The interior of the bus became instantly silent. Neither Tracy nor Mark spoke for a few bare seconds, as each searched the other's eyes like newly reunited lovers.

These great moments made me glad of my gift.

They both turned to me.

Mark's voice mimicked his bewildered look. "Rory thank you. I, ah, don't know what you did but, honestly, I have no words—except thank you."

Tracy mouthed a thank you, before impulsively leaning down to kiss my cheek and whisper, "Some magic you have."

"The power of positive thinking is all. I really didn't do anything."

She smiled. "Oh, I think you did. Whatever, I'm grateful."

Mark turned to the door and began to open an umbrella while

Tracy stood back and waited to follow him. He put an arm around her shoulders and pulled his fiancé into him to shelter them both. Then they were down the steps and gone into the night, strolling along the pavement, as though they walked beneath a beautiful, clear, starry sky. I knew even before looking that nearly every head on the bus had turned toward them. Already the mood on the bus had lifted. Conversation filled the air now, bright and buzzing.

11

My confidence bubbled up again. If I had managed to bring those two back together, then maybe, somehow, I could work magic and bring Mariana and I together. Her stop was next. When I snuck a glance, her head was bowed forward, and she had returned to reading her book, but she now wore a smile. I knew I had done that. Well, Mark, Tracy, and I had done that.

The traffic had thickened to a soup of flickering red and white; cars were bumper to bumper. A few minutes lay between me and connecting with the girl who'd captured my heart. My heart thumped in time with the wipers.

Whump-whump. Whump-whump.

As I counted down the yards, I ran through possible remarks to recite as our hands touched

Hope you're feeling uplifted.

Surely you don't have any troubles?

What's a pretty girl like you doing with troubles like this?

Pathetic. She'd be more likely to throw up in my hand, or I would. I'd never had a girlfriend. With my gift, relationships were too tricky. Too many emotions, but for Mariana, I'd take the risk.

Butler Road was the main street of a small village by the name of Woodbine. Small nick-knack shops, cafes and funky clothes outlets dotted each side of the street. Despite puddle-city, outside people around here wore raincoats and umbrellas in an avant-garde way like the weather didn't matter. Mariana fitted in, with her casual, cute fashion. This area was near the end of my run, which meant maximum time with her on my bus.

Her habit was to leave her seat early and wait for the bus to stop. I often wondered, as I watched her walk up the street, where she went, what her life was like.

I threw my concentration into feeding the bus into the small gap parked cars had left around the stop. Only when I'd finally pressed on the hand brake did I realize she was there, standing next to me, her hand clutching the silver pole behind my head.

If a heart can leap from a chest and dance outside the body, mine just had. The world fragmented into color and light dancing about me, blurring my vision. I turned to meet her smile, pushing a nervous smile to my lips.

"Room for mine?" she asked.

I think I kept smiling.

"Room?" I replied. "I, um ... I'm not sure." *How did she know about the attic?*

She tilted her head, squinted her eyes, and then her smile widened as though she'd just gotten the tagline of a joke. "The troubles, I mean. Do you have room to store them? That couple looked like theirs was jumbo size."

"Oh, of course. Yes, yes, there's room." I mentally checked the attic.

Mariana leaned in and held a hand toward me, our heads so close I felt our breaths merge. Somehow I managed to move, when all I wanted to do was look at her. I made a flourish of rubbing my hands together, then stretched my palm out to meet hers. She giggled as our skin touched. The energy flowed suddenly, as always.

But something was wrong.

A torrent of feelings rushed through my veins. In the distance I heard Mariana's laugh. But the sound was wrong, echoing like we were inside a cavern. I felt invaded, like fissures of emotion had spewed into my blood. How could Mariana carry these heavy troubles and on the outside be bright and breezy?

Momentarily I had closed my eyes—to the outside world for no more than a blink—but now they flew open and I stared back at her. I searched for a sign she was aware of this darkness. Nothing showed in her face; she still smiled innocently.

I returned to the troubles. Now I saw. These were more than troubles, they were something I'd never encountered before, like a dark, sentient thing. Maybe even an entity? The energy burned, first through my heart, then moved on as though roaming and exploring its new surrounds. I withdrew inside to follow this thing, every shred of will focused on bringing the intruder under control and guided to the attic.

This couldn't be from Mariana. Perhaps this was an accumulation of all the troubles I'd gathered up today. Maybe I'd overreached. One of my mama's favorite sayings seemed appropriate right then: "*Stay humble and you won't tumble.*"

The pressure inside was building like a gas main ready to blow. *What was happening?* I was now engaged in a psychic tug-of-war, with what, I didn't know. I was out of my depth and unprepared. There's no handbook on my gift. No *Hitchhiker's Guide to Troubles keeping.* I had learned by trial and error. The *error* being the worst mistake I'd ever made, but I was young then. Still, I bore the guilt and this fear kept me careful.

Then, as though the thing, the dark, *dark* thing, knew exactly where to go, the trouble found its way to the attic without my help. My breath caught. How and why had the weird trouble, energy, whatever this was gone there? I wanted to flee, grab Mariana and just get away. Of course, you can't run from yourself. The time taken to stow troubles was the blink of any eye. A strange second not touched by time, like I traveled into a railway siding for however long the event took while the world parked at the station waiting for me.

Inside the attic I surveyed my neatly placed boxes, all carefully locked and evenly spaced. Seven normal containers of troubles waiting to be sent on their way, their owners now freed.

I knew this dark shapeless thing, moving in and out of the boxes as though exploring the room, was dangerous. Soon the energy would realize this was not a welcoming place. The creature's life—and the intense, constantly fluctuating thing certainly felt alive—was about to be cut short. My presence seemed to create no awareness as yet, and I knew this was my moment to shove the entity into a box. Not a normal box though. I needed something larger, stronger, made of steel, reinforced with locks and chains. Something powerful.

Normally I had no problem maneuvering troubles into their boxes. This dark thing though, seemed a whole other beast, actually aware and scrutinizing the new surrounds. The thing shimmered as though covered with a film laced with glinting stars. The skin or covering pulsed rich black to a sparkling dark gray, then would occasionally bloom into a color so dense the burst threatened to extinguish all light.

I reached out for the thing. Abruptly the creature stopped moving to hover just above the floor. I knew then this thing had not grown within Mariana. For this thing to have lived inside her for any time, she wouldn't be her, sweet and beautiful. Left unchecked, the energy would eat you alive and swallow your soul. The more time the entity had to gather its senses, the less chance I would have of capturing this kind of intelligence I had never faced. The strongbox stood behind and I imagined the prison converted to a reinforced safe with walls so thick they could contain a bomb blast.

At that, the black thing paused and I felt studied, appraised. My skin felt as though I needed a shower to scrub the emotions away. Then the attention was no longer on me as I felt the creature swirl and focus on the box.

This was taking much longer than normal, but fortunately time meant nothing when I was inside the attic as though the outside world was paused.

My moment had arrived. I ran at the thing with all the energy I possessed. Should any other boxes split open from the force and spill their small troubles, I'd worry later. All the troubles I'd gathered collectively today would not amount to half the power of whatever this was.

I wrapped my will about the darkness, like a wrestler embracing his opponent. My intent was clear and the thing would know I meant harm. A force immediately turned on me with tremendous strength. As we met, the breath was knocked from my lungs, as a terrible fury of hate, guilt and every dark emotion entwined me. Some kind of consciousness entered my mind, prying and searching for weakness, to trip me up, force me to release my prisoner. The other mind recognized what I could do, somehow. And the threat.

The image of Mariana's innocent, lovely face gave me strength. With one almighty shove, I pushed at the thing with everything in me. Without warning, the dark thing wavered and collapsed inside the box. Despite surprise at my success, I kept moving and was on top of the prison, slamming the lid and winding chains around the exterior. Fitted locks snapped closed within seconds.

Despite the walls' thickness, waves of malevolent force emanated. In the confined space of the attic they felt disgusting, like a cloying putrid smell.

I slapped and ground my hands together, pleased with a job well done. How I'd won, I wasn't actually sure, but the sooner I could be rid of the thing, the better. Already I was in unknown territory, and that worried me. Disposing of this trouble, this dark thing, in the normal way probably might be a problem. What if, unlike regular troubles, this thing found its way back? There was something strangely sentient in the behavior. The idea of an emotional parasite looking for a host entered my mind.

Time. That's what I needed. Time to wrestle with my next move. Right now, my uninvited guest was secure, and I needed to return to the outside. A deep breath, and I was staring back at a smiling Mariana.

As brightly as I could, I said, "Well, barely a whimper of troubles. That all you got?"

She laughed. "I'm just a happy person. Not much in my life to trouble me, except maybe losing my job soon. Hey, but that's life. I feel more sorry if Mr. Sterling lost his business, than for me."

Brain, please engage, I beseeched. *Say something witty.* But all I could muster was, "Could be worse?"

"Could be worse," she echoed, but now her gaze moved downward to where our hands still touched.

"I'm sorry," I said, staring in horror at my hand clutching hers. I snatched my arm away.

Fear prevented me from looking at her again in case I saw annoyance or pity or anything that said she thought me strange. "Works better with a quick touch," I said in a rush. "I'm sorry. I don't know why I kept holdi—"

She patted my arm. A thrill shot through me. "All good, really. You've got a *nice* touch. Rory. We've introduced ourselves before, a while ago."

"Yes, Rory. Rory Fine, that's my name. Fine by name, fine by nature."

Oh, big fail on the cool factor.

Her hand traveled out again. My right hand, seemingly with a mind of its own, moved up to greet the outstretched palm. Our hands met firmly in a shake, and I chanced looking up to meet her eyes.

"Pleased to meet you, again, Rory Fine," she said "You're the friendliest bus driver, ever. You always brighten my day."

I-brightened-her-day. Wow!

I'd think about that later because this exchange had taken too long. Passengers would become unsettled, but I couldn't waste this chance.

"Thank you. Seeing you always makes *my* day better."

I was sounding *creepy stalker* again so I added, "My days are good. I mean I'm not waiting to see you. Your smile, yes, I notice your smile when you—"

I didn't finish the sentence because, thankfully, Raincoat Man brushed past Mariana and stood at the exit before the steps, his impatience clear.

"Does this bus turn down Central Street? I think I'm on the wrong bus. The rain. I panicked."

"No," I said, glad to have a reason to break from another embarrassing moment. "We're straight ahead on Eighth. Route ends North Street Terminus, near the old Westside Bakery."

"Oh, I'm screwed. Damn. Quickest way to get to Central? I got to be there in fifteen minutes."

Mariana began to move around him and toward the steps.

Did the universe hate me? I wanted to call to Mariana, yell, "*Wait, let's talk. There's something here. I felt something. Did you?*"

But I couldn't. Raincoat Man waited, expecting a reply. Mariana now stood at the top of the steps. She called back, "Thank you Rory Fine, for a wonderful bus ride tonight. Even with the rain you made this ..." She tilted her head as though searching for the right word. "... special."

Any words I had evaporated and all I managed was a strangled, whispered "goodbye."

Mariana paused at the door to open an umbrella. She didn't look back and a moment later was gone into the night, away from me, away from a moment I'd already begun to cherish. I returned to Raincoat Man and smiled. Inside, I cried.

"Okay, directions."

Moments later after my instructions, Raincoat Man took off in the same direction as Mariana. I pulled out into the traffic and slowly traveled along the street, scanning the sidewalk for her, hoping for one last look, but she was already gone.

The rest of the passengers left the bus over the last few stops. Everyone slapped, tapped, or shook my hand. All except one, who got off at the next stop from Mariana, but he coughed as he passed me and mumbled an apology. "A cold," he said, as he blew his nose. I had done a good job. All had left happier, setting out for a better evening than the one they had faced if I hadn't intervened.

As I pulled into the depot, I should have felt contented, happy, but when I thought of Mariana and our awkward interaction, I felt desperately alone. And lost.

Who keeps the troubles of the Troubles Keeper?
No one.

12

He studies the bus driver as he watches The One as she leaves the bus. He knows he cannot risk following her. There is too much at stake if something goes wrong. This man may have the power to cause him trouble, even stop him. As always, he is careful and mindful that most will never understand the intricacies of this world. The wondrous beauty and symmetry and the demanding necessities required to maintain the balance.

As she walks from the bus, she is unaware of how close she has come to their lives colliding. He takes pleasure in watching as the overhead streetlight momentarily illuminates her, light dancing from her hair as color explodes from her skin.

She disappears from view, slipping down a street, gone, and he presses his hand against the window. The coolness seeps into his palm as he touches her in his mind. Tastes her on his lips. She is special. But for now, he must let her go.

Now he must find another to replace The One, the blonde who interests the bus driver so much. He is a believer in fate. After all, fate revealed the doorway to him those years ago. Now fate has brought him to this bus, this driver, this girl. Surely this is a sign he is on the right path.

He breathes in the excitement of the near future and again wonders why the bus driver has appeared at this moment in time. He needs to understand more before his next step. Why has this Rory Fine drawn out his marker from The One? This was not his to take.

So he turns away. Tomorrow he will begin his pursuit again. This time he will study the bus driver, test him, and if need be, destroy him. His wait has been too long to fail when he is so near. Waiting one more day won't matter. He's already waited so long.

13

I'd sat there for more than an hour staring at the river, at the dark waters still churned and swollen from the wind and rain. The storm had moved quickly and had now passed. The moon peeked slyly out from behind a streak of clouds, and I felt spotlighted by its glow. The humidity had dissipated, and my body no longer felt strangled by the damp pressure.

This was my favorite part of the river, beneath the bridge, beneath the crazy movement of civilization traveling back and forth above. The swirl of the water in the current mesmerized; the sound of the distant traffic fell away, and I could almost believe I was the only person alive.

Despite feeling worn, my spirits were lifted from my contact with Mariana. Normally ridding troubles was a simple exercise, as normal as walking. Over the years I'd grown stronger, quicker and more adept.

"Troubles will eat me alive," a psychic had told me, years ago.

Maybe, but I still felt confident I could handle this dark thing I'd trapped. Usually sitting by the river wound a calm into me, but tonight I was nervous. What to do next? Instinct urged caution. This wouldn't be a simple opening of the box and casting this dark thing away.

Every trouble I'd gathered tonight was normal, except Mariana's dark thing. A heck of a puzzle. In order to understand this dark thing, I realized I must break a long held rule and look into Mariana's troubles. Why, of all people, was this darkness connected to her?

A funny idea occurred to me. Could Mariana have a latent talent like mine? I thought through the concept; maybe this somehow made strange sense. Emotions were just energy particles, so she could inadvertently have picked up this thing. I was a conduit. Maybe she was a conduit too? So then maybe I wasn't breaching my rule by looking into her troubles. These weren't her troubles.

First, I needed a plan.

Out came my notepad. Yep, I'm old-fashioned, despite the pull of the digital world. Pen and paper, that's me. I pulled out my cell, hit my torch app and focused the light so I could see. My pencil scratched rough and loud against the backdrop of the lapping river.

PLAN
1. Release other troubles?
2. Examine dark thing?
3. Release dark thing?
4. Where is dark thing from?
5. ~~Ask Mariana Out???~~

Cross that last one out. Getting ahead of myself. Way ahead.

On paper, clearly my plan contained risks. I couldn't open the box if I wasn't positive what I faced. Like opening a hungry caged bear's door, this might not end well. If her troubles had intertwined with this dark thing, then this could create a complicated problem.

So scratch three and work on four first. What I really needed was to look into Mariana's troubles. I madly scribbled on the paper.

1. Release other troubles.
2. Examine dark thing.

3. Release dark thing?
4. Where is dark thing from?
5. ~~Ask Mariana Out???~~
6. Look at Mariana's troubles.
7. What are Mariana's <u>real</u> troubles???

This would mean that after I released the other passengers' troubles, my next step would be something rather tricky. I would need to talk to Mariana. How could I ask the questions I needed answered without revealing too much?

My pencil tapped the page as though possessing a mind of its own.

I wrote Mariana's name on the page followed by a line.

Mariana—

How did I get to Mariana and create a conversation with her—that didn't seem creepy—and somehow gain her trust?

I made a sub heading.

Mariana—
How?
• Her work
• Go there

The plan could work, right?

Today she'd said she was always happy to see me. "The friendliest bus driver, ever," she'd said. But no, if I simply turned up at her work, I'd be back in stalker territory. Plus there were the variables.

Look at Raincoat Man's interruption when she and I spoke. So I needed a meeting I could control. A strategy with a higher probability of working, where I had some way of ensuring where and when. And the meeting needed to seem natural, where the words *stalker* or *coincidence* wouldn't enter her head.

What though?

From behind me the sound of the sudden angry screech of brakes caused me look back to the road. The wrenching of steel and shattering glass loud and stomach curdling sounded too brutal for someone not to be hurt. I jumped to my feet and began running toward the highway, thoughts of my predicament suspended. A cab and an SUV had collided at a traffic light. Even from several hundred yards, I saw the SUV had won. The cab looked like a failed work of crumpled, yellow origami.

Accidents weren't uncommon on my route, but I could rarely stop and help. There was my time schedule and, more than that, an accident harbored an exhausting emotional hell. Dark troubles from sudden events not only consumed people but sometimes released other deeper, buried emotions. The fragile paper of people's lives could be torn apart by a single accident even though, sometimes, accidents could pull people together.

Pull people together.

The words struck me as my mind jumped from accidents to my bus. I'd never been in an accident, not even once, but I'd broken down twice. I remembered the frustration of annoyed passengers. Moving a malfunctioning bus takes major organization. The time lag for everyone to get going again could be lengthy.

But a very human thing happened sometimes. Passengers who waited for the replacement bus would start talking with each other. The thought made me smile. Strangers no longer strangers.

My mind stopped there.

Strangers no longer strangers.

I was only fifty yards from the scene when two cars stopped, and their drivers leaped out and ran toward the accident. In the distance I heard the faint sound of a siren drawing closer. Even as I neared, a small crowd had begun to form.

I stopped and turned away. Tonight I wasn't needed. There were enough people on the scene already and I was grateful for that. Time was ticking away and I needed my energy to put the plot now forming in my head into motion. As I turned back to the river, the ideas began to flow. Yes, my strategy *could* work. Most importantly should this fail, there was little risk Mariana would think everything was about her. A ray of hope danced inside. I had a plan. Messy and risky, but still a plan.

14

Back at the river my focus now turned to my own immediate emergency. The other passengers' troubles needed releasing. I pushed the notepad back in my jacket pocket and turned my attention to the task at hand.

When I entered the attic the sight greeting me was worse than I could imagine. The box I'd shoved the dark thing inside still sat in its own corner, but had now become distorted. The exterior had grown black as though the contents had rotted and released a toxin. Like a mold. From the floor line to a quarter way up the sides, fingers of green, gray and black jaggedly extended toward the top. In some places small bulges had warped the smooth sides I'd built. Solid, riveted iron sheets buckled like they were paper.

My gut told me that once the mold-like substance had completely covered the box the gloop would eat through, freeing the dark thing within. I didn't want to know what would happen if that occurred. Thick malevolence surrounded the container as though what lay inside controlled the creeping mold.

Getting the dark thing out of the attic had become a priority. Some dirty math, based on the growth so far, gave me roughly forty-eight hours. Maybe. I was in unfamiliar territory, so everything was a guess.

Quickly I dispersed the normal troubles into the Dawson. Usually I would sit and enjoy the sparking colors swirl and swim away, until the current swept them to the deeper waters where they'd dissolve, no longer able to cause harm. Tonight there was no time.

I scrambled back up the bank and walked across the open grounds of Wentworth Place Park. Usually picnickers and strolling lunch time workers filled the space during the day, but now the area was hauntingly empty. My bike was parked on the other side; I always took the walk time to calm the residual feelings the troubles left behind.

The fallout of the auto accident was in full swing. Flashing lights of attendant police, ambulance and two tow trucks colored the scene in an eerie fog of light. Beautiful, if their presence wasn't signaling a human mishap.

The moon had arced quickly across the sky in the hours since I'd first arrived, partially dipping now behind the towering city buildings, patterned by random squares of still-lit offices. I felt small and alone, swallowed by the whispering landscape of emotions, troubles and energy barely felt by most people.

I wrapped my arms about myself as a shiver shook my body. Another siren echoed in the distance. Troubles never slept. Now neither could I.

15

From his vantage point, he watches as the driver sits by the river, curious as to his motive. Why is he here? What has he done with that which he doesn't own? He'd sent his gift to the girl and that was where his marker should have remained. Yet, now the bus driver has intervened.

An uncertainty he can't shake enters his mind, like a splinter under his skin. Annoying. The bus driver has become a puzzle to be solved. Closing his mind to wondering, he allows himself to hear the girl's breath in his ears, the gentle purr whistles through his mind. If he waits too long, the ferocity will increase until he has no choice. He must continue, but carefully. He tastes his distant home like the sweetest of rewards.

He walks along the pavement, following the river, passing the remnants of an accident. A turban-headed man gestures to two nodding police. Lights, camera, action, he thinks. As he draws alongside, he soaks in the atmosphere. Chaos. Danger. Anxiety. Fear. Delicious byproducts of the randomness of fate.

His thoughts turn to her. Not The One, but the girl he has found, the girl he needs tonight to take his mind from this confusion. Her black, shining hair like a dark rose curves around her face. That caught his eye first. Their entwined future pulls at him, a necessity like mice bred for experimentation. He's a scientist of life.

He slips through the night, through the city streets, moving masked, unnoticed by those ambling through their lives. He moves with purpose, a tiger prowling, nobody seeing him, unless he allows them to see.

Two days before he'd followed this one, watched her key the code to the front entrance. Lives are too filled with diversions to notice his watching. People live in arrogance, believing everything is certain, everything is safe. He's there to prove them wrong.

He is here, beside her. She's checking her phone. She sees him. Even nods. He nods back.

Moments later, she is inside in the foyer, even holds the door for him. He slips by like the barest wisp of a breeze. They travel in the elevator together. She still checks her phone. The elevator creaks and shakes as though protesting against carrying him. Anticipation is thick on his tongue.

The doors open and he follows. She turns to look at him. Recognizes he may not be who she believes. Now she notices. Now the world's diversions have slipped away. Now she realizes too late, she should have paid attention.

He touches her arm, and she is his. She looks down where his fingers touch her skin. "Hey," she says, then stops. He now has her words, her body, her life in his control.

He easily takes the keys from her hand, shepherding her to the entrance. A key in the lock and moments later the door swings open. He smiles.

The door closes behind them. She looks at him, but she cannot speak, although she tries. But her eyes speak volumes. This is the moment he treasures, when they recognize he is their destiny.

He pushes her back. She imagines she is free. They all do. She thinks to save herself, but she can't; only he will save her from this life. She will become more than she has ever been. Experience calculates his movements. He's done this before so many times. Her world now belongs to him.

The feeling drags at him, as always. He begins to believe *she* is The One. Perhaps the girl from the bus is just an illusion. Maybe *this one*, black hair and pale peach-colored skin will end his search. Then he can forget the bus driver, the other girl.

Hope rises. Now that she's in his hands, she feels so right.

He holds her pinned to the wall, both hands now around her neck. She kicks and pushes at him feebly, as the power of her drains into him. She wants to survive but he's practiced and certain. In moments she is completely his.

He carries her limp body past the kitchen to the small, square dining table in the open living area. Fake pink tulips, perfectly arranged, adorn the table's center. Along the wall, photographs of the girl with friends and family, amid backdrops of holiday destinations, decorate the wall.

Her body slumps neatly into one of the chairs. He rests her head forward on the table while he prepares. The backpack he carries slips from his shoulders to fall beside her. Picking up the satchel, he places the bag on the table, using the bulk to push away a vase of flowers.

From the pack he pulls his tools, as he thinks of them, and places them carefully upon the glass surface. The small, black bag. The drill. The camera. The surgical gloves.

Tearing a small piece of tape to stretch across her mouth, he presses as he goes, to ensure the cover is secure. He winds more across her chest, around the back of the chair, over her shoulders and around her arms. More tape across her mouth to be sure. He's noticed this has become unnecessary since his abilities have grown, but he's a creature of habit. This is just in case as a caution, like he's being careful with the bus driver. Cautiousness keeps you safe.

The black case, no more than an overnight zippered shaving pouch, houses everything he needs. Inside lies the syringe, white and pure. He takes out a glass vial and inserts the needle to draw up the yellow, oily fluid within. Hemlock distilled. An exact quantity mixed with complimentary additives is all he needs to ensure they cannot scream, even if he loses focus.

If he could operate any other way, with them unconscious—so

much easier—he would take that route, but he needs them awake. Needs to look into their eyes. See if they see what he sees, so he knows he is on the right path.

The needle pushes inside, smoothly and keenly like her skin is butter. He depresses the plunger and watches the yellow liquid disappear into the vein.

As though the plunge of liquid is her wake-up call, her eyes flutter open. Then close again. Then consciousness floods in and her lids spring apart. Her face muscles flicker with the effort. She sees. Understands.

He uses his smile to reassure. Still, she wrestles against the tape, against the chair, against her destiny, but as the hemlock mixture takes hold, her muscles slacken, and all that is left is her eyes to speak to him. He wills her head erect and marvels he can control to this degree and wonders from where this new ability has sprung.

Her eyes flicker and roll. The tape sucks in and out of her mouth with each breath. Her struggles lessen, her arms slump against the chair, he leans in and his palm cups her cheek. Beneath his fingertips her skin is cool. The drug moves quickly. She's almost ready.

His lips brush her ear. "Can you feel the power beating within?" he whispers. "We're going to release this from you."

He stands back, staring, as he wishes she understood how precious she's become. Reaching out, he snatches the edge of the tape to draw back from her mouth. Her lips quiver as she tries to take this chance, mistakenly believing she might possess the ability to scream. Her lips barely move.

He turns back to the table to retrieve the gloves. As he places them on his hands he speaks, soothingly for he appreciates her. They are a team.

"No need to worry. There's no more pain than you can handle. More discomfort. The rest is mind over matter. You know what I mean? Imagine there is no hurt and perhaps there won't be."

His attention is now on preparation. From the kit he pulls a gleaming, silver surgeon's knife, a red marker and a disposable razor. Again, he places them carefully upon the table, moving them by fractions of an inch until they align perfectly. The bag, the drill, the razor, the pen, the surgeon's knife. Beauty lives in symmetry.

With the knife in hand, so perfectly weighted, he turns to face the girl. Her eyes are wild, like they'll escape their sockets. He replaces the knife and picks up the razor.

"Shall we begin?" he asks. "Please remain calm."

He soothes her as he begins, continues to talk, sharing what is to come so she is prepared. The blade drags across her forehead, along her hairline. Hair fibers give way to the merciless edge as shiny strands drop into her lap. Black gossamer threads fall to the floor. Her head is shaved something like a monk to reveal an inch or so above her hairline. Beneath lays the perfect spot.

Tears roll down her cheeks and cling to her chin like miniature divers waiting for the perfect moment to launch into the air. He lowers his voice close to a whisper. "Don't be afraid. This is a gift."

A palm coasts across the bald skin. So smooth. So perfect. So ready. For a moment he admires his work, then turns to retrieve the pen. He marks the scalp, dragging the pen tip and coloring the skin in a perfect circle, so there can be no mistake.

Done with the pen, he places the implement back on the table, neatening the collection once more so they are all still perfectly aligned. Then the knife is in his hand again and he stands over her. Squaring his stance, he leans forward as he slices the knife around the circle, careful to precisely follow the line. Blood oozes from where he scores the skin. Then he peels off the flap of skin. Perfect. He's become so precise.

Next the drill with its core bit, its handle snug in his hand. A press of the trigger and an instant whirring fills the air. He rests the bit gently within the half-dollar size circle. He's tried other sites, other sizes, but this seems to be the nearest for what he needs. Each time he's failed, he learns and comes closer to perfection.

This girl may not be The One. He senses this through his fingers now. She will become practice, preparation, a refinement of his system. He's thinking of this, his mind drifting, when he presses the trigger. A split-second later the resistant pressure drops and he pauses. Blood has sprayed across her face, across everything within several feet of the chair. Blood, bone, brain matter.

He ignores the gore and resumes his task. The tip re-enters the skull. Her pupils are large and dark. Emotions leak from her every pore as every cell in her body releases its story. He drinks the vitality in, welcomes the energy into his core.

He tilts his head, examines her. Watching. Waiting. Blood flows in thick, dark ribbons from the wound. Tears mingle with the blood and track down her face.

Now the needles. He reaches for them, six inches long, fine and sleek. They slide in smoothly. Like a master, his fingers grip the ends and turn. This way, then that, until like a talented locksmith, he feels the click of perfect placement.

He stands back to examine his work, then turns to scan the room. Nothing has changed. The lights still glow dull yellow-white. He looks beyond her. The air is static. She is still alive, but her chest is barely moving. She hasn't long. So then neither does his chance of making everything right, of opening the door.

Disappointment seeps in; cold, blue and dull. His finger finds the trigger and the drill buzzes alive again. He moves the whirring point to another position near the original hole in her skull, excising the bone, widening the impression. Perhaps a micro-inch to the left might change everything. But she is not The One, of that he is now certain.

Her eyes beg him. Their eyes are all the same. They want to live. But so does he.

16

A bad plan is better than no plan. Mama always said, *"Always have a plan or you'll always wish you had."*

Well, a bad plan would have to do today.

Since I'd started today's route, my ribs felt every heartbeat. Every time I thought ahead, my heart smacked a little harder. There were so many factors, like playing with chess pieces that kept moving out of their squares. If Mariana didn't catch the bus today, then I'd be forced to move to Plan B. And there wasn't a Plan B.

The side issue of the dark thing didn't help. Last night I'd barely slept. Sleeping with something lurking inside felt akin to sleeping with the enemy. Whenever I checked, the mold stuff had progressed further in dismantling the prison. The slender fingers of black and dark-green now grew half way up the walls, slipping along the corner joints like sick, ivy tendrils. In places, the walls had mottled like rotten banana skin.

My time to act was tick, tick, ticking away. Forty-eight hours, thirty-six, twelve. Who knew when the thing would work free from the chamber. There was no science to call upon, nothing I could Google.

I'm in over my head revolved endlessly through my mind like a way-too-commercial pop song.

Mariana *needed* to be on the bus today, not tomorrow, not next week—*today*. Each time my mind strayed to everything failing, I ran my plan through again, imagining each step as though the preceding one succeeded.

Mariana smiling at me.

The dark thing's rotting form flowing down the river.

Me laying down to sleep, safe in my bed, knowing I had won.

Let's hope that would become my reality.

At each stop, my usuals boarded: Mr. Ogilvy, Mrs. Daley, Tracy and Mark—holding hands again—Ellen, the lovely septuagenarian with her warm smile. Headphone Boy, the man with the cold, his face still buried in his hanky, a few others. Sprinkled among them was today's strangers, tourists and casual riders.

Each one I greeted the same way: a smile, a nod and a good afternoon. Occasionally I'd throw out Jim Carrey's *The Truman Show* phrase, except with my own slant. "Good afternoon, good evening, and a trouble-less good night." People laughed despite the corniness.

My usuals from the evening before were noticeably happier. Mr. Ogilvy and Mrs. Davies sat together. That was new. He leaned toward her as he talked, with a smile wider than I'd ever seen on him. She laughed every now and then and played with her hair. The weariness, normally worn like a heavy coat, clearly absent.

Was she flirting? Happy days for him, perhaps. His son's loss had grown weightier lately. Each time I lifted his troubles, the sorrow felt thicker. Sometimes snatches of details filtered through. His twenty-three-year-old son, a cop, had been killed responding to a robbery. Inexperience met a single fatal shot. Today though, there seemed no sign of this burden playing on his mind.

Mark and Tracy held hands, she occasionally leaning into him, as he kissed the top of her head. Engagement obviously back on.

When you freed troubles, other forces came into play. Unrestricted possibilities scattered and fell to create a new set of destinies.

I couldn't stop the smile on my lips as I returned my attention to the road.

As each stop added more passengers, my mind returned to my plan. Failure would mean I would need my own troubles keeper. As I drew closer to the most important stop on the route, my mind became more focused, clearer, as I readied myself to do what was necessary.

After the deluge the night before, the fine, warm weather, without a hint of humidity, was a welcome change. Wisps of clouds sat low on the horizon as though they were too lazy to climb any higher. The setting sun painted their undersides deep pink as the sky above melted into a dark evening blue. Through the dimming light, Mariana's stop emerged ahead. Several figures arose from the bus shelter and moved to stand at the road's edge. I couldn't tell yet if she was one of them. My heart beat out each yard the bus traveled.

Fifty yards.

Forty.

Thirty.

I made out four people standing there. One usual rider and three I didn't recognize, including a tall man, a good six-feet-five, who I'd seen maybe a couple of times before. Perhaps even yesterday, though I couldn't be sure. With yesterday's events, my memory was not good, my mind fuzzy on details.

But Mariana wasn't there.

Where was she? The thick feeling in my throat dissolved into a scratchy, sharp pain like I'd swallowed glass shards. This was a disaster.

Plan B. I needed a Plan B. And quick. But what? I wasn't a superhero accustomed to saving the day. Yes, I had a gift, but fighting evil (or dark things that felt pretty damn evil), my power was barely better than useless. Great at throwing me into trouble but not so great at getting me out. I couldn't think; my mind was awash with panic. I just needed this shift over, so I could take a moment to create a new plan. Maybe I could locate Mariana's address on the transit pass database, visit her house, and ... and what? I just wasn't good at this.

I pulled into the stop on autopilot. In the distance I heard doors open and I half-smiled at each boarding and alighting passenger, not consciously registering their response. I hit the door release and felt the doors begin to swing shut.

This shouldn't have happened. Where could Mariana be? I thought fate and I were buddies, a team. Disappointment felt raw in my chest.

Then she was there.

Like a dream, a movie cliché. She stood on the other side of the now closed door hand on hip, half bent—panting.

"Oh," fell from my lips, like I'd been hit on the back and the air was knocked out of me.

I fumbled for the release, missing twice, before my hand connected and pressed down quickly like I had smashed a game show buzzer. *Yes, I know the answer. I win the prize.* The doors whooshed open.

"Thank. You," she said, the words coming out between breaths as she climbed the steps. A large black slouch bag hung from the crook of her elbow, and she pushed the strap back up to her shoulder. Messy strands had fallen from her ponytail.

"I almost missed you," she said, her cheeks flushed. "My gosh, thank you for waiting."

I wished I could say the truth: *I'd wait forever for you.* What I did manage was a decent smile and a "No problem." I was just grateful my voice didn't squeak.

Mariana casually acknowledged my smile, unaware of how happy she'd made me, then proceeded down the aisle. I waited a moment, gathering myself, watching her in the mirror, before I released the brake. My mind raced ahead, checking off my plan details while I steered the bus back into traffic.

Every stop I glanced in the mirror checking on her. A teenager with headphones and short, spiky, multi-colored dreadlocks partially blocked my view. His head bounced and swayed in time to beats only he could hear. But I could see the side of her face and a shoulder, and that was enough.

We were coming to the route's halfway mark. This was where I would put my plan in motion. I'm not an actor, per se, but I'd learned from a young age to explain away the results of troubles keeping by various means. Deny, deny, deny, usually worked well. The trick in convincing others, I'd found, was to commit totally. I had my arsenal of responses.

No, I didn't do anything special.

Simply the power of positive thinking.

Just a kind of hypnosis.

If they were persistent in questioning me, throwing in an element of truth usually helped.

Sure, I've a special power. Just watch me lift this car, or *I am reading your mind right now. You're thinking of cats.*

I didn't like lying, and I was about to. Mama used to say: *"If you mean well, you'll be forgiven most things."* I certainly hoped Mariana was the forgiving kind.

Five twenty-seven.

The deeper into the city I drove, the more the traffic grew thicker with cars now stretched bumper to bumper. My first problem arose. I needed physical distance to begin my move.

I eased off the accelerator, nothing obvious, just a gentle slowing, until thirty yards separated the car in front. With the descent of night, a snake of glowing red and white lights curved before me. I prayed another driver wouldn't decide to fill in the inviting gap.

One final glance to check on Mariana. Dreadlocks had moved slightly to the side, so part of her face now came into view. Her head was down, probably reading.

Most passengers were seated. Good. Injuring a passenger was one of the variables for which I couldn't plan. Only three stood, all near the central door: a man in a suit who was a twice-weekly passenger, a sweet mid-twenties woman, and a teenage boy with a backpack. All appeared to have a good hold on the silver metal railing near the exit. They should be okay.

I pulled in a breath like this might be my last and exhaled slowly.

I willed clarity into my mind just like I did whenever I gathered troubles. Only doubts pushed back.

This is a flawed plan. I have no other ideas.

You will fail. For Mariana, I'll make this work.

You're no secret agent. I know.

We neared the spot I'd decided was my best choice to execute.

The voice inside had grown urgent. Screaming for me to stop. *Just drive past. Think of another plan.* I almost listened. I almost did continue on, but I had to do this.

So my crazy idea that had my heart racing began.

My foot tapped the accelerator. Then released. Then tapped again. Then released. The bus shuddered and jerked.

A collective "Oh," came from the passengers.

Somebody called out, "What the?"

Another voice: "Shit."

"Fate be my friend today," I whispered under my breath.

My foot bounced on the accelerator again.

Somebody screamed.

17

The bus lurched like a trapped animal attempting to gain freedom. I continued pressing and releasing the accelerator. Those aboard would repeat later that the bus clearly had a mechanical fault. Some even applauded the way I'd handled the beast in dense traffic.

An increasing murmur rose from the passengers. The standing, suited man in the aisle toppled forward, his fall averted by the quick reflexes of a younger man to his left. A couple of teenage girls burst into giggles as they fell onto each other. The twentyish girl almost landed in the lap of a passenger, before catching herself by grabbing a handrail. Mr. Ogilvy put an arm protectively across Mrs. Daley's chest.

My few-second surveillance in the mirror assured me everyone was still okay. Rattled, yes, but no one had incurred any injuries I could see.

Luck was with me. No one was near the front of the bus. So nobody could later say they saw me surreptitiously dip down and securely grasp the gear lever.

In my head I counted: *One. Two. Three.* Then I slipped the bus out of gear. The vehicle bucked and shuddered, the noise the roar of a wounded, angry animal. In seconds, the bus came to a grinding halt —with the emphasis on grinding—the gears crunching angrily as I pushed through them for maximum effect. I'd steered into the side of the road, to ensure safety for the passengers. To everyone aboard, the bus appeared to have experienced disastrous mechanical problems. For a few moments I made a great show of playing with the dashboard and gears, as I pretended to be as surprised as everyone else.

Now for show time.

Putting on my game face I turned off the engine, twisted out of my seat to stand up in the aisle and face the back of the bus. Some passengers had already begun to gather their belongings, checking bags, rubbing arms or legs that had bumped against railings. Many though, including Mariana, looked at me expectantly. Each wore the same look. *What the hell just happened?*

My hands flew up in feigned exasperation.

"Houston, we have a problem, right? Sorry everyone. This happens occasionally. I apologize for the delay and inconvenience. This should take only ..." I paused. Another lie coming. If Mama was still here she would have clipped my ears. *"A Fine does not mix fact and fiction."* But when stakes are this high, you do what you gotta do.

I continued, my guilt mitigated, "... around fifteen to twenty minutes to get another bus to us. Then we'll have you on your way. I'll just radio now."

At my words a collective sigh rose like a badly tuned choir. A tide of complaints followed.

"Typical."

"I'll miss my train connection."

"Just my luck." To which someone quipped: "So this is your fault, then."

With that, a smattering of laughs erupted, which broke the tension that had swooped in like a storm. Those sitting near the jokester swung around to see who'd spoken. A regular, his name was Barrett *something* with a hyphenated Smith. Like Barrett-Browning-Smith—although that wasn't right, but close. Barrett-*Something*-

Smith was an impeccably-dressed lawyer, whose nose lived in papers he would fish from his beautiful, richly leather-clad briefcase.

When I'd first learned he practiced law, I reached out, thinking he must bear the huge weight of others' troubles. Surprisingly though, not so. Perhaps his job gave him the same insight as troubles keeping.

Today, again we might be kindred spirits. He'd done a good job of relieving the mood. I bowed my head to Mr. Barrett-Something-Smith, a gesture which said, *Thank you. Great help.*

"Thanks for your patience, ladies and gentleman. Like I said, twenty minutes, max."

This was not true. A replacement would be more thirty to forty minutes, maybe even an hour at this time of day, but I needed to ensure Mariana didn't seek an alternative way home and would wait for the replacement bus. This was all about her.

I continued with the subterfuge. "To expedite everything, could we please vacate the bus and wait outside on the pavement?" I angled my head toward the vista outside, to a small coffee shop, Sweetheart's Bakery.

Adding a surprised tone, I said, "Look at that, the Breakdown Gods have smiled. We won't starve. Sweetheart's serves a cheesecake like you've never tasted. So if I was you—."

A voice called out, "It's an ill wind."

Laughter filled the air along with an approving murmur, which seemed to signal: *time to move.* Passengers rose and filed off. I slid back into my seat and pretended to give the controls a once over, a delay tactic until the last person was off the bus. My call back to base would likely reveal a replacement vehicle was forty minutes to an hour away, exposing my subterfuge should anyone overhear.

The center doors remained purposely closed causing everyone to walk past me. Should anyone seem overly agitated, I wanted to be near enough to reach out and calm them. I didn't need to be putting out fires. My time and focus needed to be free to speak with Mariana.

Mariana had waited until most of the others had left before gathering her belongings to make her way down the aisle. My heart bounced out of control, so when Mariana passed me, I couldn't trust myself to speak. What I'd done and what I planned to do suddenly felt terrifying and overwhelming. So I didn't look up, instead I continued the pretense of checking the dashboard switches. From my peripheral vision I saw she paused near me. I wanted to look up, to smile, to speak to her now, but the time wasn't right.

She stepped down onto the pavement, and then, with the bus finally to myself, I quickly closed the doors and flicked a switch on the radio to call into the depot.

Cathy was the name of Central City Buses' receptionist whose smile said *I like people and I like my job.* I'd never practiced troubles keeping with her, because there'd never seemed the need.

When I explained the situation, her tone immediately lost the delight always there when she recognized my voice.

"Oh no Rory. That bus was just serviced two days ago. Oh, phooey for you. And the passengers."

"Yup," I answered, guilt swimming through my veins, "I'm two blocks north of Burns Street, just past stop 638. Gears sound gone. Put my foot on the gas and nothing. Chugged a bit, was okay, and then do not pass go, do not collect any more passengers."

"The passengers?"

I looked through the door at the congregation milling on the pavement. Some had already made their way into Sweethearts Bakery.

"Yep, they're all off now."

"Give me a sec Rory. I'll check replacement time."

The radio squawked, then fell silent.

My gaze followed Mariana as she moved through the small crowd at the door of the café. A pang hit my stomach as I lost sight of her when she entered Sweethearts. I fought the impulse to get off and put the next step into motion. But at least she hadn't walked off.

"Are you there Rory?" Cathy was back.

"I'm here."

"Bad news, I'm afraid. Forty to forty-five. Maybe an hour. Sorry. Timing is bad. All drivers are out. I caught one of the guys just clocking off. He's coming out with a replacement. Hang tight. I'll radio follow-on buses on the route, but I think they'll be at max, so probably no help to you. Of all the places for this to happen. At full capacity. A few stops on and we could have scooped them up."

"Yeah, go figure." (*Well figured*, I thought) "I'm good, Cath. If things get rowdy, I'll just tell a few jokes."

She laughed. "I hope not. Your jokes are bad. Really bad."

"Thank you. Feelings officially hurt. Gotta go now and soothe passengers."

As Cathy had pointed out, breaking down outside Sweethearts Bakery was the perfect place to trap passengers en route. My thoughts exactly on choosing here. As I flicked off the radio, I wondered how many passengers would need pacifying once the waiting time slipped past the fifteen-minute mark. Juggling any troubles keeping patchwork would need to take backseat to implementing the next part of my Mariana plan.

I reached below the seat to grab my jacket. When I turned back to rise, Tracy and Mark stood there. Mark wore an ear-to-ear smile as though he'd just won the lottery. Tracy looked a hundred times cheerier than she had yesterday. The air about them was of sweet happiness.

Great to see them happy—they were a cute couple—but this was about to mess with my plans. Standing and putting on my jacket, I glanced over their shoulders, desperately hoping to keep an eye on Sweethearts' door in case Mariana left. Unfortunately the pair blocked my view. All I caught was a glimpse of the bottom half of the café's awning with the bright blue letters spelling out "Sweethearts Café."

Time counted down in my head, as though each second that ticked by fell away into a bottomless pit.

Mark reached out a hand. "We want to thank you."

His clasp was strong, and his handshake enthusiastic as though he'd just met a childhood sports idol.

"You're welcome, I guess." I smiled, inside simply repeating, *Please don't let this take too long.*

He continued, "If not for what you did yesterday, we would have been, well, Tracy and I may have .... We're engaged, you know, and yesterday, well, yesterday things weren't good."

Mark let go of my hand, stood back, and looked over to Tracy. He slipped an arm about her shoulder and hugged her to him. Her eyes met his, and she gave him a look saying more than words. Turning back to me he added, "And now we've realized nothing matters except what we have."

"Happy to help," I replied, trying to sound casual, even though the seconds were disappearing far too quickly into that pit.

"Just a game," I lied, "throwing troubles away. My mama used to play the same little mind play with me. I'm glad I could help though."

Tracy flipped her long ponytail over her shoulder, which then hung luxuriously down over her chest. "No, more than a game. I'd call this a wonderful thing," she said. "Mark and I had a heart-to-heart last night after the bus ride. Worked through everything. That wouldn't have happened if not for you and your ... game. Personally, I thought you *did* take my troubles. I felt, well, we both felt like we could breathe again. In catching our breath, we saw how stupid we were being."

Tracy turned and looked up into Mark's eyes. He nodded at her as though giving permission to reveal a secret. "The worries, the anger, what we were fighting over seemed gone. Just like you said."

"Yes," Mark added "Kind of miraculous."

I was happy for them, but the tick of those dripping seconds seemed louder, intrusively so. *Tick. Tick. Tick. Your chance is falling away.*

I needed to extricate myself. Immediately.

"Seriously, it was nothing. I'm glad to have helped. And now ..."

As though I was a preacher about to deliver a blessing, I extended my arms and brought a hand down on each of their shoulders. "All part of the service. If you'll excuse me, I must check if any other passengers need help with a miracle after this darn bus has given up the ghost."

I gave them my best reassuring smile and applied increased pressure to their shoulders. I hoped they'd get the idea I needed to get going.

They didn't move.

Tracy's eyes narrowed. "So how *did* you do the thing?"

"Tracy, we weren't going to—" Mark said, now looking embarrassed.

Maintaining her piercing gaze on me, she replied to him, "I know, but I *want* to understand Mark. The feelings are far too real." Then she addressed me. "What kind of voodoo did you use to make us feel better, take our troubles like that? Because once we got off this bus, before you did whatever you did, Mark and I were over. Our fight was serious. Later, after we'd talked about what happened, I told Mark you must have used hypnosis. I've read how some people can do that. Mass hypnosis. Because I felt something. So did Mark. We felt, well, we felt changed, almost in a physical way."

Tracy fixed an expectant stare upon me. Wrong time for an interrogation, not that I didn't get them sometimes, but right now, this was the last thing I needed. Some people felt troubles lifting. They were just more sensitive. Those who did would dismiss the feeling. Occasionally I'd be asked this very same question. None though, had held me with as determined a look as Tracy.

"Really just a parlor trick. Something like the power of suggestion but not hypnosis."

Anyone thinking I used hypnosis was a risk. I kept my profile as low as possible. No Facebook. No Twitter. No Instagram. The last thing I needed was a good news story shouting headlines like: *Bus driver hypnotizes passengers.* I couldn't afford journalists digging into my abilities.

Tracy's eyes grew to dark slits.

"A parlor trick? I don't see how that's possible. You did something. Something real. I think we have a right to know."

Mark was the one who saved me. Maybe he detected my reticence. He squeezed Tracy's shoulder and insisted, "Honey, I think if Rory says he didn't do anything, then I think we have to accept his word."

Tracy continued to stare, lips clamped firmly together as she mulled over Mark's words. I went to go around them, but she stood her ground. I could see she wasn't convinced.

"Thanks, Mark. Great you understand. Gotta go now and check on everyone." My voice sounded two octaves higher.

With a big *that's all folks* smile, I patted him on the shoulder. Tracy looked uncertain. I light-footed around the two, escaping on Mark's side. Getting off the bus had become my single goal. Relief was all I felt as I placed a foot on the pavement. Behind me, Tracy's voice: "Mark, you know something *is* strange."

She could think me strange and pummel me with questions tomorrow, but today I had one urgent mission. Since grounding the bus, I'd checked on the dark thing, and things had grown worse.

Oily-looking thickened tendrils were now more than three quarters up the sides of the box. The temperature in the attic had risen to that of a sweat box.

On the pavement I found myself amid a milling crowd of passengers. I searched for Mariana, without making my actions obvious, by turning side to side and touching people's shoulders, apologizing as I made my way through.

"Excuse me," a breathless, concerned voice came from my side. I turned to face a middle-aged man smartly dressed in a deep-blue sports jacket, with a perfectly placed bright red pocket square peeking from his breast pocket. I didn't recognize him. No, wait, maybe a few weeks back, he'd caught the bus. He looked even more harassed than I felt.

"Is there a bus route near here to take me north to Mandalay? I've called my wife. She'll pick me up on her way from work, but I need to get to Loxton Road East. This is the third time this has happened to me—broken down bus, I mean. Replacements never come in less than forty minutes. I'm not waiting."

I hoped no one had heard him. A woman with a toddler in tow and another man in a t-shirt and jeans stood just behind. They appeared to be eavesdropping, thinking I had some news to impart. This information traveling on crowd grapevine, I didn't need. I couldn't have Mariana getting the same idea as this man. I needed her to wait.

With a reassuring smile and in as loud a voice as possible without sounding like I'd gone crazy, I said, "Just sharing what HQ tells me. Definitely fifteen minutes, max. Sorry for the inconvenience."

Turning my back to the mother and t-shirt man, I leaned in to this passenger and said in a much quieter voice, "The bus you need runs along West High Street. Two blocks that way." I pointed across the street. "Runs every thirty minutes."

I made a point of checking my watch, even though I didn't actually know its schedule. I simply wanted him and his knowledge of timings gone.

He looked across the road for just a moment, then took off at a stride, throwing me a "thanks." His jacket flapped behind him as he jogged away.

I returned to scanning the crowd. The exchange had cost me more time. People had dispersed into smaller groups. Many had moved into Sweethearts—at least I hoped that's where they'd gone. I'd seen Mariana go inside and I just hoped she hadn't come out while my attention was otherwise occupied. I scanned the crowd but didn't see her. Please let her be inside.

Barrett Something-Smith, the lawyer, emerged from Sweethearts carrying a take-away coffee cup. He slurped through the plastic hole of the cover as though he was dying of thirst. He saw me looking toward the door from which he'd just exited and started toward me.

No, no, no. I couldn't be stopped again. I had to get to Mariana. I'd thought this through during my sleepless night. This was the only way I could think to create a chance to speak to her in private, which would seem natural and not stalker creepy. Bus breaks down. Annoying, but realistic. Bus driver strikes up conversation. Not suspicious, natural. After that?

I hadn't got that far.

Something-Smith was a few feet from me, but I managed to dodge around another passenger, sidestepping, and then moving purposely through the crowd. I felt his stare follow me as I placed a determined look on my face as though I'd been called inside Sweet-hearts on urgent business.

I'd reached the door, and in an uncharacteristic move, shoved past an exiting Mr. Ogilvy. He carried two bottles of water in his hand. I smiled, but ignored his, "Hey Rory." No, I couldn't afford any more interruptions. I pushed through the door.

Once inside I was immediately enveloped by the chatter and tightness of the room. Strangely the mood felt upbeat, the breakdown seemingly creating a camaraderie.

My gaze flowed over the heads, madly scanning the room. The half dozen tables to the left were all full. The high counter to the right had disappeared behind a group of animatedly chatting passengers. Two twenty-somethings, a pink and blond-haired girl, and a guy with black gauges in his ears, moved quickly between coffee machine, cash register, glass pastry shelf and the counter. Clearly they hadn't antici-pated an onslaught of customers at this time of night.

Mariana wasn't at the counter, so my search returned to the tables. Seconds later I'd established she wasn't sitting at any of those either. I was confused. She didn't seem to be inside the café. *How* had I missed her?

Tracy and Mark had stopped me for two or three minutes, then another minute giving directions, but no more than four to five minutes delay before I'd gotten inside. How could she have disap-peared in less than five minutes? Maybe we'd passed each other somehow. My mouth felt dry. My throat raw. The conversation buzz disappeared into a muffled drone. I felt as though I stood in nothing-ness, black and empty. Now I would need to find another way to deal with the dark thing without gathering any more knowledge or help, a frightening prospect.

When Mariana casually walked out from a doorway toward the back, I felt the breath pulled from me. Until I looked above her at the bathroom sign the thought never occurred to me there was one place I hadn't searched.

Not wasting a second, I weaved my way through the people obstacle course, but was stopped before reaching her. A man in his late twenties, short, perfectly molded hair as black as boot polish, waved to her and held out a coffee cup. His leather jacket looked more expensive than my entire wardrobe.

Where had this guy come from? I had never seen Mariana with him. Could he be a boyfriend? I don't know why I had even thought someone as beautiful as Mariana wouldn't have someone. My chest deflated, but just as quickly a steely resolve pushed back. Whoever he was, boyfriend or not, I needed him away from Mariana. This wasn't about my feelings for her. This was about something dark and dangerous.

18

F or me, thinking on my feet was akin to thinking on my knees, crawling. My mama used to say: *"Rory, if you take any longer making a decision, you'll need to shave again."* My indecisiveness came from all the emotions spinning inside. Sometimes they cluttered my mind.

No inspiration came, so I simply barged toward them, hoping in the seconds I crossed the crowded room, brilliance would hit me on the head.

Even at a few feet away, I smelled Leather Jacket's overpowering aftershave. Up close, the jacket looked expensive to clean if anything should spill on the shiny leather. An idea flashed in my mind. I stopped abruptly and swung my body one hundred and eighty degrees back toward the door. As I did, I flung my arm outward.

"Do you want milk and sugar?" I shouted to an imaginary person at the tables, before feeling my hand connect with the coffee cup in Leather Jacket's hand. Hot, black, burning drops splashed onto my skin. I didn't mind. Anything was okay at this point. I yelped, louder than necessary, as I turned and feigned surprise.

"What the hell?" Leather Jacket didn't hold back his anger. A yellow-brown stain now patterned the stylishly cut shirt beneath his jacket. Small droplets hung from the black sleeve and dripped to the floor. He still held one cup in his hand, while the other now lay between our feet in the middle of a brown puddle.

Silence consumed the previous rowdy chatter as I felt all eyes turn to us.

"Sorry," I exclaimed, not daring to look at Mariana standing a few yards away. I kept my gaze on Leather Jacket. If he overreacted, I would reach out with my rapidly reddening hand—the coffee was super-hot—and calm him down.

"You're a joker, right, buddy?" His face had taken on the same pinkish hue of my burned skin.

"Oh, no," said Mariana. Her hand, which had covered her mouth, now reached into her bag and pulled out a small packet of tissues. She retrieved several and promptly handed them to Leather Jacket. Without even a thank you, he took them and dabbed savagely at his shirt as though he was trying to kill a bug.

He looked up at me like I'd assaulted him, and through gritted teeth said, "Seriously, are you for real? First, your bus breaks down and strands us. *Then*, you spill coffee. All … over … me. I'm placing a complaint, asshole."

I was acutely aware of how close I stood to Mariana, her proximity making me dizzy, and with his anger directed at me, I felt like I was caught in a chaotic ocean of emotion. I reached toward the angry man. All I needed was to touch his skin and this would go away. But he stepped back, before my hand reached him, like I had swung a punch.

"Whadya think you're doing pal? Are you crazy?"

My plan seemed to be unraveling. A thought struck me, through the chaos:*Forget him. Mariana is what matters.*

I turned to her, ignoring Leather Jacket, and said. "That was just an accident. I didn't purposely mean to—"

She stared at me, expressionless. In those moments my heart stopped beating as though a hand had reached into my chest and squeezed tight.

Behind me an angry voice demanded my name and number to

place a complaint. *Like a bus driver is a cop with a badge number.* That was almost funny, if I had time to laugh. Then a small smile eased across Mariana's face. She winked at me, and the hand inside my chest released, so my heart could beat again.

Mariana addressed him. "I don't think Rory meant to spill the coffee. He's the sweetest bus driver in the city."

A warmth spread through me. Mariana remembered my name. *She actually remembered my name.*

"Yeah, he's a real sweetheart," guffawed Leather Jacket. He looked at her, pausing, head arched back, as though thinking something through. "You know what? Screw this."

He turned, still wiping at a stain, which wouldn't be improved no matter how long he attacked the spot, and began to walk toward the exit. Several steps on, he stopped, swung back to Mariana and said, "I'm not waiting here. We can split a cab—he knocked the cup on purpose, you know."

Mariana stared after him, rolling her bottom lip beneath her teeth. Then she looked across to me, hesitating for long seconds.

Choose right, please Mariana.

I didn't know who Leather Jacket was to her, but he was all wrong for her.

The ticking of valuable seconds pounded in my ears again. I'd come to believe my life might be in terrible danger if I couldn't discover the thing's source before moving the thing on. I wanted to reach out to Mariana, grab her hand, and pull her back toward a corner of the room, away from everyone. Away from Leather Jacket.

People had formed a small space around the clearly volatile man, who stood like a statue glaring at Mariana.

"Coming?" he said, like he was speaking to a dog. The guy was obnoxious, times ten.

Mariana shook her head slightly as though she didn't want to say no, or maybe she shook her head at his attitude.

Leather Jacket waited a few more seconds, then, he too, slowly moved his head side to side and said, "Thanks for the attempted coffee. Next time, maybe we won't be so rudely interrupted."

Mariana gave a whatever-shrug. I loved her even more in that moment.

Leather Jacket pushed past two middle-aged women standing near the door. They stood back, tutting as he exited. If the door didn't have a slow-close mechanism, it would have slammed.

Crazily, the first part of the plan had worked. Somehow, Mariana and I were now side-by-side, both staring after him. "What a charmer. A friend?"

Mariana answered without turning. "No, I don't even know him. He stood in front of me in the line and asked if I wanted a coffee. I was desperate for the bathroom, so I thought 'that's nice' and said yes. I don't even know his name. So I don't, really, understand his problem." She shook her head slowly as she spoke.

Relief hit me like light summer rain on hot asphalt, cooling and welcome. I wondered at his possessiveness. His behavior was bizarre as though *I'd* interrupted *his* important plans. Still, he'd done me a huge favor. Like the passenger had said earlier, *it truly is an ill wind that blows no one any good.*

Turning to face Mariana, heartened by this new turn of events, I asked, "Since I'm responsible for the spilling of your coffee, can I get you another?"

Mariana tilted her head, pausing as she chewed again on her bottom lip. "Hmm, seems convenient."

My stomach lurched. "Convenient?"

"Yes. You spill my coffee, like he said. Now here's your chance to offer me a coffee. Very suspicious Mr. Bus Driver, Trouble Taker-Awayer."

Moments passed, as I felt my confidence slip away like I was losing grip on a rope. *She had seen through my plan?*

She continued, "You must have really enjoyed my worries yesterday."

I looked over to the counter, gathering my thoughts, then began to stutter a reply. "I, uh, I, don't know what you—"

She stopped me with a laugh and a playful smack on my arm.

"Don't look so worried. I'm joking Rory. You don't mind if I call you Rory, do you?"

"Sure. Sorry, excuse me, I'm a touch on edge with the bus and everything."

"Don't worry. The bus breaking down isn't your fault. Besides, anyone who was on the journey yesterday certainly won't care. Not after what you did."

I felt suddenly warm. "You think so? I didn't really do anything. Just played a mind game."

I had spent the past twenty-four hours regretting what I'd done. Now as I stood here actually talking to Mariana, the girl I'd never dared approach until now, I saw yesterday's events in a different light altogether. In fact, the circumstances felt fateful.

"You did so do something," she said, grabbing my forearm, sending wild tingles through my skin. "Everyone, including me, was down in the dumps. Could have been the weather. But the minute I boarded the bus there was something heavy that came over me. Go figure! But you Rory, gave us all a wakeup call. You were right. We shouldn't carry our troubles home with us. That's not fair. You shouldn't even need to remind us. We should just be throwing our own troubles in the Dawson each night."

I felt a gentle squeeze on my forearm. *More crazy tingles.*

"What a wonderful thing you did. Wonderful. And way cool."

A glowing smile lit her face. Her smile made me ache.

"I should buy *you* a drink," she said, letting go of my arm. "What do you want?"

I held my face rigid, attempting to shield how I felt. She didn't know I had dreamed of this moment for so long. All she knew was I was some guy who drove a bus and who'd spilled coffee on a jerk. So I tried to shrug her offer away, tried to act cool even though my emotions simmered unchecked.

"That's kind of you. But you don't have to get me anything. Really, that was nothing. Besides, I'm on duty. I need to be ready when the replacement bus arrives."

I was to learn Mariana's determination was rarely halted by mere words.

"No way. I won't take no for an answer. Let me guess. Black coffee, one sugar." She made a mock *ta-da-I'm-psychic* gesture with her hands.

I didn't have the heart to tell her she was way off. I didn't drink coffee. Or tea. Hot chocolate was my winter drink and in summer, just plain old water.

"How did you know?" I said, maybe a little too gleefully.

Everything changed in that moment, my nervousness disappeared, and suddenly the most natural thing in the world was to be here talking to Mariana. Just as I'd imagined. Better than I'd imagined. If only I could have reveled in a dream-come-true, but I needed to steer the conversation to yesterday. With caution though, so everything seemed natural.

"If my mama knew I let a girl I'd just met buy me a drink," I said, "I would never have heard the end of it. So, please allow me."

For long, wonderful moments we both stared at each other as though we were alone in the room. She rolled her bottom lip, then laughed, and said, "Okay, skinny latte, no sugar." She looked around the bustling, noisy café. "But I think I'll wait outside. A little crowded in there."

She turned and wove her way through the crowd to the door, leaving my heart in a mush. As she left the room I realized my mistake. I couldn't waste precious time standing in line to get coffee.

Pushing my way to the front of the six-deep line at the counter, I excused myself to an office-attired woman, whom I'd seen occasionally on the bus, and said, "Excuse me, but do you mind if I order before you? I've got to get back to the bus."

"If it gets us on our way quicker, then yes, go right ahead."

Minutes later, two hot coffees to-go in hand, I emerged outside, more in control of my emotions. I'd checked on the dark thing. Still inside the box. Still grotesque. Still growing. And feeling even more threatening.

For a mad second I couldn't find Mariana. Then through the

milling but thinning crowd, I saw her standing near the front door of the bus. Maybe she realized that's where I needed to be. Everything was coming together, more through happenstance than my planning.

There was a distinct and unusual mood among the passengers as I moved through them. They should be annoyed, frustrated, all the negative emotions experienced when plans are disrupted. Instead people talked animatedly, smiled, even laughed. Strangers were actually connecting as few stared down at their smart phones or tablets. I smiled inwardly; some of this was the hangover from yesterday. Those passengers I'd touched were still experiencing the benefits, and moods are contagious. The physics of emotional energy.

"Excuse me Rory." A woman's voice to my side stopped me. Mrs. Daley stood near the central door of the bus beside Mr. Ogilvy. Immediately I saw there was something different about her. She glowed with happiness when most days she looked tired and beaten, the physical strain of her cleaning job weighing on her like a heavy winter coat. The pair stood intimately close. Prior to yesterday I'd never noticed them even speaking to each other, let alone touching one another. Mr. Ogilvy's hand rested gently on her back and her fingers brushed lightly against his sleeve.

"Yes Mrs. Daley?"

"You're such a sweet boy. So good with our names. We just wondered how much longer, honey. We're thinking ..." She nodded in Mr. Ogilvy's direction with a warm smile. "...we might grab a cab together. But if the bus is here shortly, we'll wait."

I'd played cupid yet again, an occasional byproduct of troubles keeping. When people are given space to open up to the possibilities surrounding them, sometimes there's magic. Mrs. Daley and Mr. Ogilvy certainly deserved happiness.

I glanced to either side, ensuring I wouldn't be overheard, then leaned in close to the woman who today appeared ten years younger than her graying, short-hair portrayed.

"You know Mrs. Daley, replacement buses can sometimes take a while. Especially at this time of night. I'd share that cab."

Mrs. Daley gave me a look that said she liked my answer. She regarded Mr. Ogilvy, who also seemed to stand a little taller, a little less weighted by his loss.

"See, I told you Arthur." Then, addressing me, "Thank you, honey." In an impromptu move, she reached over, brushed my cheek with a kiss, and said, "And yesterday, thank you for that too. You are surely a blessing to this world."

Funny, those were my mama's exact words. A sudden rush of emotion, happy and sad, came over me. I missed my mom.

Standing back, even closer now to Mr. Ogilvy, she looked down at the two coffees in my hands. "Sorry, we've interrupted you. You'd better get those to their owners."

"Yes, I'll see you tomorrow. With a bus that will get us from 'a' to 'b,' I promise."

Then, as an afterthought as I walked away, I said, "Have a wonderful night you two." A girlish giggle followed me away.

In a matter of yards I'd responded to the same question—*how long before the replacement bus?*—several times, before planting a *stop me at your own risk* look on my face.

Mariana faced down the street, staring after the slow moving traffic. She didn't hear my approach, only turning when I was a few feet away. She smiled. She *always* smiled. Tiny tremors rocked my heart. My hand reached out with the cup.

"One skinny latte, un-spilled."

"Thank you. Like the Beatles' song 'Love is All You Need,' for me, sometimes, coffee is *all* you need."

She took the coffee and immediately took a sip.

"Cute," I replied, lost for anything wittier. In my mind, "Got To Get You Into My Life" began to play.

Now I'd somehow executed my plan to find a quiet, unthreatening moment with Mariana, the pavement seemed to rock beneath me.

Deep breath. Exhale. Be at peace, I told myself as I always did when stressed.

"Can I ask you a question?" I asked, sounding more confident than I felt.

"Sure." Mariana gave me a dimpled smile as she took another sip.

"What I did yesterday, did that really help you?" I tried to keep my tone serious. I didn't want her to think this was some kind of flirtation.

She looked to the side, biting on her lip as she considered the question.

"Um, yes, yeah. I guess, when I think about it I really *did* feel kind of different, kind of funny. Good funny, as though a weight had lifted. After was when I realized there had even been a weight. Now you've got me thinking, I kind of felt free. I guess you just don't realize how much the day builds up on you." Then she looked directly into my eyes. *Melted heart puddle time again.* "Rory, such a lovely thought. To do that … for everybody."

I eased into the conversation I'd planned to have, careful not to reveal too much, too soon. "I guess with my job I see people wearing their troubles all the time. I'm like a fly on the wall. Sometimes they take their frustrations out on me if they've had a bad day."

Her brow wrinkled. "Hardly your fault if the bus is late or their day isn't great."

She sipped at her coffee again. I hadn't touched my prop coffee. I continued, "Some people can be downright evil on occasion."

My plan was to angle the questions around to her customers. After great thought, I'd decided the most likely scenario was the dark thing belonged to someone she'd interacted with shortly before I trouble-kept the passengers.

"Yeah, I get that. We get those kind of people where I work too. I put on happy music after they leave. Something upbeat. Clears the bad vibes. Talking music all day, helping people, normally great fun. Mr. Sterling, he's my boss, is a sweet old guy. He's owned the store since the eighties."

"Did you have a bad customer yesterday?" I ventured.

Mariana cocked her head to the side. "That's a funny question. No, can't say I really did. Yesterday was a good day in fact. Why do you ask?"

I shrugged my shoulders, aiming at casual. "No reason. You just mentioned a weight being lifted."

She stopped and looked down at her cup, and judging by the frown on her face and the far-off look in her eyes she was thinking back to the day before.

"Hmm, now that you say that I did feel sad. No, not sad. Odd. Really odd. Off kilter. Until you did your *I'll take your troubles and throw them in the Dawson* thing. Now you've got me thinking, when I walked up to you before I got off, I remember trying very hard to hide the feeling. Pretend everything was okay. Was I so obvious?"

"No, of course not." How could I reasonably tell her some kind of dark evil thing was captured inside her. "You normally seem light as day." Quickly I added, "Not that I keep an eye on you or anything, not like a stalker. I just notice people, if you know what I mean."

Her face relaxed. "Don't worry, I know what you mean. Anyway, you don't look like a stalker. You look like a sweet, kind guy. Stalkers don't usually take people's troubles and throw them in a river. More a fairy godmother, sorry, fairy godfather thing." Realizing what she'd said, she stopped and laughed. "Not a fairy thing at all. Oh, you know what I mean. Don't you?"

She pushed her hair back behind her ears with her free hand and smiled hopefully.

Was she flirting with me?

Before I could respond, a faraway look came into her eyes, and she added, "I'll admit to one thing though, thinking about yesterday, I felt normal until I caught your bus. Actually, the bus ride changed my mood." A raised eyebrow replaced the thoughtful look. "I wonder why. Can a person walk into a space and immediately feel bad, like there's something in the air?"

That question and the way she spoke, the open look in her eyes, made me believe I could take a chance. Before I'd even considered whether the next thing I said was a good idea, I was saying things I hadn't planned, taking a risk I'd never before taken with another living soul, and probably putting my foot squarely in the wrong place.

"What if I told you I really *could* take people's troubles, rid them of the bad feelings? Temporarily, at least."

"Hmm." Mariana tilted her head, pushing at a stray blonde curl that had determinedly fallen back on her face from behind her ear. "I think I'd say that was a pretty neat trick." Then brightly, "How would you take people's troubles? Something psychic like mind control or hypnosis?"

"No, not psychic or hypnosis. Play along with me for a minute. What if we just accepted I could take people's troubles. Just a thing, you know, a person is born with. And say, one day, a rainy day, something went wrong. Something unexpected. Say instead of normal, everyday troubles, I picked up something not right, something dark from someone. Do you think I should tell them?"

"Rory, that's a really weird question. In fact, this is kind of a strange conversation."

"Humor me."

She took another sip of coffee as she considered the question. "Okay, well, I guess I'd want to know. But wouldn't someone already know? Wouldn't they be feeling the *something dark?* Feeling things weren't right?"

"You didn't know how bad you felt yesterday until I did my thing, did you?"

"Good point. I felt okay before you made me realize I hadn't felt right before."

Mariana clutched her cup tighter and frowned. "You sound like a therapist. I feel I should be lying on a couch with my eyes closed."

"Not a therapist. A troubles keeper. My mama's name for me. For what I do. Whenever she felt down, which was rare—trust me, she had the best attitude to life—but even when I was very young, she'd take my hand and tell me just that small act made her troubles drift away. One day she said I reminded her of a goal keeper, keeping those troubles under control, deflecting them from scoring a touchdown, and sending them away where they could do no harm. In my head the name stuck. *Troubles Keeper.*"

"If yesterday is anything to go by, you're a very good troubles keeper. You should give up bus driving and have your own show like that guy on cable who can talk to dead relatives. What's his name? Oh yeah, John Edward, or that new young guy, Tyler Henry. He's *really* amazing."

"Yeah, I don't think what I do would make an interesting show."

Close, even though Mariana had joked, not realizing I'd actually shared the truth. Troubles keeping was probably some kind of psychic thing but without the spirits. I didn't understand the process myself, and I'd never questioned the exact workings. Until now and the dark thing, which had become agitated since I'd come into physical proximity of Mariana. Was there some kind of recognition of her? The idea forced me to move forward with the conversation quicker than I'd hoped.

"I wondered about you," I said, lowering my voice. "Yesterday, something happened. I don't think those feelings, the mood you experienced, were you. Or the mood on the bus, for that matter."

She raised her eyebrows in response. I tried to sound light and breezy, like maybe this was a joke too.

"Troubles keepers know these things. Code of conduct type of thing."

"You know what Rory, you did help. The notion never occurred to me until right now. When I got off the bus, *no*, when I touched your hand, the effect was instant. The world seemed brighter like the sun had come out from behind a cloud. I could have skipped off the bus. I remember thinking, *Wow, the power of positive thinking.* Like Star Wars. The force be with you."

"Yes, that's right. The force is with us troubles keepers," I agreed.

She grabbed my arm and gasped. "Wait a minute Rory, do you think something happened on the bus? Do you think there was a dark force waiting there?"

Before I could answer she continued, as her mind traveled back to the day before, observing the events from a different perspective.

"You know, if we're throwing around ideas of good force, bad force, this is going to sound crazy, but something could have happened on the bus yesterday. Now I'm running everything through my head, I felt fine, I mean totally fine, until *them*—"

"Them?"

"Do you remember a group of people boarded a stop after me. I sat in the aisle seat. I think I was reading my book. Then someone brushed past me. Straight away I noticed, like a zap by static electricity. Really hurt. I reacted straight away, but I looked *out* the window, at the storm. I thought there'd been a lightning strike near us. When I saw nothing, I looked behind, down the aisle, but most of those who'd gotten on board had already sat down. Then I looked out the window again, the storm was close, and so I decided the weather had to be the reason."

"What about how you felt? You said you felt normal until then."

"Yeah, that was definitely weird." She continued to shake her head as she spoke, like she couldn't believe she had missed something so important. "My mind took off on a tangent. That doesn't normally happen to me. I'm pretty happy-go-lucky."

I wanted to say I noticed, but of course that would be *stalker behavior.*

"I began to remember all the terrible things that had frightened me in my life. Nearly drowning when I was twelve. My dog hit by a car and dying in my arms. Being betrayed by a friend who'd merely befriended me to get to my brother—he's cute, but that's still wrong. Being frightened, angry. In fact, for a moment, every terrible emotion you could imagine had been stirred inside me, like one big emotional blender. Just like, oh, what's the word? Claustrophobic."

I'd begun to realize what might have happened and, if I was right, this wasn't good.

Mariana clutched my arm again and squeezed, now looking directly into my eyes. "Oh, and something else I just remembered. I'm embarrassed to even say, but I guess since we're talking honestly—"

"Go on, you can tell your troubles keeper anything." I made a zipping motion across my lips. "I'm bound by an oath."

"Okay, but don't think me crazy. I had this awful feeling I was going to die, that I was on death row or marked or something weird like that." Her eyes searched mine. "Believe me, I'm not like that. I'm happy with everything in my life. Yesterday, for a few minutes though, I thought Death could be sitting right next to me. Then, like a miracle, you just made the feelings all go away, and I hadn't even thought about how I felt until just now. What do you think happened? I sound crazy, right?"

I knew she described the dark thing, and I knew *exactly* how the energy the thing exuded felt. Mind you, locked up, the nasty dark force energy remained isolated.

"You're not crazy. There are more things on earth than we can ever understand."

Her eyes searched mine. "What do you mean?"

Mariana waited for me to say something. This seemed like the perfect moment to explain the details of troubles as I understood them; she might listen, might actually believe me.

I began: "What I'm about to tell you requires you to trust me. You see—"

Before I could complete the sentence, there was a tap on my shoulder. When I swung about, Leather Jacket was so close I felt his breath on my face. He did not look happy. Then again, this seemed his general disposition.

"You know Mr. Bus Driver, we've been here, *waiting*, for over twenty minutes. You said *fifteen minutes. Max.* Four buses have gone by, packed with people who are *getting home*. None of them stopping. Like we've got the plague. So, ah, your watch is a little off and your company's service is pretty raw. Rest of us are not getting paid to stand around hitting on pretty girls."

Who was this guy?

"I understand sir. Can you just give me a minute, and then I'll contact the depot and get an E.T.A. update."

"I'd say you make that contact right now. I think we've given you too many minutes of our time already."

As much as I wanted to ignore him, he was right, I couldn't delay this any longer; I had to head off any frustrations gathering in the crowd. If I had just a few more minutes, everything I'd hoped to achieve might have come to fruition, but he didn't look as though he would be leaving us any time soon.

I turned back to Mariana, and the words I'd spent months repeating in my head tumbled out.

"Meet me? Later? I'm off at seven forty-five. Please, this is important. Actually *very* important."

Mariana though, misunderstood my intentions.

"I'm okay Rory. I'm not going crazy. The dark mood's gone. You don't have to worry about me. Really."

"No, no, I didn't ask because of that. There's something else. Something we need to discuss. I don't have time here, and I don't want to say, because—"

"Because what? Rory, is it something bad?"

"Just meet me. Please? There's a Chinese restaurant on Eighth Avenue. Mr. Wong's. Eight-thirty. Can you?"

I hoped the urgency in my voice would propel her into agreeing.

Leather Jacket piped up with, "Oh brother, give me a break. Seriously?" He waved a finger in my face. "And I know you spilled the coffee on purpose. *I know.* You're up to something."

As he turned and walked away Mariana opened her mouth, then without speaking clamped her lips together. She suddenly seemed uncertain. The spell about us had collapsed. Mariana looked so beautiful standing there in the street light. Her lips so naturally red, her lightly blushing cheeks, her innocent eyes like green pools of brightness. The dark thing wasn't from her.

Regrets ran through my mind. I shouldn't have told her about the troubles keeping, even jokingly. I should have found a different way to interrupt Leather Jacket and her conversation. I shouldn't have rushed asking her to meet me. She didn't know me. I was just a friendly bus driver with whom, until ten minutes ago, she'd never shared more than a few words. But this was my chance, probably my one chance, and I couldn't let the chance go. If she decided I was really the creepy, weird driver, then she might never catch my bus again. I had to give her a chance to know me.

So, heart in my throat, I said, "You'll meet me then? Please? Promise, I'm not a serial killer."

She inhaled deeply and sighed, then the hint of a smile played at the side of her mouth.

"I hope I won't regret this. Okay. I'm intrigued. Make it eight-fifteen though. I'm not good for anything if I don't get eight hours sleep. Tomorrow we're stocktaking, so I start at seven."

"Good. Anytime is good. Yes, eight-fifteen. Thank you. I'll see you then."

Reaching out, I touched her hand; just to allay any fears she might have. What I did find made me smile. She carried just one small trouble.

Ignoring my self-imposed rule to not look into people's private lives, I checked the trouble before sending the small worry to the attic. Extraordinary circumstances called for breaking of rules. When the person you love is in danger, nothing that might help is off limits.

The energy flowed through me, tickling its way to its own small box. Even as I examined the worry, I still felt guilt, but the happiness at my discovery made me want to dance down the street. Maybe I'd even store the trouble for a while, as a reminder that sometimes you *can* just get luckier than you deserve. Like Barrett-Something-Smith had said earlier on the bus, *it's an ill wind*; this dark wind, which had blown into my life had also kicked up something incredible.

You see, Mariana's trouble was centered around me.

She had hesitated to say yes, because she thought if I got to know her I might not feel like she did, that my feelings might not be reciprocal.

Mariana liked me. She actually liked me.

19

The bus driver intervenes, interjects himself where he doesn't belong. So easily he deceives the passengers, but not him, for he has watched carefully since understanding who he is and what he can do. For a moment, he'd wondered if the broken-down bus was actually a ruse to seek him out, that the bus driver has recognized him.

Until he saw the man's connection with the girl he hadn't understood. The bus driver must see her as The One. Despite his distance, he still feels the energy emanating from her. He fights the overwhelming urge to reach out and touch her skin. She is such a beautiful, shiny magnet.

Though he's not afraid, he feels relief to realize the bus driver's subterfuge must be due to the man's interest in the girl.

He follows them outside. A few minutes they talk, and he moves closer to eavesdrop and to be closer to her. Her energy ignites a flame within him. He hears only snatches. Too many people. Too much traffic rumbling by. Pieces of phrases and words drift his way.

Crazy. Mr. Wong's. Eight thirty. And *Please.*

Now the bus driver leaves her and boards the bus again. She is alone.

Looking up and down the street, she sips at her coffee; her gaze flickers around the crowd. She smiles randomly at others, then pulls out her phone. He finds his way to her. A thread so strong, he feels the tug at his core, making moving away nearly impossible. He stands behind her, so close he could, if he chose, run his hand over her curls, rub the strands between his fingers, grip chunks in his palm and pull her back to him. He breathes in the scent of her goodness, the urge to reach out almost unbearable. Like sweet pain. A hungry, demanding need bangs in his chest.

She has no idea what she is. But he knows. She is the answer for him. And the bus driver? What purpose does he serve? What if he needs the girl for himself? What if the bus driver uses her before *he* has a chance to take her?

As the bus driver leaves her he touches her hand. The slight glow, the blue, tender strings of energy passing between their skin mimic yesterday. Today, the color is deeper, stronger, as though the two of them combined create something new and more powerful.

He wonders if the bus driver has sensed the game. Maybe he'll even allow the man to find him so he can learn about this adversary. This is wise, he thinks.

He smiles. Okay, bus driver, let's play.

20

The replacement bus arrived forty-two minutes after I called in the breakdown. Most passengers had found other means of transport. A precious piece of my heart traveled away with Mariana when I flagged down a near-capacity bus and beseeched the driver to squeeze a few more passengers on board, one being Mariana.

The mechanic who arrived an hour after we'd stopped gave me a raised-eyebrow, bemused look when the lame bus miraculously started without a problem.

"You must have flooded the engine, I bet. You gotta take off gently, bud," he said, scratching at the back of his head, as he tapped the steering wheel with a spanner. "I'll give this one a good once over tomorrow."

By the time I pulled into the depot it was close to seven-thirty. To rendezvous with Mariana at Mr. Wong's I needed to develop super-speed. Breakdown procedure was to check in and file a report on the route anomaly. Office manager Beth Ann was a stickler for procedure.

Though she was assistant to the depot manager, Beth Ann pretty much ran the entire business, keeping us on time and managing staff and schedules for the week. Even though the company employed cleaners, she would often still be up and down the buses checking they were up to scratch. "People don't want to sit in other people's mess," she'd comment any time something didn't meet her exacting standards. Beth Ann had a low tolerance for the jettisoned scraps of people's lives.

If she had awareness of the emotional scraps left behind by those around her, she wouldn't fuss quite so much. For every angry word or outburst we have, the collateral damage can be incalculable. Strong enough emotions lingered sometimes on surfaces like a nasty virus waiting for a host.

"Rory, did you make us proud?" Beth Ann asked. I was in the process of packing up my bag and unlocking the cash box from its tray to carry in with me when I heard her at the bus steps.

"Tried my hardest."

"And, what *have* you done to our bus?"

"What has our bus done to *me*?" I replied, turning to face the stout woman standing at the bottom of the front door steps. She wore a do-not-mess-with-me look. Her hands were positioned on large hips, which her too-tight bright orange skirt did nothing to conceal. She slowly inhaled enough air to release a long, disapproving sigh, then gave me what I called her Mona Lisa smile, which conveyed not a hint of what would come next. A hug or an earful. Terse and unforgiving as she seemed to most, to me she was the mom I wish I still had, all one hundred fifty pound, five feet two inches of her. We had a banter created through fondness.

Beth Ann hoisted herself onto the bus and walked up the aisle, her head turning left, then right, before pausing at the fifth row, where she squatted awkwardly and pawed at something under the seat. As she rose holding a crumpled candy wrapper, the thought this might be her only form of exercise occurred to me.

"You do know you're putting a cleaner out of work, Beth Ann?"

"Yeah, well, some of them deserve to be out of work."

Two more steps along and she leaned over again. This time she held out an arm as though she was a ballerina pirouetting, and kicked one thick, stocking-covered leg beneath a seat. An apple rolled out into the aisle. Another leg swing and a half-eaten bread roll appeared.

"Tsk, tsk. Now what kind of passengers did you have today Mr. Fine? Messy little varmints let out of the zoo is what this looks like."

"Oh, probably worse," I replied, trying not to smile. "I'd be using a stick, if I was you."

"Perhaps we need to put sawdust on the floors."

"Again, I repeat, what would the cleaners do?"

"Oh, I'm sure they'd find something more meaningful given the chance. So, what the heck happened to the bus then? Was the problem the animals or the mechanicals?" She paused for a moment and smiled at her own joke.

"Not sure, actually. Could have even been me. Apparently I might have flooded the engine. Honestly, so weird."

"Wouldn't be like you Rory. I wouldn't put anything past that Rennie fellow. He's not driving with all the gears. But you ..."

As much as I enjoyed Beth Ann's amusing takes on the transport business and people in general, I was already way behind schedule to meet Mariana.

"Let's hope he has his brakes well serviced then," I said. Beth Ann, I'd love to stay and discuss the mating habits of the urban commuter and be the recipient of your keen observations, but *I've* got a date tonight."

Her mock stern countenance immediately brightened with a broad, dimpled smile.

"Oh, do you now," she said, continuing toward me, holding the wrapper and the mangled bread roll at arm's length. "Hmm, I'm pleased to hear. I've told you enough times to find a nice girl and settle down. Glad you finally listened. Who's the lucky one?"

"Just a girl. Nothing serious."

"Name? Description? Come on. Spill."

"Mariana. Beautiful." And even though I needed to hustle out of there like ten minutes ago, I had an urgent need to share the thrill of finally connecting with Mariana. Even if our *date* wasn't on a strictly romantic basis. At least we were meeting. So I added, "Can you keep a secret?"

Beth Ann cocked her head to the side. Her grin instantly grew larger and she laughed. "Course not, hon. Me, keep a secret? But now you have to tell me regardless, you big tease."

"She's a passenger, I've sort of, kind of, had a crush on for months. When the bus broke down, well, we just got talking."

"Ah, so it's an ill wind then? You couldn't have planned the whole thing better?"

Why did everyone keep saying that today—*an ill wind*—like there was a message trying to get through?

"Meaning?" I said.

"The bus breaking down. Good to see a little calamity can turn up something good. You deserve someone wonderful, my boy. I was telling that son of mine the other day—miserable slacker he is—'try and shine a bit,' I said. Takes after his father. I suggested he needed to be more like a young man I knew. I told him straight, when Rory Fine walks into a room all your troubles seem to fade."

Suddenly I felt bad. Her son couldn't be compared to me with my gift. That was unfair Beth Ann comparing him to me, but then she didn't know my advantage.

"Oh, real sweet of you. I'm sure he loved hearing that."

"I don't care what he wanted to hear. I mean it. You just shine up a room, and that's something wonderful. You're special Rory. Don't you ever change or lose the thing you do. You're one of the good ones."

My hands closed over my heart. I leaned forward and swooped a kiss on her cheek.

"Beth Ann, I think I'll cancel my date. I've just realized I love you more than I'd ever love any gorgeous, curly, blonde-haired perfect girl I happened to meet during a bus breakdown."

Beth Ann pushed me away. "Don't even joke. I wish I had a daughter I could marry off to you. Now, get out of here, you tease."

"Okay. Just know I'm a loyal guy. You're forcing me to do something I don't want to do."

"Rory Fine, I'll give you the same advice I'd give my own son, hopeless and undeserving as he is: Go find someone who makes your heart sing. If this girl is the one, then I am sleeping tonight with my fingers crossed."

I missed my mama more than my heart could stand at times. A palpable ache erupted inside. I leaned in and hugged her.

"I wish I *was* your son, Beth Ann. I really do," I whispered.

She pushed me away. "Go, boy. Meet your girl. I'll write up the report on this cantankerous bus and check in the cash box."

I hesitated to leave her with my work. I knew she'd been here since eight this morning.

With an authoritative tone she said, "Go."

I checked my watch. Yes, I *did* have to go. And fast.

As I leaped from the bus, I turned to wave goodbye through the windows, but Beth Ann had already turned away and moved to the rear of the bus, her head ducking up and down as she searched out discarded trash.

I jogged to my motorcycle parked in a back corner of the lot, which seemed the safest area to avoid any accidental mishaps. This was my one luxury since Mama's passing. If I'd bought a bike when she was alive, I don't think she would have been happy. If you rode a bike, according to her, that made you a biker, with the accompanying criminal lifestyle.

Every time I climbed on and started the engine, a feeling of invincibility came over me; one I never felt in a car. A biker though? One look at me would have ruled that out. The 400cc 1993 model ZX-11 Ninja wasn't the most powerful of bikes, but as a ride sure was fun and quick.

My mood on the ride home should have felt light and filled with hope for my imminent meeting with Mariana. The feelings though, were tempered by the knowledge I had just gleaned from my touch of Beth Ann. What a capable actress to put on such a brave show.

But I had this gift, and even a poker face can't fool a troubles keeper. The day's events had left me susceptible to accidentally pulling in energy, even when I was unprepared and not open to random emotions. Beth Ann's troubles flowed in loud and clear as we hugged. I'm sure she received some comfort when I'd lifted her sadness. The overwhelming feelings would come back though. A few days' relief, tops. This one was never going away, no matter what I did.

Beth Ann was dying.

Ovarian cancer had metastasized in her bones, and like a stealth invader, the disease had riddled her body. She hoped for more time. She hoped nobody would suspect until she found a way to share the terrible news. She hoped the end wouldn't be too terrible for those who loved her. She hoped her son—the miserable slacker, she loved very much—would be okay without her.

I hoped so too.

Troubles keeping gives you a perspective on life very different to most people, who can't see past their own troubles. I usually viewed fate as an impartial judge, that set wheels in motion and then watched from on high. I was often reminded of the famous quatrain in *The Rubaiyat of Omar Khayyám*:

> "*The Moving Finger writes; and, having writ,*
>   *Moves on: nor all thy Piety nor Wit*
>   *Shall lure it back to cancel half a Line,*
>   *Nor all thy Tears wash out a Word of it.*"

For the briefest of moments, I looked at life like most people do. The unfairness hit me like smacking into a wall. The sudden emotion floored me. So much so, I slowed until a car's honk reminded me I was traveling well below the speed limit.

Maybe too much had happened in the past twenty-four hours and my psyche had been worn down. I didn't want to accept, as I usually did, that fate had a right to make the rules. Soon another person I had come to love would be gone, and the only way I could help her was with my light-weight ability to lift away fears. In doing so, I would endure confronting them myself.

Sometimes troubles keeping sucked. Sometimes life sucked. If I could find a way to grab the moving finger, I'd snap the damn thing in half.

21

He's more cautious since seeing The One and the bus driver together today. He feels a need to practice one last time before he takes this rare, irreplaceable gem. The perfect One, the girl with the blonde curls. Years might pass before he finds another so right. If one even exists.

He wonders if the bus driver had sensed how close their proximity was in the crowd. He'd waited for the replacement bus to arrive once the girl left on another. He watched with intrigue as the bus driver moved among the passengers, touching them. The fine filaments of light dancing between him and the others.

So by the time he boards the replacement bus, he has already chosen the one with whom he will practice.

He sits beside her. At first he stares out the window, breathing in the slim fingers of energy wafting from her. He makes conversation. Light. Unthreatening. Innocent. She talks. He talks. As she reaches for the rail on the seat in front of them, he admires the way energy dances from her hand to travel along the silver metal. He wants to reach out and soak up the lively, flickering power and lick it from his fingers, but that would come later.

The bus empties more each stop until only a handful of passengers remain aboard. He and the girl and three others. He senses her pleasure in their conversation. He chose her because of the openness in her soul that glows from her.

He barely listens to her words. A hairdresser. A job interview this side of town. A just-missed bus before this one. "Fate," she says, while he thinks: *more than you will ever know*. When their fingers touch, the slightest glance, instead of seeing he feels the symphony of light. Inside, he sighs with anticipation. He yearns, in this moment, to peel back the layers of her life and peer inside.

They get off at her stop and walk along the street, just a normal couple taking in the night air. She's smiling. He's smiling. Not long now. He can hardly wait.

22

Her eyes focus upon him. She stares expectantly and waits for his next move. He has tried to explain the possibility he offers. She doesn't listen. He feels her mind constrained by this world and its limited dimension. So he must simply proceed, as always. He regrets again she, like all the rest, cannot see the beauty in his work.

He depresses the drill's trigger lightly, feels the vibration of the whirring bit, and revels in the pulses as they travel through his hand and up his arm. There's something comforting in the subtle displacement of air.

These moments just before are like waypoints, places where he inhales a breath until finally his work in this world is done and he will be home.

Her eyes roll wildly and he reaches to her; his hand now rests upon her crown, as he runs his palm through what's left of her hair, feels the smooth coolness of her extended forehead. Leaning in so his eyes are level and inches from hers, he tries to soothe her. Without words, he attempts to convey with a gentle smile the wonder he has for her and this experience.

He touches his fingers lightly to her forehead, then down over her lids, as though he is closing the eyes of one freshly dead. *Stay closed,* he wills. When he pulls his hand away, her eyes do as they are bid.

This is something new. Since the bus, The One, the driver, everything has changed. He feels a buzz inside his head, a hum filled with particles of swirling energy that can travel wherever he needs. The power travels into this one to close her eyes or hold her head with just a thought.

The girl on the bus, he thinks. Maybe her or the bus driver or the proximity of both work like a vortex of energy he's absorbed to transform him to create this new skill.

He taps the drill's trigger again. On. Off. On. Off. Before he presses down hard and the motor comes fully to life in his hands. Clasping the back securely, he tilts her head upward. She doesn't resist. Cannot resist.

He brings the whirring bit toward the pink-flushed skin, reddened by the drag of the razor. There's a dull, thick sound and then a small pop as the circular teeth break through bone into the soft tissue below, as its silver head now turns a liquid red. Instantly he releases the trigger and the drill whirs to a halt. There was a time, early on, when he missed this sound, an indicator to stop. Now he is mindful because he needs them alive if there is any chance of success.

Wiping the metal tool with a cloth, he carefully cleans away any embedded skin and blood, checking for any telltale viscous, gray matter. Holding the instrument up to the light he notes, yes, his timing was correct.

He places the drill on the table. When he returns her eyes are open again, moving from side to side.

His voice is calm, soothing. "You need to keep your eyes closed. This will be beautiful, trust me." He hopes she will see. "Patience," he whispers, more to himself than to her.

Patience and precision are necessary, because a half inch separates the most important organ in the body and death. Such an oversight of nature.

She wears a mask of red as blood rolls down her face in crimson rivulets.

Next he inserts the needles. One through five.

He waits, hoping and watching for the slow transfer of vitality and the shimmer of the opening to the other world.

But she is empty, carries nothing, not even a smidgeon of what he needs. Sometimes there is some movement, some slight variance in the air, but not here with her. He takes a step back, dismayed.

Her lids fly open and her eyes roll wildly in their sockets; tears travel down her cheeks, diluting the blood. The One would see. She would understand. She would not fear.

Pulling a chair forward, he sits opposite her to study his work; the neat circle rimmed with the white of the skull peeking through pulsing gray-cream brain below. He notes a slight bubbling of viscous matter and clear liquid. He has released the power held there at least.

He holds a final long, thin needle between them.

"How does that feel?" he asks. "Beautiful? A small adjustment I've made especially for you should open your mind. Free you."

By the look in her eyes he realizes that no matter the perfection he's created, she remains like the rest. Ignorant and empty.

"I'm sorry." He says this with his hand positioned over his heart, as he poises the needle mere inches above the fresh wound. The shaft seems to hover mid-air and vibrate with its own will.

"Scream if you feel the need," he offers, though he knows this cannot happen.

Her eyes scream silently. They always do.

23

When I entered Mr. Wong's, my emotions began to flit about like a firefly. Spending even an hour across a table from Mariana would be enough for me to die happy.

The dark thing in the attic felt stronger by the hour. On my way there, I took quiet moments when stopped at lights to check in. Since saying goodbye to Mariana its determination to escape had seemed to have increased. The box walls had begun to buckle with the pressure.

My trepidation had built in the last hour. For tonight, for the second time in my life, I would share the truth of my gift. My mama suspected, I'm sure. She never mentioned her thoughts to me, but sometimes her comments were too on point.

When I complained about anything as a child, she'd comment, *"Troubles are a tunnel with a pit at the end. Best get off that train Rory. I think you know the station."*

Never once did I hear her complain, not even as she lay in the hospital bed days from her death, tubes sticking out of her arms, nurses and doctors flitting in and out checking medical notes hung at the end of the bed like an award you don't want to win. When I'd reach out to comfort her, she'd push my hand away. "My worries are my worries, my darling."

She may not have known exactly how troubles keeping worked, but she knew I was different. Mothers accept their children, no matter what, but as I stood at the doorway of Mr. Wong's bustling dining room, I wondered what the only other woman I had loved in my life would think.

Noise from conversation and the clatter of chopsticks and spoons was like walking into a Chinese New Year's party. The walls wore quirky red and orange owl motifs looking over black-clothed tables with velvet, high-backed chairs, reminiscent of an eighties disaster makeover. Most of the patrons were Asian, indicative of the food being authentic and good.

There didn't seem to be a single spare table and I realized my mistake: I should have booked. Then again, I had no idea my plan would work. The exotic spicy smells and sound of food frying in hot woks had me salivating. I wanted to begin the conversation because my stomach was in knots, but I realized part of the churning was due to hunger.

I stood at the unmanned register, just inside the door, while wait staff moved efficiently and unsmiling from one table to another. My gaze traveled around the room, searching for Mariana. Where was she?

Pulling my phone from my jacket pocket I began to check for messages, then slid it back away realizing my second mistake. Mariana didn't have my number, and I didn't have hers. For all I knew, she could easily have rethought the whole thing. My mind started going through my backup plan. I even pulled out my quickly scrawled list from the day before.

1. Release other troubles.
2. Examine dark thing.
3. Release dark thing?
4. Where is dark thing from?
5. ~~Ask Mariana Out~~???

6. Look at Mariana's troubles.

7. What are Mariana's <u>real</u> troubles???

Number five stood out from the page like a big scary monster. In the last twenty-four hours, based on what I'd seen of the dark thing's behavior, *big, scary monster* wasn't far off. What I needed to know now was, where did the dark thing come from and why was this entity attracted to Mariana? Of all the people on the bus and all those with whom the dark thing's creator must have interacted, why her? And finally, if I moved the thing on, what would happen to the energy once free? What kind of danger would there be to me and the world?

"Rory."

My mind had been by the Dawson, wrestling with a shapeless dark creature, so I jumped when I heard my name.

I turned to face Mariana's beautiful smile. Her shoulder-length curls pulled up in a ponytail of ringlets, hanging like glorious, golden wisteria. My hand went to my chest as I said, "Oh, you scared me."

She nodded into the dining room. "Hope you made a booking."

"That would be a negative." I grimaced. "Pretty stupid, right?"

Mariana shrugged. "Spur of the moment. I get it. Not like you planned for the bus to break down, us to start talking, and then end up here, right?"

My heart kicked. "Yeah, what a crazy plan." My whole body felt as though my very pores exuded the smell of guilt.

"What about Frankie's Place?" she asked. "It's only two blocks. A cool little bar, and they serve light snacks. They do great nachos, actually."

"Sounds great."

Mariana had walked, and even though my bike was parked nearby, I decided a stroll would be the perfect opportunity to talk. As we walked, I stole glances at Mariana. The evening had taken on a surreal feel, and I felt an urge to keep checking I wasn't imagining her here beside me.

We made small talk. Even discussed the weather. Until, suddenly

Mariana grabbed my arm, not in a romantic way, but in an enough-is-enough move.

"So Rory, what's going on? You've got me worried. I don't usually agree to impromptu dinners with strangers. But I'm going out on a limb here and, actually, I don't know how to say this without sounding weird. For some reason, you don't feel like a stranger. Ever since yesterday, when you did your *I'm gonna throw your troubles in the river* thing, I've had this funny feeling, like we're connected or something. I know that sounds crazy. I don't want you to think I'm talking a *romantic* thing or I've ever said this to anyone before, but—"

I wish this *was* something romantic, I thought. Maybe Mariana referred to the dark thing, felt the presence somehow. I had to be careful now. I didn't want to reveal too much, too soon, but the writing finger had writ, and I needed to catch up before this conversation took off in a direction that would spell trouble.

I tried to keep my voice confident and in control, trustworthy. "Not weird Mariana. Maybe I can explain part of this. Why I wanted to see you. It's complicated though, so I'm not sure where to begin."

"How about starting with how you do your little trick? You use some kind of static electricity thing, right?"

Narrowing my eyes, I feigned offense. "Trick, huh? Is that what you think?"

"Sorry, I didn't mean to make fun. This is a really lovely idea, pretending to take people's troubles so they don't carry them around. Sure worked for me. I felt instantly better. Other people seemed happier too."

"Trick is fine. Nice idea is fine," I said, agreeably as possible.

I really wanted to share my secret with Mariana, to tell her yesterday *was* real, she wasn't imagining the feelings. I'd never told anyone before for very good reason. Talking about troubles keeping made you sound crazy. Even to me. Sometimes this was dangerous. Fifteen years ago someone died.

I'd thought long and hard about the next step if my plan made it to the next step, that is. Surreptitiously discovering how the dark thing had attached to her without being honest didn't seem viable.

Telling her guaranteed nothing, either, but if I was careful to only share so much, maybe this might work.

But I needed her alone, sitting across from me, so I could watch for signs she wasn't believing me, maybe reach out and take away her concerns before they took hold. I reminded myself I knew from Mariana's troubles that I'd taken, she *liked* me.

"So how then Rory? Hypnosis?" Enthusiasm enveloped her words. "I bet that's it. Wow, you *are* good."

"I'm also psychic," I said, with an assured smile and a nod of my head across the street.

"Really? Psychic? I believe in it, you know." Her eyes grew bright and her face glowed. "What kind of psychic are you?"

I stopped walking. "I'm a navigator psychic."

She frowned. "A navigator psychic? Hmm. I've never heard of that. What do you do?"

I nodded across the road. Since we'd turned onto this street, she'd been so engaged with our conversation, she'd barely looked up.

"Yeah, I can navigate my way to places I've never visited. Like Frankie's Place over there."

Mariana's gaze traveled across the street, then she turned and hit me gently in the chest.

"You. I actually believed you. You're a funny man Rory Fine!" We changed direction and headed toward Frankie's. As we did, she shook her head and, this time, gently punched the top of my arm.

I rubbed the spot and contorted my face in a mock grimace. "Ow. You've got a good punch."

"I really believed you. Wow, I'm just so gullible."

As we arrived outside Frankie's ornately-carved, oak double door I heard Mariana chuckle. "Psychic navigator. L.O.L."

"I'm a bus driver, right, so I know most of the city," I said. "Sorry, probably a dumb joke."

"You've got a silly sense of humor Rory Fine, but you know what? I like that about you."

I'd heard of this place, supposedly a pretty cool hang out. A long way from my type of joint, so I'd never been inside. Above the door flashing pink lights spelled*Frankie's Place*. Crowning the name was a lit outline of an angled man's fifties-fashion, dark blue hat. White lights ran around its edges to give a 3D appearance. By the style of the hat, I gathered *Frankie* was Frank Sinatra.

A large window to the right of the door revealed a cozy, dark space inside filled with the moving shadows of clientele. A gray etched outline of another Frank Sinatra hat filled a glass panel of the entry.

I pushed on the door and held it open for Mariana. She slid past me, wearing an impressed smile, seemingly surprised by the gentlemanly gesture. If I ignored the high ratio of young guys in business suits, Frankie's could almost be called romantic. The dark lowlights of red, orange and blue created colored circles on the floor and counter. Square, tall tables, barely big enough for two, furnished the room, along with intimate booths. A painted picture of Sinatra filled one whole wall with a scrawling of one of his sayings:

I feel sorry for people who don't drink. When they wake up in the morning, that's as good as they're going to feel all day.

Soft, pleasant jazz filled the room and mingled with the conversational murmur, giving the place quite a buzz despite the half full capacity. I could almost pretend this was a date if I ignored one pesky detail: the dark, terrible entity holed up in the attic, readying its escape. No, if there was a date in our destiny, it wasn't tonight.

"Looks good," I said, allowing the door to close behind us.

Now that we were here, my resolve, which had enjoyed a roller coaster ride since Mr. Wong's, had turned to jelly.

As we settled into a booth, Mariana turned and stared, her eyes searching mine. "You sound disappointed Rory. I'm sorry, we can go somewhere else. I like the music, though. I've been here a couple of times with a girlfriend. You don't get bothered so much with a jazz background."

"No, really it's great. Maybe I'm just tired," I said, rubbing at the back of my neck. Actually I was a *lot* tired, barely grabbing two hours of sleep since yesterday.

"Oh good. Not good to the tired bit but good you like this place."

"Maybe I'm a little nervous, as well," to assure her I didn't mean being with her made me tired.

Mariana tilted her head to the side like she was weighing me up, and said, "If I'm being honest, I'm nervous too."

"Really? You? Why?" I said, picking up a menu and pretending to read.

"You've made everything sound so mysterious. I can't imagine what you have to tell me. But like I said, there's something about you."

There's no good opening sentence to share that your skillset could be featured on a Sci-Fi Channel show or in a poor man's version of the X-Men. But the best way to tackle a high cliff jump is to step off the edge. Time wasn't my friend. The dark thing had almost engulfed the box with its now toxic-waste glow, black and dark green form. If I was also being honest, I'd suddenly, desperately wanted to share what I'd guarded for so long. My secret gift.

"I think you might need a drink first. And a snack. Are you hungry too?" I said, motioning to a waitress as she walked past our table. An obliging girl took our order returning less than five minutes later with two cokes and a bowl of steaming nachos smothered with cheese, jalapeños and guacamole.

Later I couldn't remember a thing we'd discussed in the time before I began my story. Sitting across from Mariana, watching the sweet dimples appear every time she smiled, my mind was lost. I *had* planned to hint around the troubles keeping, make what I did sound as though I was simply good at picking up vibes, a cross between hypnosis, as she suggested, with maybe a touch of psychic thrown in. Non-threatening. Fueled by wild nerves, that's not what I did.

"What I'm about to tell you sounds crazy. But you have to believe I'm not crazy."

She leaned forward and placed a palm over my hand rested on the table.

"Rory, I don't know you very well, but it's okay. Hurry up though, you're making me nervous. The thing you did on the bus yesterday was lovely and generous. I feel I should trust you."

I sucked in as much air as my lungs could take and breathed out slowly.

"Mariana, this is about yesterday. What happened might seem lovely and generous. I acknowledge what happened, what I did, was a good thing. I *always* try to do good things. I know the act looked like a performance, I guess. How could someone actually take people's troubles and throw them in a river? Right?"

Mariana nodded. "Um, yeah, I guess. That would be impossible. Okay?"

She leaned in, her chest pressed against the edge of the table, as though we shared a conspiracy. "What are you trying to say Rory?"

Another deep breath. "Not impossible. What happened yesterday on the bus was real."

Mariana's forehead furrowed in thought. "Real? You actually, for real, took people's troubles, my troubles? And this is why we all felt ... so much happier?"

"Yes, it's real," I said firmly. "Let me explain."

Mariana grabbed my hand and said, "You'd better."

24

In the next half hour I shared everything I felt safe to reveal. My childhood, stories of some of those I'd helped, my mama, then yesterday and what happened on the bus. Mariana barely moved, her eyes hardly blinked. She listened with an intensity that surprised me, her hand on her chin, her arm resting on the table in between sipping on her drink. I couldn't tell what she was thinking, except she *was* thinking.

Finally I nervously asked, "Thoughts?"

Minutes that felt like hours passed before she spoke. I must have been breathing too deeply without realizing, for she asked, "Rory, are you okay?"

"Yeah ... yes, I'm good. Sorry. I'm nervous. I've never told anyone. I know how insane this sounds."

I'd shared everything with Mariana, except the dark thing. Every way I ran that conversation through my head, this information *did* sound crazy. And alarming:*Hey, not only can I pick up troubles from others, but yesterday, I picked up this evil, dark thing now munching merrily on the walls of its prison. And guess what? It came from you.*

No, that conversation needed to come later. Let her process this information first.

"I don't know what to say," she said, looking down at the table, then back up at me, "And Rory, you're biting your lip. *Relax*. Look, we're agreed on one thing. Your story *does* sound insane. Other than you being a friendly bus driver with a sense of humor, I don't know you well at all, really."

My heart sunk into my lap. The next line would be something like: *After that story, I don't think I want to know any more about you.*

Her face grew serious and here came the bad news. "Rory, I should get up and say goodbye."

I braced myself: *Goodbye Rory. Thanks for sharing, but no thanks on the crazy trouble-keeping stuff.*

"But, yesterday," she continued, "I can't deny, I *did* feel something. Call me crazy too, but what you've told me kind of makes sense. I thought the feeling was the lightning. Somewhere I'd heard electrons during a storm can affect your body. Then the strange relief when you did your thing, which felt like a gentle draining away of the emotion. That was no lightning or the electrons though. That was you?"

Slowly I nodded, as my heart climbed back into my chest.

"Guilty," I replied, bowing my head like an actor in a curtain call.

"Like I said, I do kind of believe in psychic stuff—I guess that's what you do ... a version of a psychic thing?"

I nodded. Sounded as a good description as any.

"I'll tell you why I believe. When I was a teenager, a bunch of us visited this palm reader. Chris Lamben was his name. I didn't believe in any mumbo jumbo stuff but my friend insisted. The psychic lived in this normal house in the 'burbs. Pass him on the street, you wouldn't look twice. I'll never forget what he said to me, how he spoke as though everything was an absolute fact. He knew things about me, my family, my friends, as though I'd written them all down on a piece of paper which I had handed to him. Freaked me out, actually. My friends thought the readings were fun and exciting, but somebody knowing everything about you, well, that just makes you wonder how much else you *don't* know."

Mariana held a palm to her forehead, sweeping her hand back

over her hair as her face grew serious; the memory clearly troubled her.

"Then he told me about my future. This time he talked about things I couldn't believe. Until they happened. Sometimes years later. He told me I wasn't going to college. Correct, even though I'd planned to. But my mom got real sick, so I stayed home to help her. Breast cancer, but she's okay now. Then he said he heard music when he looked at me. Something to do with my work—a store I owned. I told him I didn't own a store, didn't know anyone who owned a music store. He simply said: 'One day.' Now, I *do* work in a music store, but I'm not the owner. Until last week, that was. My boss Mr. Sterling calls me into his office looking all serious. You know what he told me?"

You're the best looking employee he'd ever had?

"He told me he had no children and no close friends who'd be interested in keeping the business going. If we could keep the doors open, despite the downturn with streaming and iTunes, he would give the business to me when he retired next year. He said I was like a daughter to him." She paused, her eyes widening. "Kind of pretty darn close to what Chris had said, don't you think? How could he know five years ago, if he didn't have some kind of psychic thing happening?"

I shrugged. I didn't know how these psychics did their thing either. Seeing the future seemed a particularly useful tool. I wish I'd been in the psychic handout line. Warning people even before they found trouble sounded a lot better than scooping emotions up afterward.

What Mariana's story did explain was why she hadn't shunned me instantly. I'd always imagined psychic energy as one big super river and some people had the power to literally tap into the flow. Emotional energy transferring wasn't too much of a stretch from a psychic predicting your future.

"I don't know how they know," I answered honestly. "I met a tarot card reader once in a market. She knew things she shouldn't know too. Scared the heck out of me."

I thought back to that market years ago.

Most psychics *are* phonies. Takes one to know one, or to know one who isn't one. This woman sat at a foldout card table inside a cream canvas tent at a market stall. I was still looking for people like me with some kind of gift, but they always turned out to be fake. She didn't wear the usual get up: colorful, oversized, flowing clothes with clinking bracelets up the arm and big, round, hoop earrings. This woman wore a simple t-shirt and jeans with her hair pulled back in a no-nonsense ponytail. Her single piece of jewelry, a silver cross on a delicate box-link chain.

This one—I never did get her name—had only drawn one card between us when she stopped, looked into my eyes, and grabbed my hands to hold them a few inches above the table. For long, uncomfortable seconds she stared straight into my eyes, like she could see my soul.

Then she said, "You're connected. More than anyone I've ever read. You have more power in your little finger than ten psychics, like me, have in their whole body."

Her hand stroked the back of my right hand, while she continued to stare. Slowly she placed my hands down on the table and let go. Then her face changed, grew grim, as though her muscles no longer had the strength to hold up a smile.

"You must be careful. You're playing with something you cannot control. You think you can. *You can't.* This gift will bring grave danger. Has already brought danger to others. You know what I mean. Your friend at school."

I did know what she meant. I would never get over what happened.

She tilted her head to the side as though sizing me up.

"Troubles are your business, aren't they?"

I'd kept my gift hidden for ten years by then, and she'd uncovered my secret as though merely peeling away a Band-Aid.

"Not like I had a choice," I replied defensively. "More like this thing chose me."

She shook her head as though I was a foolish child, lying when caught out.

"You always have a choice. I'm telling you, stop. Stop using your power and it will fade away like unused muscles. The doorway will close. The hinges will rust. This is no power for you. No power for anyone. The more you dabble, the more that will come your way. I suggest you stop, young man. This is not a game to be played."

Who was she to tell me what to do? Her insistence got my back up. So using a special ability was okay for her but not for me?

"If I don't stop?" I asked, the tone of my voice implying whatever she said next wouldn't affect my future actions in any way.

"You've seen the destruction this can cause. What can happen. Your friend. Your future not your past should concern you. Troubles are coming that will eat you alive."

I was young, thought I was invincible, and still playing with troubles keeping. So I wasn't about to listen. I simply got up and walked away, shaking my head in an exaggerated way, so she knew what I thought of her advice.

Troubles will eat me alive. Really? I'm sorry, *too* non-specific.

I didn't heed her six years ago. Now though, just like Mariana's psychic's predictions, her warnings had begun to make sense. I still didn't trust psychics, most were frauds. I was about to caution Mariana on not putting too much stock in her reading from this Lamben guy when she asked, "You know what else Chris told me?" Then as if she was talking to herself, "I haven't thought about this in forever. Now with you and this troubles keeping, what he said makes weird sense."

"What did he say?" I hoped she would say he'd told her one day she'd meet a tall, red-headed bus driver and fall madly in love.

"One day, he told me, I would need to make a choice. Between what I thought I knew and the unseen. He said my choice might be between life and death. His words: choose wisely."

Just like all fakes, I thought, a vague prediction. I tried to keep the smirk out of my voice. "Really cryptic. Perhaps he saw you as a cave explorer?"

"Ha, ha, very funny Rory."

The waitress interrupted us with another serving of drinks. I'd had enough to drink, but Mariana picked up her glass and took two large gulps. I took a mouthful of the sweet soda, but my nerves made the sugar taste overpowering. I pushed it forward and away and wished I'd ordered water.

"He told me something else too," she continued. "Maybe you can explain, because he wouldn't elaborate. I returned a few weeks later specifically to ask him what he meant, but he still wouldn't tell me. Said he couldn't remember. Every reading was unique."

"Sadly my specialty is not explaining psychics." My words and tone came out flippant, which I instantly regretted when slight worry lines appeared on Mariana's forehead. She'd earlier picked up a napkin from the table and had twisted the paper cloth into a neat miniature roll, untwisting and then twisting again. Now she played with the crumbs she'd created.

"What he did tell me was all this strange stuff, I didn't understand, about another plane, reverse energy, windows. I can't remember everything exactly. Then he stops and says, 'Oh, yes, interesting' like he's talking to someone else. When there's just us. He looks me straight in the eyes and says, 'He'll be looking for the window, if that makes sense.' For a few seconds I smiled at him, imagining that being a window was something good. Then he ruined the image when he said, 'A darkness is coming. A dangerous darkness.' Then he refused to say anymore. Said he didn't know anymore, but I got the feeling he did. The whole thing was way weird. What do you think this means?"

In light of the dark thing, this Chris Lamben reading made a funny kind of sense. The window reference, I didn't know, but he'd pinned the idea of *darkness coming* and *danger*. Although, again, psychic vague-babble, which could be simply a good guess.

'Window' rolled in my mind, but I still didn't understand. If I worked on the theory this thing didn't originate with Mariana—and there was no way, ever, I knew that in my heart—that someone gave this dark thing to her. In the same way I took the energy away, someone transferred the thing to her. *Why?* I wondered. The group of boarding passengers she mentioned before her mood change, could one of them have actually followed her onto the bus? I'd worked on the hypotheses that this had been a random interaction. Maybe not. Should I share this with Mariana when I wasn't certain of anything? The napkin she'd been handling now lay in tiny shreds on the table.

"Are you listening to me Rory? You seem to be in another place?"

"Sorry," I answered, looking into those beautiful green eyes and telling myself I'd do everything and more to protect her. "I was thinking about the psychic. I don't know what to tell you. You're too nice (I wanted to say lovely) to be—" I stopped. I'd intended to say 'be a window to or from darkness,' but how could I say that? A window to a beautiful soul was how I'd describe her. Nothing to do with the creepy, slimy dark thing I held in the attic.

Mariana filled in the pause. "Rory, you're the sweetest guy I've met in forever. If I'm honest, and I feel like I can be with you since you've trusted me with your secret, that bus breaking down did me a great favor. Being here with you just seems right. Ever since Chris Lamben and his freaky prediction, I've occasionally felt something bad hanging over my head, like a sword of death. You know they call it the Sword of Damo-something."

"*The Sword of Damocles,* I think you mean. But, Mariana, seriously, I wouldn't believe too much."

Maybe now might be the time to hint at the dark thing. Really, the concept did fit if you stretched your imagination around the prediction. So I decided, here goes nothing.

"Mariana, something else happened yesterday I haven't told—"

But I was stopped by the image on the screen twenty feet away above the bar. A news bulletin had caught my attention. We were too far away to hear anything, but the woman's picture on the screen stopped me. I studied the image. Yes, that *was* her.

When the revelation occurred, my first impulse was to grab Mariana and run. Run back to my home, grab my belongings, and get away from the city. Far away from here. Suddenly I understood what the psychic meant when he used the word 'dangerous' all those years ago.

25

On the screen, a gray-suited reporter stood outside an apartment block with a generously proportioned entrance lawn and garden. Behind him, several police cars were parked in the street, one still with its blue and red lights flashing. Crime scene investigators in white suits with hoods covering their heads, along with men and women whom I presumed were detectives, moved around behind a temporary boundary of yellow crime tape.

A woman's photograph alternated on the screen between the panning footage of the entrance and the activity. Crawling below the images was the caption:*Possible Fifth Trepan Killer Victim.*

What had stopped me was that the woman was Sandra Swift, one of my passengers. I'd just spoken to her earlier that day at Sweethearts Café. A twenty-something girl with a friendly smile, she always thanked me for the ride. She caught the bus once or twice a week to work a part-time job somewhere uptown, if I remembered right. I'd joked with her once asking if Taylor was her sister. *Taylor Swift. Sandra Swift.* "I wish," she'd replied. "Can't sing to save my life." Exactly. If she was a Trepan Killer victim, then singing wouldn't have helped her.

Last time I saw Sandra she was standing outside Sweethearts. I shuffled through my memories, trying to remember the earlier events, but at the time getting to Mariana had been my sole focus.

By now, Mariana had followed my stare and also now watched the screen.

"What's wrong Rory? You look like you've seen a ghost?"

I couldn't answer. My mind was retracing those thirty, forty minutes. Who had Sandra been with on the sidewalk? Rising from the table, I moved toward the TV, excusing myself to several patrons sitting at the bar. They, too, now turned to the bulletin. I felt Mariana beside me, but the screen was a magnet.

"... the police have released the victim's photo and identity quickly in the hope witnesses may come forward and assist the investigation. One neighbor at the scene claims the woman, twenty-six year old Sandra Swift, is possibly the fifth Trepan Killer victim. This has not yet been officially confirmed. The terrible discovery of the woman's body was made by a female relative who had arrived to visit Miss Swift for dinner.

A neighbor who had assisted the relative immediately after the discovery has spoken to this reporter and claims Miss Swift's body carried the trademark disfiguring hole in the forehead of the previous Trepan Killer victims.

The Trepan Killer has targeted this state's southern region over the past five months, murdering his victims—all women—in a bizarre manner by drilling a hole in their skulls and inserting needles into their brains, in a similar fashion to the ancient practice of trepanning. Fossil evidence suggests trephination occurred from prehistoric times from the Neolithic period or Stone Age onwards. This unusual mode of disfiguration has been revived in recent times by a few rare supporters who claim this practice to be a means of expanding the brain's capacity.

Certainly the police investigators appear particularly attentive here tonight, not just because this is a terrible murder but because Miss Swift could prove to be another victim. Further news on this latest death, as information comes to hand. Following this newscast we are pre-empting scheduled programming to air our special report, 'The search for the new mind: Trepanning through history'."

The screen flashed to more images of the scene, then returned to sports news, which seemed oddly incongruent with the previous two minutes of alarming footage. One minute, death and a city on alert, the next, two commentators discussing batting averages.

"Who is that?" Mariana's hand rested on my forearm. When I turned to her, her face looked pale. "I think I know her but I don't know where from though."

"You do. Sort of. She was on the bus today. At the café."

"Oh my God." Her hand moved to cover her mouth. "Yes, now I remember. I think she's even sat next to me a few times. I think her name was Sara, no Susan. Oh, I can't remember."

"Sandra Swift."

"Oh, yes, Sandra. How awful. How could that happen?"

Thoughts chased around in my head and then paused on the one I couldn't avoid: *this could be my fault.* Stopping the bus may have put this girl in the path of a killer. And what did that even mean?

That the Trepan Killer had been on the bus? In the café? Maybe he'd followed her from the café?

An artist's sketched impression of the mutilation of the Trepan Killer victims that had appeared in the paper a few weeks back flashed in my mind. The image was a black-and-white speculative facsimile from descriptions pieced together during police media releases. Though not a photograph, the detail was still horrible. Brutal.

A woman, her head partially shaved above her forehead, with a hole drilled through her skull the size of a large, round lapel badge, endured six long needles protruding from the brain. Reports even suggested the women were alive during the entire procedure.

Sandra Swift did not deserve to die like this. Nobody did. The floor seemed to disappear beneath my feet and the room spun. I reached out to clutch the edge of the bar. This *was* my fault. I put her in the wrong place at the wrong time.

Mariana's voice entered my guilt-filled, spiraling thoughts. "Rory! Are you okay? You should sit down. You've gone white."

I looked at her, and for a moment imagined the victim could have been her. Then a tide of gratefulness overwhelmed me. Mariana was okay, but I quite possibly had done something terrible.

Clawing back my composure I replied, "I'm fine. I'm just processing."

"Rory, we should contact the police. Tell them she was on the bus. We saw her. Maybe we were one of the last to see her ... alive." Then Mariana's mind finally traveled to where mine had just been. "Maybe the killer was on our—?" Her jaw dropped, and she paused. "Rory, do you think the killer was on our bus? We might have actually walked past him. Maybe he was sitting near me."

Suddenly everything made sense. The dark thing, the strange, gray mood on the bus with all the passengers, Mariana's role.

The killer *had* been on the bus yesterday. And he'd been there today. Mariana had picked up the dark thing from him. This was as plain as day to me now.

The Trepan Killer was one of my passengers.

26

Suddenly the air in Frankie's Bar felt too thick and claustrophobic to breathe. I needed to think this through, to decipher what was actually going on. How one simple trouble keep could go so wrong, and how the Trepan Killer could ride my bus without me even realizing.

I slipped my hand into Mariana's, not worrying anymore if she thought the action too forward. We must move.

'A darkness is coming.'

If Mariana's psychic was right, then maybe this was what he had predicted.

A-ha, I said to the dark thing, as I checked in yet again. *Now I know who you are or at least where you came from.*

Cracks running up the sides of the box had widened and angled fissures like fractured ice now splintered the surface. The dark-green and black ooze, which had begun to pool around its base like sticky tar, had expanded. Disgusting fumes of menace emanated toward me. The thing meant harm, and I knew my time was close to done. Now I was in the peril zone with maybe only mere hours. The entity must be destroyed. *How* was the million dollar question.

"Rory? Rory! My hand. You're hurting my hand."

Mariana shook my arm attempting to free herself. I hadn't realized I'd dragged her down the street like we were fleeing a fire. Immediately I stopped, suddenly embarrassed at the intimacy of holding her hand, and let go.

Two weeks ago, two days, two hours ago, I would have felt joy at touching her, at this intimate and tenuous connection. Now all I wondered was had I endangered her?

"Please stop Rory. You're frightening me. Where are we going?"

Forcing confidence into my voice I didn't feel, I answered as best I could. "I don't mean to frighten you, but you need to trust me. If you believe in Chris Lamben, if you believe in my troubles keeping, then you must believe there are forces around you most people cannot see or feel, let alone understand. I haven't told you everything. Something happened yesterday on the bus that up until now I hadn't understood."

We had stopped beneath a streetlight. In the muted orange glow she looked more beautiful than ever and now more vulnerable. If circumstances were different, I might have even risked a kiss. This was the perfect setting straight out of a romantic film, but until I'd freed myself of the dark thing and destroyed the energy, I needed to remain single-minded.

I reached out to grasp both her hands, pulling at any fears for our circumstance and what I was about to share. As I gathered the energy from her, I felt her concern wasn't for herself but for me. Her response was to my fear. Instantly she looked more relaxed.

"Rory, are you doing the thing again? Troubles keeping?"

I nodded. "I'm, I'm just trying to help."

She snatched her hands away.

"Don't, okay? I'm fine. I'm tougher than you think."

"I'm sorry Mariana, about a whole load of stuff that you don't know. I thought I could handle this myself, but this has become bigger than I imagined."

Her eyes widened. "What can't you handle? Tell me."

"It's complicated."

"What, more complicated than taking people's troubles away?

Than that woman's murder? If I can accept all these complications in one night, then I think I can accept pretty much anything. And without your troubles keeping help, thank you. Now we need to go to the police. *Right now.*"

"No! No police. Not until I've—I don't fully understand what's going on myself. For the past twenty-four hours, I've been trying to work out a lot of things. Now with Sandra's murder, I'm not certain of anything."

"Rory, if you know something about the murder, about what happened, we *must* tell the police. You may have information that can help them. Maybe I do. We don't even know what we know. Could be someone on the bus has video on their phone or a photograph of the killer. Or saw something. Why can't we go to the police?"

"Maybe we will. I need to think and there's something urgent I need to do. And the police can't help."

"What could be more urgent than this? Are you involved some-how? You need to tell me." She leaned back and held up her hands like a barrier between us. "And don't take anything from me. I'm okay. Worried, but okay."

Are you involved, she'd asked.

Yes, I was involved, but even I wasn't sure exactly how. I couldn't tell Mariana she was also involved. Even as I stood, gently connected to her by an ethereal thread of energy, I grew convinced the dark thing being passed to her was no accident. If not for my impromptu game yesterday, the entity would have stayed because the dark thing had connected to her. What I wanted to understand was why.

Every time I was in Mariana's proximity, the dark thing stirred, pulsed with a recognition as though a predator scenting prey. My fear now was in freeing the thing instead of destroying the energy, the entity might seek her out like a diabolical homing pigeon. Then what would happen? I didn't know, but I was positive the outcome wouldn't be wonderful.

Mariana stared at me, tiny worry lines appearing on her forehead and the side of her mouth, as she waited for me to explain. My response was a reflex. Before I knew what had happened, I'd reached out and run the back of a hand down her cheek. I wanted to smooth those lines away, make all of this disappear from our lives.

She didn't flinch and she didn't back away. I pulled her into my arms, and for long, incredible moments, held her so tightly I felt as though I could press all her troubles away instead of drawing them out with my gift. The rhythm of her heart beat against my chest, and the thump of my pulse matched hers as though harmonized.

Drawing the lingering troubles away from her came automatically, and I welcomed the tingling sensation of the passage of energy. The fear firing inside her, the apprehension of the unknown, of discovering she felt something toward me, all the uncertainty swirled through me like a flock of tiny birds, swooping and diving. I pulled them into the attic and a waiting box, locking them away where they wouldn't bother her anymore. Unlike before, I ensured I took everything. I couldn't bear for her to suffer.

She pulled back and stared into my eyes.

"You just did your thing then again, didn't you?"

I barely nodded, uncertain if she would be angry.

"I felt something. There's a lightness, a freeing. I still feel terrible about the murder, and I *am* still afraid, but they feel like memories of emotions. How strange. I know I told you not to do it again, but thank you. I know you meant well."

The smallest of smiles touched my lips.

Then Mariana took a step back, pushing my hands away. Now she wasn't smiling. Her eyes flashed.

"Rory Fine, let's get this straight, here and now. I don't want you to *ever* do that again. How I feel is how I feel. I'll take the good with the bad. You've got to promise me to stop. Didn't someone teach you some kind of etiquette with being a trouble-taking person, or whatever you call your special power?"

"Troubles keeping. Which makes me a troubles keeper. There's no official name and no rules or etiquette. I'm the only one. This isn't something handed down from generation to generation. I was born this way. I've had to work everything out for myself. I don't know how I do what I do. Maybe I'm just a freak."

Mariana moved back toward me, her face softening, the fire in her eyes extinguished.

"You're not a freak. Don't ever say that. You're a lovely, kind person. Someone else might use a gift like this to make money or for their own benefit. You just share your talent with others to help. And that is a wonderful, caring thing."

She wagged a finger at me. "Still, I don't want you to do *it* with me. The trouble ... troubles keeper thing. I like to solve my own problems."

Her face grew serious again. "I don't want someone to save me. If you knew me, you'd realize there's more to me. The curls, I always think, are the problem. They make me look so girly. Underneath, I'm tough."

Mariana grasped my hand, held the palm up to eye height, and studied it. "Hands show so much. They can be raised in violence, entwined in love, in kindness, in friendship, in passion. People say eyes are the windows to the soul, but I think hands tell a lot about a person. You have good hands."

Her touch and words made me feel as though I could do anything. Mariana had in her own way, a troubles keeping gift.

"I like you Rory. You're different from other guys. What you can do is extraordinary. If I hadn't experienced what you do myself, I wouldn't have believed any of this."

She gripped my hand harder, shaking it slightly. "But this is too much to take in at once. You, that poor woman murdered, being close to something so terrible, and now there's *something* you're not telling me ..."

Mariana's words faded into the sounds of the street as though my body had traveled away. My mind narrowed in on my hands. What had Mariana just said? *Windows to the soul.* Layered on top of these words were those of Mariana's psychic. *"Looking for a window."*

Knowing what I knew now, could this possibly make sense? Or was the psychic's predictions the usual generic mumbo jumbo sprouted to take money from the gullible? Maybe this Chris Lamben had foreseen the dark thing, all the events of the past twenty four hours. My brush with the psychic in the market all those years ago had proven some people did have insight into something ethereal, into this world in which I lived.

Another plan formed in my mind. I'd never had any help in the past. Who would I have asked? But this dark thing was outside anything I'd encountered.

"Mariana, wait a second."

Her eyes widened, and I realized my words had come out a little harsh, rushed, but I had a new plan and that plan involved her. I needed Mariana's help, now more than ever. I wanted to talk to this psychic Chris Lamben, like yesterday. Tonight even. The dark thing wasn't waiting until morning, that I knew

"Do you still have your psychic's address? His phone number for starters?"

"Chris Lamben? Why? I told you I went back just one more time and he was no help. He's what I meant when I said people using their powers for their own gain. I think he just said whatever he thought would get me back."

"But do you have his number? It's important."

"Maybe. A couple of my friends still visit him every year. They think of him as some kind of infallible guide when it comes to big decisions in their lives. A copout, I think—but why do you need his number?"

"Because, I think he may have been on to something."

"I don't see where you're going with this."

"I don't totally either," I said. I was flying blind, but I certainly was learning how to think on my feet, something that wasn't my strength. "I'll explain everything soon, once I work out a few things. Right now though, time is not my friend."

The image of oozing black muck spreading in the attic loomed large in my mind.

"Trust me, okay? Like you said before, this isn't about me. I'm trying to help others. Have you got his address?"

Mariana seemed to wrestle with the question, wearing a little tension line on her forehead, which I'd come to realize signified she was thinking.

"Come on Mariana, please."

The line relaxed and a short, sharp sigh erupted from her lips.

"Okay. Okay. Call me nuts, but I do trust you. I think. Don't get me into anything crazy." She shook her finger at me again. "Let me check my phone. I might still have his details stored."

She didn't have his number or his address, but a text to one of the friends who thought he was the guru of gurus supplied what we needed in minutes.

"Now what?" she said, after reading out the address and checking the time on her phone. "It's nine fifty-eight. You don't expect he works after hours, do you?"

"I don't know what I expect, but I need to speak to him as soon as I can. If he's there, and he'll see me, then tonight is perfect."

"This is crazy on steroids, Rory."

"I know. Trust me—remember? Give me the number. I'll do the talking."

Something told me this guy was probably in the game for the money. So maybe I'd have to offer overtime pay commensurate with the hour.

Mariana called out his number and I dialed. She backed up and stood at a little distance, nervously pacing, like she worried we were about to get ourselves into trouble. I didn't like to tell her we were already in big trouble. Whatever path this dark thing had been traveling, I felt strongly the energy wanted back on that road and needed something from Mariana.

Chris Lamben's phone buzzed several times, then picked up. I opened my mouth to speak, then realized the call had gone to an answer machine. The voice on the message—presumably him— was smooth, soothing and calm. Perfectly polished for a psychic. Or a conman.

At the tone I tried to sound smooth and calm too, but the words came out in a rush: "Mr. Lamben, my name is Rory Fine. I desperately need to meet with you to discuss—."

I paused, uncertain exactly what to tell him. I looked over at Mariana, her arms wrapped protectively around her body as she continued to pace on the spot beneath a street light. I turned my back to her, so there was no chance of her overhearing.

"Mr. Lamben, I need to speak to you urgently. Tonight if possible. I'll pay extra. I have a friend. Mariana. You saw her a few years ago. I think she—we—need your help. Might even be a matter of ... life and death. Please call me back. Please."

I left my number and hung up.

"What did he say?" Mariana asked as I walked toward her.

"He didn't pick up. I left a message. You're right. It's late."

She checked the time again on her phone.

"Yeah, just after ten. I should get home. I'm kind of freaked out. Will you walk me? I'm a few blocks from here."

We slipped easily into a rhythmic gait, side by side. At some point, as though my action was the most natural thing in the world, I slipped my arm over Mariana's shoulder. Nothing more than a protective gesture to ward off the dark mood that now hung over us. As we continued to walk, the world began to feel totally right— except for one dangerous little fact. There was a serial killer loose, and for some reason he'd marked the girl I loved. Whether by accident or intention, I didn't know, but I needed to find out.

Mariana didn't object to my arm. Despite the unusual circumstances that had brought us together and the events of the night, somehow I managed to push all thoughts of the dark thing out of my mind. For the entire journey to her house my mind ventured elsewhere. Just for those moments, that short walk, I wanted to stay there. I wanted to be that guy, the regular guy, walking home the girl he adored, wondering what the future held for both of us. I didn't want to wonder if either of us might not survive.

27

At the entrance to her apartment block Mariana reached up and pecked me on the cheek. My six-foot one stature required a tiptoe reach from her. She stood back and studied my face, looking at me as though I was a precocious child.

"Rory Fine, you're a strange one. Despite the nuttiness of this evening, this has been certainly by far the most interesting date I've ever had."

"Not a date, you know," I said.

She looked puzzled. Maybe even a little disappointed.

"No, I don't mean what you're thinking. Look, I'm not much of a ladies' man, but I know how a date should go. This didn't go anywhere near a date. Tonight was about something else."

I saw by her look I wasn't explaining myself well. So, I suddenly added: "I wish this *was* a date. Really, a date with you is my greatest dream. I promise, if you can wait, there'll be a date—if you want there to be a date. I'm not presuming or anything."

She still looked at me, the small furrow in her forehead deepening. Now I was proving I wasn't a ladies' man but I found courage to speak how I'd felt for all these months.

"I mean, you're wonderful, and this wasn't a date, like I said, because I want, what I *really* want is to make our first date incredible. I promise if you will go out with me—after this is over—I'll make the evening amazing. Really amazing."

Mariana tilted her head to the side. The furrow in her forehead still lingered. I couldn't breathe, waiting for her response. Then she tiptoed up again and landed her lips on mine. Just a moment, a fleeting touch, but a tiny spark of emotion passed between us. Warm and wonderful. Roses—I even smelled roses.

"I'm holding you to that. Will I see you on the bus tomorrow? If I stay on the bus until the end of the route and refuse to get off, will you tell me then what this thing with Chris Lamben is all about?"

"Well, if you stay on the bus and won't get off, you know what happens to difficult passengers who don't follow the rules?"

"Oh yeah, what happens? You gonna throw me off?"

"No, we usually force them to go to dinner at a very nice restaurant with the bus driver on the route run. Usually puts most passengers off trying anything."

"Hmm, does sound terrible. I'll have to make sure I catch the right bus. Wouldn't want to go to dinner with one of the drivers old enough to be my grandfather."

"I wouldn't want that either. Better make sure I'm on time then."

She laughed and the worry line was gone.

"Good night, strange and mysterious man."

I was about to reply, *Goodnight, beautiful window to a wonderful place*, when my phone buzzed in my jacket pocket. We both stopped and stared at each other, realizing at this time of night, the odds were the call could be only one person. Sliding the mobile from my pocket, I pressed the answer button.

"Hello."

"Mr. Fine, is it?"

"Yes."

"Chris Lamben. You left a message? Life and death, you said." The voice, though deep and certain, sounded urgent, concerned. "Would that friend be Mariana Brown?"

At her name, I felt a thump in my chest. I wasn't expecting he would remember her. Not all these years later.

"Yes ... but how—?"

"I'll explain later. But you don't have a moment to waste. How much I can help, I don't know, but you should hurry. You have the address?"

"You mean come now?"

"Sooner the better. Is she with you? You need to bring her too."

I looked at Mariana, standing by the entrance, nervously twirling a blonde curl between her fingers.

"Yes, she is."

"Good. As soon as you can. You must bring her. Understand?"

"Can I ask why?"

"Like you said, this *is* a matter of life and death. I knew this would happen. I knew I should have told her back then. But I just didn't want—oh, it's too late now. She's in danger. Terrible, terrible danger."

He hung up without saying goodbye. I walked toward Mariana, not sure what I would tell her. What had we gotten ourselves into? *True love never did run smooth*, so Shakespeare wrote, but this was getting crazy.

28

From the entrance of the darkened alley opposite them, where shadows are his friends, he sees the glow, feels the energy. Slender, blue filaments stretch tenuously between the two. When their lips meet, a vibrant glow surrounds them. He feels physically ill.

This feels unexpected, precarious, unvisited. He wonders what the new event means. She is The One—he's certain now—and he must be careful. Perhaps they are aware of him. Suddenly he is unsure of his moves, as though everything he's practiced, everything he's learned, was for naught. Many wrongs have taught him to recognize a right, and he's always been so sure in his search. Never doubting The One was there, waiting for him. Just as much as he searched for them, he felt sure they waited for him.

This bus driver will not give her up easily. Shame, he possesses a talent, which he fritters away with aimless ease. If he understood what lay beyond, what he truly holds in his hands. In fact, he finds this lack of awareness peculiar.

He wishes now he hadn't squandered his time on the other woman, but he felt panicked, uncertain, his mind split between what he thought he knew and what might be undetermined. He simply required a release from being so close to the end of his quest.

Now as he watches, his mind spirals, caught in the possibility of failure. His future decisions come down to questions of: Are they aware of him? Do they seek him? When the time comes will the bus driver stand in his way or understand the greater possibilities? If anyone can understand the stakes it should be this man.

The bus driver seems about to leave, and he feels gladdened. No more time to be wasted. Now he will claim her. His heartbeat rises in anticipation. But now he sees him take a phone call. The conversation lasts a minute, less even, but that minute will change the night.

Now together they walk to the end of the street and wait. Five minutes and a cab whisks them away. He smashes his hand against the brick wall. A pain flares in his wrist. Foolishness. The violence did nothing to quell his frustration. He thinks to follow, but again, he reminds himself, first he needs to learn.

He can find them anytime; they are inside his skin. The bus driver cannot keep what he does not own, and she is his. Soon he will go home to where he belongs. Fate may have been thrust upon him all those years ago, but today he feels destiny coming for him. This time they'll meet on his terms.

29

Mariana snuggled beside me, both of us silently lost in our own thoughts. We'd taken a cab to where I'd parked the bike, and I'd persuaded Mariana to climb aboard. She objected at first, saying she'd never ridden one before and had promised herself she never would. I wanted my own transport and to be ready to leave at any time. This took some convincing of Mariana, but finally she agreed with "just this once." Now that we were here, waiting in Chris Lamben's unusual outdoor waiting area, she admitted she'd enjoyed the ride.

Chris Lamben had texted after the call, requesting we wait outside in the garden and not ring the bell. He would collect us once completing his preparations. As time ticked by, I fought the desire to bang on the door. His mysterious, little mind games added to my growing distrust.

I think I was actually fuming a little, when Mariana's hand came to rest on my knee. As though she also had troubles keeping powers, I suddenly relaxed. The night seemed to glow with warmth. I moved my hand to cover hers and squeezed.

"I won't let anything happen to you."

Mariana sat back, her hand still resting in mine, and stared into my eyes. "Yes, I know. This is all so odd and crazy, but I've got a soft spot for odd."

I felt weak. For a wonderful second the air pushed me forward and I felt as though I was falling toward her, and I never wanted to climb out from wherever I would land.

The tan wicker outdoor two-seater where we sat took up half the square area of the tiny garden. If you could call this space a garden. In reality this was a white-stoned, paved alley, running up the side of a house. A four-foot tall smiling Buddha squatted on a pedestal across from us, looking down in judgment. *What are you doing here non-believer? What have you begun?* Multi-colored pots filled with varieties of herbs and small flowers lined the length of the fence, some mounted on top of pedestals or metal stands with others grouped below. Every available space was filled.

Most likely the decor was meant to give the impression to those waiting they were in some ancient Asian space. The impression felt plastic and fake, further confirming my doubts about the psychic's authenticity.

On the ground next to the door sat a large, round, shallow bowl, filled with more than a dozen tea-lights. Despite the late hour, Chris Lamben had thought to light them. Might have been just as easy to leave the porch light on, but then again, theater probably mattered in his game. Mind you, at this hour, I would admit the warm glow they distributed did create a peaceful atmosphere. Until my mind wandered to the fact the time was eleven o'clock at night and we weren't here for the fun.

Mariana clearly didn't share my cynicism. Her face looked soft and peaceful in the golden light as she stared up at the star-strewn night sky. Any other time I might have appreciated the setting as possibly romantic, stolen a kiss, and seen where that took us. After all, didn't night sky and candles and a few nicely-placed flowers scream romance?

This wasn't the time though. My mind continued to burst with too many unanswered questions that felt treacherous like hidden, sharp stones beneath shallow water. Each one waiting to unbalance and topple a misplaced foot. How did this psychic remember Mariana after all these years? What did he know about the dark thing? What exactly did he mean when he called her a window? *A window to what?* And did he know anything about the killer?

The only reason I even considered this route was simple. I had nothing else. I realized Mariana knew nothing about this dark thing and had become an unwitting conduit from a killer to me to whatever I decided to do next. Whether Chris Lamben could or would help was a whole other question. If he was in this for the money, maybe he'd milk our visit, and I didn't want to cause Mariana to totally disbelieve in psychic ability. The next natural step might be to question me and troubles keeping. Sitting amid Lamben's carefully created Buddha garden my doubts began to grow.

"This is weird," Mariana said, glancing around the alley garden.

"Really? You looked like you were enjoying the atmosphere."

"Yes, this is okay in the day, but at night ... kind of creepy. That Buddha is staring at me, and I can't help thinking he's wondering what we're doing here in the middle of the night. Then that makes me think, why would Chris Lamben agree to see us at this time? Well above and beyond the call of duty, no matter how psychic you are. Then I'm thinking, maybe there's something bad. And this is why he's seeing us."

Great minds think alike, I thought. I still hadn't shared with Mariana my conversation with Lamben. Not freaking her out was high on my priority list.

So I said, "He mentioned he's a night owl and sees special clients at night. He vaguely remembers you and wanted to see how things had worked out."

I felt as though my nose had grown as I spoke, but Mariana seemed pleased to be remembered.

Five minutes prior, I'd checked on the dark thing. There was no box to be seen anymore, just a melting cube of the black goop. More alarmingly though, the size had increased to become larger than the original box. I tried to overlay more reinforcement, but the emanating, heavy energy had grown to become too oppressive, to the point where I could only remain in the thing's presence for short moments.

Having never dealt with this kind of power before, could the growth actually be the result of my attempt at constraint; the thing stretching against my will. A pressure was building that I didn't like and I wasn't sure how much longer I could fight the influence. Every time I visited the attic, the entity seemed increasingly more aware of my presence. Like a caged animal looking up to a keeper who delivered the daily feed, it seemed to pause all activity to study me.

Along with its struggle to be free, I felt there was another purpose, another desire served. There seemed a trickle of energy conveyed to somewhere outside. Faint and almost imperceptible, I attempted to intercept the flow, maybe understand with what or who the thing communicated, but I failed. One thing I understood—the dark thing wanted out.

I was mildly startled by an overwhelming sense of another presence nearby. The Moses beard I noticed first. Of course, what else would a psychic have? A man with graying, long, straggly hair, tied back in a small ponytail, smiled a knowing smile at us like we were lost children who'd been found.

"Welcome, my friends."

Mariana gasped and leaped to her feet, dropping her bag. Her wallet, lipstick, and phone fell and scattered on the white stones. I bent down, scooping the items back inside and handed her bag to her.

"Ah, a true gentleman," said Chris Lamben. Somehow the compliment sounded condescending. The psychic, dressed completely in white, wore a flowing knee-length smock hung over baggy, cheesecloth pants. He held an outstretched hand toward the inside of the house.

"Please enter. You're welcome in my home."

Mariana led the way, and as she passed him he reached out and touched her arm. "Hello Mariana. So good to see you again."

To me, he directed a limp smile. Then he took hold of Mariana's hand and led her down a darkened corridor lit by the soft glow of candles grouped randomly around tables along its length. A mix of spices and what smelled suspiciously like recently smoked marijuana shrouded us. He'd certainly gone to a lot of trouble to create an eerie, haunted house feel.

"It really is good to see you again Mariana," he said, before bending to whisper something into her ear, which made her laugh. My skin prickled. My dislike of Chris Lamben psychic, didn't creep up on me as much as the thought crackled into existence like a sparking gas flame. He thought himself far too smooth and was too familiar in the way he pawed at Mariana's arm.

At the end of the hall he stopped at a large, unusually weathered door. Then made a real show of leaning across Mariana to allow her entry. "Entrée, mademoiselle," he said, even though with a name like Lamben, I felt fairly certain he wasn't French.

I watched him, my annoyance increasing, as he observed her in an almost predatory manner as she entered. The word *creep* entered my mind.

"Mr. Lamben—" I began, but he stopped me with "Please, call me Chris." I couldn't place his accent, but he sounded like those movie stars from the forties and fifties with a transatlantic inflection, a cross between a British and American accent. Another part of his theater perhaps?

He followed Mariana into the room, his back turned to me like I was a manservant just there to carry her bag. If I could, I would have grabbed Mariana and left, but with Plan B not really having any substance, I would need to let this play out. I could throw a little theater around myself. I hurried through and caught up with Mariana, who had settled herself into one of two orange material-covered, waiting-room chairs. Placed at perfectly-matched angles facing a slender antique desk, they were dwarfed by Lamben's high-back, leather, brass-buttoned antique number, which looked far too large and out-of-place for the desk. Anyone seated in that chair would certainly appear intimidating. No wonder his clients felt as though he held their future in his hands.

"Chris," I continued again, trying to wrench back his attention.

"Thank you for seeing us. I'm surprised you would see us at this time of night."

He tore his gaze away from Mariana and looked at me as though he'd just realized I was there.

"Ah, but Mariana is special. Now I've met you, I see you also are special." As though she was a magnet, he turned back to Mariana and began making small chat like we were at a cocktail party.

I gave up for the moment and took the opportunity to take in our surrounds. Behind him stood a ceiling-high bookcase filled with thick, leather-bound volumes. The gold wording on some spines was so aged they were difficult to read at this distance. Interspersed between the tomes were modern titles like *Your Life In Numbers, The Ancient Tarot, Protection Against Bad Luck, Wiccan and other Ancient Religions.* I scanned the shelves searching for a book entitled *Troubles Keeping for the Modern Man* or *Dummies Guide to Troubles Keeping.* No such luck.

The positioning of the titles, as though they were arranged for maximum effect to display his deep knowledge of all things supernatural, only managed to make me warier and even more skeptical. In odd contrast to the hall, the lights in this room were not dimmed.

Abruptly he broke from the inanities directed at Mariana and addressed me. "And you Mr. Fine—can I call you Rory?—you are here to help Mariana? Yes? She certainly needs your help, I believe."

"You could say that. We're just after some answers on a few odd things that have happened in the past two days."

"You were right to contact me. This is urgent. Isn't it Rory?"

This statement might have sounded particularly aware, but I had told him that on the phone. He nodded knowingly at me as though we were in a conspiracy. I snuck a glance at Mariana, but she seemed entranced. Was she actually buying this guy's schmooze act?

"I'm worried about you two," he said. "That's why I was happy to see you at this late hour. 'Life and death,' you said, and you were right."

Mariana turned sideways in her chair. Her voice was tense. "What does he mean Rory?"

I didn't dare look at her, but I felt her glare. Lamben had taken me by surprise and I used every ounce of willpower not to turn to Mariana and say: *Don't trust this guy. There's something off.*

I continued to play the staring game with him and didn't turn to Mariana when I answered her. I was going to move this along, let him know I would run this show. The last thing I wanted was for him to alarm her or insinuate I had kept something from her.

"I'm not sure if I know Mariana. I know what *I* know. I'm not exactly sure what Mr. Lamben knows."

The fake too-white smile still hung on his lips. "Rory, as I said previously, call me Chris. Despite how you're feeling you can trust me. I do want to help you, and I think I can help you."

"I'm not so sure," I said, surprised at how resolutely I stood up to him and how instantly he'd gotten under my skin.

He broke our stare and looked back to Mariana, and as he did he brought his hands down on the table, clasping them together as though in prayer.

"When you came here Mariana, years ago, I realized you were special. I'd hoped this gift might bring a good life. Happiness. Now I see, not in your immediate future. You will have to fight for happiness. There is danger around you."

I glanced at Mariana, concerned of the impact of his words. A crease etched deeply in her forehead, and her face had paled. Her words were barely above a whisper. "I don't understand."

"Mr. Lamben," I interjected, to put a stop to this part of the show. He gave me a remember-call-me-Chris look. "Ah, Chris, can we get to the point? Please. And maybe less of the, you know, melodramatics and more of answering our questions."

"Perhaps you aren't asking the right questions."

"The right questions?" I said. "Can't you just tell us the right questions? Better still, just answer them." Through gritted teeth: "We don't wish to take up too much of your valuable time, of course."

"Good things in good time Rory." Then to Mariana: "He's an impatient one, isn't he?"

I could have kissed her then and there, when she answered him with, "I'd like to know too."

"You should be first asking why you're here right now? What sent you here?"

What was he talking about? The dark thing? The Trepan Killer? How could I ask him his meaning with Mariana sitting next to me without alerting her to the nature of the dark thing and what I believed was a link to the serial killer?

Instead I played dumb. "We're here because something happened on my bus today. I'm a bus driver, if your psychic powers hadn't already told you. A woman was taken after she left the bus, and she was—"

"—murdered," he said. "The Trepan Killer. Yes, I know."

30

How did he know? I refused to believe he had any supernatural ability. No person with true power would go to so much effort with their appearance and surrounds.

Mariana gasped, obviously impressed by the revelation. This information though, could have come from the same news report we'd seen in the bar. I'm sure he was talented at putting two and two together. Let's see how he handled my next question.

"We think the killer was on the bus the day before too. We thought maybe you could help us discover his identity, because we—"

Mariana interjected, her voice bright and firm. "We want to know what you meant when you told me years ago 'he was looking for a window' and something about defending against the darkness. What did you mean, exactly? You never did tell me. I know that was a long time ago, but do you remember?"

She'd taken the words right out of my mouth. Maybe she also wondered why he beat around the bush years ago and now.

He gave her that used-car-salesman-trust-me smile and said, "My dear, this is simple. You're a rare creature." He side-nodded toward me. "Like him. In all the readings I've done in all my time, I've only ever come across one other like you. Haven't you felt this with each other? The pull?"

His mind seemed to travel away as his gaze left Mariana to look sideways like someone stood there at his shoulder. He nodded a few times as though listening to sage advice. Then he continued.

"The world is simply a mass of interconnecting energy. Like attracts like. You know the cliché. When you're unique, the attraction will be increasingly compelling, unmistakable and eventual. You would call this fate. Now think of another energy that is incompatible but is drawn to this unique energy. Maybe like a meteor happily orbiting until suddenly there's a pull from a planet that the object cannot resist. Now they'll collide. What if in the collision something new is created, something more powerful, and the meteor requires this to continue on, albeit in a new form? And you have your question *and* your answer."

Glancing at Mariana I checked to see if she understood him. By the way her hands fidgeted in her lap and the blank look on her face, I presumed she wasn't getting his oblique message either.

"Still confused," I said. "Mariana too, I think. Who or what are we talking about?"

Chris looked at me as though I was a simpleton. Perhaps I was less 'unique' in his eyes now.

"Why, the Trepan Killer, of course. He sees her as an opportunity. He is drawn, no, compelled by her."

This was strange. I too, had felt the compulsion of the dark thing, a deep need, the feeling of excitement near Mariana. I wished this conversation was between him and me alone. Mariana had little understanding of this unseen world, and I could imagine her alarm.

Chris's hands snaked across the desk, reaching toward Mariana. "Give me your hands, my dear."

Mariana obediently submitted. The light-yellow spark, which erupted in the instant their hands met, blinded me. My hands went to my eyes and rubbed the sting away.

I'd seen this before, and I'd given the effect a name: spark of life. Really, they were just energy particles colliding. Each form of energy had its own unique color. Troubles and negative emotions were a light to dark-blue shade; happiness and positivity, pink to purple; illness, especially emotional, a deep green; and this yellow, just a mess of energy mingling before settling into its own pattern based on the dominant emotional energy.

This didn't always happen, otherwise I'd be walking around blinded by colorful sparks. Just sometimes, depending on factors I'd never been able to nail down. I sometimes thought the moon or the sun were involved, but I'd given up experimenting, because everything seemed so random. Like now.

Chris Lamben closed his eyes and I thought I heard him whisper, "Oh, dear." Mariana didn't seem to notice and continued to stare at their hands, barely moving, hardly breathing.

A moment later his lids sprung open and his eyes looked up to the ceiling as though drawn there by something important. He continued to stare while lowering Mariana's hands back to the desktop. She looked uncertain what to do next. Leave her hands there or pull them back? I wanted to pull my chair over to her and put an arm around her shoulders, reassure her.

As though dragged back to our reality, Chris Lamben's head snapped forward and his gaze leveled at us. I had begun to believe he did have some kind of connection to the world in which I traveled, but his histrionics again seemed overblown.

"I'm sorry," he said, his words spilling out, "I'm so sorry. They've asked me to warn you. I'd hoped last time I was mistaken—I thought maybe I was wrong. You have no idea what you are up against. Maybe this is even too late. You are both unprepared. Darkness is coming."

"Up against *what*?" I demanded, already having a pretty good idea what he meant by *darkness is coming*. Was he referring to the dark thing? He must be.

"You mean the Trepan Killer? Why would he be after us?"

"Her," he said, motioning with his hand toward Mariana. "He's watching her. In fact, he's *marked* her. Well, he had, until ..." He looked back at me and said as though asking a question, "You intervened?" Then like the words were drip-fed to him: "He knows about you too. That stopped him for a while. Gave him pause, but now, he's coming."

"We'll find him first." The words burst from me.

Chris guffawed. "No, you don't understand. He's not your garden-variety evil. You're not dealing with anything you can comprehend. You're dealing with darkness with an agenda."

"What kind of agenda?" I asked. He'd gotten the darkness bit right, so now I was prepared to listen, although I still didn't like him. "What has Mariana got to do with him?"

"I thought you would know Rory. You're a similar soul to him. But where you deal in dispersing dark emotions—a conduit, I guess is a good word—he deals in collecting them, absorbing, for his own ... yes, his own use. With Mariana, she possesses something he needs."

"Are you saying Mariana carries some kind of dark emotions he needs? I can assure you she is nothing but light."

"No, this is not that. There's something about her uniqueness, which will allow him to harness the power he collects." He sat back in his chair. His shoulders slumped and he relaxed as though he'd been switched off. "I'm sorry, I've tried to ask more, but this is all I can decipher from what my guides tell me."

Mariana looked at me as though I could explain his words. Her voice was barely a whisper when she said, "But I, I feel so, so—so normal. How can I have some kind of power when I don't feel anything? Wouldn't I know?"

Lamben addressed her, as a teacher to a student: "If you look at a wall, viewing the length from the corner edge, a window looks no different to the wall. You can't see the detail because the pane sits inside the line of sight. Only when we change our perspective and stand before the window, do we see its ability to show the garden, the river, the rooftops, the views of the world outside. This is when we see its true potential. I imagine that's why you two found each other. You're both windows of a different kind."

I refused to believe him on this point. My attraction to Mariana was a normal human emotion, nothing to do with his exaggerated ideas about energy meteors colliding. So way off course.

"And Mr. Fine, you've already had your own encounter, yes?"

This guy was certainly good, but everybody has encounters every day. Easy to make something mystical of the normal. I don't think I would ever trust this guy.

"Encounter?"

Instead of answering my question he deflected: "You haven't told her, have you? She can handle the truth, you know. Let me rephrase, she will *have* to handle the truth. You're waiting for the right time, but that time may never be right. You can't protect her like you imagine. This thing is powerful and determined."

He leaned toward me and in a conspirator tone added, "He's very aware of you too. There's some concern for him. I don't know exactly why. I can't see why. I'm never shown everything. I just work out the message from symbols I'm given."

"Aware of me? Concern? Yeah, okay, I don't think we are on the same wavelength with your, ah, symbols. We came here because you told Mariana something years ago and I wondered if you knew something about ... well, do you know what I mean?"

I didn't want to give away information about the dark thing and make this easy for him.

Lamben settled back in his chair, an assured smile crept across his face. "I can help with the problem you are facing. A certain cleansing is necessary. I can see by your aura. A dark shadow lingers there."

Okay, close. Now he had my attention. I heard Mariana say, "Rory, what does he mean?" but I remained focused on the psychic.

"A spiritual cleansing is required. I've done plenty of those. People pick up all sorts of nasty things as they live their lives. This is like straining dirty water. You've just got to be careful not to spill anything you catch. Not nice stuff, and in the wrong hands, well —nasty!"

He'd just described a version of troubles keeping. As much as I didn't like him I had begun to think this guy had something. I was still a long way from believing everything that came out of his mouth. The last thing I wanted was for him to mess around in my private territory, especially in front of Mariana. I didn't think he fully understood what he was dealing with either.

"And how would you do this?" I asked.

"The guides. They help me. They're the ones who talk to me, aid me in delivering information to clients."

"So you talk to dead people, like a medium."

"No, no, they talk to those passed, and then convey to me what needs to be shared. Like I'm plugged in to an imaginary wall socket, and that socket connects to the free flowing energy surrounding us and the world. A humble conduit is all I am."

Hardly humble.

Guides would be a nice addition to my life. I wondered where I could apply.

Mariana's voice interrupted my thoughts. "Rory, what's he talking about?"

I saw fear in her eyes. This wasn't how I wanted her to learn about the dark thing, and Lamben wasn't going to be the one who would tell her—I was. I pulled my chair closer, swiveled, and wrapped my hands around hers. My voice was calm, even though inside a sick claustrophobia slowly crept through my body. Between the psychic, the dark thing and the connection with the killer, my warning-this-is-not-good needle was nearing red.

"Mariana, remember yesterday when I offered to take everyone's troubles and throw them in the Dawson?"

She nodded her head just the once, her eyes studying mine, as she seemed open to listening to every word. My heart felt glued to my ribcage.

"Well, there's something I haven't told you. This thing is the reason I wanted desperately to speak with—see you tonight."

"So not my charm?" She gave me a mock coy smile. I hoped she still kept that smile when I'd finished.

"Well, there was that. Still is that. Definitely. But yesterday, something happened that had never happened before. I didn't just take troubles. Something else came through. Something dark. And dangerous. Something I'd never encountered. *Ever.* Like he said, this is a form of energy." I threw a nod toward the psychic. "Seems one of the passengers carried something that feels evil. When I picked up all the troubles, I collected the thing too."

Her hands tensed between mine.

"Something evil and dangerous? Dangerous for who? Is that what happened to that murdered girl? Did she die because of something you did?"

"No, no, I didn't do anything to that girl. Well, maybe, I was responsible in that I may have put her in harm's way by accident. I couldn't have known what would happen. I don't really understand what is going on myself."

"But where did the evil-something come from? Do you know who's responsible? If this thing was on our bus, then the presence must have something to do with the murder. Surely not a coincidence."

"Oh, yes, I think the murder certainly has something to do with the thing and my bus." I lowered my voice. "Mariana, there's something else. I don't want to frighten you, because I've worked some of this out. I thought coming here I might learn more. But ... this also has to do with you."

"Me?"

"Yes, I think the dark thing, as I call this energy, came from you."

She pulled her hand back from my grasp and covered her mouth.

"No. Oh my God, how? I didn't have anything to do with what happened. I'm not evil. You're mistaken."

I grabbed back her hands between mine as though I was trying to warm them.

"Not you, the dark thing didn't originate from you. I know there's no way this could be you, but I think the presence became attached to you somehow. The heavy feeling you talked about after the group of passengers boarded; one of them, I believe, is the Trepan Killer. Somehow the dark thing slipped to you, then was picked up by me."

She yanked her hands away and they flew to her mouth. "No! Oh my God, I feel sick."

Mariana looked down into her lap, her forehead worry line again prominent. When she looked up again the words fell from her mouth. "Did you throw this horrible thing in the river with all the other troubles? Is it gone? For good?"

I shook my head slowly. How was I going to tell her the dark thing was here in the room with us without freaking her out any more than she was now. I heard my Mama's words: "*Let your fears in life fall where they may, then at least you'll know what you have. You can't deal with maybes.*"

I'd been dealing with maybes for too long in the past thirty-six hours, so now was the time to throw everything out there. I was getting nowhere keeping everything to myself. So I answered Mariana with the truth.

"No, I couldn't treat the thing like normal troubles. Doing that felt too dangerous. I have the energy trapped in a special place."

I could see by the furrow of her brows she didn't understand. "Safely I promise, for the moment, where I keep all the troubles. But I need to send the thing away soon. I've wrestled with telling you but this is not from you. I know that absolutely."

I stopped short of saying I must get this dangerous, evil dark thing out *real* soon. I didn't want to alarm her anymore with the gory details of what the dark thing had done to my box prison.

"After Sandra's death, I just couldn't release our dark friend like I normally would—I usually throw them in the Dawson, that part is true. But this thing needs to be destroyed, otherwise I think the force inside might actually survive and hurt people. There's an intent, a purpose, I feel. What purpose I haven't figure out yet.

"If I could interject here."

We both turned toward Chris Lamben. I'd almost pleasantly forgotten he was here. While my focus had been on Mariana, he'd pulled out a small hand-rolled cigarette, and by the sweet, pungent smell I knew the substance wasn't bought from a shop. He took a deep drag, held the breath, and then exhaled slowly. More theater, perhaps?

"I can help you with some of those questions. My guides are powerful. And on the side of good. Our side. This dark thing, as you call the entity, seems to be from a different place, another realm. I sense this is becoming urgent."

I gave him a contemptuous look and said, "Do you need to be stoned to connect with your guides?"

"This?" He extended his arm, holding the smoldering, white stick out as though appraising the smoking tip. "Actually helps me enter a meditative state. Opens the channels to the guides."

I had no doubt by now he had *some* abilities. The unnecessary show was what I couldn't handle. Maybe I was a shade jealous, I realized, by the way he looked at Mariana.

"What do you suggest we do? Toke away and relax our way out of this?" I said.

Chris smiled and ignored my comment. He rose and walked around the room, lighting candles and incense sticks, pausing before a picture of a god I didn't recognize, where he whispered something under his breath. Then he moved to a light switch and flicked. Shadows rushed into the room. The golden flickering light of the candles played with the darkness like they were reunited friends.

Mariana reached over to me and clutched my hand as though the touch was the only thing holding her in this life. "What's happening?"

The psychic reseated himself and closed his eyes, placing an outstretched finger to his lips to suggest we remain quiet. Then dramatic seconds later: "I need silence to begin. Once I'm connected to the guides, then you can talk all you want."

Maybe thirty, forty seconds passed before his lips began to move. A stream of unintelligible words followed, first at the level of a whisper, then growing. I looked over at Mariana. Her eyes were fixed on him, her hand gripping mine even tighter.

Suddenly Lamben shouted. Mariana jumped and let go of my hand. If he played to his theatrical strengths, I'd imagined a foreign accent or a strange, hi-pitched ethereal voice would issue forth next, something that worked with the lighting. Surprisingly his voice was his own, but more confident, strong, purposeful like a TV game show host. The tone though, was unemotional.

"I'm here. These are friends. They need your help. They're special."

I gazed around the room, searching for something he might use to augment whatever he had planned. When something began to happen, I realized this couldn't be all coming from him. Part of this must be real.

Ice traveled through my veins, because whatever energy he'd evoked I could feel the power move around my body. Instead of entering via a touch, I felt as though a blanket had been thrown over me and then melted into my being. Within seconds I realized something unknown had emerged in the attic. One moment I was in the room with the psychic and Mariana, next I was inside the attic facing a stranger. In my own personal space, the haven I had created, no longer was I alone.

31

The being had taken on a version of human form, but this must have been a struggle as the persona shifted and fluctuated as though I was viewing the entity through wafting curtains. The appearance wasn't quite ghost-like, more like something had one foot in this dimension and one in another.

Behind the being the dark thing remained contained, although now the malevolence had extended even closer to the ceiling and seemed to exert an invisible pressure against the barrier. The box had morphed into a misshapen blob of unrecognizable black-green, sitting amid an ever-growing pool of dark viscous fluid. A sudden sharp, uncomfortable tingling in my feet caused me to look down. A nasty liquid surrounded me like a puddle of rancid oil. A trail traveled back to the misshapen box, and the tendrils of the line seemed to grow as I watched.

I lifted my feet in an attempt to move away, but felt stuck as though in molasses, which definitely wasn't sweet. The floor began to undulate in tiny ripples like a wind had blown through the room, even though there were no windows. A sense came over me that if left much longer the black thing would consume me just like the prison. The growing strength of the force was palpable, and I realized how naïve I had been to think I could contain this unknown energy. A throbbing, rhythmic beat echoed in my head. *Thump-bang. Thump-bang.*Building. Building. Growing more powerful, louder. My own heart began to throb. Not in unison, no, in fear.

Should this thing escape there was a good chance the intent was to cause hell, and Mariana was seated right next to me. The psychic would be no help. Whatever power he might have, he didn't strike me as a Gandalf-type wizard. As I slowly made a revolution taking in my predicament, I knew I was lost, so out of my depth I could cry. How could I have lived in this world of troubles and emotions and not realized there was more out there? How could I not have prepared for something like this? Perhaps practiced some kind of defense in the same way I created the attic and the boxes.

Without warning and from no detectable direction, I felt a sweet, fresh breeze wafting through as though a window had been opened. The shimmering entity now moved to hover at the side of the room momentarily, before moving toward me. I felt suddenly infused with a strength. Now the being was by me, suspended in a white-gold aura. Close up, the angel-like creature appeared soft, with a sparkling shimmer to the skin and exuding a feeling of serenity. Could this be one of Chris Lamben's guides?

Go figure, he might just have told the truth.

The light in the room had turned bleak gray, growing darker with the evolution of the dark thing. The guide's emanating light now penetrated the gloom as the form left my side to move effortlessly around the interior, then began to circle around the mangled box prison, barely containing the thing. Around and around the entity flew, until a small, sparkling mini-tornado had formed.

I sensed an awareness from the dark thing that the guide was an enemy. Black, string-like tendrils reached out as though dozens of spiky fingers clutched and clawed at an invisible tormentor. I wanted to leave, to warn Mariana to get as far away from me as possible. But I couldn't leave the attic; witnessing this battle held me spellbound.

A prickling itch in my feet caused me to look down. The black sludge had begun to wither like a leaf drying up, turning pale green to dark brown, then gray. The changes were mesmerizing and I understood, somehow good and evil forces, energies, if you will, were doing battle. When troubles keeping, this idea of being engaged in the same battle had never occurred to me. All these years what I did had seemed so innocuous to pick up troubles to lighten their owners' lives. Now I saw this battle as troubles keeping on steroids.

The guide had created a whirling light around the dark thing. From where I stood there was no sound or sense of rushing wind even though that's how the movement appeared, the scene almost serene. Then the guide stepped out of the whirling light, and as though the dark thing was made of nothing more than mist, the form moved into the darkness and disappeared from sight. Seconds later, the two forces, dark and light, appeared entwined, oscillating within each other, expanding and moving faster and faster. Who was winning, who was losing, was impossible to tell.

A sudden screaming sound erupted from the silence like metal cladding wrenched from a wall. The air density increased just like the pervasive sense just before a thunderstorm, like breathing through thick cotton balls. An explosion felt imminent. Instinctively I ducked. My hands flew to cover my head.

If the guide didn't win, then I was in *real* trouble. Possibly the world was in real trouble. I dared not think what kind of devastation the dark thing might unleash if released. Unconstrained, I doubted I could recapture the dark thing.

In mere seconds the two had become all but invisible amid the now spinning ball of energy. Dark and light. Light and dark. My mind felt pulled and jerked as though the twisting mass was beckoning me forward.

Perhaps what happened next was due to fear, not for myself, but for Mariana. All I cared about now was her. I'd promised I would never let anything happen to her and I intended to keep that promise. Standing by and hoping for the guide's victory was no longer an option. I had to help. I had to fight, even though I had no idea how to intervene or what would happen if I did.

I ran toward the struggling forces, the gray dead crust of the dark thing's shoots, which had, moments before, held me prisoner, crunched beneath my feet. Without thinking I thrust my arm into the middle of the swirling ball, seeking the dark thing with my mind, tearing at the enemy with all the strength and love I carried for Mariana. My body was pulled erratically, torn forward and back, as though I was the rope in a life-and-death tug-of-war. My strength quickly drained as though I battled a fierce sandstorm.

The image of Mariana's beautiful, smiling face the first day I saw her waiting at the bus stop, all golden curls and stunning smile, entered my mind like a welcome mirage. I wanted to see her again. I wanted to know what we might become. This wouldn't be the end.

Mentally I gritted my teeth, reached deep inside, pulled out everything I had, my very will to live. My body felt ragged as though every hair, every cell, every inch of me was stretched to breaking point. I would die, I felt, torn from this realm and flung into the next.

Then everything dissolved into black; a cold, enveloping black, without a micron of light. For the barest moment I understood this was where you go when your soul departs your body. I wondered if the guide who'd fought so valiantly had survived, and whether the entity's next move would be to take me to my next destination.

Then I was falling through the blackness, bottomless blackness, and I could barely breathe. With a thud that shook my body and exploded every nerve with pain, I landed. Still blinded by the dark I lay there, aching, my heart barely beating, uncertain if I was still in my body.

I could breathe though, and I gulped in huge mouthfuls of air, which seemed to barely fill my lungs. Cold ran through my veins, as I felt the life in each cell ebb away.

My heart and soul reached for Mariana, for the image of her face. I wanted for her to be the last thing I saw, even as I yearned to say goodbye. Tell her what she had never known: I loved her; I would have given my life for her—*had* given my life for her.

As I lay there awaiting my mind to blink out, angry that the God-awful, evil dark thing had won, there came a warm embrace. Every fiber of my body, every muscle relaxed with the calming touch. Any residual fear or pain, even the anger melted dreamingly away.

Dying felt kind of pleasant.

A distant voice, too muffled to understand, echoed in my head. I was reminded of my mother's kindest, most soothing tone when I was sick as a child. The voice flowed through me and into me like a soft, undulating ribbon. Could this actually be my mother come to meet me in a heaven she'd always believed in and I never did?

I searched in the darkness, straining to find her. A tiny, white spark discharged in the distance. Squinting, I looked for the face I had so deeply missed all these years. As the persona drew closer, I realized with sadness, this wasn't Mama, but the white entity, the guide.

I understood, even before the rich blackness began to miraculously clear as though a brush dabbing light particles painted around me. The guide had fought on against the dark thing, after my intervention. Somehow, our combined energy had been enough to unbalance and force the thing back to wherever evil lived. The place didn't feel as though part of this world, but more an incubator that spawned this thing into our world, where the creature's life force grew.

Relief flooded in where the darkness had held me. I saw Mariana's face and I nodded to the guide hovering before me.

"Thank you," I said. "I'm grateful."

The words came to me, not as a sound, but more like a knowing, a déjà vu moment.

More coming. Grow. Prepare.

"More?" I asked.

Then the angel-like energy was gone, like a wisp of cloud separating in a breeze. I was alone, lying in a corner of the attic. No boxes. No damage. Most marvelous of all, no dark thing.

As I pushed myself up to sit, I tried calling out to my protector again.

"More what? What do you mean?"

Only my voice echoed back. My thoughts instantly turned to Mariana. I closed my eyes and willed myself away from the attic, back to the room where she waited with the psychic. All she would have seen was my eyes close for a moment, if she noticed anything at all. So I thought.

When I opened my eyes she was beside me just as I knew she would be. What I didn't expect were the tears in her eyes as her hand gripped mine. "Rory? Rory, are you okay?"

My body felt heavy and weighted in my joints, filled with sand. I replied the only way I could, with a nod. Just moving my head felt as though inside was filled with stone. I tried to reassure her with a smile; whether the smile made my lips I had no idea.

"You disappeared on us. You were there, then you were gone. Like you'd left your body for just a minute. More, maybe. I wanted to shake you. Wake you up. Chris said to leave you. He said—" She looked over at the psychic who watched us both in his know-it-all way. "—you were doing battle with inner demons. Rory, what did he mean?"

I couldn't find the strength to speak a single word or even squeeze her hand to reassure her. The battle with the dark thing had drained every ounce of energy.

"Give him a minute," I heard Lamben say. "I'm informed he's been through a great deal."

Mariana continued to hold my hand and rub her palms up and down my arm as though to infuse life back into me. Slowly energy seeped in, enough at least for me to speak. The first words I had though were not for Mariana. We would talk later. I would share everything with her. She deserved to know.

I slowly looked over at Chris Lamben. I now knew there was more he hadn't told us. My voice shook as I addressed him, "Mr. Lamben, what did the guide mean by 'More coming?' and 'Prepare?' More of them, did they mean? How am I meant to prepare if I don't know what I'm preparing for?"

His face looked drawn, his bravado gone. The fake mid-Atlantic accent disappeared. Now, as he spoke, he sounded like he came from somewhere where 'surfs up' was a common phrase. His eyes looked fearful.

"Everything, all, is coming. I've never seen that happen. I don't know what you did, or how, but they are with you now. The guides. You need them more than me. I realized this when you opened your eyes again. Like I knew what I knew, and then it was gone. Memories erased like they never belonged with me."

His gaze traveled frantically around the room like he'd misplaced something valuable. "Yes, they're gone. Gone!" Then he stared back at me: "But they want you to know. No, they asked I implore you to listen. They said: *He knows you.* Does that make any sense?"

Then he looked at Mariana. Her hand tensed instantly as though he held a gun pointed at her. Then he turned back to me. "He knows about her too. She's The One. I don't know what that means either. He's coming. They're coming."

"The dark things? The Trepan Killer? Give me something. Please!"

How could I prepare to fight something like this? If not for the guide, I don't think I would have survived.

"I don't know, but this is something powerful. Something bigger than you or me."

"What am I meant to do with this?"

The psychic shook his head. "I don't know." Tears formed in the corner of his eyes.

"They must have said something. Otherwise, why would they have helped me?"

"I don't know Mr. Fine. Maybe you should pray."

32

He feels the damage. This is not catastrophic, but when the connection ceased he felt a sudden deadening around him, a weakening in the atmosphere. The bus driver has now made this game so interesting. He finds this opposition even fitting.

The emptiness of the night streets cloaks him like a comfortable jacket. He passes a homeless man curled in a darkened doorway, a threadbare, patterned red and black blanket pulled over his body. The covering can protect him from the elements tonight. But not from him. He stops and stands over the man. He stirs. Even asleep he senses the power, the energy radiating around him.

He studies the man as the blanket rises and falls with his ragged breath. A sense of divinity fills him. He has the power to decide this one's fate. He reaches down. His fingertips trace the lines of the face until he knows this man, knows his life. What he has won and ultimately what he has lost. He pulls at the man's life and how easily the essence comes away. This has never occurred before. Surely this is testament he is on the right path. Each one he has taken has added to him. Perhaps when he leaves for the other world he will be altered, with greater power than he first imagined.

He stands back, then turns and heads away. His mind is on her.

She can wait a little longer. Now he's met Fine on his own ground, he understands his enemy. He will be better prepared.

His mind seeks back in time. To before. Before the darkness. He remembers being a boy, dreaming of being a man. He remembers running in a field, calling to his dog, swimming in creeks, walking to school—and living. Just living with no purpose.

Then this knowledge entered his life. Such a shock initially to see further than he'd seen before. The first time he'd realized what he now possessed was during the walk in the woods later that night. In anger, he'd run, horrified at what he'd witnessed, how the events had made him feel. The memory of what he had found so vivid still. The animal's body. The smell of death, of rotten meat covered in flies, bloated and black, a mass of maggots crawling, seething in the orifices, staking their claim on the flesh.

He had retrieved a knobby stick nearby. Even now he recalls the twisted undulation of the knots, the smoothed skin, how pleasant the branch felt in his grip. He'd grown from the first time. There came a glimpse of the world, even from that rudimentary experiment with the stick sharpened accidentally by a break. How old had he been? Eleven, twelve? A life ago. He could not remember. So many lives later, he had still managed only small success. Short glimpses of what he sought.

Until her. Now his hunt is nearly over but complicated by this bus driver. But he can wait and watch until he's certain. One careless mistake and his punishment might be to live forever knowing he possibly missed his one chance. A few nights, maybe only one, and he will be home. No one will stop him. Not even Rory Fine.

33

We left Chris Lamben's close to one. As we climbed on my bike, Mariana wrapped her arms around my chest and I almost felt human again. The feeling I was a melon used for basketball practice had faded, but my brain ached in places where I didn't think I had cells.

Before turning the ignition I took a moment to luxuriate in Mariana's closeness, smell her perfume, a light floral scent with a hint of spice. The dream I'd most desired had come true; our bodies touching, sharing experiences, albeit not the type I'd imagined. Again my mama had things right. *"Careful with your wishing. God's got a sense of humor."*

The engine rumbled alive, but I wasn't there on my bike anymore. My mind surrounded us, looking down on Mariana and me as though drawn from my body. A strange sensation crawled over me, first in my neck, then all over. Somebody was watching. Somebody was smiling. At us. I searched the street, up and down, but there was nothing and nobody.

Then I was back, Mariana's body warm against me. Slowly I accelerated, glancing left and right, checking the side streets as we passed, unable to shake the feeling of being watched. By the time I turned from the road I'd convinced myself the feeling was an illusion, the result of the encounter with the guide and the dark thing. Lamben had gotten under my skin. Processing everything would take a while, I knew. So I would take nothing at face value.

Besides, I wanted to enjoy the feeling of having Mariana so close, her arms snug around my chest as though I was some kind of red-haired action hero. She hadn't spoken since we'd left the house, and I wondered whether whatever may have begun between us might be tainted by the events that had just occurred. Maybe upon arrival at her apartment she would tell me 'adios amigo.'

Who could blame her? Tonight had been crazy, even for me. The depth and power of the dark thing, its malicious intent and desire to fight, frightened the heck out of me. How would the experience be for someone who'd never experienced the world in which I lived?

I'd felt something else during the battle. A desire for instability. The idea occurred to me that creating stability was a by-product of troubles keeping. Most people, when enveloped by misery, talked of feeling off kilter. In a way, they were correct. Energy sought balance. Good and bad. Free-flowing and solid. Happiness and sadness. Too many troubles had a way of overbalancing everything. They were ever-changing, with an ability to grow into something that could become difficult to manage.

When I took people's woes, even temporarily, this restored some equilibrium. If the dark thing was a means of destabilization, then the Trepan Killer was an agent of unbalance. Was this result purposeful? Did he know what he was doing? Maybe I'd ask him one day, because if he was coming for Mariana, certainly he would need to go through me.

Mariana lived in a three-story walk up on the east side of the city in a quiet tree-lined street, not far from the depot. I imagined this a village, where neighbors nodded to each other on the street and kids played in the park on the corner. After the night we'd just had, every parked car harbored something or someone ready to leap out and knock us to the sidewalk; every window concealed watching eyes that willed us harm. I felt weak and worried, but for Mariana I put on a brave show.

As she climbed from the bike I fixed her with my best confident smile. She pulled off her helmet and her curls fell gently around her face. At some point during the evening her ponytail had disappeared.

She stared at me, arms crossed, her eyes searching mine. She wanted answers but I had none. Since we'd connected nearly ten hours ago in the crowded café, things had continued to spiral. Now the reality came down to one thing: some kind of evil stalked her. I still had no idea why.

A window. A powerful energy. Spirit guides. All these things sounded like something out of a horror film. How was I to reassure her there was nothing to fear?

"Mariana, I'm so sorry."

"Why didn't you tell me about this dark thing? It *came* from me? How? I have a right to know. What were you thinking?"

"Protecting you, is what I was thinking. Would you have listened? Or thought I was crazy? We barely knew each other."

"We still barely know each other."

She looked down at the pavement and the familiar worry line ran across her forehead. What was she thinking now? I need to lose this guy? Worst first date ever—even though this wasn't a date? Too much crazy? I certainly couldn't blame her.

She looked back at me and said, "This is all too strange. I'm having difficulty processing. First, you tell me you have some kind of strange psychic thing I've never heard of, trouble- picking-up."

"Keeping," I corrected.

"Yes, troubles keeping. Out of left field for me, without any of the other stuff. I mean, I thought, here's a sweet guy, drives a bus, kind to old people, a lovely sense of humor. Next minute we're at a psychic's house, who I haven't seen in years. Then you phase out and when you come back you look like you've run a marathon. Now supposedly, some terrible thing was inside me. You sucked the evil out, or something like that, and stored the thing away. Now, poof, all gone. Where? And, to make everything just fine and dandy something is after me because I hold some power, some secret window that I don't even know about. I'm expecting someone to jump out and yell 'punk'd'. This is insane."

Insane. Yes. We agreed. I wanted to tell her I had the best intentions; my feelings for her weren't insane; I would protect her and we would work this out together. I dismounted and stood before her.

"I know, I'd think the same if I was you and I hadn't spent most of my life in this world. Let me explain this way. Imagine you're swimming on the ocean's surface and what's on the surface is all you see. Below though, there's another world, a whole ecosystem of life and landscapes. If not for the world below, the surface world couldn't exist because each system lives off the other. That's the balance and energy flow of the universe. Everything, including emotional energy, is interconnected. If you give me a chance, I can—"

She suddenly grabbed my forearm, her grip firm and determined. "I'm just going to say one thing, and you'd better listen. I get it, but I don't ever want to see you again Rory Fine."

My heart fractured; I wanted to dissolve into the pavement, fall between the cracks, never to reappear. My worst nightmare. I started to open my mouth to beg her, but she squeezed my arm tighter with a signal to say she hadn't finished.

"—unless you promise to never ever keep something from me that *involves me.* Supernatural. Freaky, evil energy stuff. Troubles keeping, dead people hanging. Anything at all. Are we clear?"

Slowly I felt myself breathe again. I looked into eyes I could drown in.

"You forgive me? You know I did what I did because I didn't know how to explain. I've kept this a secret all my life. Not even my mom knew. But I've known you were special from the first moment I saw you."

"Sweet talking won't save you in the future, either." She gave me a smile. I could bathe in that smile. "As I see things, I have two choices. Go along with this wild goose chase with someone I only really truly met yesterday, who's already lied to me. Or file this under *a crazy evening I'd rather forget* and start catching a different bus."

She unwrapped her arms and took a step closer. "But, you, nice bus driver with a magical gift, have caught my curiosity. And I kind of like wild geese, even if they are wrapped in weird dark thing energy stuff."

Just when I was thinking this might be a good time to pull her into my arms, she stepped back.

"It's late. I need to process this. You, and everything that's happened. I hope you understand."

I did, but I didn't think she understood the danger she was in. Whatever attracted this dark thing to her—and I hadn't worked that out yet—this wasn't going to stop.

When whatever this thing was found her, I needed to be there armed with whatever defense I could prepare. Thinking this reminded me of the guide's words: *Prepare. Grow.* What the hell did that mean? What was my next step? I didn't even know how much time I had. I needed to research this thing, if I even could, then find out everything about the killer and why he would target Mariana. Was this random or was there something to Chris Lamben's warning of her being a window? A window to what?

Insecurity twisted about me. Who was I to fight this thing? I was just a bus driver with a gift. I wasn't superman or in possession of any ability that would give me an advantage in a fight against some kind of evil.

I took a step toward Mariana, not wanting to end the evening this way.

"I'm sorry, Mariana. You don't know how sorry. Maybe I caused this, but then maybe I just uncovered something that was always there. Or maybe we were meant to come together, because I needed to be there to help you. What if this thing is bigger than us?"

Mariana bit down on her lip. "I don't know what to think Rory. I know I'm tired and I have work in a few hours. I'm saying goodnight and maybe I'll see you tomorrow. With luck, perhaps I'll wake up and this will have been a dream." After a pause she added, "Except for the dinner."

A faint, wistful smile touched her lips. Before I could say

anything, she turned to walk up the double flight of stairs to the apartment block entrance.

I followed her up and waited and watched as she checked her mailbox. Apartment thirty-three I noted. "I'm sorry," I called after her as she turned to the glass entry door. As she pushed through the entrance, I called out, "Thanks for the dinner compliment."

It sounded lame, hanging out there between us as my final words before we parted. So *not* a romantic hero.

She didn't look back but I thought I heard her laugh. The door swung closed behind, the sound loud in the quiet emptiness of the street. I'd never felt more alone in my life as the silence seeped into my skin.

The guide's words wrapped around my mind. *Prepare. Grow.* They could have been slightly less cryptic. Sure would have been a help. Then I heard the Chris Lamben's words: *Pray.*

Yes, that I could do. Who to though? Now that was the question.

34

Sometimes I wondered if Beth Ann was psychic. On form today, she greeted me with: "What's the matter, my boy? Seen a ghost?"

She must have interpreted the surprise on my face as something else, because she quickly added, "Date didn't go well?" Then she smiled. "Or did go very well?"

When I shook my head, her smile instantly faded. "No, I had a good feeling for you. I'm sorry. You were so excited."

Beth Ann hugged the clipboard to her chest. "You want to talk about it, hon?"

How could I talk about what had happened?

I answered with another shake of my head. The feeling of something dark hanging over me, which had settled like a blanket the minute I'd awoken, had stayed with me. I'd barely slept for a second night in a row, so if whatever was coming came today, the enemy would have an advantage. I'd Googled into the early hours looking for something about this dark force and how this power fit in the world I knew and could be wielded as a weapon. All I found was stuff on *The Secret*, some positive thinking book and video, and page after page of *Star Wars* 'Let the force be with you' articles.

In all my troubles keeping experience I'd never come across

anything sentient with willpower. Not saying this couldn't happen, because clearly something had, but I kept thinking there might be a more realistic explanation than a sadistic killer sics his pet evil spirit on us.

Beth Ann stood staring at me, eyes bright in anticipation, awaiting an answer. As much as I would love to confide in her and ask her advice, I had nothing I could share without giving myself away.

"Nothing to talk about, Beth Ann. Everything's *fi-iiine*. Date did go in an unexpected direction,"—well, this was true—"but I'm sure I'll see her again. So ..."

I touched her arm in a thank-you-for-your-concern gesture. As I did, I gently pulled at the troubles she concealed so well. The familiar feeling of loose, prickling energy slipped into my fingers and traveled quickly to the small box in the attic. A thankfully clear attic, thanks to the guide's intervention with the dark thing.

"... no need to worry."

She smiled and said, "You know, I don't know what it is with you but sometimes, actually most times I'm with you, I instantly feel better. You must have one of those special gifts that can just warm any heart."

Beth Ann touched my hand still resting on her arm and squinted at me. "And I have one of those gifts where I can tell when someone's not telling the truth. Whatever is bothering you sweetie, talk it out with someone. If not me, someone else."

I wished I could talk this out with someone.

"Yes Mom," I said, picking up the prepped change box. Beth Ann pointed to the staff logbook and I signed my name. I itched to be on the bus and get the day moving. Mariana would be on the five-ten, and already I could barely breathe thinking about seeing her again. So I headed out quickly without looking back.

Half-way to my bus I heard footsteps moving quickly behind me. I swung around, the hand carrying the change box raised, ready. If swung with enough force the metal container could be a weapon. *Prepare.* the guide had said.

Beth Ann shuffled toward me holding out a slip of paper.

"Rory, wait up!"

Walking fast did not agree with Beth Ann. She barely managed to pant out, "I forgot to give you this, hon. Somebody called this morning. Wouldn't give his name but asked me to give you this message."

I looked down at Beth Ann's familiar scrawl and read the message twice. Even after a second read, the words still made no sense.

We have a mutual friend. If you're free, can we meet tonight? Twinkle, twinkle, little star

   133 Station Way Road, West End

"I don't understand," I said, staring at the page before looking back at Beth Ann. "Who's this from?"

"Wouldn't say, hon. Must have asked him three or four times. He said you'd know what he meant and it was a surprise."

"He didn't say a time?"

"Nope, but he did sound like a very nice man."

"Old? Young? Pretend you're Miss Marple."

"Miss Marple? Maybe not Miss Marple, but he did get me curious, so I did discover one thing. He's a passenger on your route. I searched our system using his address. If you use a TransWest Travel Card the system will track and store all passengers' journeys in the previous three months. So our mysterious caller is male. I don't have his identity because he's ticked *anonymous* on the account. I don't know why they let people do that. Perfect loophole for terrorists, in my opinion. One thing I can tell you though, he's traveled on your bus twice this week. And last week."

I didn't believe in coincidences anymore—if I ever had—so I asked, "Twice this week? What days?"

"I knew you'd ask. So I printed out a report." She slipped her glasses from the top of her head to her nose and held up a printout.

"Hmm, let me see. Here we are ... he caught the four-twenty day before yesterday. Before that, on Monday, Wednesday, the week before." She stared at the sheet for a moment before continuing. "No, there's no set days I can see. But you know what?" She looked up and held out the sheet. "Have a look at this."

I looked down at the printed page to the spot where she pointed. "Yesterday! He was on the bus yesterday. If he knows you, why didn't he speak to you?"

I thought back to yesterday's run. I'd been preoccupied with executing my plan, so if the person was someone I knew, I could have easily missed them. Still, this was curious.

Taking the words straight out of my mouth, Beth Ann said, "Curiouser. He gets on at Ebsworth Street, stop 602. Then off at Butler Street, stop 1080, every time. Just not the same time each day. Funny he should have no routine. Most passengers have a routine." She looked up at me. "Do you know him?"

I thought through my regulars and my usuals. I was good with names and good with faces, but I didn't recall. Glen March, tall, thin and always on his iPad boarded at 602 yesterday. I remembered, because he thanked me profusely for the throw-your-troubles-in-the-river event. He actually delayed the boarding passengers behind him. At the time I worried I might be late and miss Mariana. No matter how many times I said, *no problem*, he just kept shaking my hand. Until finally I nodded behind him to the waiting passengers. This behavior was unusual for him, because he never talked, usually kept his head down (shy I figured). By then I paid no attention whatsoever to anyone who climbed on at that stop, wanting to just get moving.

Leather Jacket from the Sweetheart's Bakery popped into my head. What was he doing hanging around Mariana? And he did seem ridiculously annoyed they'd been interrupted. Could he have gotten on there? Was he on the bus the day before? I recognized him yesterday as an occasional passenger, but I couldn't be certain. If the message was from him, I couldn't imagine he wanted to catch up with me to share how much he enjoyed my driving.

"No," I answered honestly to Beth Ann. "I really don't know who this could be. I know many of the passengers but possibly not this guy. Maybe if I saw him."

"Mysteries abound with you today. Dates you won't talk about. Mysterious messages. What next? A secret mission to save the world?"

A secret mission to save the world.

There she was again. Those words got me thinking on how powerful the dark thing had grown. If the entity kept growing what damage might it do, not just to me, but to everything?

"Beth Ann," I said, "I gotta go or there'll be a manager annoyed with me for running late. Not to mention passengers. I'll share my secret mission secrets when the world—or at least part of the city, doesn't depend on me to get them somewhere on time."

"Yes, good excuse. Get off with you then."

I turned and half jogged to my bus. To keep to schedule I needed to pull out of the lot in two minutes. The moment I was behind the wheel three questions hit me. Would Mariana be waiting at her usual stop? Maybe would she, after sleeping on the previous night's events, decide this was crazy? Who was this mysterious messenger? Was I prepared for whatever was coming?

Only one question could be answered. The last. The answer: a resounding *no.*

35

Passengers on. Passengers off. At every stop I studied each commuter, wondering if they were the mysterious messenger or the master of the dark thing. The latter unlikely, I figured. Surely if he'd found and followed Sandra Swift from my bus, he wouldn't come back a second time.

During my lunch break I checked my phone for the updated news feeds about Sandra.

Trepan Killer Digs Another Hole

Such a catchy headline and a reason for the news outlet to add horrific images of trepanning. Police had issued a statement revealing the victim had gone missing after six that evening. Her cousin had attempted to contact her several times via her mobile; they were meant to eat out together. When Sandra didn't answer she had made her way to the apartment on a hunch something was wrong and made the grisly discovery.

The pictures on the page stayed in my mind for the next few

hours. The thought that the person responsible could have been on my bus, near Mariana, completely unsettling.

When I began my final run for the day, Mariana's route, I made mental notes of every male passenger I vaguely remembered from the previous days. I don't think any of the regulars had actually realized Sandra had been on the bus yesterday. If they did, nobody said anything until Arthur Ogilvy climbed aboard. This sweet, sad man had caught my bus regularly for the three years I'd been driving. I'd trouble kept his worries many times, but the pain always came back.

Arthur climbed aboard, shoulders hunched, his face drawn and flushed as though the surface was brushed with a cellular version of paint thinner, so every tiny blood vessel glowed dimly against paper-thin skin.

His voice was flat and dead. "Did you hear? That young girl?"

"Yes, on the news last night."

"Can't believe this ... such a lovely girl. So full of life. She reminded me of my son, before he ... I went straight to the police and told them I'd seen her. I saw her walk away from where the bus broke down yesterday. That's the last time I ... What's happened to the world?"

I shook my head, guilt welling inside, knowing I was responsible for Sandra's path crossing the killer's. Without waiting for my reply, Arthur turned to walk down the aisle. He seemed lost in his terrible world, a world that he now knew held even more death.

Instinctively I grabbed his arm. "Arthur?" I pulled at the sadness within him. His shoulders relaxed instantly and his face softened. The rigid, hard lines of sorrow smoothed away, but his eyes remained dark and lost. Some troubles were so deep to be unreachable.

"I'm sorry," I offered, knowing those words were of little help.

His voice sounded lighter as he answered—I had helped somewhat. "Yes, I guess you never know when your time is up. I keep thinking that if I'd talked to her like I did sometimes. But I got talking to Ellie, ah, Mrs. Daley ..."

He turned and gripped the metal handles of the seats, as though they were ladder rung holds to help pull him up the aisle, leaving me with a grim determination to put this right. That thought consumed my mind as I ran through the past forty-eight hours looking for clues. Until, as though I had emerged from a tunnel, I realized Mariana's stop was just ahead.

Like I did every day that I approached this stop, I began scanning for her. Months ago I'd developed a superstitious habit: if I didn't look for her, she wouldn't be there. I was desperate to share the mysterious message. "No more hiding the truth," she'd said, and I intended to stick to that.

My superstitious trick though, failed. Mariana wasn't waiting at the stop.

Panicked thoughts rummaged through my mind. Uppermost that something terrible had happened. I should have taken her number. Like, that's the first thing you do, right? In case of emergency; in case you need to call because a serial killer is stalking the girl you love; in case you receive a mysterious message and you need to tell someone you trust. I'm a troubles keeper though, and when it comes to the girl I love, the only girl I've ever loved, I didn't read the manual.

I would finish work in an hour—sooner if I sped up a little—then I could go straight to her apartment. If she was annoyed with me, I'd plead my case. I knew I could convince her to trust me. She *had* to trust me.

We have a mutual friend.

The words on the page Beth Ann handed me circled my mind. Maybe the message had something to do with Mariana. Maybe she had just missed work or the bus. Perhaps this person could help. Otherwise why now? He'd been on the bus and had to know something. Everywhere I turned seemed unknown. Unknowns were drowning me.

36

The moment we were alone Beth Ann's smile disappeared. Her demeanor instantly became business-like. "Rory, I've been waiting for you."

"Me? What have I done?"

A knife twisted in my heart. Mariana? But that couldn't be right; Beth Ann didn't know her.

Beth Ann came around from the back of the desk to stand before me. A pen, inserted into her dark, home-dyed hair (complete with the white demarcation at the scalp) seemed to bother her. She kept pushing and pulling at the implement, until finally she pulled the pen out to hold tightly in her hand.

"The police called earlier. Did you know one of your passengers was murdered yesterday? Within hours of her getting off your bus— the bus that broke down. The one Jim said, after he checked the mechanics over, had no problems at all."

She stuck the pen back in her hair. "They've impounded the bus. Fingerprints, the whole works. They think the killer was on the bus. Your bus Rory."

"Gosh, really?" I said, playing dumb.

"Good luck, I told them, if they hoped to take fingerprints." Beth

Ann had regained her composure as though sharing the news made everything less shocking. "Do they know how many people travel on our buses in a single day?"

Her eyes grew wide. "They think it's the Trepan Killer. Police didn't say, but I saw the news. Did you know her? I know you get to know a lot of your passengers. Some of them have written lovely emails about you. How you brighten their day. Make the ride so pleasant. They even said they sometimes waited specially to catch your bus."

"Yes, I caught the news last night. She did look familiar." I didn't want to give anything away. "Maybe I even spoke to her once or twice, said 'hello, how's your day been?' You know."

She moved forward and placed her palms on my cheeks. "Listen to me Rory. This whole thing has got me on edge. You're a special one, and I know everyone's life is precious, but, well, I don't want anything happening to you. If this killer was on your bus, well ... he's ruthless."

She left the last thought hanging in the air between us. I knew all too well how ruthless and evil the killer was, not just from the dark thing, but the murders had been widely reported. There'd even been a documentary covering the past seven years of his trail of disfigured bodies, male and female, young and old, not just in our city but across the country. He'd even been linked to disappearances and murders in other countries. The carved circular hole found in the center of the victims' foreheads led expert commentators to suggest the killings were connected to some kind of ritualistic cult behavior. This was no cult, I knew.

Worry etched Beth Ann's face.

"Beth Ann, don't worry. This doesn't mean what you think, I'm sure. The police are probably checking many different leads. I'm the bus driver. If the Trepan Killer grabbed me in front of sixty passengers, how would he get home?"

"I bet that's what the woman thought yesterday—something like this couldn't happen to her. All I'm saying is be careful. There's more good in you than most people Rory. Seems to me when bad things happen, they happen more to good people, *really* good people, who never deserve what comes to them. You're probably right. Excuse a silly woman. I guess I let my mind run away. I know you'll take care. You are too special Rory."

My turn now to reach out and touch a palm to her face, calming her as I did, the concern flowing back through my fingertips. Tingling blue-gray sparks only I could see traveled beneath my skin to the attic. There was something else too, a pulse, a throb of energy in my core, peculiar and yet, comforting. There was no time to ponder the sensation. I needed to move.

An invisible hand seemingly smoothed the lines on Beth Ann's face, so she looked more at peace. The pale pink blush of color returned to her skin.

She opened her mouth to speak, then stopped, searching my face, while shaking her head side to side. "Darn, every time I'm with you Rory, I feel lighter, better able to cope. You bring the sun out on a cloudy day."

"Ah, that would be my magic fingertips." I held my hands in the air and tensed the fingers into claws, which opened and closed like I was massaging the air. "I also give great shoulder rubs."

"I might need to avail myself of one of those shoulder rubs. Migraine coming on. Soon as you're out of my hair, I'm heading home to an early bed."

I picked up my carry bag. "I'd give you a magic massage now, but for that mysterious message. I'm dying, um, curious, to know who left the message. And I've got another errand."

"Don't mind me. Nothing a good sleep won't cure. The girl from the date?"

"What?"

"The 'another errand?' Is it the girl?"

I put a finger to my lips and pretended to turn a key. "I don't kiss and tell." Soon I would meet up with Mariana but I had a clear sense she was fine. That same premonition though, urged me to visit the unknown person because something or someone important awaited me there.

"Well, if she has any sense, she'll see how special you are. Give her one of your magic touches. That'll win her."

I returned her warm smile. I wished I'd said something meaningful like, "You're special too, Beth Ann."

This woman had been a second mom these last few years. She'd invited me to Christmas and Thanksgiving, treated me like a son. I wish I'd said more than a banal "Don't fuss, woman. You watch too much *Law & Order*."

Later I would revisit these moments, thinking if I'd done something differently maybe she might have gone home immediately. Instead, maybe taking her troubles had helped her headache, so she'd stayed where she shouldn't be.

When guilt again crowded my thoughts, another of my mama's thoughtful sayings gave me solace.

"Don't worry about what if's; they're already spent."

37

He watches the woman. His plan was to follow him, the bus driver, the question mark. Instead though, he stays waiting and watching the woman. Keep your enemies close, he thinks.

Again, as he's done with so many, the bus driver took the darkness from the short, round woman, seemingly he makes no effort to conceal what he is, visible to all through the tall glass windows of the office. In a way, he's begun to understand this man. Perhaps they are more similar than he had first imagined. This man also seeks. How he has changed.

There is something else there. Something of which he cannot be certain as he observes them. There seems a strengthening when he touches her, a glowing interconnection like a chain linked fence. From her the bus driver gains something. He grows.

He decides then to stay and waits because he has a desire to learn. He's torn. He wants to finish this. Isolate The One and end his search. Yet, the curiosity is peculiarly exciting. So he waits across the way until she is alone. He is patient. Ironic, a passenger awaiting a bus is the best camouflage—hiding in plain sight.

The rest of the staff has left. The night descends and she is alone.

Cameras don't see him if he chooses not to be seen. Light is malleable, just another energy form.

When he enters, her back is to him. A coffee cup in her hand, she places the mug on top of a filing cabinet before opening one of the drawers and rifling inside. Where he senses all, they have so little awareness. She doesn't even feel him despite his proximity.

She doesn't look up or around as she retrieves a file and returns to her desk, mug back in her hand. Now seated, she stares at her screen, her view of the world so limited.

She notices him now.

The recognition of his presence is in the shrug of her shoulders. She hesitates. Then looks up. Her eyes immediately widen, questioning. She knows he is no friend. Then he has her, already in control. He is with her. She the puppet, he the master. This ability is becoming second nature to him and the skill is proving so useful. He wonders how this skill has slipped into his repertoire.

"Stay," he says, and she must. "Relax," he says, and she does. "I want to know about the bus driver."

He sees struggle in her eyes. He moves over to her and pushes his thumb into the soft joint between her shoulder and her chest bone. Pain travels down her arm. He feels the burn in his fingertips. Her eyes crazy with the hurt.

"Imagine that sensation in every part of your body. I want to know about him. And your connection."

She doesn't speak. She cannot speak unless he allows her, but her eyes tell him what he needs to know. He sees now that she doesn't even understand the bus driver. To her he is just another one of them.

He gently strokes her cheek. Some fear and pain travels through him, but this is good. Something to remind him of his past and how far he has traveled.

"We're connected, he and I. We've always been entwined. I just want to know if he knows," he tells her as he walks back to the doorway. His bag is there, deposited from when he'd entered. He gathers his things and when he turns back to her, he adds, "Yes, there's him and me and his girlfriend. We're like beautiful circuitry."

He secures her with duct tape wrapped around her body and the chair. This is becoming increasingly unnecessary, but he errs on the side of caution. Minutes later he stands before her, neatly laying out his tools. Her eyes grow wide when she sees the drill. He clutches her will to him. He finds this power liberating to realize he can hold her with just a thought, so less complicated than before.

He touches her forehead, feels the smoothness of her brow, feels the illness eating away at her. Now he sees and wonders if this has something to do with what passed between her and the driver. Bending to her, he searches her eyes.

"Oh, I see," he says. "Well, well, you're dying. No need to be afraid. At least now you will serve a purpose."

38

One Hundred and Thirty-Three Station Way Road was a two-story warehouse conversion in what was once the humble side of West End. Once a semi-industrial area on the outskirts of the inner city filled with warehouses and workshops dating back to the beginning of the twentieth century, the landscape had been creatively transformed. Fifteen years ago the local government sunk a load of dollars into refurbishing the area, converting the rundown, disused warehouses and ramshackle buildings into glistening, modern apartments. Young professionals and double-income-no-kids couples had moved in, making this an expensive and desirable place to live.

This section had a not-quite-finished feel. Rundown bungalows squatted between apartment-blocks, which, though newish, clearly enjoyed less investment than the more luxurious abodes two blocks away.

I'd never personally traveled to the West End before, except occasionally running the route when the usual driver was away. I parked my bike outside the house and stared up at the building. After all the surprises of the past two days, a foreboding I couldn't shake crept over me like I was about to collide with something I wouldn't like—not with danger, but something unsettling.

Who lived inside and what did he want? And did he have something to do with the Trepan Killer? Surely nobody with good news leaves a cryptic message.

We have a mutual friend.

If he was a friend, surely he'd leave an understandable message. *My name is so-and-so, and I know you from blah-blah. We should meet. Here's my address and number (so you can call me and make a time, like normal people).*

Made sense.

A solitary light glowed in the home's ground floor window. I climbed the stairs as a breeze whirled behind me causing fallen leaves to dance about my feet as though racing me to the door.

The door-knocker, a uniquely carved key-shape of burnished dark-brown larger than a man's fist, hung vertically above the door-knob. The appearance was of a lock to a giant antique closet. My hand enclosed the middle section of the key; it squeaked loudly as I pulled the weighty thing back and rapped several times. A metal tone resonated eerily through the door and I fully expected a pale-faced butler with slicked back hair in a dark suit to answer the door. My pulse increased ever so slightly as I waited and wondered who would open the door.

"Hold on. I won't be a moment." Surprisingly the voice sounded normal, even friendly.

Then came the crisp snapping of a double-lock releasing, and moments later the door swung open. No pale-faced Addams Family Lurch stood there. Just a meek-looking balding man in his early fifties. He wore casual dark-blue tracksuit pants and a white t-shirt. A smile lit his face, which looked intelligent and keen. He seemed excited to see me, and even before I had a chance to say hello and introduce myself he leaped forward and shook my hand.

"That was quick. I expected you might be busy and unable to come so soon. Thank you. Great to see you Rory."

Words stuck in my mouth. He spoke to me as though I was a returning prodigal son or an old friend. Though there was something familiar about him, I didn't know him. Beth Ann had said he'd caught my bus several times, maybe that was why, but I couldn't place his face on my bus. A deep memory swam to the surface, but floated annoyingly away where I couldn't reach.

"I came because of your curious message. I'm not sure how I am supposed to know you."

I stared hard at him, searching his face. The more I looked at him the more familiar he became. "Do I know you from ... where do I know you from? A long time ago, I think."

He grabbed my hand, shaking vigorously. After what happened on the bus, my instant reaction to this stranger was to close myself from his troubles. I'd just rid myself of something terrible. I didn't need to fight off some other unknown thing.

"Oh, excuse me. I guess I've aged. I thought you'd still recognize me. Daniel Starsey."

Daniel Starsey? The name didn't ring any bells, no matter how wholehearted the handshake. His enthusiasm made me hesitate to question him further. He seemed so certain I should remember him, and I did in a funny way. Maybe he had some kind of information he would only reveal if he thought I was a long-lost friend. So I played along.

"Oh, yes, of course," I said, perhaps not as enthusiastically as him. "Great to see you again."

He firmly grabbed the arm he'd just shook and pulled me inside as though afraid if he let go I might make a run.

"Come in Rory. Come in. Lots to catch up. I was drinking wine, but I've coffee if you prefer."

"Water, please. I'm not much of a wine or coffee drinker." Stimulants and drugs messed with my troubles keeping. I liked to keep my full faculties when dealing with troubles.

The narrowness of the hallway forced me to follow close behind, and as I stared at the back of his head and the way he walked, the feeling of familiarity intensified. Like déjà vu, but I just couldn't put my finger on why and where.

He turned into a small sitting room furnished with a leather sofa and recliner. Piled high on a coffee table, which sat between them, lay a collection of *National Geographic* and old *Omni* magazines, along with a half-full glass of white wine. Running one full wall was a floor-to-ceiling bookcase; a far too large piece of furniture for such a small room. Papers and books sat piled haphazardly on some of the shelves.

As I made my way around the back of the sofa, I purposely passed by the bookcase, searching for photographs or anything which might give clues to his identity. All I knew so far was he knew me, seemed friendly, drank wine in the evening and wasn't a neat freak.

Daniel Starsey stood before the recliner staring, smiling, nodding like he couldn't believe I was there.

"Rory, please, make yourself at home. Seriously great to see you. Let me grab that water."

"Thanks," I said, seating myself on the edge of the lounge. Starsey paused at the doorway, staring blankly at me. My skin crawled. *What was he looking at?* A feeling of being a trapped animal sized up by a hunter came over me. Then a grin lit his face.

"Really is so good to see you again. Rory Fine. Wow. I've looked forward to this ever since I saw you on the bus."

I gave him what I hoped was a *me-too* smile. He didn't seem to notice the lack of genuineness, but clapped his hands together and bunched his shoulders; he really did look thrilled, but he gripped those hands so tightly his knuckles were white.

"Right. Lots to catch up. Back in a moment."

The second he'd left I was up and moving and checking out the room. There were no photos or personal knickknacks to shed light on who was Daniel Starsey, so I made a beeline for the unkempt book-shelf. The thing was overcrowded; not a spare space in sight. On some shelves books stood neatly, spine out, looking perfectly aligned and untouched. A light layer of dust laid testament they hadn't been moved in a while. Nearly all of the books were on sciences. Thick, heavy tomes with titles like *Physics and the Universe, The Elegant Universe, The Hidden Reality, Introduction to High Energy Physics, Theories and Experiments in High Energy Physics, The World Beneath.*

I pulled *The Elegant Universe* from the shelf and shuffled through the pages. I'd heard about the author. Brian Green. He'd been a guest on several late night talk shows, but I couldn't remember his angle. Something about string theory and quantum physics. I had enough physics going on with troubles keeping without worrying about the scientific theories that powered our world. I knew what I needed to know.

On most other shelves books lay haphazardly stacked in piles. Scientific looking papers, with what seemed like calculations lay on top of some stacks or layered in between.

The *Elegant Universe* was still in my hands when Daniel Starsey reentered the room, holding a glass that tinkled with ice as he placed it on the table next to a nearly empty bottle of white wine. His face lit up when he saw me at the bookcase. Seemed everything I did made him *very* happy.

"Ah, you've already found my favorite book. Green's string theory is fascinating, yes? You're familiar with the concept? They thought Stephen Hawking answered everything, but he's a lightweight when his theories are compared to these concepts. Green has nailed the true theory of everything, don't you think?

I had no clue. "Um, I've not read anything like this. Anything above high school science and math are a little above my brain grade."

He tilted his head to the side, appearing to study me once more. The feeling of spiders crawling on my neck was immediate. "Yes, of course, I remember now," he said.

Who was this guy? I was nearly positive I didn't know him, yet there was just something about the way he moved his hand in the air as he talked, as though physically punctuating his sentences. His enthusiastic manner was almost theatrical. Usually I was good with faces. Usually. Until now.

Daniel Starsey seemed likable, harmless and decidedly happy to see me. Certainly there was none of the animosity and distrust I felt when I'd met Chris Lamben. At some point soon I'd need to disappoint him and explain he had me at a disadvantage in the memories department. I decided though to wait a little longer in case his identity came to me from something he said.

He scooped up his wine glass and held it out in a toast.

"Here's to old friends." Then he took several sips before sitting and motioning me to also sit. He now rested his clutched glass on his knee. His eyes sparkled with enthusiasm.

"So, you're a bus driver. An interesting occupation for someone with your talents."

Talents? Rather left field. Now there was a waft of Chris Lamben. He couldn't possibly be referring to troubles keeping, could he? Mariana was the only other person with whom I'd shared this knowledge. Possibly the psychic had a rudimentary understanding after last night. That was all. Wariness began to rise in me.

"Mr. Starsey," I began. I was about to reveal his mistake, explain he'd traveled on my bus and must have gotten me mixed up with someone else. Someone else with a *talent.* As I said his name out loud though, the memory hit me like an electric jolt.

"Mr.—Starsey? You're ... Mr. Starsey! The teacher. Right?"

"Ah," he said, nodding slowly, working his mouth into a large grin. "You didn't remember me? Oh, sorry. I should have reminded you immediately. I guess I thought you'd recall that year because that time is fixed in my mind like yesterday. I was thirty. Then again you were just a kid. So, understandable. I have wondered about you for years."

I couldn't believe this. Daniel Starsey. School was so long ago and seeing him here was completely out of context. Like he said, I was a kid. Maybe eleven, twelve. He was a teacher at my school. He'd never taught me directly, but I'd seen him around the school. As I shuffled through my memories, I found difficulty in matching this Daniel Starsey with *the* Mr. Starsey I'd known. He had hair then, for a start. If I remembered right, he also had been on the heavy side. He'd slimmed down about as much as he'd lost the center thatch of hair. Enough weight loss anyway to make him nearly unrecognizable from the man of fifteen odd years ago.

Time has a way of fixing memories so they have their own truth, even if years later they deceive you. Now everything made perfect sense. Doing some quick math, I calculated him to be mid-forties now, but he looked much older.

I remembered him with a wild, dark blond mass of waves escaping from a ponytail. The cool, laid-back teacher, who wore jeans and t-shirts with fun slogans. Though I hadn't recalled him exactly, I had vivid memories of the shirt slogans. They were pretty cool, science-based, and emblazoned in black-and-white with pictures of Einstein's face and *MC2*, fluorescent formulas on black, and there was one I never forgot: *Don't let gravity weigh you down.*

This was crazy, out-of-the-blue and still puzzling. His enthusiasm seemed overly high considering he'd simply been a teacher at our school. I'm sure we hadn't shared any bonding experiences. The *Twinkle, twinkle, little star* line made sense now; he used the nursery rhyme line to help kids remember his name. I remembered a friend shouting the words to him one day when he walked past. Why he thought I'd remember something so obscure and use the phrase in a cryptic message was puzzling, but I didn't get the feeling he'd done it purposely to mislead. He thought I'd understand and remember.

"Mr. Starsey, wow, sorry, I didn't recognize you. You're, ah, out of context."

"Context?"

"Yeah, like you're not walking down a school corridor."

"I guess that was silly of me to imagine you'd remember. You were eleven I think, last time I saw you. I had more hair and more body back then." He chuckled and took an eager swig of his wine.

"Certainly been a while. You still teaching Mr. Starsey?" I nodded toward the bookshelf. "Physics? Science now?"

"Yeah, still at learning and passing on knowledge. Good guess on the science and physics. Western Dale University. Science has become a passion. Oh, and, please, my friends call me Daniel. I don't even allow my students to call me Mr. Starsey anymore."

A wistful look colored his face as he said, "You know my career change was all due to you; I fell in love with physics in all its glorious miracle and mystery."

"*Me?*" I blurted, completely confused. A seed of something sticky and hot had embedded in my stomach. Around this age was when I discovered the dangers of my wonderful, little gift. Although at the time, '*gift*' was the last thing I'd call what I did. Nineteen ninety-nine. I was ten.

"Mr. Starsey—"

"Daniel, remember."

"Daniel—" That sounded weird. I suddenly felt ten again. "I don't really get the physics connection. And actually, I'm also curious why you left such a cryptic message."

"Well, the message got you here, didn't it?"

"I guess, but why now, out-of-the-blue?"

He smiled a knowing smile. "Because now you need me."

"Need you? Now I'm *really* confused."

"Rory, you caused me to question everything I knew about the world. How everything fit together."

The sticky, hot sensation in my stomach hardened into stone.

He knew. About the troubles keeping, he knew. *How?*

I picked up the water I hadn't intended to drink and swallowed half in one gulp, and then slowly drank the rest to buy some time. As I placed the glass back on the table, I tried to look as though I had no idea what he meant.

Deny, deny, was my default position over the years, if ever questioned about the strange emotional effect I had on people.

"I'm not very sure I understand Mr. Star ... Daniel."

"I think you do Rory. In fact, I think you'll appreciate that fate has brought us together. Don't worry. Your secret's safe with me. I totally understand why you wouldn't share this with anyone."

My breath seemed suspended before me, a white mist of incomprehension. Could he really be talking about troubles keeping? Why was he so certain?

Deny. Deny. "Honestly Daniel, I don't know what you mean. I was a kid and that was a long time ago. So you'll have to be more specific."

He still maintained a friendly smile, and that smile, with so much unsaid, caused those imaginary spiders to crawl under my skin.

"You don't need to be nervous. You can trust me."

At this point, with all that had happened, I wasn't trusting anyone, least of all an old school teacher who'd just suddenly reappeared.

Daniel Starsey leaned over, placed his wine glass on the coffee table, and fixed me with a solid stare. The smile had disappeared. "I guess you want the whole story, right Rory?

No, I didn't think I did want the *whole story*, because the *whole story* was there in his eyes. He knew about me. That knowledge in a stranger's hands was a very, very dangerous thing. History was my proof.

39

September fifteenth. I'd never forget that day, etched in my mind like the first time you break a bone, or the pet you love dies, or you realize you're different from everyone else. You discover what seemed like a cool little game is a dangerous snake, which will bite you and anyone nearby.

The school kept an official report. So did I, staying up into the early hours, writing down every detail, so I didn't need to rely on my memory to work out what had happened. Seems the day had had a similar impact on Daniel Starsey.

"Kids don't perform miracles, do they Rory?" Daniel Starsey said, leaning forward. "Not ordinary kids, anyway. If you don't believe in God? What is a miracle? I'll tell you, a miracle is science we are yet to discover."

As he talked, I began to understand, you can never cover all the angles. I didn't realize he was there, a witness to what had occurred. Where he thought he'd seen a miracle, I'd experienced a horror story.

Suddenly I felt exposed, vulnerable, as the memories flooded back. I thought I'd put the event as far behind me as I could. Occasionally the memory would filter into a dream or a wistful moment, but I'd come to terms with what had happened. There was nobody to blame, just kids being kids, innocent and unsuspecting. In my case, how could I have known what power lay in my fingertips?

Deny, deny wasn't going to fly. I saw that now. The determined look on his face told me he did know. What I needed to understand exactly was what else he knew and how his knowledge related to what was happening now with Mariana and the Trepan Killer. This clearly was no coincidence.

I tried to control my breathing, act calm, meanwhile my heart galloped. "Okay," I began, my voice sounding weak, but growing firmer. "Let's say I know what you're talking about, what happens now?"

He threw back the last mouthful of wine and said, "Now we talk seriously about what's happening. I want to help. The balance is out. I don't think one man, even an extraordinary man like you, can right this current imbalance on their own. The nature of energy is of seeking equilibrium. Should that balance not reset, and if what I understand to be true is correct, then the world we know will be changed forever."

"I'm sorry, I don't follow," I said, honestly. My response had nothing to with *deny-deny*. I really didn't understand.

The overhead bulb's harsh, white light shone over him, glancing off his forehead like a lead actor pinned by a spotlight making his words even more dramatic.

"There's darkness coming Rory, and I'm not sure either of us has the power to prevent what that darkness will bring."

40

Daniel Starsey just used the word *darkness?* Yeah, he didn't say trouble or misfortune or even evil. He said *darkness.* Why would he use that word, the same word I used to describe the thing, the hitchhiker entity I'd just wrestled from the attic?

"I know, I sound crazy. Then again an every-day guy with an ordinary job like, say, driving city buses, who can transfer energy from a mere touch, sounds pretty darn crazy too, don't you think?"

Gloves were officially off now. My expression hardened. I wanted to know what he knew before giving anything away. I was Clark Kent revealed, and I didn't like the feeling much at all, no matter how well meaning he appeared.

"Okay, so what do you actually think I do? Because, truly, you've lost me." I tried to keep the panic out of my voice. He could be fishing. Maybe what he thought he knew was something else completely. "I'm a bus driver, pure and simple. If you mean the little show a couple of nights ago on the bus, well, that was a game. People will believe what they want to believe. You've heard of *The Secret,* haven't you? That just comes down to positive thinking. If you tell someone they'll feel better, they usually do. You tell people you'll take their troubles and throw them in the river, ninety percent will go along with you."

Starsey picked up the wine and angled it over his glass only to discover it was empty. I wondered if his confidence was contrived. As he replaced the bottle, he fixed me with a stare and tilted his head as though he was examining me.

"But the number isn't ninety percent with you, is it? Every person you touch *does* feel better. In fact, they don't just feel better, they're changed on a deeper level."

How could he know?

Suddenly I couldn't catch my breath, so I took a few seconds to answer.

"If this is true, how? You tell me. Hypnosis?"

"Rory, you don't have to be afraid. You and I both know this isn't about hypnosis or tricks. The magic is you. I've wondered for years if you truly understood something that came so naturally. Did you see the big picture? I really pondered this."

He paused as though carefully choosing his words. "I have a question, and I'm thrilled to have you sitting here after all these years. If I'm honest, I never thought I'd ever get to ask you. I'm your biggest fan after witnessing the event the other night. I see now what you've done with your gift. The good you do. Especially after what happened all those years ago."

Now I was a deer caught in headlights, the car bearing down on me. I couldn't move, couldn't look away and couldn't formulate an escape. How could he know with such certainty?

The day to which he referred was over sixteen years ago. I'd convinced myself there were no witnesses. Nobody there except Mikey, Stevie and me. Now forced to face that memory, I felt physically ill. Guilt and sadness filled my heart, replaced by a sudden anger toward Daniel Starsey for bringing me here covertly, then throwing that day at me. Perhaps what had happened posed a fascinating question for him, but for me, that day came at an age when living should have been about fun and friends. Instead, I'd faced one of the toughest lessons of life. And I had faced those events on my own.

When I spoke I didn't recognize my own voice. The anger had welled up inside, coating the words leaving my mouth.

"If you're talking about Mikey, I've come to terms with what happened. I was just a kid dealing with something unknown, bigger than me."

His face softened and he put up his hands in a placating gesture. His voice was quiet, filled with contrition.

"I understand now. Of course, I'm not blaming you. Clearly everything then was unintentional. You were a child. I didn't know what to think myself. I never told a soul. Not *one* living soul. I left the school a month later and, for a while, teaching, because of that day. The faculty thought it was some post-traumatic stress reaction to what had happened on my watch. The guilt. You and what you did was what I couldn't resolve in my mind. You'd ignited a curiosity, which became a decade long search to understand. Out of a terrible tragedy came something good."

"Good?" I said, puzzled by the shining delight on his face.

"From mistakes Rory, we learn. Maybe there are things I've learned that I can teach you. The universe demands symmetry; in fact, needs equilibrium to maintain stability. So, occasionally necessity throws up someone like you, who, by your very existence, balances the inequities."

While I still digested his words, he added another wild card: "You're not the only one, you know."

"Not the only one?"

"No, you're not the only balance check. Your girlfriend, for instance. Don't you wonder how you found each other? An attraction of forces, of course."

My heart took off. "Mr. Starsey—"

"Daniel, remember."

"No, actually, can I call you Mr. Starsey until I get used to the idea you're someone else other than a teacher I hardly knew from my past."

"Sure, call me what you like, but I am a friend. I can't tell you how much I admire you and your ability. How you go about life as if you're just a normal human being."

Years I'd been careful. My secret, mine alone. Now within a twenty-four-hour period I had shared my secret and was now tempted to share again. Mind you, Daniel Starsey seemed to know more than me about me, which was a freak-out. I wasn't sure if I should be relieved or concerned. He seemed genuinely excited and, despite how I'd felt when I first entered his home, I didn't feel threatened anymore.

"Rory, I urge you to trust me. I promise you I'm here to help. In fact, fate, the universe, whatever you would call it, threw us together all those years ago. I believe for a reason. I'm not sure exactly how this works for you, and that's what I want to know. I need to know as much about you and your girlfriend as I can. According to my calculations, a threat is coming. You're going to need all the help you can get."

"Darkness is coming," I said to myself.

I thought I had whispered only to myself, but maybe not, because Daniel said, "Yes, darkness is coming, so we need to start now to prepare. First, tell me what happened that day at school. I've always wondered the catalyst. Call my curiosity scientific."

The same words Mariana had recalled Chris Lamben saying years ago. The same words the psychic had told us last night, and now Daniel Starsey. The universe sending a message? I felt compelled to open my ears and my heart, despite the risk, and share what I knew, and listen to what he had to say. I wasn't throwing caution to the wind. I would simply allow my sails to be filled with wind and travel a little down the river.

I drew a deep breath. My mind traveled back. When I chose, I could recall everything that day in all its vividness. Always the memory was there, like a Netflix film just waiting to be streamed.

"Okay Daniel. You want to know about that day?"

He nodded. A satisfied look spread across his face. His eyes shone in what I imagined was years of anticipation, while he had no true idea what a painful memory he'd forced me to recall.

"That day was the first time someone else learned about me, what I could do, you know. And for me, the first lesson in what not to do."

My cheeks burned with shame and I lowered my eyes. I didn't want to look at him. Since he'd clearly been there, he knew what I'd done. The sounds of the playground all those years ago filled my ears. Children calling to each other, balls thwacking against walls, a freshly mown grass smell, birds chirping from trees surrounding the playground. The bell ringing declaring time to go back to class. A teacher calling to students to "pick up your trash." A cacophony of normal.

Then I looked up and stared straight into Daniel's eyes, surprised at the pinch of sadness in my chest as I said, "I didn't mean for anyone to die."

"I know you didn't," he said gently. "I know."

41

My first few weeks at school were not fun. Kids are touchy, feely creatures. They push, grab, and prod each other. This is the way they learn boundaries, relate to others and discover how best to express themselves. The tumult of emotional explosions randomly picked up, before I understood what was happening, terrified me.

Troubles were like the shock of static electricity on a windy, dry day. Uncomfortable, unsettling, sometimes painful, I soon learned caution in whom I touched. Or allowed to touch me.

Not all feelings hurt. Light, warm, tingling feelings of my mama's loving touch felt like soaking in a luxuriant bath. The warmth entered my body, gently flowing through my skin, until somewhere in the center of my being the feeling would stop and snuggle down inside, only fading hours later.

Eventually I learned a few things: slowing the energy enough to take control, examining the feelings and glimpses of lives. Trying to understand experiences and emotions was years beyond me.

Everything changed the night I watched a Sunday night wildlife show documenting animals taken cruelly from the wild and shipped around the world for profit. As I watched hunters capture animals, place them in cages and then large wooden boxes for transport to zoos, the idea struck me. Maybe I could do the same with the troubles and feelings—place them in boxes, hide them away. Later I learned, in psychological terms, this was called partitioning. Then I read a book about a girl who hid in an attic during the German Nazi occupation. While her experience was a terrible thing, there was safety in that attic. She did survive. The idea caught my imagination. So *the attic* was born.

With practice, I became adept at pushing and leading the troubles into little wooden crates (just like the wild animals), and sometimes colorful boxes, if I felt creative. Eventually though, the attic became full. Next challenge: removing the troubles to make way for more.

First time I offloaded the troubles was with Bluey, a small, fluffy, blue bear with a white nose and beady black eyes. My father gave him to me the day I was born. One night, snuggled up to Bluey in bed, so exhausted even lifting an arm seemed too much, I knew I needed to do something urgently. The attic was full, piled high with boxes. The more the space filled, the more the tiredness grew, like the slow loading of scales with weights.

Hugging the little blue toy tight, I imagined him as part of me and all my feelings and confusion flowing into him, just so I could rest.

A strange prickling began deep inside my head, a swirling, sharp feeling traveling from my core, to the fingers clutched about Bluey; he was a magnet, the troubles metal filings. In the darkened room, Bluey began to glow like a faint, eerie nightlight. Pulling myself into a sitting position, I held him out from my body and stared at the now incandescent bear.

Was he coming alive I wondered, as characters did in movies? Excitement in me grew as I imagined a new friend like Woody from *Toy Story*. When after several minutes he did nothing more than just glow, I rested his body against the bedhead and pushed at him.

Nothing. He remained squishy and soft. Then the light faded and my heart crumpled in disappointment. Finally having a friend with whom to share my world had, for a moment, become tantalizingly wonderful. By the time I lay back, the glow had disappeared completely, leaving no sign anything had happened. I wound my body around Bluey and fell asleep, curious and filled with a shady sadness. In the morning I awoke excitedly grabbing for Bluey to check. Overnight, I thought, maybe he had miraculously come to life. But no, he was still ordinary Bluey, a stuffed teddy bear.

What I began to realize had changed was me. A sense of lightness and contentment filled my core, and when I checked in the attic, the boxes were empty.

Next time I faced an overflowing in the attic I was at my cousin Scott's home. Amid our rough and tumble in the yard, he fell over a jutting tree root and fractured his ankle. My aunt grabbed me as I kneeled over a screaming Scott. That contact was enough to dump her fear and panic into me. The power-jolt to my system was unexpected and shocking. Now not only was Scott screaming, I now joined him. My aunt, on the other hand had become calm, while I wailed like I'd broken a bone too.

When Mama reached me, she cuddled and rocked me to composure, giving me the break I needed to gather myself and stow the intense emotions into a box. The attic was already full though. The sudden addition of this trouble made for an uncomfortable half hour until we arrived home. I struggled to contain the energy as the emotion leaked and melted into my own, but I wasn't managing well. So I spent the time shifting uncomfortably on the train ride home as though I had to go to the bathroom.

The relief to be in my own home sent me straight to Bluey. I wrapped my arms around the bear and cuddled him, squishing his body into my chest, as I willed the terrible, painful feeling to leave. Like a granted wish come true, moments later the pent up energy flowed away. I felt light and relieved. When the emotional dregs had disappeared, I laid Bluey beside me. He glowed a beautiful, iridescent blue again, just like before.

Then and there I understood how I could manage the buildup of troubles, of how to clear the attic. From then on, anytime I picked up troubles—which was a daily occurrence—I placed them in the attic until I could return to Bluey.

The feeling of freedom felt so good I began taking Bluey to school. Eventually, Mama persuaded me somewhere around third grade that Bluey needed to stay at home. "He's already smart enough. Let's have him stay home and keep me company," she'd said.

To my mama, my obsession with a teddy bear must have seemed curious, maybe worrying. Most days after arriving home, I'd bolt to my room, drain the troubles energy into Bluey's little, fur-covered body, and fully breathe again. The feeling was one of taking a big gulp of fresh air after hiding inside a dusty, old cupboard.

By the beginning of middle school I had mastered reasonable control of my gift. My mama was the one who caused me to think of my ability as a gift. She began to repeat how instantly better she felt whenever I was nearby. Troubles keeping was sometimes purposeful and other times accidental. I hadn't yet learned to fully temper my power. Mama kept calling the way I made her feel 'a gift of my nature.' That label stuck in my mind. I liked the idea of this being a gift of my nature.

What I didn't know was the more the gift was used the more powerful the ability would grow. Something that, as I grew a little older, became a game for me that would end in tragedy. The day to which Daniel Starsey referred, was the day I learned you can't take gifts for granted. When kids screw up, feelings get hurt, windows get broken, sometimes bones. Those can be mended. The one time I screwed up, someone died.

42

The months following that day I played the *what if* game. Had I done this or that might he have survived? Twelve years old, full of my own invincibility, unaware of my vulnerability, by then I'd played with the power of troubles keeping for several years. On the precipice of teenage-hood, hormonal, confident, I acted first and thought later.

By then, I'd managed to make two friends, oddballs like me. Mikey, skinny, weasel-faced with black hair that had a way of flopping over his face like the fibers had their own will. He rarely had much to say, but somehow that made him good company.

Stevie was the polar opposite—loud, round, and always telling jokes, which were funny because they were so unfunny. When I drew out his troubles though, I saw tragedy cloaked by the humor. An alcoholic father. A mother with prescription drug demons.

On that terrible day they were there, Mikey and Stevie. I never saw Daniel Starsey but, of course, in the chaos of those few minutes and the aftermath I wasn't exactly focused on witnesses.

The day was stifling, the kind of heat where wiping sweat from foreheads and above lips just seemed an invitation for more to form. Usually recess involved a gulp of a sugary snack and a round of tag.

Not that day though. On that day, our break became the disaster, which began with me and Mikey calming, or attempting to calm, a hysterical Stevie.

He'd been cornered in the bathroom by the *buglies*—our name for the biggest, meanest, ugliest bullies in the school. By the size of these guys, they should have been in middle school. They'd shoved Stevie into a wall, delivering a bloody nose and a scraped knee, followed by the head in the toilet trick. He'd been done over good.

His hysterics weren't the result of his encounter or the indignity of being bullied. His fear was he would be noticed by a teacher. From his injuries anyone could see he'd been in a fight, and snitching would catch you something worse. Arriving home, obviously beaten up, was what truly had him in hysterics. There would be no sympathy. Everything that went wrong was his fault. No excuses.

When he found us in the playground he smelled of piss, masked somewhat by the even more toxic stench of vomit. Our first mistake happened then. We, inadvertently, had returned him to the scene of the attack. The bathroom.

While Mikey stood guard by the door—we didn't need the buglies back for a second round and we didn't need witnesses—I cleaned him up best I could. I couldn't calm Stevie, who'd grown even more hysterical. His mom would kill him for messing his shirt; his dad, because he'd allowed someone to get the better of him.

There are certain moments where anguish and emotion are too volatile to handle. I'd learned this, so I kept touching to a bare minimum. I couldn't help my friend until some of the emotion had subsided. At that age, I simply didn't have enough handle on my gift.

Stevie's shirt was off. He stood, with his kid-roll of fat bulging over his pants, staring in the mirror, scrubbing at the blood on his face. I had his shirt in the basin, rinsing the material as best I could in the small space and with my lack of cleaning experience. Globs of sick came free from the shirt and stuck in the plug hole's metal strainer. I gagged at the nauseating smell and image and held my forearm beneath my nose, swishing the shirt with the other hand. Gradually the smell dissipated as the puke disappeared down the drain.

Mikey had given up guard duty and now had wads of wetted tissue clenched in a fist as he wiped at Stevie's legs, removing the oozing blood from his wound. I guess we all thought, the quicker we got out of there the better. All hands on deck—or all hands on Stevie, more accurately. By the time I had the shirt held under the hand dryer, we almost had everything done. Stevie had begun to calm down and things might have been fine then. We would have headed to class—slightly late, but Stevie had been sick, a reasonable excuse, and the day would have played out like any other.

After everything though, the stress of seeing Stevie that way, of being caught, or facing the buglies ourselves, Mikey piped up with: "We should report this. I've had enough. Those kids deserve to be pummeled into the ground. Shits."

Well, that started Stevie off again. His sizable chest began to heave and even quiver as though his lungs were a paper bag blown up, ready to be popped. A loud strangled-cat sound slid from his lips. Big, juicy, panic-fueled tears rolled down his cheeks. If the kid didn't calm down, we weren't going to have a choice about who knew what. The whole school would know. We might as well have put an announcement over the school P.A.

"Shhh," Mikey hissed. "If you don't stop, then everyone will hear. I don't want those buglies back here looking at me."

Stevie didn't hear a word. He continued to wail, which caused Mikey to look more annoyed and increase the volume of his shushes. This was turning into a mini-disaster of a cover-up. Mikey tried again, this time more forcefully, pushing his hand over Stevie's mouth, and through gritted teeth his words sounded like he was some kind of a gangster.

"Calm down, Stevie. Zip your mouth. You're okay. We're not telling. You just gotta calm."

Stevie wasn't hearing him. His eyes were crazy marbles rolling in their sockets like the beating had knocked the orbs loose. Now his breathing was panicked. In-out. In-out. The blue of his lips and white of his face, suggested he wasn't giving the oxygen enough time to get to his lungs.

What I did next was instinctive. He needed my help. My hand reached out to him and I grabbed one of his flailing arms. The words, "Stevie, calm down. You need—" were all I managed, before an avalanche of emotion hit me and I felt as though I was tumbling down a slope, miles high, gathering speed as I fell. Fear, upset and outrage sparked through my hands, then my body. Orange, red, indigo: colors I'd never before seen in troubles. As they shimmered and sparkled under my skin, coursing through my veins, I panicked too. An emotional electric jolt I was unprepared to handle had hit me full force.

Like never before and never since, the emotional power literally knocked me off my feet. I was under the basin, my head smashed against the pipe below. Bright lights circled around me like a multi-colored moving tunnel. Just as I marveled at the colors, the tunnel became a velvet-black with twinkling, jagged, fissures stretching far ahead. *Death,* I thought. *In a bathroom. Mama would be upset.*

Then hands were on me. They pulled at my arms, and I felt myself traveling through the tunnel at light speed toward cracks of light glowing above me. I wasn't dying, I realized to my relief, just momentarily unconscious.

And if Mikey had just left me, nothing would have happened. We would have simply looked back on this day and probably, as time went on, laughed at how I was taken down by a basin. But Mikey being ever-helpful Mikey, grabbed my arm to help. As he did, the turmoil of energy, the panic, and every last ounce of trouble I'd collected from Stevie and anyone else that day, shot from me to him like the explosion of the biggest damn firecracker you'd ever seen.

I knew something bad had happened from the snap in my head, like giant hands had smashed together. When I looked up, Mikey was enveloped in a blue glow, like a ghostly cloud of fairy dust. His star-tled face froze in an image of horror like he'd just seen his worst nightmare. Or felt his worst nightmare.

Poor Mikey. The kid with the perfect family, the kid who was loved unconditionally and wanted for nothing, who'd never experienced the kind of achy childhood Stevie endured—to which he'd gradually learned to adapt, as kids do—suddenly copped everything. Whammo. All Stevie's anguished and conflicted years invaded Mikey in one single shock.

The energy had knocked me on my ass, for him the impact must have been like a truck had struck him. He no longer stood above me, but as though slapped by the hand of an invisible giant, he slammed backward, smashing a cubicle door inward. The door whacked the thin wall behind like the crack of a whip.

Mikey landed on the floor, his back against the bowl of the toilet. He clutched at his chest like a heart attack victim, and then stared down, eyes wide, unblinking, as though looking for a bullet wound. His mouth opened and shut, opened and shut like he had words, but had forgotten how to get them from his brain to his lips.

I scrambled across the floor to him, reaching out, thinking I might be able to take them back, calm him down, make everything right again.

"Mikeee," I called. "You okay?"

Behind me, Stevie, free of his troubles, joined in.

"Yeah, Mikey, you don't look too good. What's wrong?"

That was an understatement. Mikey looked bad. The white face of seconds ago had turned a peach red like a fire had ignited from within. Agony etched his contorted face. Glistening tears rolled down his flushed cheeks to pool beneath his nose and chin. I was reminded of a baby throwing a tantrum, although Mikey wasn't in there anymore. He'd become a vessel filled with terror and emotion.

"Don't know," he said. "What happ ... ened. Feel, no, ... don't feel like me. Don't feel right."

"It's okay," I soothed, holding my hands just above him. Even at a distance, I felt heat on my skin. Touching him again was out of the question. Anything might happen.

As though imaginary strings controlled him, Mikey grabbed the toilet seat and hoisted himself up effortlessly to stand above me. He stared blankly through the open door at the wall ahead above the basin. Now a boy who had the look on his face I'd seen in horror movie characters, the ones who were about to die. He leaped over me, as I still sat on the floor, like I was nothing more than a large carton, and disappeared out the bathroom door. Stevie and I had no time to stop him.

Alone suddenly, we looked at each other. Stevie, despite his tear and blood-streaked face, looked as together as I'd ever seen him. The shock and my troubles keeping must have knocked the panic out of him. He leaned over and held out his hand to help me up.

I stared at the offered hand, but I'd learned my lesson. "Nah, I'm good," I said, shaking my head. Quickly, I climbed to my feet and together we ran after Mikey like we had a race to win.

Now as I sat with Daniel, recalling that day as though the events had happened merely hours before, I realized, perhaps there had been a sense of someone at the door as we ran past. I was so focused on catching Mikey, everything around me had disappeared in a blur of motion.

I stopped talking and stared at the man who knew too much about me and my gift, and a shock of recognition traveled across time.

In my mind, I turned to look at the shadowy figure standing just up the hall as we stampeded from the bathroom. I saw Daniel Starsey off to the side. The image of him back down the hall near the lockers had been buried as unimportant beneath what ensued in the next few minutes.

"That was you."

He smiled a knowing smile. This time it wasn't touched with enthusiasm; instead his eyes filled with sadness.

"Yes," he said. "That was me."

43

"I don't understand," I said to Daniel. "Why wouldn't you say something? After everything that happened, you didn't say anything. Didn't talk to me. Why?"

"I've thought on the same question all these years. Lived with the guilt of remaining quiet. If I'd just grabbed Mikey, stopped him maybe. I did call out, but you just kept running. I think I said something inane, like 'What's your rush? It'll keep.' If I'd followed you even and your other friend—what was his name again?"

"Stephen Graham. We called him Stevie."

"Yes, Stephen Graham. If I'd come after you, instead of thinking another teacher could solve the problem. I was a laid-back kind of young guy then, and I'd selfishly thought if whatever was happening was important, then I'd be the one writing up the report. If. If. If. *If's* will drive you mad. I didn't know what I'd seen, and if I'm being honest, I think I was afraid."

"Afraid? Of three kids?"

"Not afraid of you boys. No, I was afraid of what I saw. I'd been walking along the hall toward the bathroom, maybe ten yards away, when I saw a blue flash of light. Initially I thought there must be an electrical fault. I'd just gotten a few yards from the door when Mikey

Hale ran out in the opposite direction. Then you and Stephen followed straight after. You and Mikey were what stopped me. There was this weird blue glow about you both. First him, then you. I can remember thinking, 'What the hell kind of paint does that?' Followed by, 'What the hell *mess* had you made in there?'

"You ran, I thought, because you heard me coming. So first, I checked the bathroom. Other than puddles on the floor though, there was no explanation for the light. So I did go looking for you. I know kids can be kids, so I wasn't in any hurry. If only I had been, maybe I could have done something."

He looked wistful and even more grieved. I'd beaten myself up for years after but eventually I'd come to terms with the randomness of fate. Necessary when you have my talent.

"Don't blame yourself," I offered. "What occurred wasn't your fault. They were just dumb random events piled on top of each other starting with Stevie actually. No, really, everything began with the buglies. If not for them, nothing would have begun. The funny thing is, now I don't even remember their names."

Daniel moved uncomfortably in his chair as though he had just realized he'd sat on a patch of prickles.

"I appreciate you saying that, but I guess what happened after changes you forever. Least for me it did. I did my own investigation of what happened after you ran from the bathroom. I knew about the bullies and I know you never reported them. I thought bullying was the reason Mikey did what he did. I thought they'd attacked him and Stevie. But that's not what happened. Mikey, by all accounts, was the last kid alive who'd kill himself. That's what happened ... suicide, right? The police labeled his death an accident, but they didn't see what I saw."

"No, I don't believe he killed himself," I said. "It *was* an accident. I guess a *purposeful* accident. He couldn't handle what happened. We tried to catch Mikey but he ran like crazy. Maybe he heard us behind him and didn't see the car?"

"I know that's what you told the authorities, the principal, everyone, but I know what I saw. He waited."

Then I was back there, next to Stevie, both of us calling out to Mikey, who was just a little ahead, screaming, "Mikey, wait. Stop." I knew what he felt, what he might do. Not for certain, but I'd felt his feelings, his desperation, and I knew his head must be spinning and the emotional pain had taken a stranglehold on his mind.

Mikey turned back to us just for a moment. If you could call someone alive a ghost, he was that. His eyes were hollow, as though in just those few minutes his eyeballs had sunken inside his head. Black, bruised blotches colored beneath his eyes, like he'd run into a door.

He didn't acknowledge us, didn't say goodbye, wave or even say *sorry, I'm going to haunt your dreams forever.* I don't think he really saw us. I think he just saw a way out. Seconds after he looked at us, he turned to the road. He seemed to look left and right, like you should when crossing, then he just stepped out in front of the car and turned to face what would be his death.

I could still hear the sound of the brakes screaming like they, too, were terrified. Then the thick thud. Everything that followed felt highlighted in vivid color and slowed down for our viewing pleasure.

His crumpled body landed almost without a sound on the other side of the road. The blood on the hood of the car, rich, ketchup-sauce red against the pale cream enamel imprinted on my brain as we ran past toward him. The woman's face as she climbed out of the car, like she'd walked into a nightmare, staring at us as though we were ghosts. The way Mikey's body lay sprawled, one arm swung across his stomach like he had an ache there, the other above his head, twisted and broken. His head though made us both turn instantly and retch by the side of our friend. The skull had cracked open, right across his forehead, just like an egg. A horrible pool of blood surrounded his head like a pearly, red picture frame. His hair, matted with the blood, for once sat back off his face. His eyes gawped, motionless, across to the stationery car as though to say: *There lies the cause of this.*

Of course, I was the cause of this. Me, my troubles keeping, and the naivety of youth.

The driver claimed Mikey had just stepped out in front of the car and she couldn't stop. What happened was just a terrible accident. We said nothing, too traumatized by what had happened. Anyway, who would believe an eleven-year-old kid would purposely step out in front of a car?

Support hovered over Stevie and me: counselors, priests, teachers, and my parents. Stevie's life was already a big, steaming mess. He seemed to get over just about anything quickly and he appeared to absorb the nightmare as just another *thing* added to his collection of dark childhood mementos.

We never talked about that day together, but sometimes when we passed the spot where he died, I saw something in his eyes. He knew. Like I knew. A terrible thing had gotten into Mikey and that thing wasn't from this world, well, not the world he understood. Within a day, he was back to his old self; loud and talkative Stevie, but now he seemed to watch the world as though at any moment the very air might transform into something that would bite him.

Dr. Katie Ambrose, the school psychologist, gave me coping tools I still use to this day. "Terrible events," she said, in that quiet, gentle voice of hers, "are sometimes not for us to understand. We must put them away somewhere and drain their energy so we can give good energy to our lives." She never knew how true were those words.

Daniel Starsey's voice overlaid the memory of Dr. Ambrose. "What happened was a terrible event," he said, "but his death was no accident."

"How much did you see?" I asked, meeting his stare as I reached over and picked up the near-empty water glass and drained the last few drops. My tongue felt raw and dry and I really needed a drink.

"Most everything. I saw Mikey step out and the car hit him. From where I was, he looked to wait for the car. I was the one who called for help. Clearly he needed medical attention, and I thought better to get help, before coming to you. Then a crowd appeared in minutes, and I thought they didn't need another body in the way."

He stared at me as if looking for more answers. I met his stare. "Mr. Starsey, what do you want from me? That was years ago. Why now?"

"Time's relative. Seems like yesterday to me. That day I knew what I'd seen, or I worked out later what I'd seen. Then I began watching you. You weren't like any child I'd ever met. My curiosity was a drug. I never got too close. I wasn't even sure if you weren't some kind of weapon. I know, based on what you really do, that's kind of funny. I couldn't tell anyone or they'd think witnessing a traumatic event had made me delusional. But I saw what you had Rory. You had, have, a gift. I saw how sometimes when kids were upset or worried, you'd touch them, their arm, their hand, their head, and the reaction was immediate. Suddenly they'd calm. The crying ones didn't shed another tear, like they'd forgot what had upset them. I knew I was witness to something incredible."

"A very long time ago," I offered. Why was he only now sharing this knowledge? Until I knew the answer, I had to move with caution.

"Maybe, but fate brought me to you again," he said. "And there was the other night, wasn't there? You have a power. You take something negative and help people. With Mikey, something went wrong. I've been researching ever since. You, that day, Mikey's death, this is what got me involved in physics. More precisely, high energy physics. Particle physics, I guess, in layman's terms. For a decade, I've studied the subatomic elements of matter and radiation and their interactions. You'd find the science fascinating stuff. I've got a feeling you probably don't realize what you do is grounded in science. To most, you would seem to possess a kind of psychic ability."

"So I'm like a science experiment gone wrong?"

Daniel laughed. "No, I think you're a conduit. I was so in awe of what I saw you do, I stopped teaching a year later, completed a master degree in biology and quantum physics and a PhD in molecular biology. All because of that day and you and the blue light. I wanted to understand exactly how you do what you do. To do that I needed to understand the world on a molecular level."

My curiosity burned. I never imagined there could be a logical, well, scientific reason why I had this ability. Over the years, this way of life had become second nature and I no longer wondered or cared. Troubles keeping was what I did. That was that.

"Did you figure out how I work?"

"I've a pretty good theory."

"Even if I admit to what you think you saw, even if everything was true and I had this ability, why have you waited all these years to contact me? Why now?"

He leaned forward, pausing before he spoke. The room seemed to shrink around us; the light in his eyes moments before, gone.

"Because I think you're in terrible danger. If my theory proves correct, and I'm almost certain I'm right, then the world is also at risk. I mentioned string theory before, but do you know what it is?"

I shook my head. "No."

"Only the theory of everything, of how the universe operates, how everything from a sub-atomic particle to a planet behaves. How life exists. The concept is complicated and simple, all at once. But first, this also involves your girlfriend."

"My girlfriend?"

"Yes, Mariana Brown. I've been following her for a while. Finding you was just a lucky happenstance."

"She's not my girlfriend." Her smiling face as I'd said goodbye last night flashed in my mind. "Well, not yet."

"Well, your girlfriend-to-be, also, is very special. I could explain why in physics and formulas, but it boils down to this: She's as special as you, but in a different way. She's part of a puzzle. Both of you are like keys that fit into the DNA of the world, if you will. Without you, the energy circulating in the world isn't balanced. With Mariana though, she's like a membrane between dark and light. Something dark needs her to complete their own puzzle. My thoughts are—"

Something dark.

I abruptly interrupted him. "You mean the Trepan Killer, don't you?"

"Yes, except he's not a killer. Not in the sense of the word as we understand. He's something else altogether. Another part of the way the world works is the best I can explain. We must hurry though. The best thing for now is to get to Mariana. I'll explain everything to both of you then."

I had so many questions, but I couldn't deny my gut told me everything he'd said made a strange sense. Without acknowledging I agreed with everything he'd told me, I stood and said, "If she's in danger, we must go."

Daniel Starsey rose. "I hoped you'd say that." Then, as we both headed for the door, he added like an enthusiastic fan, "I've a thousand questions for you Rory."

"Ditto Mr. Starsey. Ditto."

44

A memory returns from a murky past, swimming on the periphery of his knowledge. He hesitates because something else has come, something disturbing, causing his concentration to become foggy. A buzzing is in his head where there is usually clear, sharp thoughts building since the woman at the bus depot. He thinks back to when the sensation began, when he had touched the needles he'd inserted into her brain. A sound had come like a screaming banshee, tearing into him. He had fallen backward, his hands groping at his head. Dizziness had swamped him along with feelings of confusion.

Something had thrown everything out of balance.

He had struggled back, pulling himself forward to her. He reached out to one of the needles, seated so carefully in the anterior fontanelle toward the center of her skull, the sweet baby's spot as he always thought of the position. This was the place where everything that was her would have helped him toward his goal. Some helped more than others. His fingertips had enclosed the needle's head, and again the sound had come, increasing in pitch until he felt pain. Then, as though the needle had vibrated through the skin of his fingertips, he had felt fine shards in his blood; cold and sharp. He had snatched back his hand in surprise.

Something had gone wrong. Something had gone *very* wrong. So he'd left, alarmed and wanting to be away from her, so he could think on this new development.

He leans against the wall of his small apartment, his sanctuary against the small-minded creatures who live their lives outside not seeing what is right beneath their noses (or really in the very air around them). What has he missed? What has changed?

He thinks about The One and the bus driver, and now this, which must be a sign. A force, an energy of some type has been initiated as though the three of them are ingredients that, once combined, will give birth to something completely new. And powerful. Control of his victims' bodies with a mere thought is certainly a useful new talent but, until now, what never occurred to him is that he might not be the only one with a new faculty with which to play.

Something pushed back at him through the woman at the depot. He would normally find this fascinating—the multiplier effect— except now he is less certain of what he faces.

He sees more than he has ever seen before, as though he is connected to the future as well as the past, but he doesn't like these changes when he is so near to success. Something is misaligned and he knows this isn't good. He feels them coming, becoming aware. Quite possibly he's squandered his advantage, his ability to see more than them, his knowledge of what lies beyond. And he just wants to go home, to where he belongs and that gives him the strength to move.

Soon is all that consumes his thoughts.

45

Daniel insisted we travel together to Mariana's apartment. By now it was near nine-thirty. After the trip down memory lane my mind had returned, as always, to her. The why of her absence at the bus stop earlier had grown into a nagging doubt that I had made a mistake and should have gone to her first. The confident feeling I had had before, that she was okay, was fading rapidly.

Daniel as an ally and his apparent desire to help gave me some confidence. Although, if he came with me to Mariana's, he might convince her I wasn't one of nature's freaks. His conviction was compelling. A sneaking doubt played in my mind: Was he involved with the killer and here I was foolishly leading him to Mariana, giving him easy access? So I refused to leave my bike behind and was just as adamant he follow me.

Mariana lived a five-minute drive from the depot; I always felt this was a stroke of lucky geography. Once she'd boarded, she remained on my bus for almost the rest of the run. That's why as we neared Mariana's apartment, fate intervened. My mind had entered auto-pilot as I took the time alone to ponder Daniel's revelations and, out of habit, I turned toward the depot. Only as I neared the perimeter fence, which ran the boundary of the premises, did I realize my mistake.

I knew something was wrong. There was no reason for me to think this. I'd never been psychic in the sense of *I can tell future* or anything close. Yet, as I drew near my workplace, tiny, little lights, which reminded me of fireflies, flitted across my vision. A pain had invaded my head, as though I'd driven through toxic fumes, the kind that gave you an instant headache. I knew in this second I needed to stop. Beth Ann needed my help.

Something was going on inside my head, something that had begun the minute I'd picked up the dark thing. I hadn't had a chance to think everything through, but I'd begun to realize, somehow, I didn't always need to touch someone to feel their troubles. The air swam for me with the emotions, an unseen current of sensation. I'd noticed after this happened impressions of people's lives would travel through my mind.

With so much going on I'd dismissed the random thoughts, telling myself this most likely was my way of processing all that had happened in such a short space of time. I'd felt something, a kind of knowing, last night with Mariana, but I'd put the sense down to the intense emotions of being with her.

The ringing in my ears now felt like a warning, a kind of Spidey sense shouting at me to stop, go help Beth Ann. What had happened, I didn't know. All I knew: She needed me.

Lights blazing in her office way past civil working hours was not unusual, but she'd assured me she would go straight home.

"Migraine coming on. As soon as you're out of my hair, I'm heading home to bed."

So why would she be there all these hours later when security was her big thing? Nobody would be allowed in her office in her absence. At this time of night, the only people on site were two mechanics servicing the buses, getting ready for the next day. They would be in the garage, a large shed out back, a hundred or so yards from the offices. Why would they be in the office? That made no sense.

Daniel followed me and I motioned back to him that I would turn into the yard. Moments later I pulled up at the side of the office and Daniel parked alongside. Beth Ann's car was there, but the blinds of the large glass window, from which she normally kept an eye on the comings and goings, were closed. My sense of dread grew.

"What's happening?" Daniel asked, as he joined me at the door to the office. "Shouldn't we be getting to Mariana's?"

As we walked around to the front the crunch of the asphalt beneath our shoes, loud in the dead quiet, echoed as though we were inside a massive box.

"I don't know, call me crazy, but something's not right here. I just had this odd feeling I needed to check on my boss. She shouldn't be here. Maybe a break-in."

A few yards away, a yellow sliver of light along the edge of the entry revealed the door lay slightly ajar. My newly discovered buzzing firefly sense now fired on super-strength as I pushed open the door and entered. Before I'd even put a foot inside, the sensation hit me like a thwack somewhere in my mind's recesses: Somebody who wasn't meant to be here had intruded. A pervasive darkness filled my head, rushing over me like a wave of bad, putrid air.

I reached out to Daniel and put my hand across his chest to stop him from taking another step. "Something's wrong here."

"Or," he replied, "someone's simply left the lights on."

I lowered my voice to just above a whisper. "No, that's not what happened. Maybe lights left on mean nothing, but not lights on and door open in this particular office."

The reception area looked perfectly normal. Two dated, worn material-covered chairs separated by a small, chipped, wood-laminate table looked untouched. Behind the front counter stood three desks, their chairs pushed neatly beneath, the domain of the small band of office staff who worked alongside Beth Ann. Blank computer screens stood as silent witnesses, surrounded by stacked trays of papers, empty coffee cups and personal nick knacks.

The room looked so normal. Something was off. The atmosphere just didn't *feel* normal.

I walked past the counter and the desks toward Beth Ann's office in back. The door was slightly ajar, just like the entrance, but only a dim light shone beneath, as though there was just a desk lamp on inside. That wasn't right either. She would never leave her door unlocked. The safe was in there and she was a stickler for procedures and security. Even if she was in there, with just a lamp, the radio would be on.

"Music makes the world go 'round," she would say, even though refugee-from-the-eighties Beth Ann was the last person you'd suspect of loving hip hop and the latest tunes. That dial never moved from XKR100.1 'The Hits before they're Hits.'

The room sounded unoccupied, but I knew that wasn't true. The fireflies buzzed a warning. These sensations were new, but I somehow interpreted the message.

I felt Daniel behind me, but all I saw was the door growing larger, darker, more threatening as the buzz grew to a deafening roar calling to me. *Come in here Rory and your life will change.* My life had transformed enough these two days and I wasn't particularly anxious for anything more. But Beth Ann might be in there hurt, needing my help.

Fluorescent lights hummed overhead joining with the firefly buzz like they were part of an orchestra; music from instrument laid over instrument until they created something recognizable. Who the conductor was, I didn't know. All I knew was that I was the audience.

I pushed at the door. Something cold and dark awaited behind there, I knew this as a certainty. I didn't fight the thought or try to reason the idea away. The door hid a terror I must face.

The door swung open and I flicked the wall switch. Light overwhelmed the room, and I saw her immediately. I didn't stagger backward, even though the strength in my knees had dissolved. I didn't cry out; I took the scene in like you accept the fantasy of a dream as your reality. Because even before I saw her, I knew what I would see. The buzzing fireflies had shown me. Beth Ann was there behind her desk, but she wasn't about to greet me with a smile and witty quip.

The woman I thought of as a second mom sat strapped to a high-backed black chair, held upright by gray-silver duct tape. Empty eyes stared at me, fear embedded in them, so tangible I felt dragged inside her pain. Her scalp and face were ravaged, her skin peeled back around the circular wound, which oozed fresh and now-congealing blood down her cheeks. Blood had dripped from her face to pattern the front of her shirt. Protruding from the circular wound were a half dozen thin, silver needles.

The violence and atrocity stopped me for a second, as though I'd hit an invisible barrier. You cannot enter, you must watch in captive horror. I knew this was about me. A nasty little present left as a calling card. *For you,* the message said. He wanted this terror and chaos and he wanted me afraid.

"Oh ,my, God, she's alive."

The voice was Daniel's. Then I saw what he saw. A flicker of an eyelid, a slight rolling of an eyeball, like she was about to have a fit. I was across the room in three strides, bending to her, searching her eyes.

"Beth Ann, can you hear me?" She stared up at me, barely breathing, her eyes fixed, not on my face but somewhere above my head, like she saw something there standing over me. I turned but saw nothing. No ethereal creature, no dancing blue lights, even my fireflies had lowered their drone.

"You'll be okay," I kept repeating.

From behind, Daniel said, "I'm calling an ambulance."

I touched her arm, urgently pulling at the fear and terror within her, bracing myself to accept whatever came. The pain and horror fled inside as though they were desperate to escape, to find a haven away from this poor, haunted woman. The sturdiest box I could imagine awaited. I funneled all the emotions inside within moments, slamming down the lid with all the force I possessed. I stood in the attic studying the box, hoping this wasn't another version of the dark thing. The box glowed a deep burgundy, then faded to pale crimson, then a light apricot, then was gone like a torch run out of battery. A dark and agonizing trouble? Yes. But a dark thing? No.

Immediately Beth Ann calmed; the fear on her face dulled, but her eyes never left mine. I saw she knew I'd done something. Later I'd work out how to explain.

"It's okay, Beth Ann, you'll be alright. Help's coming," I said, frantically pulling at the tape to free her arms, then the restraint across her chest. Her mouth opened and closed as though she was trying to talk. Once free, I held her limp body against the chair. She seemed to have lost any control. Maybe this due to shock, or perhaps the effects of a drug. Or something else I couldn't put my finger on, but the firefly feeling tingled again.

"Don't try to talk. You're safe."

The needles protruded from her forehead, like they were part of a hideous pincushion. The Trepan Killer was sick, truly evil, but then I already knew this from my up-close-and-personal.

I kept talking to Beth Ann, soothing her, assuring her she would be okay. I hoped my voice concealed the tremor of anger pulsing in my heart. From behind me I heard Daniel on the phone with the authorities, his voice urgent and tense.

I was so focused on Beth Ann, when his hand crushed into my shoulder, I jumped. In a whisper in my ear, so Beth Ann couldn't hear, he said, "She's in a bad way. I think we should move her, maybe. Lay her down. At least we can immobilize her head."

Together we carefully moved her from the chair and lay her limp body on the floor. Daniel held her head gently, with a hand on each side, over her ears. The needles looked angry and precarious, and I prayed they hadn't caused brain damage.

Terrible as that would be, at least she had a chance, unlike my passenger Sandra Swift. Two people connected to me, targeted by the Trepan Killer. I examined the facts. This was my fault. Somehow, whether because of Mariana or the dark thing, the killer and I were entwined. My tingling little fireflies told me so. How though? Only the killer knew the answer.

Emotions welled, a torrent of fear and anguish pushing at me.

"I gotta take a moment," I managed to gasp as I stood, my hand wiping across my face.

"Yes, of course," said Daniel.

I walked toward the door and stood with my head resting against the wall. The room disappeared and I was in the attic standing at the box where I'd stowed Beth Ann's troubles. Seemingly such a simple thing to capture these emotions and hide them away. Thank goodness I was here to do this, to help Beth Ann. Right now though, I needed to be with Mariana. I should have gone there first and not to Daniel's. The sense I had before that I needed to follow my intuition disappeared and I crumpled to the ground. What if the killer had been the one who had led me on a wild goose chase, first to Daniel's and then to here?

Then the answer struck me, even more terrifying: I was exactly where he wanted me. An image of Mariana flew into my mind and I felt the air vibrate, then begin to close in as pressure built about me. I pushed against the unseen force with everything I had, until I felt the tightness lessen. I felt surrounded by the dark thing. The evil wasn't gone; a sense of something lingered, more powerful than before the guardian had banished the first horror A terrible scent remained with Beth Ann like a calling card.

I opened my eyes in a rush. Daniel Starsey stood over me, his face knotted with worry.

"Rory. Rory? Are you back with us? What's happening? The medics are coming in now."

"Danie—" I couldn't finish, because the fireflies buzzed again. So beautiful, so golden and yet so urgent.

Danger. Terrible danger. The words repeated in my head.

"Don't talk Rory. There's time." I heard Daniel's words in the distance, but I was mesmerized by the words of the fireflies.

I strangled out the word "Danger." He didn't understand my meaning, what I'd learned.

"Your boss will be okay," he continued. "I'm sure she will. You too. You're not, we're not in danger right at this moment."

Only I knew what needed to be done. "No. No, not ... me. Not Beth Ann."

"What Rory? Take it easy. You've had quite a shock."

"No, we must go. You were right."

"Right?"

"Mariana. She's in terrible danger. Something stopped him here before he'd finished and he's not happy. I don't know how I stopped him, but something's changed. Something with me has changed too, and that's what saved Beth Ann."

"How?" said Daniel.

"I don't know," I said, honestly. "But I'd better find out. Pretty sure this talent that I didn't know I had will be needed again."

46

We were gone before the medics had even begun attending Beth Ann. I felt she would be okay, but there was no time to wait and be sure. Later I could check. Right now, my focus was on getting to Mariana.

We bolted from the building. From behind, I heard Daniel's breath as he tried to keep up with my pace. As we arrived at my bike and Daniel's car, I made a quick decision.

"We should go together," I said, as I ran around to the driver's side. I held out my hand. "Give me the keys. I'll drive. We'll be quicker."

Daniel stared at me for a moment before throwing the keys toward me. I caught them and, for a few moments, fumbled with the unfamiliar lock. All I could think about was Mariana, and that gave me darn nervous fingers.

This was no random act. The killer had left Beth Ann where I could find her, where I could be delayed. He'd learned about me via the dark thing. I understood that now. Perhaps what he hadn't factored was somehow the knowledge went both ways. I now understood more about him.

Images like jumbled pieces of a shattered jigsaw traveled around in my brain. I tried to piece them together, but they didn't fit, as though the pieces had no grounding in life. Whatever he was, the killer didn't think or operate like a normal human being. Like Chris Lamben had said, Mariana was the key or a window or something else. *Window* was the wrong word. More like an interface. I still hadn't worked out what this meant, but messages seemed to be filtering through; I just had to learn how to catch them and understand their meaning.

"What's going on? You look like you saw a ghost, like you were in a trance. I thought you'd fainted," said Daniel, as I pulled out of the lot.

"I can't explain what happened very well. Seems more like *seeing* than feeling an emotion. Kind of like knowing something now that I didn't know before, but nobody told me. I didn't get everything either. Snatches, at the most. Mariana has something the Trepan Killer needs. This is all I know. And he's not planning to take what he wants by asking politely. We need to get to her, then get somewhere safe until I can work this out."

"I think I know what he wants," Daniel said.

I glanced across. He stared straight ahead, lips tight and his brow furrowed.

"What? You need to tell me everything you know. No more alluding."

"That won't help."

"What won't help?"

"Getting her to somewhere safe. You don't know what you're up against."

"Something to do with a window or, maybe, like an interface?"

My focus returned to the road; a couple with a dog strolled along the sidewalk. A man on a bicycle rode beside us before falling behind. Everything looked normal outside. No darkness, no weird other worldly creatures flying through the night sky. Yet I felt as though something was about to pounce. I knew Daniel had kept some knowledge from me. I didn't know what and I didn't know why.

He hesitated before answering. "Maybe a window, of sorts. That's an interesting take. More accurately, I believe you're dealing with a sub-atomic anomaly. I hadn't finished explaining why I left teaching to study science. When I witnessed Mikey's death, then observed you those weeks after, I realized everything I knew about the world, the laws of physics, no longer made sense. There were other powers intervening that I'd never imagined."

"Still, what does Mariana have to do with any of this? Please."

"Her molecular makeup is unique, like a freak of nature. Think of her as a light bulb. Without electricity applied to the bulb, you only have a piece of glass with a filament or gas inside. Nothing spectacular and apparently serving no purpose. Apply an electrical charge and suddenly you have a chain reaction, agitating the gas or heating the filament. The result? We have light. The light bulb becomes a whole different object."

I began to understand what he meant and the puzzle parts fell into place.

"She's a conduit. That's what he's looking for. Someone who's a closed circuit for the energy. Like the light bulb."

"Exactly. You're similar, but slightly different, like diverse breeds of birds, if that makes sense. Varied singular channels for the current. You, with what you do, are like a filter or transistor that feeds energy away. I watched you do your thing so many times at school. I didn't understand what you were doing at first but later, years later, I began to understand. The day Mikey died, I believe you drew in all of Stevie's fear and emotion, then accidentally dumped all that negative energy into Mikey. His mind became a balloon stretched too far and literally exploded."

"An interesting theory," I said, thinking this concept made as much sense as anything I'd ever thought myself.

"You've learned to control your ability since, built your own resistors, so to speak, to control the energy."

"I've come to terms with the gift. I'm careful," I said, but as I spoke, the thought crossed my mind, how had he *noticed* anything about me?

I turned to ask the question, but the buzzing returned in my brain, the fireflies had risen en masse. They circled before my eyes, obliterating everything around me in their golden glow, which abruptly transformed into a whirling flash. I tried to return my focus to the road ahead, but the view moved in and out of perspective like a distant mirage momentarily blinding me.

Then my sight settled and I was at the entry to Mariana's street, but the car was moving too fast for the corner. Removing my foot from the accelerator to push on the brake didn't work. In fact, the action seemed near impossible. The pedal fought back every time I attempted to release the pressure, like invisible glue held my foot down.

The back of the vehicle began to swing out and the world moved sideways. I played with the wheel, attempting to wrest back control, but a determined power fought me. The car began to fishtail wildly and there was no way of stopping what came next.

A parked sedan filled my vision as though the vehicle had miraculously arrived via a time portal. I knew we would hit, no matter what I tried to do. I pulled madly at the wheel in the hope I could do something, but I had nothing. The world was moving too fast, I realized, even if I could move my foot. I braced, gripping, white-knuckled.

Daniel cried "Oh, my God," before the sound of the impact wiped out anything else he might have said. We hit the car before careening off to the other side of the road. A wagon awaited us there in the perfect spot for our car to sideswipe down every panel of one side. The sickening sound of shattering glass and metal tearing on metal enveloped us. We were spinning in the worst dodge-'em ride ever. My first thought: *Who will protect Mariana if we don't survive?*

Through all of this, I determinedly kept at my attempts to move my foot to the brake. As we skidded onward from the wagon at dangerous speed, the pressure released and my foot came free enough to skim across to the brake. I threw my entire weight on the pedal until we came to a sudden stop. My body flung forward as though hurled from a height. The sound of the exploding airbags filled the cabin, and if not for them and the seatbelt, I hate to think where Daniel and I may have landed. An instant sharp pain flared at the back of my neck, and I reached behind to feel if anything had pierced there, but there was nothing. Whiplash probably.

I looked over at Daniel. Blood trickled from a cut across his forehead and his arms looked grazed and already showing signs of bruising, maybe from hitting the dash. He didn't look like he was bleeding badly though. The window beside him had come off worse. The pane had shattered and hundreds of small pieces covered his lap and the foot well below. A spider web of cracks spread out across the windshield making viewing through to the outside impossible.

"Are you okay? Your head?"

His hand rose above the airbag to his forehead, his fingers prodding at the injury. He pulled them away sharply and looked down at his bloodied fingertips.

"Ow. I think so. Hurts, but I'm okay." He felt around his arms and chest. "Am I bleeding anywhere else?"

I studied him for a moment. "No. Other than a cut above your eye, I think you're okay."

I unbuckled my belt and pushed at the airbag sitting in my lap as I twisted in my seat to face the door. A stroke of luck; the door seemed undamaged. I pulled the handle and shoved. The door opened halfway, albeit, with a grinding complaint. Once outside, I saw the back end, right hand side of the car had buckled from the impact. We were lucky to have not come off worse but the car was a mess. Drivable, but not in great shape.

Quickly I moved to the other side and pulled at Daniel's door. My neck burned, reminding me to be careful. *I'd be careful later.* Now I had to hurry and get Daniel out; we needed to get inside the building. I pulled again, throwing my weight against the panel as Daniel heaved from the inside. The door wouldn't budge. The passenger side had taken more of the impact's brunt and the door had buckled inward on the hinges.

"You'll have to get out the driver's side," I said. "No-go here."

Daniel clambered across and, with my help, was out of the car thirty seconds later. I was already turned and moving toward the steps of the entrance to Mariana's apartment block. I wanted to get away from the accident. Someone would invariably call police and then we would waste too much time with what followed.

We needed to get to Mariana immediately. Something had caused my concentration to waver and then prevented me from controlling the car. Something didn't want me to get to her.

Jabbing my finger on Mariana's buzzer, I ignored the impolite ten o'clock hour to be calling on someone.

"Maybe she's not home," said Daniel, when there was no answer.

I pressed again. That's when the panic truly set in. What if *he'd* gotten to her and she was inside, her skull torn open? The image of Beth Ann's terrified eyes searching mine became Mariana's eyes.

I turned to face Daniel. "Where is she? God, *where is she?*"

But he wasn't behind me anymore. He stood a few feet away at the locked glass door entrance to the apartments. In his hand was a small electronic device, which at first glance looked like a mini-iPad. This one though, had three small metal antenna attachments sprouting from the top. Daniel's finger swiped around a mid-screen digital dial. Numbers ran around the circumference like a tachometer.

As he moved his fingertips around, lights followed his touch. Then the dial turned green, and he stood back and held the device toward the door. After pressing a button at the bottom of the device, a small buzzing sound emitted. I heard Daniel count down from five under his breath. At *one,* a row of numbers and letters printed out on the screen but from where I stood I couldn't make them out exactly.

"She's been here recently," said Daniel.

"How could you know?"

He turned to face me, holding out the instrument. "This! The SQUID. Super-conducting quantum intercept device."

"Okay, now in normal non-scientific people talk. SQUID?"

Daniel hit a few more keys and the electronic thing emitted a beeping sound. As he held the iPad-like thing to the door, he continued to talk.

"Yes, the science is complicated; that's why I named my invention SQUID; less of a mouthful. The short version: this device picks up energy signals on a sub-atomic level. That's the quantum intercept part. Same way you can draw in the negative energy from others, this measures energy resonance. This is how I found Mariana and then, as a side discovery, you. I wasn't looking for you, or her, in fact. I was following him, the Trepan Killer. He has an energy B.E. Print I've never encountered."

"B.E. Print? Explain, please." I looked at the door. "And hurry."

"Yes, I know we need to hurry. I just need another thirty seconds." He continued to watch the screen as he spoke.

"One of my research grants funded a study on the energy field of murder victims. The theory is there may be a way to identify a murderer by their bio-energy imprint—B.E. Print for short. Actually a variance of Kirlian photography, which is basically a method of filming life force or life energy, dating back to the mid-1900's. Some research claims the equipment simply records the moisture content surrounding living objects and this has nothing to do with life force. I disagree. I've worked on the technology now for nearly a decade, and I believe pretty much perfected the science, although I can't seem to convince anyone. So I thought by finding and identifying the Trepan Killer I could prove my invention's value. But the concept came from you originally. I spent the next ten years after leaving school, studying and researching, so I could better understand you. This gadget is a byproduct of my research."

"But how do you know who owns the imprint?" Once I released troubles from the attic, I couldn't tell one from the other. They simply became a jumble of energy.

"No two people have the same bio-energy field. They are as unique as a fingerprint. I can tell how long since someone has passed by a geographical position based on the strength of the energy trace too."

"And the Trepan Killer?"

"Yes, that's how I came across you and then Mariana. I was tracking his B.E. Though his B.E. was like nothing I'd ever seen."

As he talked, he adjusted settings on the device.

"I have his imprint stored. If he's been here, his B.E. will be picked up by the SQUID. This is what I'm doing right now."

He continued to hold the device against the door. A steady stream of beeps emitted from the machine, like the sound of a high-pitched Geiger counter. Instead of crackling static, waves of quite a musical sound filled the air. Daniel pulled back the device and stared at the screen.

"And?" I asked, my heart racing as though also picking up energy emissions registering off the scale.

Daniel looked up at me, his face saying everything I didn't want to hear.

"Yes," he said. "He's been here."

47

My decision was obvious. Since Mariana wasn't answering, we had to, at the least, get inside the apartment block and to her door. Once there, I'd work out the next step.

I'd seen what I planned to do next in movies and I hoped this would work for me. I addressed the panel of thirty odd apartment buzzers and pressed them one-by-one as quickly as I could. Within a few seconds, the speaker crackled alive and tinny-sounding voices answered.

"Who's there?"

"What?"

"Yes?"

With each reply I said, "Allen here. Apartment twenty-three. Door key isn't working. Buzz me, please?"

Seven apartment owners answered before I heard a buzz from the door and the latch unlock. I swung around and rushed for the entrance. Daniel had moved through and held the door for me. The elevator wasn't our friend, taking forever to arrive and then an eternity to travel to her floor. I angled sideways through the opening doors even before they'd slid fully across.

Seconds later I was banging at Mariana's door, and I mean banging. The sound echoed loudly in the corridor, and I imagined if she didn't come to the door, a neighbor would be checking on us real soon.

I whispered to myself as though the words were a magical chant: *Let her be okay. Let her be okay. Please let her be okay.*

After waiting ten, fifteen seconds, there was no answer.

Let her be okay, I repeated.

I banged again, my palm flattened against the door. Desperate now, I called, "Mariana. Mariana, it's Rory. Are you okay?"

Please let her be okay.

I turned to Daniel, panic in my voice. "What do we do? If she's in there, hurt ..."

My voice trailed off as the image of Beth Ann in her office, the needles and blood so vivid, morphed into Mariana. Now I imagined Mariana's face looking up at me in horror.

"One moment," said Daniel, moving past me to hold the SQUID to the door. Moments later—moments, which seemed an eternity—the machine beeped. He turned back to me, his mouth grim. What was he about to tell me? The killer had been here? The readings were off the scale? *What?*

She's okay, was all I wanted to know, all I wanted him to tell me, if his machine could even do that.

"Whhaaat?" I said, fear strangling the word so it sounded like a whispered scream.

Daniel raised an eyebrow as though I'd asked him a difficult question. His gaze traveled behind me down the corridor.

Something was there, behind me.

I swung about, my hands up, ready to fight, ready to defend my life, Mariana's, if she was alive inside. I was ready to face the Trepan Killer, ready to die if need be. I wasn't a fighter, but love turns you into a greater version of yourself.

All the breath was sucked from me. My hands dropped to my waist and my head shook from side to side, as though on auto-pilot. Words escaped me as they usually did when I saw her.

Mariana stood ten yards away, holding a cloth carry bag. A loaf of bread and a bunch of flowers peeked from inside. She wore the same puzzled look on her face as Daniel.

"Rory? *Rory?* What are you doing here? And how did you get into the building. It's nearly ten-thirty."

"Mariana. You don't know how glad I am to see you. I thought ... I thought something-had-happened."

"Happened? No, I'm okay."

"You weren't on the bus today."

"I know, I'm sorry. A customer came in just before closing and couldn't decide between two Beatles albums. I was the only one working and, well, of course, I didn't have your number. That was a real plan fail."

She then looked at Daniel, frowning. "And you brought a friend?"

"Oh, yes, this is Daniel Starsey," I said, nodding toward him. Then with a little pride, because even late at night, carrying groceries, her hair in messy tangles around her face, Mariana was still a breath-taking sight. "Daniel, this is Mariana."

Daniel leaped in. "Mariana, good to meet. But I'm afraid we don't have time for pleasantries. We shouldn't stay here. You ... we are in danger."

Mariana looked back at me, the worry line deepening in her forehead.

"We should listen to him, I think," I said. "He seems to have answers."

She looked back at Daniel, then returned her stare to me. "So, I run out of milk, slip out for groceries and somehow you have gotten inside my apartment block. And someone I've never met before in my life tells me we're in danger. Now I'm supposed to what? Run off with you in the middle of the night?"

I reached to touch her arm to assure her, but she pulled back.

"Uh-uh, I told you about that."

"Okay, then," I said, "trust your instincts. You know what you felt last night, what you felt on the bus. Something's going on and we are *both* involved."

She stared into my eyes for the longest time, then as though scolding a child, she said, "Rory Fine, you need to work on your courting skills. Excuse me, please."

This didn't sound good.

Mariana turned to her apartment door and, while juggling her groceries to her left hand, slid a key into the lock and stepped inside. Daniel and I looked at each other; his look matching mine: dumbfounded. How could she ignore our warning?

I opened my mouth to implore her again, but she turned, still holding her groceries in one hand and the edge of the door with the other. Her face looked serious as she sighed, short and sharp like when you blow out candles on a cake.

"If I'm in danger, then probably its best we don't stand in the hall. Now I think I *am* crazy, but I'm actually going to listen to you."

48

To Mariana's credit, after putting away her groceries she stood in the kitchen and listened. When I asked should we sit, she replied, "No, I do my best thinking standing. Comes from working in retail."

As Daniel explained his research and theories on sub-atomic particles, the special characteristics of life energy that the SQUID could detect, B.E. prints, and even showed her the readout from the Trepan Killer and how the energy signature differed from an average person, she took the information in and said nothing. When Daniel stopped, having explained everything, she contemplated the SQUID for long seconds, then asked a very good question.

"If I truly have an ability to do something with energy or move something from one dimension to another—and I'm not saying I believe any of this—why would this ability, and the killer or whatever he is, just appear now?"

I jumped in to deliver my thoughts. "Why did my troubles keeping only seem to start when I was about ten? There's no clear answers. What would make life easy was a Harry Potter type school for people like us." I shrugged and gave her my cheekiest smile.

She laughed. "This story would make a good book."

Daniel and I both stopped short of telling her about Beth Ann. Later, I'd share this, but for now persuading her to believe in us was enough. She seemed at least partially convinced of the science.

Daniel said, "I believe the Trepan Killer has followed you. That's why he was on the bus. Then something happened. I don't know what. And he stopped. Like he's playing around the edges, observing. He comes in, then moves away." His tone became urgent. "Now, you see why we need to get going?"

"Not ... totally," Mariana said. "Why can't I just lock the door or call the police? Or just be really, really careful until he's caught?"

Daniel tapped the SQUID device. "This is never wrong. And I don't want to alarm anyone, but he's been here." At the shocked look on her face, he added, "At least he's been near the door to your apartment. In the hall. Recently I'm afraid."

Mariana's hand reached to cover her mouth. "You have proof? We should contact the police immediately."

Daniel shook his head. "Any way you explain this our story sounds crazy. I've never even managed to get a paper published. My peers think I'm chasing a scientific wild goose. Then there's Rory. How would we explain him? What he can do? They'd just label us as kooks."

Mariana held a palm to her forehead and pushed back her hair so curls fell across her head to the side of her face. She looked at me. "Rory? I don't know what to do."

"Trust him. He's right. I've thought through this since Daniel told me. The concept does spin your mind, but I don't have any other ideas."

Mariana shook her head from side to side as she looked down into the coffee cup she'd been holding.

"Call me super foolish, but I almost believe you. Actually, after sleeping on everything, not seeing you all day, I had convinced myself yesterday was a crazy dream or a joke of some kind."

"I'd never play a joke on you about something this serious."

"Okay," she said, her voice more upbeat, "if I believe you and that *thing*—" She nodded at the SQUID in Daniel's hands. "—then where can we go? This guy sounds, well, I hate to say this, but he sounds super-human."

Daniel piped up then. He looked almost apologetic, as though everything he'd just said had been the good news. "I'm sorry, I haven't told you everything. This isn't just about you two or me. I believe the entire world is at risk."

He must have read the shocked look on our faces, because he quickly added, "I know this sounds huge and melodramatic. Don't worry. I have a plan."

Mariana and I spoke in unison. "Plan?"

"Yes, well, not exactly a plan, more like a well-constructed experiment."

"Meaning?" I asked.

"Meaning, I don't know if my idea will work, but from everything I've learned from my research, there's a good chance." When he said 'a good chance,' the words were positively upbeat, as though he was convincing us the weather would be fine on the weekend despite a contrary forecast.

I looked at Mariana, then back at him, concerned. "If your well-constructed experiment doesn't work?"

He tilted his head to the side, wavering, clearly considering the question, maybe even surprised we weren't jumping in with both feet.

"Then I don't think anything we do will matter. When you play with fire, there's always a chance you'll get burned, and we're playing with something more volatile than fire."

"What?" I asked.

"Sub-atomic particles. And when you play with those tiny fellas, there's a good chance your entire world will get burned. I think there's a real possibility what the killer wants with Mariana might be just great for him but very, very bad for us. All of us."

The fireflies began a dance in my head, and I felt drawn to look away and listen to their buzzing song. Something was happening I didn't understand, but I trusted Daniel and his science, what I could fathom.

Then a random thought entered my mind. Suddenly I knew he

was coming, not directly, not in a way so we could prepare. He stole through the city like a shadow. And we lived in the light. But he was coming no matter what we did, and he was coming for Mariana.

Without asking permission or even wondering if she would object, I grabbed Mariana's hand and said, "I'm sorry, we can't stay here any longer."

49

W hat awaited us at Daniel's home was freaky, to say the least. If he had shown me this room before I think I would have made my way quickly to the door, with a phone call to the police next.

He called the room the *haven*. To my mind, the space looked more like a fancy chicken coop. An old divan ran partially along one wall, with a folded portable dinner table resting against another wall, and beside this a white, plastic outdoor chair.

From floor to ceiling of what I presumed had been a bedroom, was a mosaic of copper-colored see-through panels. They even spread across the ceiling and behind the entry door. On closer inspection, composing each panel was a pattern of crisscrossed wires that ran from each sheet to fix one panel to the next. These wires then ran down to the floor where they disappeared between the loose carpet coverings. Through the unevenness of the floor, I realized the panels also were beneath our feet.

When Daniel closed the door behind us, an incredible claustrophobia overcame me, like the world outside had disappeared and we were trapped. Mariana gripped my arm and moved closer.

"What do you think?" Daniel asked.

"I think your taste in interior design needs work."

"This room isn't about the look. The function is perfect."

"And the function is?" asked Mariana, as she slowly scanned the room from top to bottom.

"Absorption of electrical charges. I've even added some modifications and now this room offers protection against a wide spectrum of energies. Sends them to ground. You might have heard of this type of technology. This is a big Faraday cage."

I had. I'd seen one when I was a kid at a science expo, but now knowing that still didn't really answer my question.

"But why?" I asked.

"Quite fascinating really and this complements the SQUID technology. Remember SQUID measures energy resonance, the electrical impulses given off by a person, their life force. The energy you absorb when you transfer emotions is similar. In their purest form they are simply electrons, positive and negative, that interact with our brain chemistry and hormones. This cage blocks electrical charge coming from the outside. More importantly, the construction blocks any energy within from escaping."

Daniel's face lit up as I'd come to expect any time he talked about something scientific.

"Electrical charges zip through our cells. Electricity gives and also takes away, as in during an overload, like a lightning strike. The charge overpowers the body's network and stops everything, so to speak."

"I remember this from school," I said. "Wasn't the scientist Michael Faraday? He invented a cage in the nineteen hundreds to protect against electrical charges. I think I saw one at a science expo used with a Tesla coil."

"Yep, and they're in every microwave to protect against escaping radiation. Electromagnetic radiation is everywhere. If there was a surge though, that pulse could disrupt everything we rely upon for civilization. The government's been working on a response to this type of attack for years. Imagine the world without Internet, computers, phones. Every economy would instantly collapse."

"But why have you got one?" Mariana asked.

"Because of him, the killer. Once I began tracking him via his B.E. print, I realized he had a unique electromagnetic signature. At every murder scene he left traces, but his energy was chaotic and amplified, like he'd somehow enhanced the emotional charge around the victims. Remember I said electrical energy gives and takes? He's enhancing their energy—I don't know how yet—but that's how they die."

"The dark thing," I said to myself, as I thought about Daniel's words. I looked around the cage, then back at Daniel.

"So this Faraday cage will protect us from him? Is this what you mean?"

"Oh, this does more," he said. "The cage blocks him tracing us or, more essentially, Mariana. I believe he has something similar to my SQUID. Whether a natural ability or man-made, he uses this to stalk his victims. Once he sets his sights on someone, he knows where they are, like he's placed a tracking device. This is all I can think to explain some of the energy signals I've found. This will block that, because the energy impulse he sends out, or the person he's tracking sends back to him, can't get through. The minute we walked into this room, we vanished from his radar."

"So we're safe in here," Mariana said.

"Yes. I've got some bedding and food." Daniel pointed to several rolled up sleeping bags, a small cooler in the corner and a large cardboard box. "There's also a portable toilet."

"But we can't stay here forever. Comfy as this place seems," I said, in a mocking grimace.

"No, but we can stay here long enough to create a plan. He wants Mariana. Something within her will give him the energy he needs to achieve his aim."

"What's his aim?" she asked, suddenly pale.

"*That* I haven't figured out entirely. But I suspect losing track of you will frustrate him. He will be searching for us, I think. I suspect he wasn't far behind when we were at your apartment. He'd been there, according to the SQUID, in the previous hour. We may have even interrupted him."

"But the minute we leave this room he will find us again?" I said.

"Yes, but by then, we will have a plan."

We eventually settled in for the night and Daniel attempted to educate us in physics we could barely comprehend. My brain hurt as he meticulously explained the physics of the universe.

He'd fed readings from the SQUID taken at Mariana's into a data analysis software. The killer's energy levels had grown and changed, according to the program, and Daniel's theory was that the killer's power had grown from his contact with me and Mariana. Some kind of molecular energy metamorphosis.

Everything has an energy signature, he told us, so he could pinpoint the location where matter was disturbed by measuring the disruption to an object's electron field. He likened the process to throwing a pebble into a lake. The force of the pebble's impact could be measured by noting the stone's entry point to the distance between the ripples and how long before the movement stopped.

"This is where you come in," he said, his eyes firing, barely able to contain his excitement. "Dark matter and ordinary matter co-exist. They seem out of balance, with ninety-five point one percent of the invisible dark matter surrounding us, and less than five percent visible. But the universe still maintains a perfect, beautiful symmetry. If there is a god, he works on a sub-atomic level. And that's why you two are so important."

"Us? What has all this got to do with us?" Mariana asked.

"You are part of some kind of master plan of nature. I'm convinced there are others too. You're the check and balance if matter ever lost equilibrium. If that happened, the result would be the equivalent of a nuclear bomb's chain reaction. Nuclear explosions begin with an instability of nuclei and neutrons."

He waved his hands in the air to demonstrate the chaotic movement of neutrons.

"When neutrons move quickly the tiny nuclei become agitated.

This generates so much energy so rapidly the nuclear material explodes."

His hands sprung open, fingers spread wide in a dramatic fashion.

"With a nuclear bomb the explosion stops the fission. However, dark matter is the most dangerous substance in the universe. At the initial point of fission, where the two matters become unbalanced, there isn't an explosion."

Mariana's mouth gaped open. "What is there?"

Daniel stopped, taking a slug from a soda bottle sitting on the table, before placing the cap back on and shaking it. The remaining liquid churned creating a mass of bubbles. He held up the receptacle, now a creamy mess, with dark liquid on the bottom and a tawny-colored layer of bubbles above. Then he opened the cap and a spray of soda exploded from the bottle, spilling down the sides and spattering the floor for several feet. With a flourish, he placed the leaking bottle down on the table behind him.

"There's an *implosion* into the dark matter. Since dark matter is the most abundant material, like I said—more than ninety-five per cent of everything—that energy basically takes over. Everything is converted to dark matter. Nothing to stop the process because that precious four point nine percent of ordinary matter has disappeared into nothing. The universe we know and love is gone."

"But why would the killer destroy everything? He'd die too," I said.

"Hmm, good question. I've thought about this since you described Mariana as a window. What if the Trepan Killer has a way to move to another dimension that actually exists in dark matter. Maybe he's the one and only alien invader of our dimension. Or perhaps he isn't from somewhere else and just doesn't understand the danger. Either way, the ramification is not a good thing for us."

Mariana and I looked at each other, a little shell-shocked. When this all began I thought I was simply saving the girl I loved. Now, perhaps, I was saving the entire world, even the universe. I was no

Superman, so I wasn't sure if I should laugh or cry at the craziness of what Daniel had just shared.

He looked so confident, so excited at being able to share his haven room and his theories, for a moment I believed everything just might work out perfectly. And everything almost did.

50

H is eyes close as he stands immobile, his hand against the wall of her apartment. So empty. So unmistakably empty. She had been here, but now is gone. She is so near he can almost taste her in the material of the walls, the fiber of the carpet, the molecules of pale lamplight that dance around the room.

Doubt like an angry little seed blooms, but he pushes the fury away. He knows them. They do not know him. He should have ignored his curiosity, not followed the bus driver or dallied with his woman friend. He should have returned here and waited.

He feels her; not too far away. Once his, they are always his. A tenuous thread pulls; the call of her. A smile touches his lips. Calm seeps into his mind and he relaxes. Then the pressure begins as he moves his mind toward her seeking the place in her which belongs to him. Beads of excitement fill him, growing, multiplying as he travels, no longer constrained by this capsule of a body.

He reaches, stretches, seeks ... then gone. Their connection so strong a moment ago, blinks out as though he has never been with her before, never explored her life. Nothing. He jabs and pushes against the nothingness, attempting to find a way around. Or through.

The barrier feels impassable.

His search turns to the bus driver. Again nothing.

He puzzles over this as his eyelids spring open, taking in the apartment. He feels weakened; the force, which has grown since he found her, has lessened. Why, he cannot fathom.

Unable to proceed forward, he sits on a chair in her living room. He cannot go back and so he does the only thing left—to wait. He has patience and a higher perspective. Eventually he will find them. He's waited this long, he can wait just a little longer.

51

I climbed onto the bus to begin my route, stomach churning, nerves on fire, my armpits already damp. Three days ago my biggest worry was how I would begin a conversation with Mariana. Courageous wasn't a word I'd use to describe myself. Now everything had changed. Unnatural courage was all I needed to finish this day. And luck, a bucket load of luck.

Mariana was in my life, not as I'd imagined, but I'd take what I had for now. The hardest thing I'd done was to leave her that morning, not knowing how this day would turn out. She'd waved goodbye and blew me a kiss. I felt the warmth of her kiss on my cheek as surely as if we had touched. All I had to ease my mind was knowing she was with Daniel. I trusted him and his weird science, as I thought of his explanations. Weird science, which made the best sense of my gift I'd ever heard.

My eyes itched after the long night of talk and planning, discarding of tactics and the rehashing of new. I had ideas. Daniel had ideas. Mariana raised her own. In the end, what we decided upon was uncertain, and yet doing nothing would be even more uncertain. We knew we couldn't wait. We knew he would come.

Mariana had something the Trepan Killer wanted and he wasn't going to stop.

Riding through the depot gates that morning to begin work, my heart hurt instantly. Beth Ann would not be there to greet me. All we knew so far was she was alive and in surgery. Her future unknown.

The police had sectioned off the offices, but allowed the buses to still leave, continue on their purpose even though many of the drivers, on hearing the news, looked just as crestfallen as me. Brushing with evil transforms you. I knew this first hand. My entire body felt restructured, adapted somehow by my encounter. Certainly I identified with Spiderman now, except I'd been bitten by something darker than a radioactive spider.

Men in thin, white loose overalls dusted, searched and explored every inch of the area for clues. The bus I'd driven the day before yesterday, which Sandra Swift had ridden mere hours before the Trepan Killer had found her, was still parked in an isolated section of the yard. My accomplice, now alone and forlorn like a caged animal carrying a disease.

A temporary office, manned by a blonde, fortyish woman who looked as skittish as a kitten, had been set up in one of the garages. The temp secretary, Jo, complained the minute I met her how she was more accustomed to being sent by her agency to pristine offices and filing duties, not filling in for a woman savaged by insanity, who now clung to life.

When I signed for my change box she asked, "Your name Rory Fine?"

When I nodded a 'yes,' she said, "One of those detectives been asking after you. Wants you to see them ASAP. He's around here somewhere. Said to call when you came in. Something about you being the driver on the day that woman got killed. Seems like that Trepan Killer got a thing about this place. I don't much like being here, I tell you that now."

I couldn't be waylaid; I needed to run my route at least for today, so I said nonchalantly, "Yeah, give me his number and I'll call him later. Can't be late to start the run."

As I headed out toward the waiting buses, feeling as though lead weights were strapped to my ankles, I saw the image of Beth Ann standing at the window of the main office. I imagined her calling her usual greeting: *Rory, go get 'em or at least get 'em on time.*

"You can't blame yourself Rory," Mariana had said last night.

But I felt impaled by guilt, knowing my troubles keeping somehow led the killer here and to Sandra.

"I'm so sorry," I said to the imaginary Beth Ann.

"What's that? I didn't catch you?" said one of the white-clad, female investigators who must have believed my words were directed at her.

I looked over and smiled. "Just preparing to take on the world."

Her eyebrows furrowed. "Aren't you just one of the bus drivers?"

I paused mid-stride and reached my hand to cover hers, enclosed in a thin white glove. As the initial punch of emotional energy entered my skin I felt a crackling. A pale-blue light flickered through my fingers, and I looked into her eyes and saw a calm enter. A small rise appeared on her lips, the muscles twitching ever so slightly.

"Yes, but we all make differences in our own way."

She pulled back her hand and stared as though she'd just realized her palm belonged to her. "Yes, I guess ... so."

Then the twitching muscles gave in and a smile spread across her face.

"Yeah, we do," she said, as though she'd never considered this a possibility. I left her standing there and continued on. Her voice followed me seconds later. "You have a great day. Go make a difference."

I really hoped I would.

I climbed aboard my bus, but instead of taking the driver's seat I continued up the aisle to the back to sit in the rear bench seat. I needed a few moments of contemplation to run through the plan. Not much of a plan because so many things hinged on events beyond our control. I hated that part. The forensic detective was correct; I was just a bus driver, albeit with a small gift. That gift though had never required me to become a hero.

By the time I sat in the driver's seat, I'd straightened my head space, so even though from the outside I was *just* Rory Fine, friendly, amiable and happy-go-lucky. Inside, I wore the resolve created by my love for Mariana and the determination to put things right.

As I pulled out from the lot, I glanced toward my workplace. This might be the last time I'd leave here. Sadness erupted at the thought of Beth Ann lying in the hospital, the image of the needles and what that monster had done to her so raw in my mind.

As I navigated into the traffic, I tipped two fingers to my forehead in a salute toward the depot. "This is for you, Beth Ann," I said.

Today, the Rory Fine who drove this route was a me I could have never imagined. No longer mild-mannered troubles keeper. Today I would be a trouble giver. The Trepan Killer would soon learn what that meant.

52

With each stop I made, calm settled over me like a warm blanket. Doing something familiar and so ordinary as driving a bus and interacting with passengers, as I'd done for years, found me falling back into my normal cheeriness. Mid-morning until just before peak hour I rarely saw a regular. Peak hour, just after four, they would begin to appear like rabbits coming out after a storm. I welcomed their friendly smiles, made even more friendly since my throw-your-troubles-in-the-river stunt.

Daniel would catch the bus on the four-ten run, somewhere midway on the route. This would give him most of the day to prepare.

"Most important that you act as if nothing's happened. Act normal. When you see me, we don't know each other," he'd said.

Somehow, I managed to 'act normal,' and behave as though everything was perfectly fine, which made the abnormality of last night's sleeping in the homemade Tesla chicken coop seem even more bizarre.

I kept up my usual banter with passengers. There were moments where I'd catch myself and feel genuinely surprised at my coolness. Any time my mind strayed to a vision of a world sucked into a dark pit if we failed, I would switch my attention to an internal film of me and Mariana together. I'd envision every imagined event, dates, holidays, even a wedding. They all brought a silly, goofy smile to my face and helped ease the tension twisting in my neck.

If only I could pull my own troubles into the attic, things would be easier, but I'd never worked that one out. Instead, I simply reminded myself that by the time the sun came up tomorrow, this would be over.

Daniel was convinced, as was I, that the killer had been on the bus in the past week. I wondered if I'd see Leather Jacket from the café. Something about him and his reaction to Mariana seemed off. Then again, he might just be a plain-and-simple jerk. I began to study every passenger who boarded, wondering if I would feel something that would alert me. The killer could be anyone.

Tracy and Mark seemed to bounce onto the bus. Tracy greeted me like I was a brother she hadn't seen in years. She surprised me by leaning down to place a kiss on my cheek.

"We've set the wedding date. You're on the invitation list. If not for you ..." She angled her head to Mark, grabbed his hand and pulled him toward us. "Isn't that right? If Rory hadn't done what he did with the troubles. Throwing them away. We wouldn't have worked out our problems." She stared back at me. "I swear."

"I'm happy for you," I said, imagining Mariana in a wedding dress, unable to stop a smile from reaching my lips.

I observed the pair in the rearview mirror settle into their seats; Mark placed an arm around Tracy as she snuggled her head into the indent of his neck.

Near to four-twenty, as I watched another load of passengers board at a busy stop, the realization hit me. I normally anticipated Mariana's stop, but he was to get on at Madison Park. I'd been caught up with my own thoughts and driving and we were now three stops past there and no Daniel. But maybe he'd boarded via the central doors and I'd missed him. After all, the pretense was we were strangers.

I pulled on the brake, got up, and made my way up the aisle excusing myself to passengers and explaining I needed to check on something in the back. As I moved, I swung my head side-to-side, scrutinizing each seat row.

No, I was right. Daniel wasn't on board.

I checked my phone at the next stop for messages. A big fat zero. No call. No message. I tried not to panic. *Happy thoughts. Happy thoughts.* There could be a perfectly good reason. What that reason was though, I couldn't imagine. We'd been pretty definite on how today would go, running through the plan even as we parted this morning.

I needed to get back to the depot. Immediately. In the distance I heard or felt the firefly buzz. Something was wrong. Something was off kilter.

The bus was crowded, so I couldn't just pull up at a stop, get off and disappear. I couldn't even stop long enough to make a call, unless I staged another break down. But for all I knew the killer had boarded the bus and might be alerted if I tried that one again.

All I could do was text.

Where are u? Plans changed?

At the next stop, I checked my phone. No reply. I texted again—just question marks this time.

???

The phone's silence was brutal, but I had to keep driving, finish the route.

When the doors opened at Stop 1031 and Arthur Ogilvy appeared at the bottom of the steps, eyes downcast, my heart went out to him. I couldn't help myself, as he passed by I reached out and gently brushed his hand, no more than a finger touch. This contact was enough to pull the sadness from him. As I stowed his troubles in their own box in the attic for safekeeping, I noticed anger mingled in. I held my palm against the side of the box, feeling the energy. Why would he be angry? Sad, yes, that I understood, but he wasn't an angry soul.

The darkness came to me as though drawn through a straw, so thick and disgusting I tasted the foulness in my mouth, rotten and sickening. There didn't need to be words for me to understand the message.

Don't follow. Don't pursue. You will lose.

Buried within the darkness of the thing was a feeling I couldn't fathom. An image of a face distorted, but smiling, and I felt as though I should know him. Then the mirage was gone, and I was left with an echo of ... admiration ... from him. Admiration? Like I was a kindred spirit. I shook the feeling away like something disgusting coated my body with a slick of evil oil.

Mr. Ogilvy? Could the killer be him? I risked the smallest of touches again. This time I was ready, but all that came was a trickle of normal troubles. This was a message I realized. Mr. Ogilvy the messenger.

Then a whoosh came, like a pressure released, and the dark messenger thing was gone like a puff of smoke dissolving into the air. I found myself staring into the eyes of Mr. Ogilvy, eyes that now looked out on the world with a little more clarity and hope.

He turned slowly away from me, shuffling up the aisle, his body clearly not serving him without pain today, before pausing several rows along. He turned back and said, "Thank you," though I doubted he understood why he felt the need to say those words.

I slipped my phone out of my jacket pocket and checked again for messages. Still nothing. Just my messages to Daniel. I sent another.

Picking up M soon. Hope u ok!!! Text pls!!!

Several more stops and my mind had traveled ahead and was focused on Mariana. The bus had filled almost to capacity and the Sterling Records' stop was minutes away. Maybe she knew what had happened to Daniel. If she was there. If she wasn't, what did that mean? And what would I do? Where would I begin to search?

If anything went wrong we'd agreed to head back to Daniel's haven. I told myself to stop panicking and while I waited at the stop before Mariana's for passengers to board, I texted her.

Daniel not at stop. With you? Be there in two minutes.

Mariana's stop was where our plan would begin.

Daniel's words from the night before echoed in my head. *Everything is converted to dark matter. The universe we know and love is gone.*

With so much at stake, I had to push the idea of an imploding universe from my mind. That kind of pressure really messes with your head. My focus had to be on Mariana. *Save the girl. Save the universe.*

I scanned ahead toward Mariana's stop, which had now come into view, explosions and black nothingness whisked from my mind. I made out the lawyer Barrett-something-Smith waiting at the stop, along with several others I couldn't recognize as yet.

Something struck me as peculiar. The lawyer usually got on at one-one-nine in the central business district, five or six stops back; this wasn't his stop. *What was he doing here?* This didn't seem right at all.

I still couldn't identify Mariana amid the group. A peculiar lost feeling came over me, and the world seemed to have expanded and become an intimidating place working against me, against our plan. Mariana *had* to be at the stop. She needed to climb aboard the bus, sit as near as possible to Daniel, and wait, like we'd arranged. But Daniel hadn't boarded the bus, so already our plan was awry.

At some point we felt certain the Trepan Killer would follow Mariana onto the bus. Daniel had been positive from the energy traces that the killer had followed her for the past few days. We couldn't work out why he hadn't made a move, but up until last night he'd been very near. When he did come aboard, Daniel had calibrated the SQUID to alert him. He'd told us that he'd worked over the past week to narrow down the energy signature and he was sure he was correct.

The next part of the plan would then happen.

Daniel had been working on controlling the balance of matter from previous research of others. Since the sixties, physicists had believed in a small but powerful, naturally occurring force known as the Hibbert field. This barrier, though short-ranged, could be generated around an object to protect the atoms from wild neutrons, thus stopping short the Universe-destroying chain reaction. He even suggested my troubles keeping was a natural means of creating a Hibbert field. He'd pretty much lost me with his scientific-speak, but I kind of enjoyed listening to a technical answer to my gift.

He'd also created another little gadget that could create a mini Hibbert field. Once we'd identified the Trepan Killer, Mariana and Daniel would follow him off the bus and message me. Then all we needed to do was get close enough to apply the Hibbert field, take him back to the haven room, and ... well, we hadn't gotten past there.

Daniel suggested if we increased the Hibbert field, then the Trepan Killer's energy might be permanently disrupted, the electrons becoming over-stimulated and ultimately destroyed. He'd picked up the soda bottle and shook the container again to demonstrate how fizz was no longer created because all the carbon dioxide had since escaped.

Would his idea work? He didn't know for sure, but in light of the fact we had nothing else, our plan had *better* work. Of course, everything hinged on us finding the Trepan Killer and activating the field. There was a lot of *if's*. That's what worried me.

Now Daniel was missing and now seemingly Mariana too. Me on my own wasn't part of any plan.

As I pulled into the stop I craned my neck to peer over the three passengers waiting to climb on as several on-board alighted. Mariana just *had* to be there. If she wasn't, I didn't know if I could control my panic. My pulse throbbed in my temples like a jackhammer banging inside my head. When the last person boarded, I held the door open as long as I could. Maybe she was late. Maybe kept back with another late customer, like yesterday.

While the moments ticked by, I ran through alternative scenarios, plans they may have changed, thinking each one through and examining each to see if any scenario made sense. Nothing fit. Daniel said he would be there on the bus. Mariana said she would be there at the stop. *That was the plan.* I was there to help in whatever way I could with whatever my abilities allowed me to do. On my own though, useless was a kind word. With a sinking feeling, I realized Mariana wasn't coming.

"Excuse me." The voice startled me. "Is everything alright?"

Glenn, the pony-tailed software programmer stood beside me, his hand on the metal safety bar. Though not a particularly talkative regular, I recalled he'd said he did some off-site work on a local tourism website.

He reached down and touched my shoulder.

The jarring sensation was instant and violent, a static electricity shot revved up to maximum as a thousand emotions surged through me. Just like the time at school with Mikey, I felt overwhelmed, my inner circuitry blown. I gasped and gulped in air, desperately trying to pull oxygen back into my lungs.

I heard myself say "No," but the words came to me like a distant echo. I wondered if I was still conscious or even still on the bus. I felt flung into another place. Then I found myself clinging to the wheel, hugging the frame like a drowning man clinking to a lifebuoy.

What had just happened?

Glenn still stared down at me and I wondered why he was smiling. A single thought filled my mind as though shoved into me with an other-worldly force, a shouted warning.

The attic.

The energy knew exactly where to go. I raced to the attic still feeling a little woozy. Yes, whatever had been delivered via Glenn was there, chaotic and uninhibited, another dark thing shimmering in the corner, hovering calmly as though taunting me. With everything I had, I pulled at the being, and surprisingly the entity came easily. Within seconds I had marshaled the darkness into a box, which for good measure had steel-rod strengthened concrete walls. Large-linked chains wrapped around the exterior. I was taking no chances.

I stood a few yards from the box, staring, my hands shaking from the shock. Strangely, despite the surprise of the attack, this one wasn't as powerful as the first dark thing. No, this visit was intended for something else.

Hesitantly I walked toward the box and placed my hand against the side, feeling the smooth, cold gray exterior. I'd gotten good at this over the years, although I'd never had to use such security and force before with other troubles. A vibration shuddered from inside, as though the thing sensed me nearby and a thread of energy shivered though the molecules of the box. A warm tingle entered my palm. Instantly I pulled away, uncertain what I felt.

Then the fireflies began to dance in my subconscious and a knowing came over me. I don't know from where these firefly thoughts came but they were certainly useful.

This wasn't random energy or emotion but something which filled me with dread. We had misunderstood our enemy. Daniel had been right. The Trepan Killer had grown in power. I moved away to gather my thoughts, my gaze never leaving the box.

Random images appeared before me, fluctuating shadows of people I knew, people I loved, had loved. Mariana. Beth Ann. My dear mama. Daniel Starsey. Sandra Swift. My regular passengers. Places swam between them: my bus and the route, my home, that day at school when Mikey died. Then a final, powerful image of Mikey flying through the air over the car's hood, so vivid I felt as though I was there. My stomach clenched at the memory so infused with emotion that I could very nearly be sick again, just like on that day. I fought back the bile that traveled up my throat. I needed to work through what I was seeing and feeling. This was important. There was a message here.

Over the images came a fluid darkness, breaking into tendrils, which reached out into nothingness. A tiny speck of light appeared in the midst like a distant lighthouse seen through fog. This light grew quickly until the glow was a white, hot, radiating throb. Then, like a snake striking, the darkness swooped on the light. Both appeared to wrestle with one another, with neither seeming to triumph.

The killer, everything that had happened and why, all became crystal clear. My breath caught in my throat. This thing I'd locked in the box wasn't an entity or random troubles or emotions. He had sent this. This was a message, a terrible message, and if I'd understood correctly, and I think I had, then we had *definitely* miscalculated.

Now though, at least I knew where to find the killer.

53

With some dread I returned to meet Glenn's stare. I'd half-expected he might have morphed into an evil twin of himself. But, no, same Glenn: mousy hair pulled back in a short ponytail, black-hooped five cent holes in his ears that looked in a funny way like dark holes themselves.

"Man, are you okay? You looked like you were having a heart attack," he said.

My mind slid back into gear. "I'm fine, really ..."

I had to get back to the depot, but Glenn didn't move.

There was no time for my usual politeness, so my voice was unnaturally terse. "Really, please take your seat. Otherwise I'll start running late."

"Okay, but you're not gonna, like, have a fit or something and then crash the bus are you?"

"No, water— *agh-agh*," I pretend-coughed "—went down the wrong way."

I returned to the wheel, stared ahead through the windshield and indicated to merge back into the traffic before he had a chance to quiz me with *What water?*

As I waited for a break in the traffic, I spied Leather Jacket. I'd never gotten his motivation straight in my head. Seriously, who was he? He now ran down the pavement, suit jacket flapping behind him, waving to me.

Momentarily I considered keeping the doors closed and taking off, but what if he had something to do with this? The exchange at the café had played on my mind. He had seemed to zero in on Mariana and be overly preoccupied with her. As much as I would have preferred to take off and wave to the guy as I passed, instead I engaged the brake and pressed the entry release. The doors hissed open. Leather Jacket climbed on-board, nodded a *hello thank you*, as though he'd never seen me before in his life. Was he pretending? I watched him walk up the aisle and take his seat, uncertain of the meaning of his nonchalance.

The traffic had slowed; we had hit peak hour, and my progression became just a slow creep forward. My fingers drummed an impatient tune on the wheel. *Come on,* I screamed silently. Normally I wouldn't care, because normally I would still run on time with the schedule allowing for traffic. Today, my personal schedule didn't allow for traffic. Traffic was my enemy. Stopping for passengers also frustrated me. People got on. People got off. Just not quickly enough.

I didn't look for Mariana or Daniel at other stops. The plan had changed, I now understood, but not by them. The killer had wanted me to know that. Mariana's face remained fixed in my mind as I'd seen her in the missive delivered by Glenn, the killer's unaware messenger. The meaning was clear, *he* had her or would *soon* have her. Here we were naively thinking we had a plan to capture *him*. Instead, he had a plan to capture Mariana. He'd led us to believe we had some control, but the minute we'd left Daniel's haven he had the advantage.

To those departing I wanted to scream, *get off the bus.* They seemed to move in slow motion, not a care in the world, but I had a care, a really big care that with each passing minute tightened fractionally more around my chest.

How he contacted me I couldn't fathom, but those images he'd sent via Glenn were to taunt ... for fun? No, I didn't think so. To panic me, that's why. So I'd be too frazzled to follow or offer resistance. He'd snuck into my mind and I struggled to think straight. Somehow he knew when stressed I couldn't trouble keep, couldn't control the flow of emotional energy. Calm was a necessary ingredient. My mind raced with the terrible possibility of losing Mariana and the unthinkable disaster, if Daniel's imploding black matter theory was right. I began to feel weakened, like I was losing an important connection that was unraveling twine by twine.

I needed to take back control, so ignoring everything around me, I willed myself to become composed.

Be at peace. Be calm, I urged my mind. More passengers departed: a mom and her son—he talking animatedly about a guitar lesson he'd just enjoyed; her cooing about his talent—and two others stepped down onto the pavement.

My mind began to cool, distance itself from the fear. As I felt my focus return, a glowing thread came into view, wafting ahead of me, like a lit pathway that stretched down the street and around the corner. The snaking thread was beautiful and beckoning and like nothing I'd ever seen. My mind fired with hope.

He had played us, yes, but he'd overplayed, and now I had something on him. In sending me a message, he'd made a fatal error. Connecting with me via Glenn meant he transferred his message easily, but he'd underestimated me and my evolving ability. Heck, I'd underestimated me too. Maybe the connection with Mariana or the dark thing had activated latent abilities like a bodybuilder using heavier weights to enhance his muscles. I didn't know, but I knew my gift had expanded in ways I could never have imagined.

I had faith whoever or whatever created me to be a check and balance, as Daniel had said, was on my side, and that gave me strength. What I didn't have, I now realized, was time.

54

Night had begun to settle around us; twilight clouds were now just dark purple clumps floating overhead. If all I'd received was the killer's message, I may have viewed the arrival of darkness as a sign of the fate working against me. But his little game had inadvertently given me a chance. One thing I knew: getting back to the depot would take too long. Every minute now counted.

So for the second time this week, I faked a breakdown. Not original. Not a wonderful plan, but all I could come up with in the moment. I was getting good at phony breakdowns. Tap on the brake several times. Grind the clutch. On with the handbrake. Nobody hurt again. I'd worry tomorrow whether I'd lose my job. If Daniel was correct and we failed to stop the killer, there might be no job, no world, just endless black matter.

I brought the bus to a halt even before the next stop and climbed out of my seat to stand in the aisle and address the passengers. Play acting an attempt to check gauges and the mechanics was out the window. No time for artistic flourishes.

"I'm sorry everyone," I said, trying to show concern, while rushing through my speech. "Seems we have a serious mechanical fault. For your safety, can I please request everyone vacate the bus here? A replacement bus will be along to collect you shortly. Twenty minutes tops. Maybe less. I'm very sorry."

A collective sigh erupted through the bus. I noticed Leather Jacket, who'd already begun cursing—and who looked as though he could kill someone—was already out of his seat and stomping up the aisle.

"Again! You've got to be kidding me. Shit to your fucking bus service."

I ignored him and addressed everyone else, keeping my voice bright and breezy as I waved my hands toward the door like an usher.

"I'm sorry folks, really. The sooner you disembark, the sooner we'll have the replacement bus here. Thank you for your co-operation and patience."

People filed off, a few commenting on the terrible state of public transport. My regulars were more forgiving with the occasional smile and a *what- ya-gonna-do* look. I replied with a shoulder-raise and a *beats-me-we-must-be-unlucky* shrug. The very moment the last person left the bus, I threw myself back into the driver's seat, pulled the lever to close the doors, and started the engine again.

The passengers now assembled on the sidewalk would not be happy. I didn't dare look out the doors or windows as I drove away. I was pretty certain the expressions I would see.

Eight blocks later, I turned off my route and headed a quicker way through back streets to avoid traffic. A few pedestrians turned at the noise of a bus revving down a quiet street. I figured I'd save a good ten to twelve minutes taking this route.

By the time I'd pulled into the bus lot my arms felt weary from clutching at the wheel, not to mention my adrenaline-soaked nervous system. I didn't even park the bus in its assigned space but left the vehicle in the nearest position to the employee car park. Then I ran, like I was competing for gold, to where I'd left my bike that morning.

Helmet on, I jammed my key into the ignition and the engine revved to life. I was already moving, heading for the exit, before anyone would even realize I'd been there.

I tore down backstreets and even ran a few red lights, praying there were no police around. I knew where Mariana was and the more I closed the gap to her location, the stronger the feeling became, as the little psychic fireflies buzzed and glowed their little hearts out, urging me on.

As I sped along faster than I'd ever consider safe, there was just one thing on which to focus: my emotions. I needed to calm down; find some inner peace. Adrenaline, fear, every emotion fought at me, barraged me with its own draining energy. I tried to think of something bright and hopeful to chase the feelings away, to temper their tone. As much as I wrestled those slippery fish, my heart still raced with all kinds of panic.

How do you think peaceful thoughts when you're about to face true evil? As I raced toward Mariana, not certain I would reach her in time or what I would find, I honestly had no answer.

55

As I turned into the street the sense of déjà vu felt powerful, an almost physical force. Something like fifteen years had passed since I'd been here. Although I'd moved a few miles from this area where I'd spent my childhood, my adult life had never taken me back here.

Ducking and weaving and speeding down back streets like I was a movie stuntman would have seemed so out of character less than two days ago. My mama would have shouted: *"Slow down. Alive is the best time to arrive."* As I sped down the street, the houses on either side blurred. I searched ahead looking for signs he was still here. I felt him close and the fireflies buzzed a confirmation. I hadn't known I would end up here.

On the edge of cognizance lay a familiarity. The killer and I had shared something or would share something. This kinship I believed came from our ability to tap into the emotional energy of the world. A psychic power cord plugged into an energized spiritual socket like the psychic had said about his own experience. Why I was here was still a little gray in my mind, but I was certain I would soon find out.

Strong memories exploded as I slowed the bike and bumped over the curb to the pavement.

Mikey laying on the street just ahead.

A woman standing by her car, crying.

Teachers running out from the school gate.

Stevie by my side, his hands over his eyes not wanting to see.

And me, just a boy, horror written across my face at what I believed I'd done.

As I took a moment to stare at the place where Mikey had died, I knew for certain who I would face. My first thoughts were that the Trepan Killer had chosen here because of my haunted past. That he may have thought these terrible memories would weaken his adversary. Now I knew his past had brought us here. Not as friends now, but enemies.

I moved to the gate at a pace and pushed, but it didn't give. Times had changed; in my school days this entrance was never locked. Now a solid padlock barred my way. I looked up to see the configuration at the top of the high fence would make scaling difficult. I didn't like my chances of scaling the obstacle quickly and then getting Mariana back over if she was injured.

I wrapped my fingers around the chain and pulled. Something was on my side. The actual gate hinges felt loose and flimsy. Age had taken its toll. I looked back at my bike, standing like a patient steed for my return with the rescued damsel. I wondered.

56

The One is truly a beautiful portal, more stunning and powerful than he has imagined. She sits quietly in the swivel chair behind the teacher's desk, a little slumped, almost forlorn, hands resting on the arms as though in a moment she will rise and teach a class.

Today she is the student. She bows to his mind. She cannot move, for he commands her silence as he reaches inside and immobilizes her will. This ability is fresh and new and, as the power continues to grow, he's enjoyed the feeling. This new ability must be something to do with her and with the bus driver, as though the three are points of a triangle. The holy spirit of psychic power.

Now that he's here in this school, back where his journey began, he feels a curious but not uncomfortable sense of once being just a boy. He pauses a moment, taking in the room. Then he laughs out loud at how little he knew of his future. How little others knew of him. He wishes he could have his day again with the bullies who had terrorized him so. What had they called them? *Bullers. The buggees. The buglies*, yes.

He's waited for so very long, and now that the moment is here, he can barely breathe. He believes in fate. Fate had brought Rory Fine to him all those years ago. Fate has brought her to him. Now they are here, he sees the circle of life as a marvelous, beautiful, ironic thing.

Surrounding them are walls adorned with art in bright prime colors—greens, reds, and yellows daubed with the enthusiasm of a child's imprudent hand. Strangely, this feels a happy place, filled with optimism. This pleases him, matching his own triumphant mood. Papier-mâché creations—varying versions of a shrunken head–are laid out on a long shelf against one wall. Boxes and boxes of books and games fill cases that run along another wall. Every spare wall is used for storage or display. Bright, fluorescent overhead illuminations hold back the shadows, and though he prefers to work by focused light, this is no longer necessary

For years, the moments he'd experienced in this school just a few rooms away had lived in his mind, alive and animated. Mikey over him, his hand on his mouth, with the smell of his skin, the roughness of the palm pressing against his lips. *If you don't stop, then everyone will hear.* Then Mikey flying across the room like a discarded rag doll. Rory kneeling on the bathroom stall floor talking to Mikey. *Are you okay? Are you okay?* Those words have inhabited his dreams.

He feels a burning triumph in his blood when he thinks of that day when Rory Fine touched him and thrust him to a hell, which ultimately became his savior.

In that second in the bathroom, which seemed to slow to an eternity of moments, he'd been given a glimpse of the other world. He'd peered through the shimmering opening, something like a ragged door, in the dirty, green bathroom. In that instant, he was changed. He saw them too, on the other side, looking back at him. His people and his home.

Then the opening and his people disappeared. Later as time moved on, he realized the event had transformed him. After this, everyone in his life paled—his pathetic, sick family, the other moronic children, amoebic-brained teachers, every single, living human being had become pointless creatures, blind to that which exists all around them. Now he was going home. Finally going through the door.

He'd always imagined during his search for the key, the window, this world he'd glimpsed, belonged to Rory Fine. Until he saw Fine driving the bus, while he followed the girl on-board. If this other world had belonged to Fine, then why was he still here? He possessed more power than the rest of these creatures, but he was still nothing more than a pathetic shadow of what he could be as he dragged emotions from these flawed human beings. Such a futile exercise.

"No need to be afraid," he says to her.

He has repeated these words to each of them. They never understand. They don't grasp the concept, and maybe that's how the world should function. They are not like him. He'd seen the truth the day Mikey died. He hadn't stood watching in horror as everyone thought; he'd been mortified to still be trapped on this side.

"This won't hurt too much. Just relax," he says to her.

After so many failed attempts, these words he speaks without thinking, without needing to engage his conscious mind; they have become part of the process, part of the design, to bring him down to the calm he needs.

Like all the others, her gaze is fixed on him like he has the answers to every question in the world. And maybe he does. He looks upon her, marveling at the glowing energy. Just like on the bus, this close, she warms every molecule of his being.

Her eyes move to the left and her gaze lands on the teacher laying on the floor. He didn't recognize him as Mr. Starsey after all these years. Ironic because that day imprinted them, and fate has brought them back full circle; all players ready in place.

How the teacher thought he could prevent him from taking The One and finding his way back to the other world was pure foolishness. He'd found them quickly, and he will be forever grateful for the growth in his abilities. One minute: nothing. Next, they were there in his sights. Watching in amusement as Starsey prepared his mechanisms; electronic buzzing things like walking sticks for those suffering just a limp. Starsey's view of the world, too small and limited to offer any resistance. So he'd turned the teacher's technology against him. Oh yes, they were led to him, but he already awaited, well prepared.

"You're wondering why?" he asks her.

He doesn't share this knowledge easily. They cannot comprehend, but she deserves to know some, for she is different, the catalyst who will alter everything.

She continues to stare at the teacher, but he wants her to listen, to be part of what is to come, so she has a chance of seeing what greatness she holds.

"He's of no concern," he says, nodding to the prostrate form.

She meets his eyes. He knows what she thinks. Of course she wants to know the answer to the *why?*

"So very simple. This is the way of life," he says, pushing at her curls; silk beneath his fingertips. He trails his palm across her forehead. So perfectly smooth.

"You think you exist within a solid body, but everything is an optical illusion. None of this is the true reality. You're nothing more than strings of energy and matter, twirling in their own universe. Your beautiful strings are special, though you're an anomaly of nature."

Her eyes follow his every movement. The wave of an arm, the tilting of his head, the movement of his mouth. He appreciates that she knows these might be the last images she will ever see.

"Don't worry, you never die. Not really. You'll return again."

He gestures and nods as he speaks, warming to his role of teacher. "If you can imagine this is like the Earth's total volume of water. Most don't understand the quantity is finite. The molecules just cycle through forms. Rain, ice, or snow; they fall to Earth and fill the oceans, lakes, rivers, puddles, every living thing. Then they melt, evaporate, perspire, to form clouds which rain down, and so begins the cycle. The universe possesses a symmetry with matter. Like water, the perfect balance is maintained."

He thinks she understands; he sees something in her eyes.

"You're wondering why you, yes? Resonance, a perfect resonance. Each person has their own exact vibration, blame the sub-atomic strings. The one signal I need is rare, but I felt you out there."

He places a palm over his heart. "Heard you for years, but I couldn't find you. I kept looking, kept trying and failing with those others. But now we're here. You and me. Shall we make music so I can dance away?"

Something flashes, darkening her eyes. Anger, perhaps. So he says to her, "Please don't fight the process. This is the way, the only way."

He runs a stray finger down the side of her face. Her skin is soft, pliant, waiting for him. "And our friend, the bus driver, he isn't coming, if that's what you're hoping. I sent him a message and I'm certain he understood.

"You'll notice constriction in your chest. That's just me, please don't fight the feeling."

He leans down until their faces are level. She stares back, her eyes not even blinking. A small whimper like a meowing kitten escapes her lips.

"We need you perfectly still. But I can manage this without you needing to worry. Seems I have a nice little extra gift of control, courtesy of you or the bus driver or, well, I don't really know, but very handy."

He turns to his bag sitting next to the desk, retrieves the leather pouch to lay on the desk. Carefully, like he's handling a precious artifact, he retrieves the scalpel and holds the blade to the light.

"So," he says to her, pulling out the scalpel, checking the blade against the pad of his thumb. A thin line of red appears across the tip as though drawn by pen across his skin. Exhilaration bursts within as he feels the skin parting by microns. The exact balance of the implement is like a perfectly tuned musical instrument. Now, facing the key he thought he might never find, he smiles at his beautiful providence. He leans in and whispers. And the words are just for her and him and destiny.

"Are you ready?" he says to her.

57

"*T*hink *positively.*" That's what my mama would always say. "*No matter the height of the challenge you face, a good attitude makes the difference between failure and success.*"

I revved the throttle of the bike and stared at the gate. The lock didn't look too strong—maybe even kind of flimsy, even. *Yes, that was a positive.* The fence didn't appear to have been built to withstand a vehicle traveling at speed. *Another positive.* On the other side was the girl I loved. *A big positive.* I surmised if I hit the fence at speed at the right angle, just near the lock, there was a chance—no, think positively—there was *no way* the fence wasn't coming down or the gate wouldn't fly open.

I revved the throttle again, courage building until the urge to release the gear and send the bike forward overrode my apprehension.

Don't think. Go.

And I did. Gripping the handlebars like they possessed some magic that would protect me as I positive-willed the gate to fall, to offer no more resistance than paper.

The impact was surprisingly minor, just a jolt and the jangle and clatter of metal giving way. Part of the fence came down as well, dragged to ground by the weight of the gate torn from its hinges. The fence might be high to dissuade vandals, but was not sound. Positive thinking plus bike equals triumph.

There was a bump as I hit the raised pathway inside the gate, which unbalanced the bike slightly but I countered and stabilized the wobble. So then I was good. Once inside, I followed the pathway around to the side of the building.

Nothing had changed. This was the entrance where, in my first few school years, my mother would deposit me at the door to toddle my way to class, always hoping no-one would notice me or come too near.

The flaking red-painted wooden, double doors threw vivid memories at me. Friends, kindly teachers, the buglies, Stevie, Mikey, Daniel Starsey and, of course, that day. Then after the accident, Mikey's mother accepting an honorary award for her son at the end-of-year presentation. Stevie's face came to mind, solid and heart-breaking. The way he looked at me the following days was a little unsettling, like we had shared a very different experience. While I was nervous and sad he displayed a calm and quiet that wasn't there before.

I placed my hand against the door. My skin looked strikingly white against the rich-red, chipped paint. The fireflies in my head buzzed a merry little melody like they were actually happy. I felt Mariana inside the building, another strange development in my repertoire. Sensing others had never been my gift, but I felt changed, adapted. I hoped when this was over maybe Daniel could supply some answers and we would get to have that discussion, because I sensed him inside too, but the feeling was weak. I wasn't sure if this meant he was deeper in the building or something was wrong.

This ability was all very new and unknown. The killer couldn't know my gift had evolved in the last few days or surely he wouldn't have sent the message, wouldn't have allowed a tenuous contact that could reveal so much. Or this could be a trap.

Mariana's fear was a palpable force feeding through to me as though we shared an invisible tether. I felt her alive still, but I had to get inside. In a hurry. I doubted she would stay that way for long.

I tried the door, twisting at the worn brass knob. Locked. Then shoved my shoulder into the wooden door. A sharp throb shuddered down my arm.

I heard my mama's voice. *Think positively.*

But this was a locked door and far from the flimsiness of the fence, so I didn't think being positive would be the key. Then again, I had felt the jolt of the fence as my bike careened through, like the something beyond allowed me access.

But this was a door. Then again, what choice did I have?

Think positively. You can go through.

The fireflies buzzed in my vision, flitting here and there, tingling in my core. On the other side I felt Mariana's presence. She couldn't die because of a door. I turned to look at my bike sitting at the bottom of the steps. A good bike and one that had served me well.

Thinking positively had worked once. Let's hope optimism worked again. I jumped down the steps, two at a time, and noticed the dent in the front guard and the nasty scrapes along the side from the wire fence. Well, my ride was already damaged, so ...

I climbed on again and offered "sorry" to my accomplice and turned the key. The engine erupted to life, sounding deep and *positive* in the quiet of the night. Circling slowly back into the yard, I gave myself enough distance to build speed. Then I counted down from five as my wrist twisted back and forth on the throttle, the revs sounding high and loud, and even door-busting, in the quiet night air.

I wondered if he heard me coming. I hoped he did, and I hoped he knew to be afraid. This was the sound of me and *positive* thinking, positive energy and common goodness riding in to save the day and restore balance. With all this on my side how could I lose?

58

The muscles of her mouth twitch as she tries to speak. He reaches down to run a quivering finger across her lips. Her body, her mind, the window portal, now belongs to him. She glows so exquisitely; a pale pink of glorious wavering light surrounds her body, head to toe. He could stare at the light forever.

At his touch, her eyes roll in their sockets. There is a slight rise in her eyebrows and he wonders at the strength she must exert to make the movement when he has hold of her. He feels her will push at him and he is amused. Still, just to be sure, because this must be absolutely perfect, he has wound the duct tape about her and the chair.

The scalpel glints gray in the brilliant overhead lights as though the blade smiles at him with certainty. He brings the fine tip to rest against her forehead just below the new hairline, two inches above its previous position. With his other hand, he braces the side of her head.

"Hold still now," he says, calm and focused.

Anticipation is a juicy, sweet candy on his tongue.

Then, in one smooth, gentle practiced move, he runs the precision blade across the taut scalp skin. Just like drawing a pencil line. A thin crimson streak follows the knife's path as though he creates art on a flesh-colored canvas. He feels her pain sensors explode beneath his touch. Her eyes bulge as if the air pressure has increased inside her head.

Warm blood trickles over his fingertips, sticky and hot, as he angles the blade down and around in a curve. White skull bone appears for just a moment, then disappears as the redness of blood overwhelms the wound. His focus is intense. He wants this center perfect.

Then there is something ...

Something away. Distant. Something he feels in the air. Something wrong.

He stays the blade paused over the seeping half circle he's created. Something has changed in the last few seconds.

Then he sees, as the image swims before his eyes like the swell of a tide coming nearer. They are not alone. He pulls back from her and turns toward the door and wonders his next move. When the crashing sound comes, he has already begun to wonder how he made this mistake.

A growling roar like an angry beast arises from somewhere outside. He puts down the bloodied scalpel and moves toward the door. A few steps and he stops, annoyance rising, which then turns to anger. He needs peace. This is not peace. This is an interruption, confounding him with its audacity.

There's something else he's never seen, which surprises and puzzles him. He slowly turns to take in his surrounds. Colorful wisps slide and slice through the air, over the papier-mâché heads, the artwork, the desks and every object in the room. He is now unsettled.

He is still pondering the *why* and the *how* when the sound of an explosion reaches him. No, not an explosion. A crash. Splitting wood, a cascade of calamity, of something destroyed by force. A door. A wall. Outside, somewhere down the hall.

His mind spins. His mind *never* spins. The wisps have gone now. Danced away. He is again alone with her.

Then he feels him. How is he here?

He glances back at The One. He hears her name in his head.

Mariana. Mariana. Mariana. Over and over like a muffled scream. He stares longingly at her. A few more minutes, maybe ten, and he would be ready. He would be going home.

But the bus driver is coming now. An interruption. An invader. An annoyance to be dealt with before he can continue.

He sighs as he walks back to the teacher's desk. He picks up the scalpel, feels the weight firm and obedient in his hand. He stares down at the table; the drill, the six long, silver needles, his shiny pieces aligned and perfectly in place.

He turns to her, calm and in control, and he wants to say: "Don't worry. I'll be back."

But the way she stares at him, the look of triumph in her eyes, stops him. He thinks of the vision of those waiting on the other side. Calling him to home. He will not be stopped after all this time. A calm seeps into his mind. A necessary calm to face this intruder. So instead he says to her, to her glowing, hopeful eyes: "I have a reunion, of sorts, but he is not your hero. He could have been so much more. Shortly all he'll be is a dead wannabe hero who had enormous potential."

59

I'd expected to fly off my bike at impact with the door. They clearly don't make doors like they used to. *Thank you, education funding cuts.* In fact, I'd almost performed a perfect stunt jump. The skid along the hallway was what just didn't pan exactly as I'd hoped.

As the bike connected with the door, the sound was horrendous, like a mini-explosion. My strategy of aiming directly where the two double doors connected had worked pretty perfectly. The force partially shattered one door with a whopping crack, which sounded as though the building might collapse, breaking the flimsy lock.

I was through. And alive. As much as I had thrown everything in with positive thinking, surviving still felt miraculous. A split-second later though, I realized getting through the door wasn't the issue. Staying upright was the challenge.

The out of balance bike twisted sideways and traveled uncontrollably in a direction of its own choosing. I managed to jump clear, but the momentum still threw me forward at nearly the same speed as the bike. For those few seconds, as I covered the distance at a terrifying pace, I worked at my legs and arms, frantically searching for something to grab. Uppermost in my mind, I didn't want the bike going over or on top of me.

In movies, when accidents happen, everything slows to a snail's crawl, so every little detail is displayed for your watching pleasure. In real life, the event happens so fast your mind becomes blank and your vision is just a blur of color and objects moving faster than they ever should. The sound is hell, like the roar of a wild beast intent on devouring you should their jaws clamp onto any part of your body.

I was tumbling, and not in a graceful way, until a large cardboard carton stopped me instantly. The force buckled the sides inward and knocked over the box, spilling dozens of what looked like coloring books onto the floor.

The bike continued onward, slamming hard against the door at the end of the hall, which did not forgive like the gate. The bike stood upright for a moment, then collapsed backward at the entrance, with the back wheel still in place but spinning in the air. The engine stalled, and there was just me, the creak of the turning wheel, and a growing silence.

Adrenaline kicked in like a switch flicked on and all the pent-up emotion flooded into my body. My heart thumped as though wanting to escape and smash the nearest door in sympathy.

Now time *did* slow as I lay there for seconds that felt like hours and tried to find sense in what had just happened. Why I was laying on the floor; why I was even here; and why was my bike laying yards away smashed and ruined?

Then the reality rushed over me, and I climbed to my feet, unsteady, reaching for a rail running the length of the hall, which suddenly felt like a lifeline. My hands traveled frantically over my arms and legs—surely something would be broken?—but no, nothing. Except, as I put weight on my knee, what felt like fire licked through my left leg. *Oh damn.*

Gingerly I pushed two fingers at the pain, which hurt like hell, but didn't feel broken. Two-to-three-inches below the knee, my pants were torn. I pulled at the ragged hole, the surrounding material saturated with blood. The torn strips easily pulled back to reveal a four or five inch gash just below the knee that would need stitches. I tried putting weight on the the limb again. A dozen bees had taken up residence, but I thought I could still walk. Amazing how shock and adrenaline can influence a body.

I reached for my cell, thinking now maybe I could call the police as a backup. The authorities might not believe we'd found the Trepan Killer using psychic gifts, but they'd certainly believe a report of a bike crashing through a school entrance. I'd worry how to explain the why and how later.

But my cell was gone. I looked around, but my only means of communication was nowhere in sight. The force of the impact and my skid up the hallway must have thrown the darn thing from my pocket. Damn.

But *think positively Rory.*

I was all in one piece, mobile, and now inside the building. A reasonable result, even with the injury. Instantly my mind turned to Mariana. I felt her here somewhere. Felt him too.

I felt him as though he stood by me, as though I'd touched him and drawn out his troubles. What I felt wasn't troubles though, more like a mind connected to the very air around me. This was another *New.* Chris Lamben's words came to me and now made sense.

I'm plugged into an imaginary wall socket, and that socket connects to the free flowing energy surrounding us.

Maybe the guides had given me my own version of plug-in-and-play with the energy.

Vibrant memories of this hallway bounced around in my consciousness, but there was no time for reminiscing. I needed to move. I checked up and down the hall and then smiled. I didn't need supernatural ability to find the killer. A light shone from a room four doors up, which I'd only just passed flying along the floorboards. In there was the killer. Mariana too. I felt this knowledge, as though a sign hung on the door. White, beckoning light shone through the glass squares in the top half of the door and from the gap below calling to me. *Come in. Come in Rory Fine. Time to play.* I didn't know if I'd imagined those words or *he* was in my head.

First problem: no weapon. Second: no idea what to do when I came face-to-face with him in the flesh. It's one crazy thing to battle a dark entity, my temporary guest in the attic, another when you are facing the breathing, living master. Standing here though, wouldn't save her or the world, for that matter.

I began up the hallway, each step on my injured leg a slice of agony. I attempted to counter the pain by thinking of something that would compel me forward, no matter what. *Love.* Mariana was in there, and I would somehow save her.

Ten steps and I'd be at the door. *Come in. Time to play.*

"Yes, let's play," I replied, under my breath.

All I had was my gift and whatever the ability had become since this had begun. I needed my gift tuned to optimum performance, so I needed to regain my calm, slow my madly beating heart and lower my breathing rate. What I must do was gain control of my focus.

Breathe. Relax. Be at peace. Breathe. Relax. Be at peace.

I ran those words through my head, infused them into every cell like recharging a million, trillion little batteries. And be positive, I reminded myself. *Remember, the power of positive.*

My pulse slowed. My breathing eased. My mind became empty of everything except my desire to stop him. To save Mariana's life.

Relax. Breathe. Relax. Be at peace. The words began to work. A sense of calm settled over me, a blanket of solace. Even the pain in my leg eased just a little.

Now with my mind calmed, I became aware of an open door into a darkened room. I stepped sideways, into the shadows. A few more seconds were needed to fully steady my mind. Moments later and my eyes had adjusted to the dark. The irony of the room in which I now found myself was not lost on me.

Voices. Crying. Mikey. Stevie. The smell of vomit. The echo of distress in the very walls.

"*Mikey, you don't look too good.*"

Mikey's reply: "*What happ ... ened. Feel, no, don't feeel like me. Don't feel right.*"

Even the back of my head where my skull had hit the basin began to throb.

Mikey's face as he sprung up and ran for the door, his shirt flying behind him as he escaped. Here was the bathroom. There was the basin.

The terrible recall overwhelmed my mind and I began to breathe hard as my heart skipped up a notch. I didn't need this trip down memory lane right now. I needed focus, but the room kept spinning, throwing emotions at me.

Breathe. Relax. Be at peace. Breathe. Breeeathe. Relaaax.

Suddenly, through everything, I heard footsteps outside in the hall. I clawed back my mind to the present. My breath caught in my throat, and I gently sidestepped closer into the shadows behind the door. Light from the moon sprinkled through the busted door into the hall. There was a figure moving out there. Slowly, purposely. The light from the room he'd exited fell across his path.

I eased the bathroom door closed, so a small gap remained. As I stared through the slim aperture, an image from my past filtered into my mind as though the face were right there. His eyes were what I recognized, but they'd changed from when I'd last looked into them.

Stevie only came back to school for a few more weeks before his family moved. Moved is what I'd heard, anyway. Maybe they'd just taken him out of our school and placed him somewhere else nearby. Who would blame them?

Stevie and I had never spoken of that day. The memory was a silent horror that hung between us, pushing our lives apart, not uniting us as disasters sometimes do. But he'd never seemed right after that day. He'd been a bright spirit before, but after that day a shadow version replaced his personality. I figured he may have been afraid of me, of what he'd seen. Now, I understood fear hadn't transformed him.

His change had been because of me. For this I was deeply sorry. Though what he'd done with the power he must have inherited from my touch was his choosing. I wondered what could have occurred to cause him to take this path. As I gently pulled the door closed, one thought inhabited my mind: Whatever had made him this way, he chose wrong.

60

The sound of footsteps had traveled up the hall past me and grown faint. He looked for me and sensed I was near. I imagined a cloak over me, like that famous wizard character Harry's cloak of invisibility. I didn't know if the concept would work, but then until a few hours ago I didn't know I could do half the things I'd done. Which made me wonder: had his power grown and evolved like mine? Had a chain reaction begun the moment I picked up the dark thing?

Not knowing his abilities I decided my best strategy was to find Mariana and escape quietly, avoiding confrontation at all cost. But things were not going my way. My leg had begun to throb. *Badly*. This injured I wasn't going to win a fight or escape quickly. Pain had begun to whither my calm, so I wasn't certain if I could even defend against an attack by another dark thing. I had no idea if the guides had stuck around. For all I knew, I was on my own. Probably *was* on my own.

My mama's face entered my mind.

"Anything you set your mind on, you can do. Imagine you can, and you can."

I would have kissed her if she was here. She'd seeded my imagination with positive, wonderful messages all my life. All I needed was to listen.

Imagine the pain gone. That's what I must do.

I closed my eyes and reached down with my mind, just like I did when troubles keeping. A cool palm stretched out from the mist of my imagination and wrapped around my injured, swollen knee for just a moment, then moved on slowly to cover the jagged tear in my skin. The soothing cool seeped into the skin, blood, then bone and shimmered through the firing nerve and pain sensors. As I applied mental pressure to the wound, I dragged at the pain, imagining my psychic palm pulling at the suctioned tentacles of hurt feeding poisonous pain into my body. I gathered them together like they were strands of string and pulled, dragging the glowing filaments away from my leg.

At first the little suckers resisted, then, as though they knew they couldn't win, they simply released and came away. Within moments, I had ferried the strands of pain to the attic and secured them into a box as though they were simply troubles. The panels of the prison turned red, then orange, before finally fading to a pale, glowing, quite beautiful creamy-pink.

"Hmm, neat trick," I whispered, wiping my palms together. "I'll deal with you later."

When I opened my eyes and placed weight on the leg nearly all the pain was gone. Small traces that felt more like a pushed bruise ache, was all that remained; the pain no longer enjoyed over-whelming control. This relief made sense. Pain, like emotions, was simply a transfer of energy via nerve endings, so of course the feeling could be manipulated. I wondered if I could do the same for others; another string to my troubles keeping bow.

Now I could return my focus to my next move. I listened at the door for long seconds. The sound of footsteps was gone. I took a deep breath thinking: now or never. I wasn't even sure if my imagined invisibility even worked, if he actually knew I was in here and was now playing a cat-and-mouse game.

Opening the door a quarter way, I slid through into the hall like a spy in the night, gently testing my injured leg. The limb felt reasonably solid, just a slight twinge to remind me there was an injury I would need to deal with later. The light from the room ahead still glowed brightly, beckoning me.

With each step I reclaimed my calm. *Breathe. Relax. Be at peace.*

At the door I crouched below the glass panels, put my ear to the wood and listened. Mariana was in that room, I simply knew. A thread of emotion from her had tightened around my heart. I didn't want to look through those windows. I didn't want to see what could be there, what he might have already done.

My little fireflies, the same sense that had told me he wasn't in there also told me he was searching and would soon return. I didn't have long.

As I grasped the handle, I noticed my hand shaking. *Calm. Relax. Be at peace.* The doorknob turned easily, followed by the sound of the click of the released catch—far too loud. Too much a warning, a calling to him. I gently pushed at the door as my heart pushed at my chest. *Calm. Relax. Be at peace.*

The door swung open, creaking loudly, like every stupid horror movie door. Peering inside, about to enter this room, weaponless, with a killer somewhere nearby, seemed all kinds of foolish. But then foolish had been my middle name since all this started.

Inside the room my attention was drawn to straight rows of desks with chairs pushed neatly beneath. The room was a jungle of art, momentarily blinding me with color. When I looked back, I saw Mariana immediately at the teacher's desk tied by tape to a chair. She sat upright, eyes open, as though overseeing a classroom of students only she could see. Her head was upright but her neck seemed unnaturally stiff. She *must* have heard me—the creaking door was loud enough—yet her head only partially turned in my direction, like just moving the muscles hurt. What was wrong?

Blood was everywhere, running down her face, having dripped onto her clothes and the floor. My heart churned for her to see what he had done. As awful as the vision was, my all-consuming wish was granted. Mariana was alive.

My leg might not have been fit for sprinting, but I was across the room in a dash. I hurtled around the desk and swung the swivel-chair to face me and kneeled before her, careful to rest just my good knee on the floor. Our gazes met and I saw true terror shining from her eyes. Her entire body though, seemed unnaturally stiff, but her eyes were very much alive. They blinked and followed my face like I was her whole world.

Anger rose like bile in my throat at the patch of revealed scalp and the half circle carved on her forehead. A flap of skin hung down from one side around the hole, where the monster had begun to peel away her scalp. Rivulets of blood slithered from the wound and down the sides of her face, to mingle at her chin like a fork in a river, before the rich-red droplets dripped into her lap.

God, there was so much more blood now I was up close!

"Mariana! You'll be okay. We're getting away from here."

Even before loosening the tape, I touched my hand to her cheek. A single tear squeezed from the corner of her eye and traveled down her face to mix with the blood. She couldn't speak for some reason, but I felt as though I heard her in my head. She trusted me and I could not fail her. I needed the kind of courage I'd never imagined I would possess. Her troubles flowed to me as the panic and fear left her eyes. I funneled the emotions away, but there was no time to admire my neat work, as I would normally. Loss of blood could send someone into irreversible shock and I needed to staunch the flow. With her skull exposed she looked all too fragile.

My eyes never left hers as I spoke and continued to pull at the tape. "Don't worry. You should feel calmer now. Give me a second." But I needed to find something to cover her wounds. I stood and looked frantically about the room. A few necessary spent moments and then I would have her out of there.

A container in a corner filled with multi-colored material caught my eye. I dashed to the shelf, gathered a handful of what was rags turned into art material, and turned back to Mariana. That's when I saw Daniel, practically tripped over him as he lay on the floor between two front row desks. I'd been so intent on Mariana, I hadn't even noticed.

Now I rushed to him, bending down to check for a pulse. Thank God, there was one. A black, nasty lump swelled on the side of his head, but there was no other injury I could see. No terrible carving in his forehead or blood anywhere. Poor Daniel. His enthusiasm for helping us had done this. Guilt banged at me, but tomorrow I would worry, but for now I had two people to save.

As I stood from Daniel, I spied a pot of scissors on a nearby low bench. *Maybe a makeshift weapon?* I wondered how many people had saved the world with a pair of children's scissors. They didn't even have sharp points, but the blades seemed sharp.

Back with Mariana, I again squatted before her. "Everything's okay. Daniel's okay. He's just unconscious," I said, pressing one of the cloths against her head. "I'm so sorry. I didn't realize the killer was Stevie."

Stevie didn't sound right for a cold-hearted killer—*Stephen,* maybe?

"I know him," I continued. "I'll explain later, but I think I'm to blame for what he's become."

Her eyes broke my heart as they searched my face. They said more than words. She'd barely moved a muscle since I'd entered the room and I realized I might need to carry her out. My leg had begun to send shooting pain reminders that my little pain keeping trick was not a permanent fix.

"Mariana, can you move any part of your body? Try moving a finger?"

She looked down to her lap where one of her hands rested. While still applying pressure to her head, I watched for movement. There was a slight tremble in a thumb and her wrist but I realized there were forces at work preventing her from full control. I'd need to move her, and then Daniel.

I knew Stevie—no, I had to think of him as who he was now, the Trepan Killer—would return soon. Again, I felt the dark presence of him growing nearer. We really needed to move this second but releasing the pressure on Mariana's wound was a concern. Maybe I needed to do what I'd told myself I shouldn't do: deal with the killer first. If I didn't we were open to be ambushed as we escaped.

I touched Mariana's face, cupping her cheek in my hand trying to assure her. As I did, I dragged again at her fears. Her eyes told me she felt the release and this time she wasn't annoyed with me.

"Mariana, I'm going to leave you for a moment. Okay? I promise he won't hurt you anymore."

I pulled off my sweater and tied the arms tightly around the cloth on Mariana's head. The arms were long enough to tie a knot and hold the piece of art material in place. Now my attention turned inward to the pain energy imprisoned in the attic. The pain energy pushed against a container I had made quickly on the fly. With each passing second, the hurt filtered back into my body like a slow dripping tap. I tried to reinforce the box with chains and thicker walls, but the wild, energetic particles continued to leak, like they were finer than normal troubles and could pass through the barriers. My chance to do anything was trickling away right before me. I looked at the door over Mariana's head, then back into her eyes.

"I've got to find him. I'll be back."

As I turned away and moved to the door, I felt a wrenching in my heart. My knee ached nearly as much as the moment of injury, so now I had no choice but to give in to a limp. How well was this rescue going to work now? Me limping around looking for a killer. But then what choice did I have? I held out the scissors, the blades spread apart; a gun would've been nice. If I could just surprise him, then maybe, maybe this would be over. With each step, I bit down on my lip and that helped to slightly take the pain from my leg.

Once at the door, I twisted back to Mariana to assure her I'd be back soon. She gave me a faint smile, which was heartening. Whatever was controlling her was loosening its hold. When I returned to face the door, I realized my time was up.

61

I recognized him immediately from the bus. Why hadn't I noticed the resemblance, realized he was Stevie? You're just not looking for someone from your past to step on your bus, especially someone like him. Yes, he had been aboard, but his subterfuge was good.

The night I took everyone's troubles, he was the one with the cold. Here's me thinking his thoughtfulness prevented him from slapping my hand but the whole act was a ruse. When I saw him the next time, he still coughed into his handkerchief, which obscured his face. At the time, I vaguely remembered thinking *poor guy* and hoped he didn't spread a virus on every seat rail he touched. Turns out he was spreading something far nastier.

I saw Stevie now as a man, tall and confident, a far cry from the boy I once knew. His blonde hair, now a light brown, looked carefully styled and particular, which seemed ironic considering the chaos he'd created. Though we shared the same age he looked younger, like an older teenager. He'd lost the shoulder hunch of his childhood, the bodily personification of someone uncertain of life. He stood in the doorway, dressed in a fashionable suit, his tie askew, as though he'd just finished work and had switched off for the day. You wouldn't give him a second look, except for the specks of blood spattered on his white, dress shirt.

"Hello Rory. I wish I could say good to see you, yet again, but I thought I'd sent you a very clear message. Yet you've somehow come anyway. Call my contact a Freudian slip of a mistake. Possibly for old time's sake I did want to see you again. Like a class reunion."

He held his arms wide as though he was about to take a bow and lowered his head as though tipping a hat.

"You haven't changed much. Always Mr. Do-gooder, running around helping kids with your special skill. I must thank you too, for handing your gift off to me. I haven't wasted mine. I've turned my power into something more. Excuse my games over the past few days, but my curiosity was too difficult to control. What you did with all those passengers was impressive and that got me wondering if your ability had grown like mine. Then I realized *not*." He opened his palm to emphasize *not*.

I listened to him, trying to remain calm, thinking my next move.

"I don't understand why you've done this," I said. "How could you do this, Stevie? Kill all those people? Do this to Mariana?"

"Better call me Stephen now. Stevie lives in the past. In fact, he died that day in the bathroom. I take care of things in a way he couldn't. Ask those dumb parents of mine. Oh, you may not have heard? Both of them died—suicide. Too much on their plate. Or maybe over-emotional, a poor lifestyle, right? I can drain emotion too, you see. But ah, I don't worry about troubles. They can keep those. I take the good stuff."

I wanted to stall him until I thought of something or maybe Daniel woke up, or I didn't know what, so I kept asking questions.

"Okay, but why Beth Ann and Mariana?"

"Well, the woman at the depot, she was just something to prod you. See what you were made of. This one though, she's special." He looked over me to Mariana. "But you already know. She has what I need, what I have searched for all these years. A window to the other world I saw. A doorway that appeared in the bathroom, the day you changed me."

He began to walk past me as though confident I offered no threat.

"Wait. Hold on. What do you mean the *other world*?"

He stopped and stared at me, then frowned.

"Hmm, interesting. I thought you knew. I thought the other dimension was *your* world. You, a visitor like me. I wondered after seeing you again, why you had remained here on this side."

"I'm not sure what you mean"—*which was the absolute truth*—"but if there is a world you saw, and you think you belong there, why not just go and leave us alone?"

"I did try, but I couldn't find the entrance again, no matter how hard I willed the doorway to appear. Then I realized I needed you or someone like you. Someone with the power to, I guess, give me a kind of boost. So I've searched ever since. Know what I found? There's a lot of people who have a touch of what you have, and some people have more than remnants. Psychic powers, I guess you'd call them. So began a wild goose chase in a way, because nobody had enough of the necessary right energy. Until The One, your Mariana. On the bus when I touched her, I knew. Then I saw you there too. So much a beautiful perfect destiny."

He sounded insane. I was still trying to work out what to do, willing Daniel to wake up, so I continued, feeling like those police negotiators in hostage situations.

"Stevie, Stephen, maybe we can work this out. Maybe I can help you. You don't need to hurt Mariana. I don't think this is what destiny wants of you."

He shook his head. "Ah, you're wrong. Destiny has brought you here as well. Like a double package, just to be sure I have enough to get over, to go home."

My heart had begun to thud, but I heard the sound like a distant banging, as though I stood outside myself. My breath sounded like an echo, like I was trapped inside a sealed chamber. My blood coursed through my veins, every corpuscle imbued with a fiery drive.

"No," I said under my breath. "Can't happen."

I would not let him take Mariana. Or Daniel. Or anyone else. Instead of taking this gift he'd been accidentally given and doing

something good, he'd chosen to create chaos and pain. I knew he'd
endured terrible things thanks to his parents and my inadvertent
mistake, but you don't do what he'd done to Beth Ann and all the
others.

"You're not doing this," I said, my voice sounding calmer than I
felt.

I gestured toward him with the scissors, waving them as though
the tiny blades were a sword. Probably looked ridiculous, *was* ridiculous, but I needed more time. I sensed something occurring, a small
change in the density of the gently swirling air. Whether the knowing
came from me or something in the atmosphere, I no longer felt alone
in this fight.

The confident smile on Stevie's face dissolved. A steely look came
into his eyes. "I am doing this. You know I can't stop. You should
understand at least that we don't belong here. There's another place
for us."

Whatever this other world was I had no awareness of this other
dimension. I'd never seen, felt or had any sense there was something
else around us, except when the psychic Lamben's spirit guide helped
me. Even then, I didn't really understand what the glowing white
entity truly was; I just felt glad he or she had appeared at the exact
moment they were needed.

The atmosphere had grown in the few minutes since Stephen had
entered the room. There felt a slow rise like humidity creeping up on
a summer's day, except this wasn't moisture, this was a dense buildup of emotions, frenzied and thick.

"Use me then," I pleaded.

"Can't. She's The One. She has a special DNA, a power, an ability
that I've realized after all my searching and experimentation I need.
She's rare, maybe the only one. She doesn't know what she possesses,
how to use her power. Like an athlete with an innate ability, unaware
until they start training."

"But why don't you just dimensional travel yourself? Why must
you kill, since you're so supposedly evolved?"

"Oh, I would if I could. Shame you didn't hand off that ability that day in the bathroom. Maybe this is all your fault."

He paused and pointed a slow lazy-finger toward where Daniel Starsey lay unmoving on the floor. "He's interesting though. The gadgets are fascinating. Maybe one day he might work out how to cross over to the other world without the need to use ones like her."

His finger then moved to point toward Mariana.

"Right now, the only way to access the part of the brain where this ability is located is with my surgery. The right One, enough energy applied and, voila, I'm home. But I think this has something to do with you too. Your proximity has affected her."

The disdainful way he referred to Mariana like she was a thing to be used, fanned anger already burning through me.

"Pretty damn selfish of you. Killing innocent people for your own benefit."

"*You* kill to stay alive, use the bodies of animals and plants for food, clothing, shelter. Survival instinct is strong, no matter who or what you are. Now, lesson over. School was a long time ago for you and me. I will finish what you began.

He turned away and moved toward Mariana as though I no longer existed. Maybe he thought violence wasn't in my repertoire. As I took a step toward him to prove him wrong, I felt a warm energy around me. Was this his influence or something else? My fear and fury exploded into a white hot knot in my stomach as Stephen stood by Mariana examining the instruments on the desk. When I attempted to raise even a foot, something held me. I couldn't move. There was something else too; a distant buzz of fireflies assuring me to wait, to trust my instinct.

"You're pretty certain of yourself," I said.

He didn't reply but picked up the drill. The tool whirred to life; the sound dreadful and grating in the quiet room. Even from here, I saw the terror return to Mariana's eyes. Then, as though he'd noticed something not to his liking, he replaced the drill on the table and picked up the scalpel. When he turned to Mariana his focus was cold as the steel of the blade he held above her.

"No," I screamed, willing my legs to move, to break the hold I felt on my muscles. With the first step, excruciating white-hot fire shot up my leg. In that movement, the pain box had dissolved and the remaining energy had escaped. Now, minus the instant adrenaline surge from the crash, the fire-ant throb had returned to a whole other level of agony.

My leg collapsed beneath me and I tumbled, head first, into the corner of a desk. Darkness came down like a rich velvet curtain settling over a veil of gray. Before engulfing me completely I saw my old friend, now an enemy standing over Mariana. He hadn't even looked my way; for him I no longer existed.

Mariana would die, the girl I loved butchered by a creature I'd help create. I couldn't let this happen and I fought at the darkness enveloping me. *Stay calm. Be at peace. Stay calm.*

My thoughts turned inside and I pulled at the pain shooting so violently up my leg, tearing into the fiber of my consciousness.

Just a few more minutes, I silently beseeched. *Then you can lash me with all the ache you like.*

But I was wrestling a viper. The wisps of energy danced and moved around the attic, hissing at me. This was a new experience and all I had was my focus and determination, but I brought that to bear on the pain, throwing my iron will at the thing. Like a butterfly net waved in pure frustration in the breeze, I unexpectedly snared the strands. Once I'd caught one, the rest came easily and I shoved them quickly in a new prison, a stronger, more suitable box. This one was glass, with no microscopic holes through which the dark thing could escape.

Instantly the gray fog before my eyes began to clear, and my strength returned in a rush like an incoming tsunami pushing back any fear or second thoughts about what I could or couldn't do. I was on my feet and moving toward Stevie, the scissors clutched in my hand. Whatever I needed to do to stop him I would.

He didn't turn from Mariana and still held the scalpel resting on her forehead when he addressed me.

"You can't harm me. I've evolved somewhat."

His words and confidence stopped me for a second, the pathetic weapon waving in my hand. He had moved beside Mariana, having untied my makeshift bandage to reveal the wound. The tape I'd loosened still held her in place, but she had become unnaturally still. Blood had begun again to trickle down her forehead and face, and her brutalized scalp was a dreadful sight. Should I rush him though he could easily cut her throat before I had reached them.

Quieting my mind—*calm, be peaceful*—the room, the very air particles, everything around me slowed. His smiling, leering face, Mariana's blinking eyes, the movement of my own legs and arms. I studied everything within sight, thinking, thinking ... there had to be something I could do. Everything couldn't end this way. Mariana, even the world perhaps. Did Stephen even know what he risked?

The room's energy felt charged like an elastic coil ready to spring. The hair on my arms stood sharply on end, and my skin prickled as though moisture evaporated from the surface. Something was happening.

I noticed Mariana's eyes moving ... maybe trying to say something. She stared right at me, then her eyes looked to the left, then back. Then to the left and back again. I looked in the direction in which she seemed to signal.

The table. She seemed to motion to the desk. I looked over to where she indicated, searching. But what? An open case, several smaller, sharp medical implements, the needles and the drill.

What was I was supposed to see?

I systematically rechecked each item again, my gaze stopping on each one as my panic began to rise. No matter how many times I repeated *calm*, we'd gone way beyond that.

Then I saw what she wanted me to see. Of course.

Smart girl. Incredible girl. With everything happening she had still noticed what I hadn't seen. For all Stevie's superiority, his downfall might just be his own arrogance.

My hope now was Daniel really did know his stuff, that his gadgets worked like he'd said and that he always kept his batteries charged. In the next few seconds, we were about to discover if science could trump evil.

62

Daniel Starsey had explained—let's say boasted—the capabilities of the super-conducting quantum interference device. With so many uses, calling the technology a SQUID seemed a poor reference. Among capabilities like tracing energy imprints, the instrument could also emit a sub-atomic energy wave, something like an electromagnetic pulse, (the stuff of futuristic terrorist threats). Daniel had informed us he'd built this fail-safe into the unit should the device ever fall into the wrong hands.

His theory was carving a hole in a person's skull and inserting needles into their brains wasn't the main reason people died. At least not every time. No, according to him, as energy traveled via the needles the brain short-circuited like an electrical spike.

Watching Stephen hold the scalpel pressed to Mariana's face was horrific. He began setting to work on the opposite side of his original cut. Fresh blood seeped as the flesh separated. He stopped and turned his head side-to-side, examining his handiwork like an artist touching up a painting. This loss of mobility for me and Mariana must be his doing; he was far too cavalier in ignoring me, obviously believing his power infallible.

Maybe with anyone else his control would be absolute, but he had the girl I loved beneath that blade. I'd made her a promise: *"He won't hurt you anymore."* And I always keep my promises.

Mariana's stare and mine connected and something passed between us. I'll never know how I managed the move, but sheer will carried me forward as though my feet weren't touching the floor, but simply skimmed the surface. A few more inches and I would be close enough to snatch up the SQUID.

Mariana must have understood my next move. How she managed to do what she did next must have been through sheer will. The power to survive. Her gift, yet unexplored. She managed to bring one of her hands up against his arm. As she did, half-spoken words erupted from her. "Yo-ooo-aw ju'ss ee-vehl."

Stephen the Trepan Killer, the confident master of extraordinary power, actually looked surprised. That was all I needed, just an unexpected distraction, a half-second in time that caused him to back away from her.

I lunged for the SQUID and had the gadget in my hand even before he'd replied, "Evil is just a perspective."

On the SQUID's right hand corner a small rectangle glowed blue. I pressed the button, willing the thing to instant life. A row of lights on the screen's bottom systematically lit up from red to amber to green. I recalled this same sequence when Daniel had partially demonstrated what to *never* touch. Then the gadget buzzed in my hand and I hoped green meant ready. And, I doubly-hoped, the button on the right, over which my finger hovered, was the one to send the sub-atomic pulse.

Stephen swiveled and seeing the SQUID in my hand he hesitated, then took a step toward me. At least he'd moved away from Mariana.

"Wait. You don't underst—" he began to say, but far too late. I'd already jabbed the button and held the SQUID out toward him. A beautiful glowing ball of white-gold and blue light streamed from the head of the device and arced to the scalpel in his hand. The light traveled into his fingers and the skin of his palm and, within seconds, the blue glow had moved up his arm.

The superior pretense dissolved from his face like a melted wax mask. His eyes, so full of fire and triumph now held a limp, empty expression as though every particle of energy had instantly drained from his body. The blue-white glow continued, spreading quickly beneath his skin to fill his entire body, and then expanded to surround him like an aura. The colored light thrashed and leaped a few inches about him, reminding me of a video I'd seen of the Aurora Borealis. Blue became pink, then yellow, exploding into all the colors of the rainbow to then cycle back through the paler versions of the colors. The vision, quite beautiful, if not for the look of horror and rage now contorting his face.

Stephen reached out a hand as though trying to grab hold of something solid just inches from his fingers. His body shuddered and jerked, then he flew a few yards backward to land at the base of a low bookcase. Books and paper tumbled around and on him. They too took on the glow, as his body writhed on the floor, like he was in the throes of a fit.

His eyes stared up at me, accusing, as though I'd broken a cardinal rule of the psychic world. I'd no idea what had happened or what *would* happen. Whether the effect would kill him or wear off quickly and he would come at me with aggravated fury. The air in the room felt super-charged like we were inside an electrical storm.

I rushed to Mariana. This was our chance at escape and I wasn't going to blow this window of opportunity. I recovered the cloth laying on the floor, rushed to her and, once again, wrapped the material around her freshly bleeding wounds. My gaze kept jumping to Stephen, still on the floor, but now glowing like a human nuclear popsicle.

Nearby lay Daniel, but all I could see from my position were his legs and he still wasn't moving. I needed to get him away as well, in case he might be harmed by whatever was going on with the killer. I had a graphic image from one of those science TV shows of a black hole imploding, sucking everything around inside into nothingness.

Her eyes moved to look up at me and as I bandaged her head, I could see that whatever hold he had over her was loosening. There was the slightest movement in her neck and a twitch in the muscles around her eyes and brows. My hand brushed against Mariana's poor blood-stained face. I pulled again at her troubles and recognized immediately that something was wrong. There was the same shot of emotion, the surge of energy, traveling through me I had felt that time on the bus. The force knocked me backward and spun my mind.

The dark thing. Here again.

Maybe this had been a trap, or a safeguard, or part of the process. I didn't know, but this was not great, in fact I felt overwhelmed. This thing was crazy powerful, incredibly more than the first one. My advantage this time: I knew what I faced and what needed to be done. So as much as panic was my automatic response, I quieted and steadied my mind best I could.

Stay calm. Be at peace.

The world around me dissolved as I rushed to the attic. Upon entering, I saw the box already in position. This one, taller than me, and reinforced with steel and chains, from which any super being would struggle to escape.

I thought of Mariana and our future together, wonderful, bright and shining with happiness. This thing wasn't getting past me. I was done with fighting dark things and whatever the hell Stevie had become. As a precaution, I'd even strengthened the attic walls—the place was now a bunker. If I couldn't destroy the dark thing, if this enemy destroyed me instead, at the least, the energy wasn't getting out. Ever. Should I be killed, the entity would die with me.

Sucking in deep lungfuls of air and attempting to maintain my composure, I felt as ready as I ever would be to take on the predator. I wrapped my mind around the entity and hauled the dark thing into the room. As the image emerged before me, I faced my adversary square on. The thought of what he'd put Mariana through, Beth Ann, all the other innocent victims, imbued me with a strength and fury I never thought I possessed.

The ugly darkness floated before me; a shapeless, writhing mass, the antithesis of the glowing aura that held the thing's master in the outside. But I felt his connection in here with this menace. In the being's center a dark core had formed, so dense that surrounding light seemed to disappear within.

I held my arms before me, hands held aloft, palms facing the thing in an instinctive protective stance. Or maybe my action wasn't a reflex but for a whole different reason because something seemed to be happening.

Slowly I breathed in and out, in relaxed calming breaths. The oxygen filled my lungs, and I felt a power within me growing stronger, more powerful with each breath. Though I'd never felt this way before, something seemed to whisper to my subconscious, guiding my next actions.

My hands clasped together, thumb on top of thumb, two pointing fingers meeting each other and directed at the dark thing. I bowed my head to my thumbs and looked along the digits like they were a sniper sight. A sudden force welled within me, as though I'd just plugged into a tremendous but volatile power source. I hesitated, shaken by the new sensation, fighting not to collapse to the floor with the energy's overwhelming strength.

What would come next? I hadn't a clue. Was some kind of psychic weapon meant to shoot from my fingers?

When the two, white, faceless figures appeared, at first I thought they were the result of my instinctive movements, the energy flow. They quickly floated forward to rest beside me on either side, their bodies shimmering golden-white. The psychic's guardians, or my version of them? I didn't care which; I simply understood they were there for me and I was grateful. My focus returned to the dark thing, which had doubled in size, so all three of us were now dwarfed.

No longer alone I felt greater than this enemy, like I had the entire world behind me and goodness was on my side. Whatever wanted balance in the world, whoever had created dark and ordinary matter, wanted me to prevail. Maybe this was wishful thinking, but I felt a *knowing* within, like whatever I needed to triumph was there for me. This wasn't about saving Mariana or me or Daniel, this was about something greater.

My focus returned to my hands. I held them before me, aiming at the center of the black mass. There in my hand rested a beautiful weapon of brilliant-white, long like a rifle, but slim like a reed-thin pipe ending in a point. That point felt ready to fire. I don't know how I knew what to do. I just did. Expanding the energy inside me, shoving the power out, I sent the force shooting down my arms, through my fingers and out through the weapon. A silver, precise beam shot from my hands and entered the dark thing.

The sight was beautiful and frightening and amazing, all at once. *How had I done that?*

The beam continued to feed into the dark thing, at first with no result except for a slight quiver where the light shaft entered the mass. I pushed the energy with everything in me, reaching inside to fuel that beam with the love I felt for Mariana, my mother, Beth Ann and my desire to protect them from harm.

The black, dense shape began to glisten, then fade in and out, thinning, as turbulent black air that reminded me of smoke from burning tires, streamed from the core. Long streaks of the smoke seemed to reach for me, clawing in a frantic manner.

An unfamiliar sound, more like a muffled roar than words, filled the room. Second by second, the air pressure grew more dense as the thing fought to reach me. Whether the pressure or the dark thing, something seeped inside my skull, and I felt a vise clamped about my head, tightening with each breath I took.

A shard of spinning gray-green flung from the dark thing and traveled toward me, the speed too great to avoid being hit. Blinding pain pierced my body to reach deep inside my head. The agony so intense, I wondered if I would die. If I was to survive it would require determination and everything I had left inside.

"Get out of my space. Get away from me. Away from Mariana." The sound of my voice, desperate; there was so much more I had left to do in my life.

The pressure on my shoulders came so softly and gently I didn't notice at first. When I realized the touch was not the dark thing, I looked to the side and saw the guides had each placed an ethereal hand upon me. With this touch, the channeled power focused on the dark thing grew and expanded, so the attic walls glowed golden and white and warm.

The shape of my adversary expanded for long seconds as the dimming shadow grew larger and regained solidity. My fear rose as I wondered if a psychic version of an atomic bomb was about to be unleashed.

Then, as though this movement was the dark thing's last final attempt at defense, the mass of darkness collapsed back into a smaller entity, with edges simply jagged spikes of matter. Fragments broke off, rejoined and then fell, before dissolving away. I mentally dragged at the remaining thin tendrils as though they were particles of troubles.

Now several holes had appeared in the thing's body where our penetrating light was focused, so the wall behind grew increasingly visible. As I moved closer, the beam became sharper, increasing the size of the holes.

Our attack was working but I felt myself tiring. My arms had begun to shake as my concentration faltered. The painful buzz inside my head increased—a sensation of something reaching inside, pulling on every nerve sensor. In my experience, the body could contain only so much emotional energy; too much could be devastating. I had no more than a few seconds left and I realized this could still end in failure despite how hard I had fought.

The guides though weren't giving up. They were by my side again and like a turbo-switch had been flipped, power surged through my body like I'd never experienced. From my hands, an even more brilliant light exploded into a furious ball hurtling toward the dark thing.

When the energy sphere connected, the vision was actually beautiful, like a miniature star going nova. Instinctively I ducked and raised my arms to cover my head. What followed was sudden and overwhelming; thick darkness, and something loud pumping rhythmically around me.

The guides were gone. I saw nothing and felt nothing. Just the sound and the blackness.

Thump-pa. Thump-pa. Thuuump-pa. So loud in my ears it hurt.

I sensed light turning like a sphere around me, and I realized my eyes were actually closed. My lids fluttered open, and I discovered I was back in the classroom, face down on the floor, with my face turned toward the door.

Moving my head gave my body permission to begin hurting me again. My neck ached and felt stiff, as though held firm in a clamp. I pushed against the pain and managed to lift and turn my head slightly.

The cold eyes of the maker of so much misery stared into mine. Stephen, once the feared Trepan Killer, once my friend, looked oddly peaceful. He wore a slight surprise in his expression like he'd seen something that amused him.

His limbs, which had shuddered and flailed wildly minutes before, now lay stilled and askew. An inch, no more, of shimmering multi-colored light, like a magnificent rainbow, framed his body. Even as I watched, fascinated, the light faded to just a hint of color, a remnant of stirring energy, and then was gone. Stevie was now just a still and empty body. The incredible energy he possessed dispersed with his life.

I don't know why I reached out and touched his hand to pull at his troubles. Why would I do such a dangerous thing, possibly inviting the dark thing back?

Maybe curiosity. Maybe reflex, in case the dark thing was still there and I could prevent the toxic energy from gaining freedom. Or maybe because he now looked so much like the Stevie I once knew, so full of life and fun, and who had been my friend.

The troubles were faint, but the emotions of his final moments of life were still there. Dying away, dispersing into the air, leaving with his soul. The nature of them surprised me. Later I'd process what I'd learned when I had time to think through everything and understand the meaning.

Immediately my thoughts turned to Mariana. Ignoring my exhaustion and pain, I leaped to my feet and was by her side in a second. Pain screamed in my injured leg, but I didn't care. This night-

mare was finally over and I needed to ensure she was okay and
unhurt by the battle that had just raged.

The SQUID was still in my hand, and I placed the remarkable
instrument back on the desk. Thank God, for Daniel's crazy science
and his curiosity all those years ago.

Mariana lay slumped in the chair, held up now by only the tape
crudely fixed around her body. I yanked frantically at the tape,
freeing her. She collapsed in the chair like a toy bear with all the
stuffing removed. With Stephen gone, whatever power he wielded to
keep her motionless had died with him.

I pulled her into my arms, hugging her body to me as though I
planned to never let her go again. Euphoria, like I'd never experienced before, flooded through my being. Tears ran down Mariana's
face and mingled with the blood, and I felt my own tears stinging my
eyes.

"It's okay. It's okay. You're safe," I whispered, breathless, as I re-
applied the homemade bandage around her head. Pulling back, I
stared into the face of a fellow wounded soldier. Together, I guess we
had maybe saved the world.

In our embrace, her troubles, her fear, the awfulness of the
events, traveled into me, and I sent them on their way to the attic. As
they flowed, I recognized her concern for me. Not about me, totally,
but more about what would happen between us after this horror we
had experienced.

Behind me, I heard a faltering voice. "Rory? Mariana? Whaaa-t
hap'n?"

"It's okay, Daniel. Give me a minute," I said "We're mostly fine. But
he's dead."

I picked Mariana up as best I could, resting her weight against my
own body, then lowered her to the floor. Her mouth moved as she
tried to talk.

My finger pressed against her lips. "Shhh, don't use your energy.
Help will be here soon. I'll be back in a moment."

I glanced at Stephen lying there, lifeless, as I went to Daniel. For a
gut-churning moment, I expected the killer to rise again and fight on,

but he was dead like any everyday person. Passed over into another world; just not the one he had expected.

Kneeling by Daniel, I checked his pulse. Though there was a large, nasty bruise on his temple and he looked about as pale as I felt, he'd live.

"Daniel, have you got your cell? I don't think I can carry both of you out of here. We're gonna need help," I said, thinking surely the killer would have taken his cell from him.

He waved a limp hand toward his legs. "I think, think, here. My pocket."

An over confident Stephen must have believed nothing could stop him, so he'd left us Daniel's cell. I quickly dialed and gave the operator my story. Bike smashed through a door, problem at the school, two people injured. I'd come up with some reason later as to how I knew Daniel and Mariana were inside. Imminent danger imagined from the screams?

Within a few minutes, the sound of a siren could be heard in the distance, drawing nearer with each beat of a second. By then, I was back with Mariana holding her hand, soothing and assuring her this would all be over soon. We were safe and we were alive and the world felt in balance again. At least for me, here with Mariana beside me.

I gazed down into her green eyes, so beautiful and so filled with hope as she looked back at me. Nobody would ever understand what we had just endured. *We* probably would never understand. I wondered what this experience would do to Mariana's spirit? How she would now view the world. I'd lived with people's troubles moving around me, so I was protected in a way. Even though I'd never encountered the evil living within Stephen, I'd seen the darkness in souls. Mariana hadn't.

A siren blared loudly outside in the street, then abruptly stopped, followed by the sound of doors opening and closing. Flashing lights filtered through the upper windows of the classroom casting dancing colors across the ceiling. Several voices drifted through the walls, but Mariana's face was all I saw, her breathing all I heard.

"No more bus trips for you for a while," I said gently. "Ambulance for this ride."

At the side of her mouth, a muscle flickered as Mariana attempted a smile.

63

Seven weeks after the events at Doubleview Elementary, life had almost returned to normal. I'd returned to driving my route. Mariana returned to work at Sterling Records. Beth Ann had left the hospital many weeks ago, but had taken extended leave to stay with her daughter upstate. Who could blame her?

My leg took longer to heal than anything else. A partially torn patellar tendon near my knee required a splint and crutches for five weeks. The doctor said I'd been lucky. I *knew* I'd been lucky, but not in the way he meant. I'd survived. Mariana had survived. The fragile world seemed to be moving along as well balanced as it had ever been.

Today was the first time out on my route since the night at the school. I was doing okay. The psychologist—management at work insisted I see one—said to expect flashbacks and unusual and overwhelming feelings. Eventually, he had said, I'd feel reasonably normal again. Of course, he didn't realize *my* normal wasn't the *average* normal.

There's something comforting about the familiar, even if that is driving down streets you've driven a thousand times. I'd missed my regulars. I wanted to know how they were doing without my occasional interventions. I had pondered for a long time the stormy night, when I'd stood on that bus and invited them to hand over their troubles.

Were my actions foolish, considering everything that followed? Or was everything that happened unavoidable, because Stevie, Mariana and I had always been on a collision path engineered way back on that day at school?

A lot of good came from that night too.

If not for my decision to trouble keep the entire busload of passengers, Tracy and Mark wouldn't have a wedding date, and I wouldn't have an invitation to said wedding.

Mr. Ogilvy would still be staring out the bus window every trip, mourning his son. Instead, today, he and Mrs. Daley sat together, talking and smiling like they were old friends. *Or more.* I hoped more.

Glen March, the young programmer, shared with me that after I *took his troubles* he'd decided to stop worrying about change and took a chance on a job opportunity he'd never considered. His face beamed as he told me how much he loved his new job, which was just around the corner from the previous one, so he could still catch my bus.

The list went on, with each regular clearly delighted to see me and sharing his or her life changes so enthusiastically the bus was at risk of running late. They had my gratitude for sharing, for if I made a difference, like George Bailey in my favorite film *It's A Wonderful Life*, then that warmed my heart.

Daniel Starsey had become a friend. We'd spent many nights discussing Stevie—I tried to keep thinking of him as my friend from school—and what we believed had occurred. What he meant by the other world. Was that dimension real? Or imagined? Already Daniel had closeted himself away working on something new he promised to share soon. The other dimensional world Stevie thought he saw changed him so dramatically that he was prepared to kill. Daniel thought he might have an interesting answer or at least some better questions. This whole thing had brought Daniel into my life again, and now I had someone to talk to, even a father figure with whom to share my secret, unusual life.

And Mariana? She might have simply become another newspaper headline, a victim of a psychopath with her name listed under a case file number, along with all The Trepan Killer's other victims. I worried for a long time if my gift was what had brought the killer into her life and endangered her. I'd contemplated stopping troubles keeping and the new skills I'd developed, like the blue laser-light thingy or the way I could now read people's lives as well as their emotions, because I was afraid of their side effects, of which I had no idea yet. Could these abilities bring more darkness into our lives?

Tracy's words changed my mind, as she handed me a wedding invitation when she and Mark boarded the bus. In that moment, I knew that I needed to keep doing what I did best.

"You'll come, won't you?" She was like a ten-year-old handing out birthday invites. "You being there would mean so much to us. We were so worried, and then so relieved to hear you were okay. We realized we can't afford to waste another day. So we set the date. You've got to embrace your life no matter what. Who knows what's around the corner, right?"

So right. I needed to embrace what I could do, my part in the balance of life, and stop thinking about what I might not be able to do, stop fearing what lay around the corner. Taking people's troubles away, for even a short time, allowed them to look at their lives and relationships unhindered. There was no choice for me. Like George Bailey who wanted to escape his life, while fate kept pulling him back, I had to continue on, not out of obligation, but loyalty. I must continue to be a troubles keeper, because people needed my help. I owed them that.

Ellen, the sprightly septuagenarian, with skin so papery-thin every vein in her hands was revealed, patted my cheek as I helped her down the steps at her stop, her touch cool like she'd just dipped her fingers in iced water.

"Thank you Rory. How's that darling girl who was hurt too? She catches this bus. What's her name? Marilyn?"

"Mariana."

"Oh yes, Mar-i-ana." She sung the word like her name was a song. "She's a pretty thing. Helps me get off the bus if she's sitting nearby. Such a lovely girl. She's like you. Makes me feel better. Always."

When I reached the Dawson River stretch, the view hit me with an emotional punch. The way the light of the setting sun glinted off the water like sparkling diamonds. The crisp white wave tips racing across the surface. That I was here to see and appreciate this view made me pause. The mood on the bus today was the polar opposite to the night when dark, ominous clouds heralded future events that would change Mariana's and my life.

As I approached Mariana's stop my heart still beat wildly, as always, but now the skipping in my chest wasn't from nervousness but pure joy. The healing scars on her forehead were mostly in the hairline. The plastic surgeon said they'd fade over time. Mariana called them war wounds and a reminder to live each day in gratitude. She had cut the rest of her hair and wore a head scarf when she was out until the style grew in. I told her she still looked beautiful—she had a punk-princess kind of look—but she said people stared and she didn't want to answer the questions she was asked. Her hair was growing back though, just like her enthusiasm for life.

Mr. Sterling had decided to retire from actively working in the shop and had promoted Mariana to manager of the two other staff. New responsibilities were good for her. Maybe that had impacted her boss's decision, maybe he knew she needed something, which made her look forward, allowed her to heal, and kept her mind focused on each day.

"Just for the next year or so," she'd told me. "Then I'll see what happens."

There at the stop she waited and my heart danced. No need to hide my smile or how I felt. She wore a pale-pink, short-brimmed hat over her scarf. She sure was cute.

"Hello there," I said, as she climbed the steps toward me. "You're looking happy."

"I am happy." She swiped her multi-rider through the machine to the right of my seat, and then looked back at me.

"Today's a special day. Seeing you driving the bus feels like *normal* has returned."

"Yeah. I like normal. I hope normal makes you hungry."

"Are we—?" she said.

I smiled. "Yep, I made a reservation. Italian?"

"Anything."

"Reservation's at eight. I'll come by seven-thirty."

"Perfect."

She made her way to the back. In the mirror I watched my girl find a seat next to a passenger I didn't know. Who was that? I wondered. A knot formed in my stomach, but I stopped myself from taking the thought further. There was one Trepan Killer. There couldn't be more. Stevie was an anomaly created by an accident through me. My thoughts returned to things more wonderful.

My girl. Boy, I loved the sound of that.

The biggest surprise since this had happened was discovering how little Mariana cared about my gift. I always imagined I'd live my whole life hiding who I truly was. Now two people knew, and I didn't feel like such an oddity.

As the doors closed after Mariana had alighted, she blew me a kiss from the pavement and mouthed *seven-thirty*. I nodded and smiled, feeling so lucky, I could climb out of my seat and dance up the aisle.

In preparation for tonight, I'd rehearsed all day the special words I'd planned to say: *Mariana, I love you. I've loved you from the first time you boarded my bus.* I hoped for her reply: *Me too.*

The words still swam in my head as my final run for the day ended. I was on a pretty big high as I parked the bus toward the back of the lot and climbed out of my seat. Beth Ann wasn't here so I took a walk down the aisle to scan for lost property. Really, I wanted to soak up the normalcy of the day.

A flash of color against the gray and blue of the seats caught my attention. A bright, floral pink piece of material. I thought I remembered seeing the scarf around Tracy's neck when she'd leaned in to plop a kiss on my cheek. When I retrieved the scarf, a tingle of pure joy traveled into my fingertips. I smiled and thought of another of my mama's sayings. *"True love will give you tingles."* Yes, that's true, Mama, so true.

Next to the scarf, as though left there just for me, lay the evening's newspaper folded in half. The headline leaped out and felt like a punch to the jaw.

Trepan Killer from another world

A source has revealed the Trepan Killer Stephen Maslin, found dead seven weeks ago in the same Doubleview Elementary School he'd attended fifteen years prior, had for ten years been under the care of Dr. Liam Barnes.

Yet unsubstantiated claims suggest had Dr. Barnes gone to the police with information about what Maslin revealed in his sessions, many of his victims might still be alive. The last two surviving victims would also not have experienced the trauma or the disfigurement of the trepanning procedure performed on them. Trepanning is the ancient practice of carving a hole in the center of a forehead.

The source close to Dr. Barnes claims Maslin suffered from severe psychosis, believing he had traveled from another dimension and his victims held the key for him to return home. This delusional disorder stemmed from post-traumatic stress disorder, or PTSD, from a 2001 incident in which Maslin witnessed the death of a fellow student hit by a car outside Doubleview Elementary School.

Dr. Barnes declined an interview, but issued this statement: "At no point did I believe Stephen Maslin was a danger to himself or others."

I refolded and held the newspaper in my hand, not sure what to think. A creeping icy feeling traveled up the back of my neck, and I shivered.

Had Stephen really seen another dimension or did he imagine

the other world? I'd begun to believe in its existence and that maybe one day I might see the place he called home too. Or could his vision just be the result of the panic and terror in that bathroom years ago?

I ran the concept back and forth and around. Every interaction I'd had with him flitted across my mind. He'd seemed so convincing. He did have some kind of power; the dark thing was proof of that and, at the school, I had felt him in my mind somehow controlling my physical movements, fighting against me. Mariana had discussed the feeling and his power. If he was just a person who'd somehow soaked up some of my ability, which created an obsession, then was his story of the other dimension untrue?

Daniel had already begun to search for scientific explanations for everything, even this other dimension, the portal for which Stevie had searched in such a horrific way. But if there wasn't another dimension, then did his belief in Mariana being some kind of portal just another crazy idea sprung from his obsession? Perhaps she was simply a lovely, ordinary, beautiful girl. Since those insane couple of days, she'd displayed no rare abilities.

As I made my way back down the aisle, I heard voices from outside, which broke my reverie. The cleaners had arrived, and as we passed on the steps, I dropped the newspaper inside the trash bag they'd left just inside the door. I'd think about these questions later. I'm sure Daniel and I would spend many nights discussing what everything meant, if all of this actually meant anything.

Five minutes later I paused as I pulled on my helmet. I thought about Stevie and the killer he'd become and those feelings I'd pulled from him moments after his death. I'd sent them down to the Dawson a few hours later, after I was certain Mariana was asleep and safe at the hospital.

There had been an unexpected sense of balance restored in our world as I watched them float away. I'd begun to believe in his world then. Now, I questioned Stevie's idea of a portal thinly balanced between worlds. I'd begun to warm to the notion of an illusion grown stronger over the years in the mind of a troubled kid. Had I wished

I'd made that kind of difference? Fought true evil, saved the girl and the world, and won?

As I steered the bike out of the depot, I told myself this question had no answer. What did it matter anyway now that everything was over? Whether Stevie Maslin came from another dimension, saw another world or not, the Trepan Killer was gone. My immediate future tonight was about Mariana and our future. My heart and mind reached out to her. I loved this girl. I would protect this girl. Forever.

My days as a bus driver were drawing to an end. I felt this in my gut. My mama's voice whispered, as always, when I decided my days as a friendly people mover were numbered. Her last words to me were *"Rory, make sure you leave this world a better place than how you found the place. I'm leaving you here, so that's my 'better' done."*

I'd received a gift and, thanks to those few days when a killer had entered my world, the gift had grown, changed and become something more powerful. Maybe the ability had become something that might make an even bigger difference to those I encountered.

Maybe Stevie Maslin wasn't as great a supernatural force as we first thought, but one thing I knew absolutely: the dark thing I'd battled wasn't natural. The thing and the dark energy, which fed the power, wasn't from here. One thing I did know, even without Daniel's scientific theories, you can't destroy energy, because energy is fluid and will just reform into something else.

Every now and then I'd feel something; in tiny spaces between moments just before sleep when your mind wanders away to nothing. Something was there, a faint flicker on the edge of my periphery. Something dark. Something hungry. Something waiting. If I didn't go in search of this, this ... entity, thing, enemy, then I'd be ignoring my duty, ignoring the reason I might exist. Maybe this was about the balance of life. And fate. She sure did seem to enjoy her games with me.

I thought about the hospital, visiting Mariana while she healed, the moment there when an odd seed of an idea had formed in my mind. As I pulled up outside Mariana's apartment that seed sprouted and began to grow.

Even at the hospital, I couldn't help troubles keeping. For me, the action was a natural thing, an automatic response like smiling at a baby. Just a simple conversation with someone beside me in the waiting room, my elbow touching their skin and I saw a change in their eyes. The world seemed better, despite the grim event that had brought them to this moment. A helpful young doctor whose tired face brightened after I shook his hand to thank him. An elderly woman who'd just lost her husband to throat cancer, whose shoulders sagged less after I handed her a coffee and placed a palm on her arm. A nurse at reception, so short and cranky with visitors, who smiled when our fingers glanced off each other as she passed me a pen.

So many people hurting, worrying, filled with troubles, which might not leave for a very long time, if ever. Hospitals are not joy-inspiring spaces. Except if you or your loved one is leaving, and leaving healthy. Being there, over those hours, really got me thinking. I could do a lot of good if I was there every day.

Maybe a nurses' aide or an orderly.

So many people facing the worst day of their lives—the difference I could make. Not just to patients, but doctors, health care workers, and all the loved ones of those admitted or in emergency. This could work really well, amazingly well.

Many people with my gift might not choose a job where many people cross their path each day. Troubles keeping was hard work, and sometimes exposure to the deep heartache and worry enclosed in those troubles could be difficult to handle. But I did get something back; the benefit wasn't all one sided.

There's an energy when you ease someone's day, despite the mistakes sometimes, despite what happened with Stevie. I'm not perfect, but I have the courage to keep trying. My mama bred that into me. There was a framed quote my mama had hung on our living room wall, and I read those words every day of my life since I was a kid. So they were now part of me. To those words I could now truly attest. Maybe that's why my abilities had grown.

"It is one of the beautiful compensations of life that no man can sincerely try to help another without helping himself." Ralph Waldo Emerson.

As I pressed the buzzer to Mariana's apartment, my future became clearer than a cloudless sky. My decision was made. Tomorrow I'd begin working on figuring everything out. In the coming days, I'd talk to Daniel about this other world and the possibility that the dimensional realm might or might not be the invention of a psychotic man. If the world did exist, how could we find the portal and ensure the safety of our universe?

After that, I'd make some serious life changes, small as those might seem against the backdrop of searching for other worlds.

Tonight was about us. Me and Mariana. Tomorrow was a new day and something told me there was a job at a hospital and a badge with my name.

Not the End …

21st August 2016

The Troubles Keeper 2 is on the way!

Due to popular demand, a sequel to **The Troubles Keeper** is underway. Susan May is hard at work writing **The Goodbye Giver**, which will bring to life a new character with extraordinary abilities. Look out for it in 2019.

Grab a starter library of **FREE** eBooks by Susan May
www.readerlinks.com/l/490258

After, please return here to turn the page and read Susan's popular
From the Imagination Vault, where readers are taken behind the story
to share in her inspiration for Best Seller and maybe you might
discover where fiction and inspiration merge into another reality.

After the Thank You section keep reading to enjoy a preview of
Deadly Messengers.

IMAGINATION VAULT

Story ideas spring from the oddest places. Why a writer's mind will leap from something they read, or heard, or from a random idea to go on to create a story plot is as magical to me as probably to those who don't write.

The Troubles Keeper was an amazingly fateful experience from start to finish. I read a Facebook post by Elizabeth Gilbert author of *Eat, Pray, Love*—remember the film with Julia Roberts? Elizabeth shared her experience years ago on a Manhattan bus, where the bus driver did exactly the same thing as my lovely character Rory Fine. He'd noticed how miserable his passengers seemed and offered to take all their troubles and throw them in the Hudson. As Elizabeth Gilbert wrote: *"And one by one, as we filed off the bus, we dropped our troubles into the palm of this good man's hand, and we stepped off the bus with smiles on our faces."*

The moment I'd finished reading the article, I turned to my husband and said, "I've got the story idea for my next book." Now many a time an idea alights but never seeds. Story concepts must prove they're deserving. Most ideas float away never to be heard of again, while some hang around, tapping on my shoulder and asking: *My turn yet?* Then another project idea comes along and they fly away like leaves ruffled by the wind.

Not *The Troubles Keeper*. This one was a tree planted in my path, pretty well grown. Rory Fine arrived a few days after I read the article, almost fully formed as a character with a name, voice and an attitude to life I couldn't ignore. He had a story to share and he wanted that story told.

Like all my stories, long and short, this one began with a shadow of a premise; a determined bus driver who could take people's troubles, a girl on the bus he loved but couldn't approach, and a killer who was after that girl. Despite my experience in writing and the passion with which I began this story, this was a tough write. Part of the challenge was the quandaries of the elusive muse, who decided half way through the third edit I had picked the wrong person as the killer, forcing me to rewrite some of the last half. I'm glad I did. Everything now fell more smoothly into place. I do love these characters and how they interact together, so I take back every mean name I called that muse when things weren't working.

Now to the technical stuff. I love to include obscure real-life facts in my stories, which sound completely unbelievable, yet, are true. This makes for an interesting *and* scary story. One reader suggested I categorize my books no-fiction, "that's non-fiction with just a touch of fiction."

So String Theory is real. The microscopic theory of gravity attempts to provide a complete and consistent description of the fundamental structure of our universe and suggests there are more dimensions than we have previously been aware. More information on this very complex subject can be found in *Ted Talks* by Brian Greene. I barely comprehend the science.

The Hibbert field is half true. There was an instrument designed in 1911 by the name of Hibbert's Magnetic Balance. This instrument relied upon balancing magnetic forces against magnetic forces to measure units of currents and ratios of current strengths.

A Faraday cage is also real and used pretty much the way I've written, although the construction protects against electrical transmissions only. This device was invented in 1836 by Michael Faraday. You can see them usually in science museums protecting against energy dispatched from a Tesla coil. They're quite amazing and beautiful to watch in action.

Of course, Daniel Starsey's SQUID (super-conducting quantum inter- cept device) and the B.E. print gadget (Bio-energy imprint) aren't real, but I wish they were available. Sure would make catching criminals or discovering who took that last cookie a lot easier.

The most unbelievable thing is trepanning. This bizarre practice is real. People do this to themselves thinking they can attain a higher vision of the world and increase their intelligence, a bit like traveling to another dimension. There is a video I found of a guy called Bobby Lund who talks of how he performed trepanation on himself. Pretty nasty stuff, but I was looking for a serial killer who practiced killing in a way I'd never read before. Sorry, if those scenes are nasty. I tamed them down in subsequent edits.

. . .

On the psychic Chris Lamben: I did visit a psychic whose name was Chris in my mid-twenties. This character is loosely based on him, and some of the things Chris Lamben says are as I remembered from my readings. Chris was a big flirt and he would say to me and all my female friends—we discovered after comparing notes—"Might I say you are a very attractive woman."

His readings were crazy accurate, predicting many major life events, which have since come true: When I'd have my family (quite late in life) and a business I would own at twenty-seven, which would be successful. That was the darn business which kept me from writing for two decades. He didn't tell me that though. I do believe in psychics. I don't know how their ability works, but you cannot watch Hollywood Medium's Tyler Henry without feeling compelled to believe there is something real about the readings.

You may have noticed *The Troubles Keeper* hints at a sequel, and you would be right. There's something about Rory, Mariana, and Daniel I just can't leave behind for good. I'm not saying there's a book soon, but there's something fascinating about someone who can help others so selflessly. I also wonder about the other world Stevie saw. If you would like to read a sequel write me susanmay@node1.com.au. I'll include you in my early reader's club, so you'll know when I do write a sequel. Readers in this club receive early copies of my future books. And you'll simply make my day.

Which brings me to the dedication at the front of the book. You may wonder why I dedicated this book to the director of the 1946 film *It's A Wonderful Life*. That film changed my view on life when I was about twenty-three. I caught the movie as a Friday late night film. Luckily

I'd hit record, because as the tears flowed at the end, I immediately hit the replay button. Prior to this, my friends would always joke about my pessimistic view of life. What I saw in the way the main character George Bailey (played by Jimmy Stewart) helped others, was a different way to live. Instantly, I became an optimist, and I'm the most positive person you'll meet, despite the dark thrillers I write.

Of course, George didn't realize he changed lives. In fact, he begrudged a great many of fate's interventions that forced him to help others. To the point where he decided he was no good to this world and attempted to kill himself. This is when Clarence the angel literally drops in and shows him what a difference he has actually made and that he really had lived a wonderful life.

I immediately thought: *Wow/! What a difference you could make if you actually went out of your way to help others.* This movie had such an impact on me, I even named my two sons after characters. My eldest is Bailey (George Bailey) and my other is Harry (George's younger brother.)

As I write this, I realize I may have accidentally echoed that story—totally subconsciously. Rory helps people selflessly and can never know for sure what changes he has affected, but he touches lives like George did. George fell in love very sweetly and married Mary (Mariana). George adored and was inspired by his mother, just like Rory. George defended his town from ol' man Potter, a selfish, evil character whose goal was to take over Bedford Falls, and he didn't care who he harmed. George's uncle, who caused him quite some grief due to his forgetfulness, rounded the townspeople up and helped George save Bedford Falls' Savings and Loan and defeat Potter. Daniel Starsey had a touch of dither to him and saved the day with his gadgets. In the end, George was helped by an angel, and angel-like figures helped Rory.

None of this I'd noticed until the final edits neared completion. Imagination sure works in mysterious ways, and I always marvel how my mind accesses information when needed, something like a dream. Perhaps I've accidentally written an *It's A Wonderful Life* supernatural horror.

If you are new to my work, thank you for taking a chance on a writer you've never read. If you are one of those wonderful readers who have previously discovered my books and supported me, a million thanks. I hope you've enjoyed this journey too. My greatest wish is that for a few hours at least, my gang of characters and I have taken your troubles from your mind.

Maybe when life seems all too overwhelming you might take the lead from Rory. Go sit by a river, touch a palm to your heart, pull out those troubles, and throw them as hard as you can into the current. Imagine them floating far, far away.

Don't we all have a little troubles keeper inside us? For ourselves and for others? I think so. I hope so.

Until next time ...

Susan May

P.S. Update 2019

Readers have fallen in love with Rory and demanded more books. So I'm in the process of turning The Troubles Keeper into a trilogy. If you have enjoyed this book, no need to wait for number two, which I'm expecting to release later in 2020

A prequel novella to *The Troubles Keeper* is included in **Destination Dark Zone,** a collection of six twisted tales.

In the prequel novella-length **Drift,** we meet a young Rory traveling on a commuter train during a terrible snow storm. The train will never reach its destination.

Enjoy several opening chapters at the end of this book.

LOVED THIS?

What's next?

Three things you can do right now.

1) Jump into another Susan May read! There's many more novels and story collections for you to enjoy. While Susan mostly writes stand alone novels, she's currently working on a trilogy for her most beloved book **The Troubles Keeper**. Explore all available books in order of most recent publication: **susanmaywriter.net/susan-may-books**

While there check out **Destination Dark Zone**, which includes a prequel to The Troubles Keeper.

2) The Goodbye Giver (The Troubles Keeper 2) is on its way. Join **Susan May's Readers' Club** and receive two FREE books to keep and be alerted when its released. **susanmaywriter.net/free-books**

3) Do you have a moment to leave a review on Amazon? It's one of the most beneficial ways you can support an author. Every review helps —even just a few words! **You can leave one here.** Your help is appreciated. Thank you!

Connect with Susan May

Join Susan May's Readers' Club and receive two Free books
susanmaywriter.net/free-books

plus

- *Behind the Story* access to fascinating details about the writing of Susan's books.
- Contests to enter with great prizes like Kindle readers and Audible books.
- Free and discounted book offers
- And much more (we're working on the *much more* all the time)

Find Susan May every day at her private Facebook group **The Mayhem Gang.** You are welcome to join a great bunch of people from around the world, discussing books, life and other fun topics.

Facebook Susan Mayhem Gang

Susan May would love to hear from you, so email her at
susanmay@node1.com.au

THANK YOU

With each book I write, I grow more grateful for the life I now enjoy. Writing was and is my dream, and here I am living that dream. Writing novels is sometimes hard and requires long hours working in isolation, but they are joyful hours.

My husband and children are my greatest inspiration. As long as I have you I need nothing else. Thank you for giving me the time to do this writing thing.

Every time I release a novel I think of my parents who, sadly, are no longer with us. I carry you both in my heart with every word I write. If not for you Dad, I may have never discovered the joy of books. Mom, thank you for teaching me to read before I even attended my first day at school. Words have always been my life.

Then there's my growing team of professionals who make my stories and my writing world so much better for their input. Christie from eBook Editing Pro, Deranged Doctor Design, Justin at Light Free-lancing Web Design, Anne Johnstonbrown my female narrator, and the extraordinary Steve Marvel narrator of this book, and my husband Franco who gives me feedback on the second draft of my work (he's not allowed to read the first). Thank you, sincerely, to my special early readers, who read through an advance copy and rooted out all the typos and not so-poetic-sentences, as though they'd embarked on a treasure hunt (see following page).

Of course, my stories are just thoughts in my head and words on paper until readers open the first page. I've thought a lot about this lately—how I see my stories differently from when I write them to once the early reviews come in. What I think is a shaky premise (this is insecure writer mindset here) becomes something totally different when I see my creation through reader's eyes. Before my books are read, I'm like that girl staring in the mirror noticing all her body's faults that nobody else can see. A wonderful reader Loretta Paszkat from Canada suggested this to me:

Writers and Readers = a magical relationship.

You know what? I agree. Our meeting of minds is something very special. So thank you for the magical friendship across the pages or the Audible. I'm a lucky gal to have such magic in my life.

Susan May

To the Hawk Eyes...

After I'd finished this book I sent the manuscript out to my early reader group. These are wonderful people who love my books and, as they read through the early readers' copy, kindly noted the errors and inconsistencies. The process of polishing the manuscript felt like a real international team effort, with emails arriving every few days from all over the world. The readers approached their mission with gusto like they were on an Easter egg hunt.

A special thanks to passionate Bibliophiles Diane Lybbert and Stacy Myrose who really went above and beyond the call of duty with their seek-and-destroy-incorrect-grammar mission. Then my wonderful new friend Jan E. Klein systematically went through the book removing my excess commas (apparently over the years I had become quite the comma-adder, but no more). She also educated me on some grammar concepts that I'd never fully understood. This book reads so much better thanks to Jan and all the passionate readers.

However, everyone listed here also contributed in polishing this book. I thank everyone for their generosity and care for my work. You all truly humble me.

Julie Wall, Sandy Jones, Jane Culwell, Loretta, Bill Craig, Sandy Good, Carrie Werner, Faouzia, Irene, Mike Rice, Jim Phillips, James Hayward, Christy Mun, Annelien Mes, Tracey Allen, George Lopez, Jenelle Roberts, Brenda Telford, Jan Paramski

QUESTIONS! QUESTIONS! QUESTIONS!

These are questions from early readers of this book that I thought you would find interesting. Thank you to Judy Clay (NY, USA), known to her friends as the Basement Mistress, for supplying most of these. If you have any questions please write me at susanmay@ node1.com.au I'll possibly include them in updates of this book.

Were you influenced by Caroline Kepnes' "You"? How the killer is written reminded me of her style (I liked it, just curious).

No, I wasn't, although I love that book. "You" is so original. I wanted my killer to have a very distinctive voice. I struggled all through the first draft to find that voice, writing in many tenses and points of view. I tried every single one and none of them felt right until near the three quarter mark when I tried third person present. "You" is written in second person present. Rory is written in first person past tense. Once that clicked I had to go back in second edits and transform all the tenses. I missed a few, so my poor editor had to work out the confusion.

An author will change many things during the draft and edits, and I'm sure I speak for all writers in saying that we always miss a few consistency errors and that's where the editor comes in. Quite a few times my editor marked things and said "not sure if this works." Invariably the error would be a leftover section that should have been altered.

I changed the identity of the killer in the second edit because I couldn't get him in the right place at the right time. He was in another geographical place in the story. Then I hit upon the character who eventually became the killer. Everything fitted perfectly, as if I hadn't previously seen what was right before my very eyes. Writing is like that. You uncover so much in second edits; themes, character motivation, little pieces that you can fit in better and expand upon.

Second edits are hell with so much work. Imagine walking into a house that looks as though someone's had a party. Stuff is everywhere. You have to systematically go through every room and work out where everything is meant to be and if this fits in that place or needs to be thrown out or moved somewhere else. By the third draft writing is pretty easy sailing. You are just checking that the rooms look beautiful and rearranging furniture and decorations. I enjoy the fourth. That's just dusting out the house and moving a few small things. Then you turn the key and open the door for the readers to come in and enjoy your creation.

Some of my early readers knew that I had a different killer in the first two drafts of this novel and Jan Klein asked, "Who had you originally picked as the killer? I can't picture it being anyone but Stevie; unless it was the teacher?"

You would be right Jan. Daniel was the original killer but I couldn't work out how to have him with Beth Ann doing the nasty deed and also with Rory at his house. Then how would I have him run across town while at the same time stalking Mariana?

Initially, the time line seemed okay, but I then wanted the scene with Beth Ann occurring simultaneously while Rory met with Daniel. In fact, the Trepan Killer first attacked Beth Ann in her apartment. She'd gone home with that headache.

When I couldn't work the timings out, I thought back over the characters and wondered, if not Daniel, then who? Then the idea struck me that the killer had to be Stevie. I instantly knew the book had moved to another level of thrills. Everything made perfect sense.

As this was the second draft, I had to go back and change a lot of things and do some rewriting. However, this is normal for second drafts and the process didn't take too much time. Most scenes are the same but I had to write Daniel in as unconscious in the school room climax scene, and change all his gadgets for use in the positive and not evil sense. Then I needed to have the Trepan Killer's psychic ability grow in power since he no longer had gadgets available. Those gadgets would now be used against him. I cannot imagine the killer as anyone else now. It was like a puzzle piece falling into place perfectly. And this is why I write. These moments feel like you've just dived a perfect ten!

Were you influenced by Hannibal from Thomas Harris especially with the Trepanning? I thought it was awesome and I kept seeing Ray Liotta in my head.

I remember reading Red Dragon by Thomas Harris when the book was first released. I'd heard the story contained the most gruesome, scary scenes you could read and, once read, you would never feel safe again. "Yeah, give me that," I thought. All the books I've read in my life influence my writing. Everything is in my head somewhere, but I try not to repeat anything I've read or seen in film.

Of course, every serial killer book has a sadistic killer. That's not new, but an author always seeks to find something new in the character.

With casting my killer, I hunted around for the creepiest, most macabre way of murdering people. If you checked my Google records they would put me on a serial killer wannabe watch list. Somehow I came across trepanning. I watched a few videos and thought 'yuk' these people are crazy to do this to themselves. However, I also thought what a great thing for a serial killer to do.

Why he would do this was what I had to work out. That process took some time and, again, there was a lot of reworking of those pages. This killer has been the hardest character I've ever written and I've probably written nearly a hundred with my short stories. By the way, I've never watched the Ray Liotta scene in "Hannibal" where he feeds the character his own brain. That image is just too awful for me. I know this sounds weird that I can write dark and evil scenes, but I don't want to look at confronting gruesomeness on a screen. Yuk!

Perhaps a bit of King's Needful Things? Just wondering.

And no, on the Stephen King 'Needful Things.' I actually had to check that book after this question. He's written so many I couldn't remember what the story was about. I don't think I've read this book or I've forgotten the plot, which is more likely. Now on my reading list though. Sounds great. So that is a definite no on any inspiration from King's novel.

I did not like the character of the psychic, Chris. I did not think he was needed at all. He dragged the book for me.

I needed Chris Lamben in there because he's a linking, information character. You need them in a story or your characters can't gather information in a realistic way to move forward. He's meant to be unlikable. The real life psychic Chris, who I visited a couple of times in my twenties, was rather creepy and smug. Most of the things my character says are what I remember Chris saying. The idea of plugging himself into a big energy river he actually shared with me, delivered in his smooth manner.

If you mean he slowed the plot down though, sorry, my bad. I needed him there, otherwise the characters couldn't have gathered some of the information and Rory wouldn't have been able to progress with his attic visitor or to gain an ally who helps him later (don't want to give any spoilers). There's also a fine line between getting straight to the point and taking readers on an adventure. Sometimes digressions are about just enjoying the ride. Ask Stephen King; he's always digressing. Sometimes they work. Sometimes his don't and are just waffle. With Chris, I kind of enjoyed writing him because the scene took me back to my earlier years. That's his real garden I described as well.

But! I loved Daniel. Great introduction to the character, his motivation and what he had to offer. A true unsung hero.

I love Daniel too. He wasn't this character originally, but once I realized he was the gadget guy, I gave him a real bounce in his step. I kept imagining Rick Moranis in "Honey I Shrunk the Kids." He's the bumbling, brilliant professor who thinks what he does is normal, but his normal is strange to everyone else.

All the ancillary characters in The Troubles Keeper came from the story. I am a pantser (write by the seat of my pants), so I don't plot. Stephen King is the same. So the characters evolve over the first and second drafts and many are out of a device necessity. In this case, Daniel enjoyed the greatest evolution to the point where I could see him having his own book in the future. He's definitely back in the second book, whenever that happens. Even as I write this, I'm thinking, "Oh, Daniel, when you play with fire, you are going to get burned." With all these gadgets maybe he invents the wrong thing. Just a thought.

DRIFT

And now, enjoy the opening chapters of Drift, a prequel to The Troubles Keeper. Strap yourself in, it's going to be quite the ride.

An evening commuter train departs a city station during a wild and bitter snowstorm. Those aboard are thinking only of arriving home and enjoying a hot dinner. This train, though, will never reach its final destination.

On board, seven-year-old Rory is traveling home with his mother. A curious child, he passes the time playing a people-watching game, spying on his fellow passengers and fantasizing about who they really are behind their facades.

When a female passenger catches his attention, he finds himself unable to stop watching her. Maybe it's the annoying buzzing in his head or the woman's unusual behavior but there's something not quite right about her. Soon he'll discover there's something not quite right about this night. In fact, this night is all wrong.

In this *Troubles Keeper* prequel, we meet a young Rory Fine, as yet unaware of his unique ability. Something incredible is about to happen to change the course of his life, and the lives of many others. Heroes sometimes come in small but remarkable packages.

PROLOGUE

February 4, 1996 would not end as it had begun. This February fourth would be changed. And because of this, all the events following would be intrinsically altered forever—all because of this one day. Well, that was the hope.

PART I

1

In Chase City, the snow had fallen non-stop for three days. Small flurries of dancing flakes whipped wildly around the streets leading to the Palmerston North Station. The peak hour travelers, rushing to climb the steps to their platforms, pulled the lapels of their coats high and tugged them closer about their frozen necks, tightening their hoods and turning their faces toward the ground in a futile attempt to protect themselves from the bitter cold.

Seven-year-old Rory held tight to his mama's hand as they stood on the platform awaiting their homeward-bound train. Even through the combined thickness of both their gloves, he imagined he sensed the warmth of her skin. Now and then, she'd squeeze his fingers to reassure him he was safe and that very soon, they'd be out of the elements and in a heated car.

In the distance, he heard the faint *clack-clack* of the approaching train. His happiness and relief at the thought they'd soon arrive home made him give a little hop. On the menu tonight was his favorite, spaghetti Bolognese. Home also meant a hot bath; Rory so loved throwing off his cold, stiff clothes and sitting there in the luxurious steamy bubbles as the chill slowly drained from his body. If his mother was in a rush, they'd skip washing his hair, one of his least favorite things anyway; the soap always got in his eyes and the smell of shampoo sometimes set him off sneezing.

Every time he complained, his mother would make a pretend scowl and threaten to have his unruly, shoulder-length red locks completely shaved off. He knew she wasn't serious because moments later, she'd smile and say, "Oh, I'm joking, because then all your magical powers would disappear! You know—like what happened to Samson." He wasn't even sure who Samson was, but he thought having special powers seemed very cool, even if he wasn't certain what they might be yet.

Often, his mama would add, "You have a wonderful heart, my lovely son. Make sure never to change, because the world's a better place because of you. Rory Fine. Fine by name, fine by nature. From the moment you entered the world, son."

He wondered how she knew things about his heart. Well, how could she? It was just stuffed away inside, hidden, like his favorite meatballs after he'd eaten them. So, how did Mama know what his heart could be like? It was impossible.

When he placed a hand over his chest, he only felt a faint *thump-thump-thump* there. Nothing good about that, except it meant he was alive.

Being here today was a surprise because he shouldn't have been accompanying his mother at all. Thanks to his babysitter Carol's *emergency*, he had the joy of traveling home with his mama. He loved her and he loved train rides, so he was about as happy as Elmo on Sesame Street—maybe even a bit happier! That was why, when his usually sweet mama spoke in her cranky voice about Carol bringing him to his mother's work, it had him quite confused.

His mom worked in the mailroom of Colonial Mutual Insurance, situated on the fifth floor of a forty-story, gray, old building. It was the five gleaming elevators, though, that Rory always looked forward to riding whenever he visited. On the rare occasions he found himself there, he thrilled at riding between floors and jumping up and down as the elevator car slowed to a stop. He felt as if he was flying and the sensation always left him in fits of giggles. Today, he wondered if

Samson flew too, but without an elevator, and he hoped when he grew up that would be his power.

When he and Carol had arrived late in the afternoon, his mama appeared surprised to see them both. Then the flicker of an annoyed face replaced the rounded "O" of her lips. He thought he'd done something wrong, but as he sat at a desk in a corner—surrounded by packages and letters and piles of paper, scribbling away on a large, orange envelope—he overheard his mother telling a lady with bright pink lipstick how she "didn't believe for a second that Carol's father was sick."

Rory watched and listened, wondering what his mother meant by *something fishy*. When she saw him looking at her, a warm smile replaced her unhappy, knitted-eyebrows look. She came over to him and cupped his face in a palm.

"Sometimes, people can be silly and a little thoughtless. Always be thoughtful and kind. Be the one others can count on, okay? You know what I mean?"

Rory didn't know what she meant at all. He struggled to understand a great deal about the adult world and had almost given up trying. He hoped he'd learn soon—that the knowledge would just drip from the sky and seep into him as if he was a sponge, no effort required at all—because he didn't want his mama to think him silly or thoughtless. But although Carol may have disappointed his mother, Rory wasn't disappointed, in the slightest. Here he was, about to catch a train with his mama, having ridden an elevator up and down, and having managed to jump, not once, but twice during the last ride down. So even the terrible weather couldn't take away the happiness bursting inside him, because today seemed like a magical day. Something about it just felt good. Just like his heart.

2

Rory pulled his favorite dark-blue beanie further down, so it nestled just above his brow. He leaned out, pulling at his mom's hand to catch sight of the train as it pulled into the station. With the fading light and snow, he saw a monster with a single glowing eye coming right for them.

The monster pulled to a stop with a long, anguished screech and rattle and became once more just a train. Rory's mom held his hand even tighter as the doors slid open with a muffled gasp of escaping air. The commuter crowd pushed forward once those departing had alighted, eager to get off a platform offering little shelter from the elements. They hurried onto the train and Rory felt himself lifted over the threshold in his mother's haste to board.

The warmth of the car thawed his cold face and hands almost in an instant. He felt a tingling in his face and reached with his unencumbered hand to wipe at flakes of snow weighing down his lashes.

Rory's father had left two days before his fourth birthday. In that moment, now so faded in his memory, he still recalled a man with a sad face, crying as he hugged his son. His father had told him to take care of his mother and grow his brave heart—because there was something his father must do alone.

Then another image always followed that one, the image of his mother crying and whispering something he couldn't understand, no matter how many times he thought over it. *"What if we need you more than they do?"*

He wondered always who *they* were—and what did *they* need?

But he'd been a baby back then—not a big seven-year-old, like now. So he couldn't be sure if it was a real memory or something he'd seen on TV. But whenever it slipped into his mind, what he did know was that he felt a sadness creep into his heart. He'd always push it away because he didn't like to feel sad. And he didn't like anyone else to feel sad either. Sadness was not a good feeling.

He conjured imaginary worlds filled with adventure and heroes. One day, he thought he might go on real adventures, maybe even find his father. Then they'd be a family again and the sadness he sensed in his Mama would go away.

So, as he and his mother slid into two of the vacant seats facing the aisle, Rory leaned over and whispered, "I love you, Mama."

His mama placed her oversized handbag on her lap, smiled down at him and squeezed his hand for the second time in the last five minutes.

"I love you too, my sweet boy. You're Fine by name and fine by nature. Let no one tell you different."

As he returned her smile, Rory caught sight of a girl seated beside Mama. With her purple and blue hair sprinkled with sprays of yellow and red, she looked like one of those parrots he'd seen in a cartoon. She also had a ring through her nose, which made his own nose itchy just by looking at her. She didn't see him because she was reading a book, held up to her face with one hand.

Across from them, a boy and a girl—who looked about the same age as Carol, his babysitter—held hands. As he watched, they leaned into each other and kissed on the lips for a long, long time. The kiss lasted long enough for him to wonder if they might run out of breath and turn into statues right there. He was sure they were turning quite pale, starved of breath already.

Rory was a people-watcher. At least, that was what his teacher,

Miss Watson, called him. He'd heard of birdwatchers who stared at books and matched birds to pictures, but he didn't know if there were people-watcher books; all he knew was there was something fascinating about people's behavior. Other children might find peak hour crowds intimidating, but not him. He could play the *Story Game*, noting people as if they were characters in a book and imagine who they *really* were, because everyone had an alter ego, just like Superman.

"Ha-choo. Ha-choo. Ahhhh-choo!"

Just as the doors shushed closed, a man wearing a deep burgundy coat and black, baggy trousers, leaped aboard. As he did, sneezes exploded from him and, while still in mid-stride, he pulled out a handkerchief with one hand and blew his nose with a loud honk. While wiping his nose, he tripped and took several running steps down the aisle before sitting himself in an empty seat two rows down. He sneezed again, four more in rapid succession, before slumping noisily against the window.

Bright-colored coat, baggy trousers... and what with all the sneezing and clumsy stumbling, the man reminded Rory of a hapless circus clown. Rory watched the back of the man's head, imagining him whipping out one of those horns clowns squeezed and blowing it at the person behind him.

Honk! Honk!

Two girls, looking about the same age as his babysitter Carol, sat across the aisle but up one row. One flicked her long, blond hair behind her as if she was a horse shaking its mane. She cupped a hand over the ear of another blond girl—this one wearing a ponytail. Then they both looked over at a man with a big Santa Claus stomach, who wore a gray bomber jacket which seemed expanded beyond its stretching ability.

It wasn't nice to laugh at people—Mama always said *don't mock those who look different, we're all different*. He looked on as the girls both giggled and covered their mouths with their hands, which did nothing to stifle their laughter. The whole time, they continued to glance at the man, who looked back at them and frowned. That made them laugh even more and Rory decided they were mean, just like Cinderella's wicked stepsisters.

A bearded, dark-skinned man with messed hair, a leather jacket and tight jeans stood by the door. Covering his ears were big, black headphones, their long cord snaking down to a shoulder bag. His head bobbed up and down to a musical beat only he could hear.

Rory nodded his head in time with the man's head movements. He was like a parrot in a pet shop he'd seen one time, where the store owner had run his finger up and down in rhythm beside the cage, and the bird had followed each stroke. That was it, then! He was Parrot Man, musical super hero.

A whistle shrilled from somewhere outside, and Rory swung his gaze, about to peer out the window, looking for the stationmaster. That seemed like a good job, except in the snow. He couldn't see the man though through the falling whiteness. The train lurched as the brakes released, causing the standing passengers' heads and bodies to sway backward, before swinging again forward. They were on their way and Rory exclaimed a quiet 'Yay' inside.

A woman sat next to the kissing couple—still pecking at each other—with silver hair pulled into such a tight bun it seemed to tighten the skin over her jaw into a scissor-sharp line. When she caught him staring, the lady nodded and smiled as if she'd read his glee at leaving and agreed.

Then, still smiling, she looked toward the nodding man and wrinkled her nose as if she had smelled something bad. The wrinkles crisscrossing her face and deep lines etched sideways down from the side of her mouth to her chin made her look like the scary witch from Hansel and Gretel. He'd have to be careful of her when he got off the train. Maybe she was hunting children in the snow and was trying to lure him in with her sweet-old-lady smiles. Now, he imagined how she might make a nice soup of him later if she could only get her hands on him.

Rory looked away, not wishing to attract her attention any further. The crackling sound of a newspaper page being turned caught his attention next. Three rows up, a man in a dark suit and loose tie which hung about his neck like a necklace, was shaking his newspaper open as he turned a page. He then folded the paper in half and held it out in front of him, half blocking the aisle.

Rory noted the jumble of words and dreamed of the day he'd sit on a train or a bus and read anything at all. It all seemed very far off at this moment. Reading wasn't easy, but maybe he could be a bus driver or a train driver. They didn't need to read, did they?

Enough of the Story Game, he thought, feeling the train pick up speed. Nobody was looking at him and he'd had enough of looking at everyone else. They were all stored in his mind to use later in stories, he'd tell himself.

Rory pulled off his gloves, shoved them in a pocket and then reached inside his other pants' pocket and hunted around. His fingers clasped the cold, smooth outline of a Matchbox car. A Chevrolet Camaro slid out, clasped snugly in his palm. He couldn't say the words right, yet. *Chevrolet Camaro.* Hmm. *Chev-vro-l-olay...* The 'V' sound tied his tongue but he'd been practicing and was almost there. The Camaro bit could come later.

"Mama, it's okay if I play with my Cher-o-lay?"

"Yes. Careful, though don't drop it."

He pulled and pushed the toy up and down the top of his leg, making a *vroom, vroom* noise as he did. That car went everywhere with him and he no longer possessed legs; now, they were hills and runways to challenge the little vehicle.

When the train slowed for the next station, he wasn't even aware several minutes had passed because he'd been racing across green mountains and busy city streets. As the train's brakes squealed, announcing its slowing to enter the station, he was a million miles away, driving his Chevrolet at full speed around a bend; the noise of its brakes screeched and squealed as he made a corner and headed at full speed into a straightaway.

People crowded aboard with only a few exiting here, and when Rory looked up to check who remained of *his people,* he found his view now somewhat restricted. All he saw, for the most part, were arms and legs, jackets and gloves, and wooly scarves wrapped high and tight around mottled necks looking more and more like cooked meats. Many people were now standing and though he felt crowded, it was an opportunity to add more to his *Story Game*. He'd have a marvelous adventure to imagine tonight while taking his bath.

Three ladies dressed in skirts and sleek shirts stood in front of him talking about a movie they'd just seen. *Toy Story*. Somehow, he needed to convince his mama to take him to see it too. They rarely visited the cinema but he'd seen the posters and ad on TV and he really, really wanted to watch it. He could almost smell the popcorn, and that thought made him hungry. Then his mind went to dinner and his tummy growled again. He turned his head to ask his mother how much longer before they were home but stopped.

She was staring across the car past him, and that wasn't usual for her. "Staring and gawking is for those who don't have enough sense to know what is their business and what is another's," she'd say. So what was happening here?

He followed her gaze as if it was a red laser beam lighting a pathway. It seemed to lead straight to a tall woman who was turning her head this way and that, looking across the passengers as if searching for someone or something. Her stare bounced off each person after lingering a few seconds, but long enough to be more than an accident. Fixed on her face was a mask of deep concentration, just like his mama looked when she was reading bills. Was she counting? Maybe she worked for the railway?

Lucky she was standing in a pocket of space, allowing him to see her, the top half of her body framed through the internal window at the end of their seat. Her hair was so black it almost shone purple, and she sported a cropped boy-style haircut even shorter than his own. Her skin was smooth and white like the soft inside of an apple.

There was something robotic in the way she moved, although it was clear she wasn't a robot. Well, that was obvious; robots didn't look like pretty women, they were silver and smooth and made of metal.

But what she could be... yes, she could... she could be a scientist?

A scientist on this train, here to study people. What about a test to see how many people climbed aboard a train before it became too heavy to move? Had anyone looked into that? *If not, then they should*, Rory thought.

"I say one hundred," he whispered under his breath, smiling to himself because being a scientist who counted how many people got onto a train sounded very interesting. But her clothes didn't look like a scientist's; tight-fitting dark blue shirt tucked skin-smooth into the top of leather pants. Did scientists wear leather pants? He wasn't sure. He thought they wore white coats.

Well, anyway. Rory thought she was the most beautiful woman he had ever seen, and as if she'd heard, she swiveled her neck and her gaze landed upon him. Her head tilted to the left, and he felt magnetized by her blue-like-the-sky eyes. A wisp of a smile touched her lips. Then, she dipped her head as if in a silent greeting.

Rory considered for a moment if they had met before. He scanned his memory but found nothing of her. Yet, the way she looked at him was like she *knew* him. He didn't know what made him think this. Maybe it was from all the babysitters he'd had or the way his teachers treated him, but, yes, he thought she must know him. She *had to* know him. It was painted all over her expression, the same kind of look—but without the dread or irritation—that sweet Mama's face acquired when she crossed over the street to avoid a tiny woman who talked too much, the one they often encountered in the street when they just wanted to nip out for a quick loaf of bread. That woman who twittered on and on like a bird always showed up in the street whenever they were in a rush, never when they had time to spare. So, yes; this stranger looked at Rory as if she recognized him and they were long acquainted, just the same way Mama eyed the strange birdwoman.

Warmth spread across Rory's cheeks and neck, and thinking of his mama's words that he should never stare, he gave her a faint smile. In return, she wangled her head again, so it tilted at the opposite angle now.

He wasn't sure what to do next, so he returned his attention to his car and ran it up his arm again—but the whole time, he felt her watching him. Her eyes seared into the top of his head so he stayed looking down at his Che-ro-lay.

Rory decided he'd ask his mother about the black-haired woman, but when he looked up to catch her attention, she had her fingertips to her temples and was rubbing there and staring at her lap. *Oh dear. Mama must have a headache,* he thought. He didn't want to bother her. Maybe she'd seen him staring, and he'd upset her. So he went back to his car and wondered if Scientist Lady would turn out to be a goodie or a baddie.

Then he felt a hand touching on the top of his head, patting his beanie. His mother was smiling down at him now. No longer rubbing at her own temples, she slipped an arm around him and hugged his body to hers. It was on the tip of his tongue to ask her about Scientist Lady as he gazed up at her from beneath his fringe of curly gold-fire locks peeping out from his beanie. But her focus had left him and now aimed again toward the black-haired lady.

He felt crazy little butterflies in his stomach when he saw his mama's eyes. Rory knew that look because he'd seen it enough times when he'd hurt himself or was sick.

That was his mama's worried look.

Her very worried look.

G ail Fine didn't feel her normal kind of tired; tonight, her body was steeped in deep exhaustion, the kind eating into your bones and wrapping around your spirit. *Defeated* was one word she'd used to describe it. Days like this made her want to give up, curl into a ball and cry, just like she had done on that terrible night when it hit her that her Edward was never coming home again. Not ever.

She had still clung onto hope back then, even after that day. The plan had been for him to only leave them for a few weeks, a month at the most. But as his absence stretched into a second month without a word, the finality had hit her at 2 a.m. when the cold, empty space beside her screamed out the ugly truth. Now, some three years later, she'd mostly accepted the finality of it. Yet some days, like today, were worse than others.

Edward had promised he'd find his way home or die trying, but what else could she think after those words? What had prevented him, what had stopped him, that's what ate at her. Since she knew in her heart he would never abandon his family, that left only one answer—and she didn't want to think about how that fate had befallen him. He'd known it would be dangerous, and so had she, but there was so very much at stake at the time. So, how could she have told him not to go? Although, she'd wanted to scream it at him as he'd turned and walked out the door. But she had the care of their precious child to think about and to fill her mind. Even way back then they already had known how special he was, so she'd been faced with little choice.

Gail glanced at Rory and a wave of sadness traveled through her, but instead of weighing her down, it filled her with a fire to protect her son. He was her life now, and though she hoped he'd never face what his father had, she knew she must still prepare him.

That was all that mattered. Her own happiness meant nothing because there was too much at stake. Her husband had once said he and Gail carried the world on their shoulders; Atlas had nothing on them. At least Atlas had known what he'd faced. *She* had no idea, and that was what kept her awake at night, leaving her perpetually tired, her eyes straining to stay open during the day, and her soul too exhausted to rest even when the darkness fell.

As she ran a hand through her shoulder-length, auburn hair with its kinks and half-curls she no longer fussed over, she thought *I must get a haircut,* as her fingers snagged on several knots. Spoiling herself with hairstyles and makeup was so far from her priority list; heck, she was lucky to remember to brush her teeth. She only visited the hairdressers when she couldn't stand the mess any longer, and that was about now. Maybe next week. Or the one after that.

Gail's priority sat right there beside her, and whatever spare time she had left to her—between the full-time clerical job at Colonial Mutual Life and two nights a week, sometimes three, in the café—she devoted to Rory. The weekends were free, and that was *their* time, theirs once she'd completed the house chores, performed through yawns and little sit-downs before she toppled over.

Bless her little Rory, because he would pitch in and help—as much as any seven-year-old could—and had the nature of an angel. Maybe that was God's way of evening out the bad—evil, she often thought—which had torn their family apart.

Looking down at her thoughtful, quiet son, her heart broke. Guilt was never far away in these silly little moments. She couldn't help noticing how Rory had grown quieter over the past year. Guilt seeped into her heart as she pondered if it was his realization he was missing something important in his life, and that no matter how hard she tried, she couldn't give it back to him. The damage of not having a father and not knowing why was a heavy, heavy weight for anyone, let alone a small child.

Whenever he asked, she told him a half truth, that he had left to fight for their freedom and something had happened and he couldn't come home. She prayed she'd never need to reveal the real truth. To the best of her ability, she'd done everything possible to ensure Rory had a sense of security and knew he could at least count on her to be there and to always love him.

Gail watched Rory watching their fellow passengers, and she mused if he didn't have more of her husband's DNA than they had first thought. He looked like a perfect porcelain fiery-haired doll, with his half-smile, perfect lightly-freckled alabaster skin—made even whiter from the cold—and intelligent brown eyes twinkling with curiosity.

Oh my, just looking at him made her run all the *if only's*. If only she'd said no when Edward had asked her permission to go. If only she'd asked to go with him. If only she'd just thought the whole thing through. She saw her husband sitting there, his six-foot-two frame making their kitchen table look like a child's toy, as he awaited her answer. *Was that a tear glistening in his eye?* Did he want her to say no, make her the one who stopped him, the one who took the mantle from his shoulders?

But how could she have said no? How could she have been selfish when he was so needed, and when he might be the only one who could save them?

Yet, sometimes, anger darkened her heart at his making her the one to choose, making her his accomplice in shattering the life they had, *should have* had, *would have* had if not... if not for the misfortune of being special. This was why she didn't want that for Rory. Being special was dangerous and heartbreaking and held an unknown future.

Gail shook her gaze from her son and surveyed the other passengers in the car. It was a habit of hers, just in case he was there, somewhere among them, looking for them as much as she looked for him. As she did so, without realizing, Gail rubbed a palm up and down Rory's arm as if feeling delicate silk, in a subconscious move to reassure herself he was still by her side.

I'm surrounded by people and yet so alone.

Gail checked her wristwatch. 5:20.

Come on, she urged the train which seemed to be taking forever to leave the station. She needed dinner on the table by 6:15, her son bathed and ready for bed before handing his care to the babysitter. Then it would be a rush across the six blocks to Allegros, the café where she worked, to start her shift by seven.

When she noticed the black-haired woman staring at Rory, Gail Fine shivered as a sliver of ice pierced her heart. It couldn't be her.

Yet, if it was, that must mean something had happened. She turned away and looked down at her lap. She needed to think and to decide what she should do next. But her mind came up blank because this woman was the last person she'd ever expected or wanted to see again.

4

W ith a slight jolt, the train pulled from the station. Standing passengers swayed backward with the motion, before swinging forward again as if in some synchronized dance.

Outside, the storm whipped up a frenzy of snow flurries and an almost collective silent sigh escaped from those aboard that they were again moving. Who knew if this storm would gather momentum and close stations or lines? Not a single person wanted to be traveling in this mess any longer than necessary.

Rory twisted about and stared through the window as towering buildings slipped by, the L train making its giddy loop around the inner-city landscape. The street lights glowed a vague, muted yellow against the dark streetscape which appeared as empty as if the world had ended.

Rory looked over at his mother again who'd returned to wearing the worried look, after replacing it with a brief and fleeting smile especially for him. Her eyes now seemed as dark as the sky outside as she moved her head to peer down the car length through the gaps between passengers. He wondered if it was the Scientist Lady who worried her. He searched for the black-haired woman and saw she was still there but had moved a little down the aisle. She appeared to continue to search for something. Or someone.

Rory decided he didn't want the Scientist Lady to see his mama looking at her. He wanted him and his mama to remain invisible. So he tapped his mother's hand and said, "Mama, how much longer?" He didn't much care about the answer but it was the first thing which sprang into his mind.

His mother tilted her head to the side and stared at him, and Rory was pleased to see her eyes had again changed to become the deep, kind eyes of the person he loved and trusted most in the world.

"Hey, sweetheart, you must be real hungry, right?"

"No, it's okay, I'm just tired."

She pulled off his beanie in a playful way and ruffled his hair, then touched the back of her hand to his face.

"Soon my love, soon. Three more stations. Maybe ten minutes, if that." Then she pushed his beanie back on his head, pulling it over his ears and kissing the top.

He nodded his understanding, then glanced toward the Scientist Lady from just the corner of his eye, so she wouldn't see him looking. To his relief, she had moved even farther away, but because she was so tall, he could still see the top of her head. His gaze traveled back to his mother who now stared straight ahead, oblivious to her son's concern over a complete stranger.

But he still couldn't decide if the woman even was a stranger. Something about her also didn't seem to fit in the scene on the train, like a zebra would stand out among horses. Though she was beautiful to Rory's mind, her hair and clothes weren't all that unusual; yet there was that unsettled buzzing in his head he'd never experienced before that he felt had something to do with her. Maybe it was the way she surveyed those around her as if she was hunting, or the strange smile of recognition she gave Rory.

Good, he thought, once he knew many bodies and feet separated them, still not clear in his mind why it was, in fact, good she was now farther away, or what trouble surrounded the black-haired woman, or why he felt the need to protect his mother from her.

Sometimes, he didn't understand the way his mind worked. His mama often told him he was special, but whenever he asked why, she'd wrinkle her nose, give him a sweet look and say, "Because you just are."

Rory turned from the Scientist Lady but continued glancing over to her every few seconds or so. What could possibly happen among all these people? Soon, they'd disembark and leave the strange lady behind and he'd forget all about her. He would, wouldn't he?

Rory resumed driving his little car but had lost interest, so he drove it up his arm one last time, then down his leg on the way to his pants' pocket. He had just parked it snug away when he sensed the train slowing—and not at all at the usual speed as if pulling into a station. A squealing and shrieking came from below the train. *The wheels. The brakes.*

They had only left the last station a minute ago, and it didn't seem to him they had traveled for long enough to be entering the next, yet brakes were being applied. Rory craned his neck to peer out the window to check if their station lay ahead. It was dark out there, pitch black, a vast cavern of nothingness; night had fallen and he couldn't see much of anything. And even the thick, dense blanket of deep white snow appeared black.

His mother gasped and swung about to stare out the window too, her arm reaching across to rest in reassurance on his back and shoulder.

"What's happening here?" she whispered, more to herself than him. "Must be the storm. Problem with the tracks."

Rory couldn't see well enough, so on impulse, he crawled up on the seat to kneel at the window, pressing his nose to the cold glass. He stared out into the bleak night and saw that far below, now just slightly illuminated by hazy street lamps and maybe twenty-five feet away, lay traffic-heavy, snow-whitened roads of downtown. This part of the L was way above the street like a bridge. His mother had told him once, the city had grown so big a hundred years ago, they didn't have room to build underground or along the street, so upward had been the only way to go,

Rory had loved traveling so far up as if on a rollercoaster. Not tonight though, because with this unexpected slowing and the storm outside, he felt vulnerable and his heartbeat rose just a little. He twisted and craned his neck to look down the length of the outside of the train, and could just make out the rest of the cars snaking around a bend.

The train was still moving, but only creeping along, a sluggish caterpillar on tracks. After twenty seconds, it ground to a complete stop and the horrible screeching of the brakes ceased. Rory had just been about to put his fingers in his ears to stop the sound.

Several passengers had already stood and moved toward the door, thinking they'd arrived at the next station. Others gathered newspapers, books, and belongings, stowing them inside bags and pockets in readiness to alight.

Rory looked over at his mother again for a signal they should do the same, but she hadn't moved. She still stared out the window, her brows bunched together in that now too-familiar worried look.

"What's wrong with the public transportation system?" a high-pitched woman's voice exclaimed from somewhere in the crowd.

"I know," replied another woman, whom he couldn't see for all the standing bodies. "We got going. Now what're we waitin' for? God, I hope this isn't a breakdown. In this awful weather!"

"This happened last week," replied the high-pitched voice again, "we waited an hour until they came and shunted us to a station. Made us get off and catch a bus. That would be crap in this snow. Freeze our tails off, we would."

Someone else—another woman—piped up, "Still waitin' for my refund from the last time!"

A male voice interjected. "transportation system's gone to shit!"

The mood in the car had descended in an instant to match the darkness lying outside. Rory even imagined a change in the air, heaviness replacing light sucked clean away. His teacher had only told them last week how everything was made from spinning tiny, tiny things you couldn't see. He couldn't remember the name, but he wondered if they were spinning in a different direction now. That was how it felt to him—a change in the air.

People began to return to their seats, while others shuffled impatiently where they stood. Even more joined, to discuss what the cause of the delay might be, so that it began to sound like a busy classroom, but of adults instead of kids.

When a bump rocked the car, the unexpectedness caused a chorus of shocked exclamations from nearly everyone. Those standing found themselves propelled forward at an unexpected speed. Some stumbled over others, one or two were caught and saved by a helping hand, the rest ending up in a heap on the floor, before they immediately scrambled to get back up. A briefcase—held by the nearby businessman with the suit as he stood near the doors—dropped to the ground, making a smacking noise. The girl who'd been kissing the boy across from the man he'd named Briefcase Man reached out to grab a woman who'd stumbled and fallen across her lap.

"Oh, my God, sorry!" the woman exclaimed as she righted herself back to standing with the help of the girl who replied, "No problem."

"Shit," a kid in a school blazer said, as he fell over Briefcase Man's case and tumbled to the floor. Rory knew it was wrong to swear but if you lost your balance, it might be okay.

And Rory was sure he knew the likely cause of the bump and all the swear words he'd heard uttered about him. He'd run his tricycle into walls often enough to recognize the sensation of one solid object colliding with another something-or-other, also rock hard and immoveable. So, that was it then. They'd hit something.

After the ten seconds of disruption, a murmur erupted, then nervous laughter. Many leaned over those seated or moved to the doors to peer out the window. Even more wore confused expressions, while a few gave an excited whoop. Three or four passengers rose from their seats a second time, eager to be off the train when it arrived at the station.

Rory looked for the dark-haired Scientist Lady, curious to know whether she had fallen over. He searched the faces in the crowd, straining his neck this way and that to check if she was lying on the floor or still upright, clinging onto some piece of the train's innards.

He couldn't see her. She seemed to have disappeared, which was impossible unless he'd been right and she was a witch. But witches weren't real.

Were they?

Then, a hand was on his arm, clutching tight, causing him to yelp. His heartbeat set off like a rocket and he had a sudden instinct to get up and run.

It was 5:27 p.m.

Continue reading

for FREE with Kindle Unlimited or Kindle Prime

DESTINATION DARK ZONE

Available also in whisper-synched audible

DESTINATION DARK ZONE

ABOUT SUSAN MAY

Susan May sold more than 200,000 books and is an Amazon best-selling author, ranked among the top one hundred horror authors in the USA since 2015.

Her growing number of fans from all over the world have likened her immersive and page turning style to Stephen King, Dean Koontz, Robert Mathieson, Gillian Flynn and Ray Bradford.

Susan was four when she decided she would become a writer and packed a bag to march down the road looking for a school. For forty-six years after, she suffered from life-gets-in-the-way-osis. Setting a goal to write just one page a day cured her in 2010. This discipline grew into an addictive habit, which has since born multiple best-selling dark thriller novels and dozens of short stories and novellas, many of which are published award-winners in Australia, the U.S.A and the U.K.

Passionate film lover since childhood, Susan is also a film critic with the dream job of reviewing films for a local radio station. You'll find her several times a week in a darkened cinema gobbling popcorn and enjoying the latest film. She sees 150 plus films a year on screen at the invitation of all the studios and, no, she never tires of them.

Susan lives in beautiful Perth, Western Australia with her two teenage sons and husband, while her mind constantly travels to dark, faraway places most would fear to visit. That though is where her inspiration lives, so go she must.

ALSO BY SUSAN MAY

Explore all available books in order of most recent publication:
susanmaywriter.net/susan-may-books

NOVELS

Destination Dark Zone

Best Seller

The Troubles Keeper

Deadly Messengers

Back Again

The Goodbye Giver (THE TROUBLES KEEPER 2)

(COMING MID-2020)

JOIN SUSAN MAY READERS CLUB FOR ALERT

NOVELLA

291

Behind the Fire

OMNIBUS

Happy Nightmares! Thriller Omnibus

SHORT STORY COLLECTIONS

Behind Dark Doors (one)

Behind Dark Doors (two)

THE TROUBLES KEEPER
BY SUSAN MAY
Copyright 2016 Susan May

DRIFT
BY SUSAN MAY
Copyright 2019 Susan May

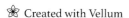 Created with Vellum

Made in the USA
Middletown, DE
25 May 2020